Safe Haven . . .

"You're shivering, my dear. Come, I'll warm you."

McLean set the candle down and lifted her in his arms. "You're cold as ice, poor darling." He carried her over to the bed and slipped beneath the covers with her.

"Your heart is racing," he said. "Are you still frightened?"

"No." Her voice was husky with desire. "I've already forgotten it. You have that effect on me."

McLean smiled. "I'm glad." Leaning down, he kissed her mouth. "You taste like honey."

"It came with the tea."

"No. It's you." His mouth was on hers this time with a flare of urgency. "My delicious Grace," he whispered. "I can never have enough of you. . ."

Her arms wound round his neck boldly. Fiercely. "Take me, then."

She wanted him to hold her, kiss her, fill her. To prove to her that he was real and her fears were not. Indeed, as his hands stroked lightly over her, the last of them melted away. The world followed. . .

ST. MARTIN'S PAPERBACKS TITLES
BY MARIANNE WILLMAN

The Wish

The Enchanted Mirror

The Lost Bride

The Mermaid's Song

Mistress of
Rossmor

Marianne Willman

St. Martin's Paperbacks

MISTRESS OF ROSSMOR

ISBN: 0-312-98132-5

Printed in the United States of America

St. Martin's Paperbacks edition / August 2002

St. Martin's Paperbacks are published by St. Martin's Press, 175 Fifth Avenue, New York, NY 10010.

10 9 8 7 6 5 4 3 2 1

Prologue

THE HIGHLANDS OF SCOTLAND, 1885
I believe that I should write down the strange events that occurred when I first came to Rossmor Manor, while they remain fresh in my mind. I scarcely know where to begin! Does my story start in Rome, where I first met Alistair McLean, or later, within the manor's haunted walls?

Neither, I think, upon reflection. I should—I must—open my narrative far in the past; for everything that has happened to me, both wonderful and terrible, began with another woman who was mistress of Rossmor almost a hundred and fifty years ago. Her name is Freya, and I know her story now as well as I do my own . . .

It was just past dawn when Freya climbed slowly to the battlements. Rain fell like tears across Loch Ross, turning the water to pebbled glass. The wind moaned and sighed, like a lover all forlorn.

Even the wind feels my pain, she thought. *Even the sky weeps for me.*

Her husband was unfaithful. To her and to everything she valued most. His betrayal had shattered her.

She had raged and wept for days, and finally put the pieces of her self-respect back together as best she could. Now she stood at the top of the highest turret, while the wind whipped at her cloak, trying to make up her mind what to do.

Waiting for a sign.

She was the hereditary heiress and captain of her clan, mistress of Rossmor in her own right. She could have married for power, but she had married for love. Now her husband was home from the bloody fray, sprawled across the feather bed in their private chamber beneath the crest that held her family's motto: "Loyalty Is All."

Their innocent children slept below in another room, unheeding of her turmoil. Where did her duty lie? Where her loyalty?

She turned and looked down at the lonely glen through the silver rain. Its beauty seared her soul. Despite the distance, she could make out the crofters' cottages, with their burnt walls and fallen roofs. Their smoke-blackened windows were like empty eye sockets, blindly accusing.

If not for me . . . she thought. *If not for me, it would never have come to this.*

The rain faded, leaving fog draped across the glen like a gray shawl. It stretched and thinned while she warred with herself, wracked with guilt and agonizing indecision.

And then she had her sign.

A sharp cry startled her. She put back her wet hood and lifted her head. The cry repeated, much closer. Freya watched as a great hawk came soaring down from the misty clouds that shrouded the mountains. Her slender body tensed.

The hawk was *his* emblem.

It flew over the loch, arcing through the sky above the Islands of the Five Sisters, untouched by the roiling passage of the storm, just as *he* had come through the terrors of the battle unscathed.

The bird wheeled and plunged down toward the nearest island where it had its home. Without warning, the clear air turned a bright, burning blue that lit the entire glen.

Lightning knifed across the sky and struck the grove on the hill. The tree exploded in a blinding white glare, and the hawk tumbled wildly, its charred and smoking body plummeting to earth.

A boom of thunder shook the glen and a blast of wind swept through. The clouds gave way before it, like stampeding sheep. Overhead the sky turned clear and bluer than her eyes.

She had her answer.

Leaving the turret, she followed the winding stair, holding tight to the guide rope strung through iron loops along the inner wall.

It wouldn't do to fall. Not now.

She went down to the chamber she shared with her husband and drifted to the bed. He was a handsome giant, and had stolen her heart long before he'd stolen his first kiss. She would not let him take her honor.

Leaning forward, she kissed his warm lips. Her own were cold as stone. "Awaken," she whispered. "Awaken, husband—and see the face of justice!"

He came awake almost at once, his gray eyes startled and wary.

It was too late. Her dagger, sharp as his betrayal, swift and deadly as a lightning bolt, had already found its mark . . .

Chapter One

Alistair McLean stood on the Palatine Hill above the Forum Romanum, beneath a brilliant lapis sky. He took off his hat and ran his fingers through thick dark hair.

If any place in Rome is haunted, it should be here, he thought.

Amid the city's domed churches and palaces and spouting fountains, the Forum was a wild and silent island of green overgrowth and shattered stone. Broken columns protruded like elegant bones through the weed-choked expanse and trees sprouted from the roofs of half-buried temples. An air of brooding melancholy hung over what had once been the beating heart of the vast Roman Empire. The ancient splendor was reduced to rubble, all the blood and glory scoured away by time.

In the proper season the site was full of British and American tourists bent on "improving" themselves, by ticking off all the "sights to be seen" as if they were items on a shopping list. But not in the brazen heat of August. Anyone with a particle of sense and the means to do so had fled the city for the coolness of the surrounding hills.

He'd purposely tried for a day and time when the Forum would be thin of visitors, in order to immerse himself in the atmosphere. It appeared that he'd chosen wisely: thus far he'd seen only one cassocked priest talking to a friar, and two small boys romping with their pup in the distance.

They were long gone and the circumstances should have been ideal. But the indefinable something he sought eluded McLean. He felt no sense of the history of the place. It was merely acres of neglected, wildly overgrown ruins, ringed by the seven hills of Rome.

Perhaps he was concentrating too much. Perhaps he should try to think of nothing at all . . .

There was movement below and he frowned. A slender young woman in crisp white and navy stood amid the ruins of the House of the Vestals, guidebook in hand. The straw bonnet that hid most of her dark hair was outmoded, but set at a precise angle and tied with a neat bow.

She came gliding over the weedy, uneven paving stones as if she were in a London drawing room. She was English—no doubt of that—and as completely out of place among the ruins of imperial glory as a tea cozy in a barracks.

McLean was chagrined. He knew her type: earnest and sincere and completely lacking in imagination. He folded his arms and leaned back against the wall, wishing she would go away soon. But no, Englishwomen of her ilk never did. Not until she'd seen every stone and column and inscription that she intended to see. She would dutifully examine each temple and arch, tut-tut over the wicked deeds of the past, read a page from her guidebook—and then go on dutifully to the next item listed under some fusty heading such as "Noteworthy Places to Be Seen by the Cultured Traveler While in London."

Except that she didn't go on at all.

She stopped so suddenly it looked as if she'd run into a solid wall. McLean drew in a sharp breath, and tried to suppress a sudden surge of excitement. He'd seen that same expression on another face many times. It was a look that, seen even once, could never be forgotten.

Shifting his weight, he watched her intently. For five years he had been trying to unlock the truth of the tragedy that bedeviled him. Could this slender, dark-haired young woman hold the key?

He frowned as her eyes went wide with bewilderment and dawning terror. He was already starting down toward the floor of the Forum, when her face went white and she raised her hand in a gesture of fear.

Grace Templar thought she was alone in the forum. She stood in the molten afternoon light and drank in the view. It was heady as wine. This was her first visit abroad, and the excitement of seeing a place she'd only read about in history books filled her.

Just past the church of Santa Francesca Romana, the empty tiers of the Colosseum rose against a sky so deep and limitless a blue it seemed unreal.

It seems almost as unreal that I am actually here!

Six weeks earlier she'd answered an advertisement for the position of companion, secretary, and chaperone for an American widow and her aspiring debutante daughter, imagining it would be her ticket to adventure. Thus far her hopes had been disappointed.

Neither Mrs. Bingley nor sixteen-year-old Miss Eliza Bingley had any interest in historic places, unless they came with an eligible nobleman—preferably an earl—attached.

Mrs. Bingley was an ambitious woman. She knew that it was easier to breach the ranks of the *ton* abroad, than in the stricter confines of a London Season. She hadn't realized, however, that the Roman aristocracy and titled tourists who were her intended prey would have fled the August heat for cool villas in the hills outside Rome. It would be September before they trickled back.

Temporarily thwarted in their ambitions, the mother and daughter spent most of their time within the walls of the villa they'd taken on three months' hire, looking at fashion plates. Their excursions were chiefly to the fashionable shops where—despite Grace's best attempts to dissuade them—they ordered expensive gowns and capes and bonnets, most of which only a courtesan would wear.

Yet here I am, at last! Grace thought.

At the present moment, the Bingleys were taking lunch at a hotel with English acquaintances whom they would scarcely have deigned to recognize under other circumstances, and Grace had the afternoon free. She was delighted to escape her difficult employer and bored pupil for a few precious hours of peace.

She descended to the weed-strewn floor of the Forum. The sun was a brass hammer, but a shiver ran through Grace the instant her slippers touched the stone. She was totally unprepared for the vast, desolate grandeur of the ruins. As she proceeded along the ancient Via Sacra, Grace felt a ripple of unease.

Two goats chewed wildflowers where Roman senators had gathered in their purple-hemmed togas. Feral cats sunned themselves on the remains of the Rostra, where the greatest orators of the empire had once held forth.

Perhaps in the far future, she thought, *visitors to England may find cows grazing near the ruins of St. Paul, or tourists sketching a heap of stones that were once the Tower of London.*

The fanciful image unsettled her. Shaking off its effects, she wandered along examining the three columns and raised dais that were the remains of Vespasian's Temple. She tried to imagine how it had looked in its heyday with marble façades gleaming in the sun and the whole of it bustling with thousands of people.

She was touched with ineffable sadness. It rustled in the heavy air around her, gathering in upon itself. Grace hesitated, then came to a full stop. She felt the weight of centuries pressing down upon her like stones. The sensation grew with every passing second.

Panic knifed through her. She forced herself to move down the Sacred Way. Suddenly her skin prickled and her hair rose at her nape. Another tremor shook her, followed by a bright pang of alarm.

Oh, no! I should not have come here!

Even as she thought it, it was too late.

The phantom scents came first, as always. They swirled around her in an invisible current. *Garlic and spices and roasting sausages . . . exotic perfumes and burning oil . . . wood smoke and incense . . . animal dung and human sweat . . .*

She tried to turn and run away. Her feet refused to move. They were as firmly rooted as the trees and shrubs sprouting between the cracks in the tilted pavement.

"No . . . no!" The cry was ripped from deep within her, but came out through her clenched teeth as a stifled moan.

Sounds filtered through her veil of fear. *The faint strum of a stringed instrument . . . the approach of booted feet . . . then a murmur of masculine voices, growing ever louder, like the brash thunder of a breaking wave against the stony shore of her resistance.*

While she struggled against an overwhelming panic, other images imposed themselves over the ruins. Monuments and noble buildings shimmering miragelike, where before there had been open sky. They took on increased solidity and light reflected from their polished travertine surfaces.

All around her she felt the presence of a bustling but yet invisible mass of humanity. Shapes grew out of the sunlight, like images of smoke. They grew denser, more real. Took on the pale, wavery tones of a watercolor wash . . .

A solemn procession . . . the grief-stricken wails of the crowd that thronged the way . . . the stern soldiers and priests . . . and then a young woman, weak and almost fainting with terror in the back of a cart, her heart-shaped face horror-stuck and gray beneath her white veil.

She had slipped away to meet her lover, broken her vow of chastity. That would have been sin enough. But she had let the sacred Vestal fire die out in her absence, putting Rome in danger. It was treason of the gravest sort.

And now she must pay the terrible price . . .

Grace felt her lungs constrict. *No!* She fought to draw in a racking breath, and struggled for control. *I must stay calm. I must concentrate on the present . . .*

She tried not to think of the frightened young girl being taken away to her death. She grounded herself in the here and now, immersed herself in detail. The heavy heat of the day. The curlicue pattern of yellow lichen encrusting a broken step and the half-buried remains of a fallen lintel. The film of light perspiration on her forehead and the prickle of it between her breasts. The tautness of the blue grosgrain ribbon beneath her chin.

It took every bit of willpower she possessed, but Grace succeeded. The scents and sounds faded, the images grew dim and winked out. The Forum Romanum was empty and in ruins once more, the shades of those long dead laid to rest.

Relief mingled with trembling reaction as her pounding pulse eased. She touched her temple. There was just the subtlest aura remaining. The slightest tug toward the past.

Dear God! It had been years since she'd received an impression so sudden. So strong! *I must leave, at once.*

She turned quickly, intending to go back the way she had come. She heard an odd sound as if a door had closed somewhere nearby, with a doleful clang. An instant later a dark bird rose up almost beside her in a great clap of wings. Grace recoiled as the air of its passing stirred the bow beneath her jaw.

This time there was no warning. She was flung back into the swift-flowing river of time. Her vision dimmed, then returned with unnatural clarity.

She looked out through someone else's eyes. She was in

a dark, enclosed space, alone. A small irregular rectangle of glorious sky showed overhead, blue as a sapphire. Suddenly a dark shape flew up against it, blotting the brightness.

A bird, *she thought, as her heart skipped in panic.*

But it wasn't a bird. It was a hand holding a stone. It settled into place, blotting out the living light, filling the final chink in the roof of her tomb.

She was buried alive.

Grace stood in golden sunlight with her eyes wide and sightless as her world went black.

The guidebook fell from her hand and went sliding across the ancient stones.

Alistair McLean was half-way down when he saw Grace sway. He clambered over a wall of stone and leapt down to the Forum floor. A bird startled up from the grass and arrowed past him. The young woman recoiled in alarm, then went rigid. The guidebook fell from her immaculately gloved hand.

The next thing he knew, she dropped like a stone.

Although he sprinted across, he wasn't in time to catch her before she hit the pavement with a sickening thud. He knelt beside her. The force of the blow had knocked her bonnet askew. Witch-black curls tumbled loose around her white face. He touched her throat and was relieved to feel her pulse.

"A miracle she wasn't killed," he said beneath his breath.

At the sound of his voice, she stirred and gave a little moan. Her eyes fluttered open. They were thickly lashed and like no color he'd ever seen before: deep green lit with gold, and just the faintest hint of umber, like warm summer days blending into autumn. Then he saw a trickle of blood angling down from beneath the brim of her crushed bonnet.

"Don't move," he ordered. "I cannot tell the extent of your injuries yet."

Grace looked up into the handsome face of a total stranger. She noted the deep cleft in his chin and eyes as intensely blue as the Roman sky. They looked familiar, yet she didn't think she knew him.

"What . . . what happened? . . . Where am I?"

He frowned down at her. "Don't you remember?"

She shook her head and winced.

"You are amid the ruins of the old Forum. You fainted and hit your head."

Grace bit her lip. "I can't recall anything . . ."

"That is not uncommon after a blow such as you sustained. Hold still a moment and let me examine you."

Lifting her hair carefully away, he discovered a graze along her temple, ending in a small crescent-shaped gash. He wadded up his handkerchief and pressed it in place gently. "You've a nasty cut, but it shouldn't scar."

"That is the least of my problems at the moment." Cold sweat beaded above her bloodless lips. She thought she was going to be sick, but the feeling passed.

Grace struggled to rise.

"Wait! Can you move your legs?"

"Yes." She wiggled her feet, then blinked a few times as her vision blurred. She sat up so abruptly that the last tinge of color drained from her face. "If you would please be so good as to help me to my feet . . ."

"Don't be hasty," he said. "I'm afraid that you hit your head rather hard. You may have a concussion—or worse."

Her unusual eyes regarded him with confused alarm. McLean wished he'd been a little less abrupt. "It's merely a precaution," he told her.

"An unnecessary one. I am quite . . . quite well, I assure you. Thank you for your concern, sir, however I believe the only injury I've suffered is to my dignity."

"Your dignity be damned," he said, and lifted her up in

his arms. She was obviously in shock and her teeth were chattering. "Where is the rest of your party?"

"I . . . I don't know. I . . . I think I came alone."

"The devil you say!" He thought quickly. "I'll take you to them. At what hotel are you staying?" he asked more gently.

Grace fumbled among her jumbled thoughts and dragged out a name. "Claridge's?"

McLean swore beneath his breath. "My dear girl, you are not in London, you are in Rome. I think it would be best to get you out of the hot sun." He lifted her with ease and stood her on her feet, but kept his arm about her for support. "Can you walk?"

Her head ached and she felt dizzy, but Grace wanted to leave this place immediately. "Yes," she lied. "Really, I feel quite well."

"You surprise me. That was quite a knock you took. Do you think it was the heat that made you swoon?"

"I never swoon," she told him a little sharply.

"You gave a damned good imitation of it, then. What made you fall? Were you startled when the bird flew up?"

Her pupils went wide and she surprised him yet again.

Instead of answering, she fainted.

There wasn't another soul around to offer assistance. McLean cursed beneath his breath, for all the good it did him: he was left standing in the shimmering heat of a Roman afternoon, with an unconscious woman in his arms.

Chapter Two

McLean lifted the crystal decanter in his hotel suite, poured himself out a stiff drink, and downed it. *This is the devil of a coil!*

The young woman had come round in the carriage—long enough for him to get her up to his suite—but her thoughts were disordered. She couldn't even tell him her name. There was no doubt at all that she suffered from concussion.

It would have gone against his principles but McLean was almost regretting that he hadn't taken her to the nearest hospital charity ward and washed his hands of the entire affair. Instead she was in his bedchamber with the curtains drawn and a cold compress upon her head.

The doctor, a thin elegant man, exited the bedroom of McLean's hotel suite, beaming. "A touch of sun and a few scrapes and bruises only. La signora will recover completely."

"Thank God!" Relief flooded through McLean. He'd feared her injury was more serious. He didn't bother to correct the man's assumption that the woman ensconced in his bed was his wife.

"She came round again as I was examining her."

"What did she say? How did she seem?"

"She was rather agitated," the physician went on. "I have

given her a mild sedative draught—short acting, but potent—and it has taken rapid effect. She is asleep, and will slumber soundly for an hour or two. When she awakens, she will be as good as new."

He looked around the elegantly appointed parlor with approval, prepared to settle in for the duration. McClain bit back the curse that rose to his lips.

He was at his most affable as he offered the physician his thanks, a glass of brandy from the decanter on the sideboard, and generous payment for his services. Since these were followed by his hat and cane in rapid succession, the doctor found himself blinking on the other side of the door before he quite realized what was happening.

It was urgent that he discover the woman's identity and restore her to her friends before her presence in his hotel room created a scandal. He was sure she'd had a reticule on her arm when he'd first seen her. If so, it was lost among the Forum's weeds and ancient stone, along with any clues it might have contained as to where she was putting up.

He entered the bedroom. Light slanted through the closed shutters and the high-ceilinged room was stifling. The woman was lying atop the burgundy brocade spread, her black witch's hair spread out over the white pillowcase like a storm cloud. He shook her shoulder gently, then with more force. She was in a drugged slumber so profound he couldn't waken her.

He hadn't had time earlier to realize how very pretty she was. Now her face was clean but scraped and bruised along one delicate cheekbone. A wad of gauze neatly affixed with sticking plaster covered the cut at her temple. He brushed the back of his fingers against her forehead. Her skin was soft and much cooler than it had been earlier. A good sign.

The doctor had unbuttoned her bodice to listen to her heart, and left it undone in deference to the heat. McClain was a man used to quick action, but now he hesitated. He couldn't very well send for the maid. It was bad enough that the young woman was alone with him in his hotel room. Nor did he want to undress her himself. If she came to and found herself in her shift, she'd likely go off in hysterics. Once the damned sedative wore off, that is.

He stared down at her, rubbing his chin. Somewhere in Rome, someone was wondering at her absence. Concerned family? Worried husband? Lover?

He doubted the last. *Too prim and proper. But she had a full, passionate mouth.*

She wore no jewelry except for the locket around her throat. McLean lifted it his fingers. The locket was small and round, with two initials carved upon its face. G.T. It was a piece of mourning jewelry, inexpensive but elegantly styled. McLean turned it over in his fingers. Inside the clear glass back was a tiny coiled braid of white-blond hair woven with raven black.

He opened it and something fell out on the carpet with a soft ping. He bent his knee and retrieved a simple gold band set halfway round with creamy seed pearls. Inside were engraved two indecipherable initials and an illegible date. McLean frowned down at it.

A family heirloom—or a wedding ring? Perhaps she wasn't really a spinster, but a young widow earning her way in a world that was hostile to pretty women who lacked the protection of a husband or the support of a family.

In current opinion, spinsters were considered safe, widows a danger to any men within the walls that housed them. It was as if feminine sexuality were a ferocious genie that, once let out of its bottle, could never be safely controlled again. McLean had no patience with such prejudice, but it was widespread.

His slipped the ring back inside the hollow space and snapped it closed. McLean looked for other clues. The few brief words she'd spoken had convinced him that she was a lady by birth. Her speech and manners were proof of that. Her garments were well enough, but not in the current mode. Her collar and cuffs had been turned once and were again showing wear at the edges.

Whatever her background, he reasoned, she was either too proud to seek assistance of her relatives—or she had none to whom she could turn. McLean pegged her as a distressed gentlewoman, traveling as companion to some querulous old lady—*who will be growing increasingly querelous,* he thought, *with every passing hour.*

A woman's reputation was a fragile thing, and he'd seen well-bred matrons eagerly dismember some unfortunate female's character and morals, like foxes tearing apart a hapless vole. Impossible to make inquiries at all the various hotels frequented by English tourists. Even if he knew them all, there wasn't enough time before evening fell.

Every minute she remained in his rooms endangered her future, and his. If it were to become known that she had been in his private quarters, he would be censured—but she would be ruined.

He shook her again, more roughly. She stirred and murmured something incomprehensible, but that was all. He feared she would sleep for hours.

Frustrated, he went out to the balcony and lit a cigar. Rome was spread out below him in splendor, all gold and ocher, dark red and dusty green. The light was incredible, the sky above the hills a deep and infinite sapphire. The massive dome of St. Peter's Basilica shone golden in the sun.

I should have taken her to a convent, or one of the hospitals run by the nuns. I would have had her off my hands now, without any further involvement on my part. Why the devil didn't I?

Of course he'd acted out of instinct and the immediate need to get her out of the sizzling noonday heat. His hotel had been close by. But as he made excuses, McLean realized that none of these factors had been paramount in making his decision. He had looked down on the Forum, wondering if he might sense echoes of the ancient dramas that had played out there, but hoping for more.

He'd gotten his wish.

He frowned, remembering the blithe manner in which she'd walked along the old Sacred Way by the Temple of Vesta. The sudden way she'd frozen in place. The complete and utter horror on her face. It hadn't been the blank-eyed expression of someone about to swoon. It had been the devastated look of someone witnessing an event too terrible to contemplate.

He put out the cigar and went back inside. She lay like an effigy upon the spread, but the wisps of hair curling away from her temples stirred in the light breeze as he closed the door. She looked exceedingly vulnerable and very young.

McLean touched her cheek. Certain people were born with talents—perfect pitch, athletic ability, a genius for numbers or painting or military strategy. Some, according to popular belief, had the gift—or the curse—to see things that were hidden to others. He was certain that she was one of them.

"What happened to you in the Forum?" he murmured as he stood beside the bed. "What was it that you felt? Or saw?"

He wouldn't rest until he knew the answer.

Chapter Three

Grace Templar struggled to awaken from a dream as bizarre as it was frightening. She was walking through the ruins of the Forum Romanum in sweltering heat . . .

She stood at the head of a staircase open to the sky. Below her were spread out the garden and pool of the complex that had once housed the Vestal virgins, guardians of Rome's sacred fire.

Grace went down a flight of worn steps and came out beside the pool. The headless statues of the chief Vestals lined the side. Beyond it groups of people waited silently, standing in ragged rows.

Waiting for her.

But as she drew closer, Grace saw that she was no longer in the House of the Vestals. In fact, she was no longer in Rome.

The scene shifted. She was on the edge of a moor. In the distance she glimpsed a manor house or perhaps a small castle, set in a vast park. The land rolled down away to her left, revealing a thin silver slice of water and green hills beyond, rising to bald gray mountains. At their base a village of drab stone houses huddled beneath the menacing brow of an overhanging ridge. The cross of a medieval church thrust up like a sword against a lowering sky.

No, this wasn't Rome, nor was it any place she'd seen before.

And the forms she'd seen weren't people after all. They were tilted headstones subsiding into the mossy ground of the churchyard.

She needed to know the names chiseled upon them, but the words were worn and weathered, their incised letters clogged with lichen and dirt. Her fingers traced over them blindly. Urgently. It was no use. The identities of those buried here had been obliterated.

"Not there . . ." a voice whispered.

She gave a start and looked around, but she was alone. Perhaps it had been only the wind rustling through the trees.

Something moved along the edge of her vision and she turned. A graveled path wound away to the right, and she was impelled to follow it.

A moment ago it had been high summer, but now the air was chill with the scent of coming rain. The path she trod was strewn with autumn leaves in rust and copper and gold. Grace followed it to its end, where it encircled a wrought-iron fence, enclosing a large obelisk of polished black granite. Names were carved upon three sides of the obelisk, she saw. The fourth was untouched.

A marble angel knelt to one side. As Grace passed by, the angel slowly turned its blind, impersonal face to her. It raised its beautifully sculpted hand toward the memorial and pointed to the unmarked side of the obelisk.

"Your name," the angel whispered softly, "will go there."

Grace sat up, heart hammering. The angel and the autumn churchyard vanished, to be replaced by a dim golden glow. For a moment she thought that it was still part of the dream. Then she realized she was in an enormous bed. She didn't know where she was, nor why, and her head throbbed terribly.

Her eyes grew accustomed to the faint light that glowed around the edges of the heavy shutters, outlining a mirrored armoire of carved satinwood, a round table, and two tapestry-covered chairs. A washstand and bureau stood on the opposite wall bracketing a wall niche containing a bronze statue. None of it familiar.

Grace stumbled from the bed to the long window and threw open one of the shutters. Squinting against the piercing light, she surveyed the view. The balcony looked out over familiar tiled roofs and domes and marble monuments. *Rome.*

At least she knew where she was now. But how on earth had she come to be alone, in this dim, masculine-scented room? She closed her eyes and concentrated. Images seeped back, like watercolors soaking through thin paper: faint, diffuse, and curiously reversed.

The scent of summer, the shimmer of dragonflies darting over the river . . . the smell of starch and green soap and a narrow dormitory with rows of beds lined up beneath the walls . . . French perfume and cigars, and a parlor by firelight . . .

She took a deep breath. All those brief scenes were familiar to her. The river had brought a feeling of joy, the dormitory a sensation of loss and sorrow, the firelit parlor anger and despair. Yet every one of those emotions seemed distant, muted by time.

These were things that have happened to me, Grace thought, *but not in the recent past.* Little by little other scenes formed, assembling themselves behind her closed lids like mosaics of fractured glass. Her breath came out in a rush: she remembered now—Mrs. Bingley and her daughter, Liza, and the Villa Fortuna!

She heard the door open behind her, and whirled around. Light from the open window fell across a fine figure of a man.

"So," he said. "You're awake at last. How is your head?"

"Aching rather violently," she replied.

McLean closed the door and crossed to her side. She looked different, firm and purposeful. Those changeable, river-green eyes were alert. And wary. He wondered what she was thinking.

Grace was vitally aware of the strong, athletic body beneath his finely tailored clothes. Of a mouth as firm and determined as it was sensual. He was darkly handsome, like a figure from a fairy tale. Whether he was hero or villain, she didn't know.

"Who are you?" he asked. "What is your name and direction?"

"I might ask the same of you," she said more coolly than she felt.

"My name is McLean. McLean of Rossmor."

"I am Miss Templar. And I wish to know where I am, sir, and how I came to be in this place!"

He raised his eyebrows. "Do you remember nothing of this afternoon's events?"

She ran a hand across her forehead. "I'm afraid my mind is a little hazy."

"You were walking through ruins of the Forum near the House of the Vestals, when you suddenly collapsed."

The scent of cloves and garlic . . . exotic incense and perfumes . . .

Grace looked away. She remembered now. It had happened again.

The vision of the Forum as it once had been, overlaying the ruins of the present. Becoming more and more real.

Slow drums and booted feet. Wails and lamentations. The helpless feeling of being trapped in someone else's nightmare, her hands bound before her. Then she was hauled down from the chariot and thrown into the dark chamber. The last stone chinked into place, blotting out the sky forever . . .

"Buried alive," she whispered in horror. "I am buried alive!"

McLean was beside her instantly. "Sit down in this chair. There. Now lower your head between your knees." He pushed her neck down and she leaned forward, gasping for air.

She felt dizzy and ill but no longer faint. "I'm sorry. I . . . I don't know what is wrong with me."

"What is the last thing that you recall?"

She hesitated. "I believe it was entering the Forum ruins, with my guidebook in hand. Yes."

He brought her a cloth wrung out in water from the basin. "Just now . . . you said something about being buried alive. What did you mean?"

"I don't recall saying it. I must have felt as if the room were suddenly airless. As if I were smothering." She twisted her hands in her lap. How could she tell this stranger what she'd seen? How could she tell anyone, and not be committed to an asylum?

His eyebrows rose. "I thought perhaps you'd been reading about the fate of dishonored Vestal virgins. They were entombed alive."

Grace clenched her hands until she felt her fingernails bite into her palms. *I will not faint. I will not faint!*

She bathed her face again with the cold towel. "Will you tell me what happened and how I come to be here?"

"You are a very fortunate young lady. You were startled, perhaps by a bird that flew up beside you, and lost your balance. You sustained a slight blow to the head and were knocked unconscious. Not having the slightest clue to your identity, I had no choice but to bring you back to my hotel and pray that your memory returned. I am relieved to see that it has—at last."

Grace's eyes widened. "Good heavens! What is the time?"

"You've missed your tea, and possibly your dinner. Are you feeling peckish?"

The clock in the parlor chimed the hour. Grace was stricken. "Food is the last thing on my mind at the moment. I should have returned hours ago! Mrs. Bingley will be exceedingly upset that I've been away so long."

"Not under the circumstances, I should hope. Your friend will understand when she learns that you have suffered an injury."

Grace flushed. "Mrs. Bingley is my employer. I act as her secretary and as a sort of companion-governess to her daughter—and she *will* be furious with me."

A governess. Yes, that fit the picture. He wondered how it had come about that she was forced to earn her bread.

"Please, sir . . . Mr. McLean. I must return to the Villa Fortuna immediately."

"I know its location. It is only a short drive from this hotel."

"Then I must be on my way. There is no time to waste." Her position with the Bingleys had been hard-won. If she were to be dismissed again, this time without a reference— no, it didn't bear thinking of!

"You are in no shape to travel just yet."

She clasped her hands together tightly. "You don't . . . sir, you cannot understand my position . . ."

"Indeed I do, madam. I am as anxious to preserve my reputation as to preserve yours. But first you must take some refreshment. I insist."

"I wish to set off at once." She took a step forward. Her legs were wobbly as a new lamb's, and it frightened her.

McLean was there to grasp her arm and steady her. He looked down at her a moment with an expression she couldn't read.

"Sit down upon this chair, Miss Templar. I'll fetch a glass of cordial to restore your spirits."

She sent him a speaking glance. "It's not my spirits that are disordered, Mr. McLean, but my legs."

"You'll feel better after you've eaten something. Bathe your face and fix your hair. I'll ring for refreshments."

He went out and Grace glanced in the mirror over the bureau and gasped. She was shocked at her state of dishevelment. Her black hair had come loose from its chignon to tumble about her shoulders, and in addition to the bandage at her temple she had a bruise along her right cheekbone.

If Mrs. Bingley could see me now, she'd have a fit of apoplexy. But not before giving me my marching papers!

Grace poured water from the porcelain pitcher into the matching basin, and bathed her face and throat. After smoothing her hair back, she twisted it neatly at her nape and secured it with her pins and combs. There was nothing much she could do about her garments, except to brush them as vigorously as she was able. Streaks of dirt showed up as gray smears along her dark skirt, and as dark marks on her white blouse, which was also horridly crumpled.

Perhaps it was just as well that the evidence of the mishap remained. Mrs. Bingley would surely be convinced that something untoward had happened.

Grace's thoughts turned to her rescuer. She wondered what had brought him to Rome at such an unseasonable time, and how he had come to be in the Forum in the worst heat of the day. *And lucky for me that he was there!*

She was grateful for that. And for the fact that she hadn't given away her secret. Her burden. That was how she had come to characterize the strange and uncontrollable ability that had descended on her after a high fever when she was still at Miss Cranmer's. Once her other senses returned, she'd discovered that she had a sort of erratic sixth sense.

At first she'd thought the flashes of odd sights were figments of her imagination, a bizarre result of the fever she'd suffered. Gradually she'd come to realize that places were filled with memories of the past, and that those memories were somehow accessible to her—and that she had no more control over them than she had over the weather.

Less, in fact. If it were raining or snowing, she could always put on a cloak and pop open an umbrella, or elect to stay indoors; but there was no way Grace knew to keep the random images from crowding into her mind and overwhelming it.

But it had been so long since the last occurrence. *Almost an entire year,* she thought. *Why here? Why now?*

On the whole, she would rather have the ability to see the future, which could still be changed, than the past. At the moment she'd give quite a bit to be able to see Mrs. Bingley's reaction when she finally returned to the villa.

When she joined McLean in the elegant parlor, a platter of bread and fruit, cheese and cold meats was set out for her. "I won't let you leave this room until you've eaten something," he told her. "Doctor's orders."

"Very well." She selected chicken and grapes and a braided roll.

He smiled. "I must confess I didn't expect you to agree so readily."

Grace sent him a cool look. "I can see that you're a stubborn man, used to having your commands obeyed. Much as I hate to reinforce your sense of authority, I'm sure it is quicker to give in than to argue the point."

There was a brief flash of surprise and a tinge of temper in his expression. "Very clever, Miss Templar. And also correct. You are not the first to tell me that I am proud and overbearing and sure that I know best."

"Alas that it did no good." She finished the light repast and wiped her fingers daintily on a napkin.

McLean handed her a glass of amber liquid. "Another peremptory order, then. Drink it down, Miss Templar, and you'll feel better straightaway."

She took the brandy as if it were medicine, with a puckered face and a quick shudder. It slid down her throat like satin, then landed in her midsection like a lighted coal. It took a full minute of coughing before she could speak. Grace took the glass of water he pressed on her and drank it down.

"Thank you for your assistance, Mr. McLean. While I'm disinclined to put any further burden upon you, I would appreciate it greatly if you could arrange to have me conveyed to Mrs. Bingley without further delay."

"I'll do much better than that, Miss Templar. I will personally see you safely delivered to Mrs. Bingley's door."

He fetched her bonnet from the table. Grace gave a cry of dismay. One side of it was hopelessly crushed.

He saw the quick regret flicker through her green eyes, to be replaced by a cool detachment. She was, he thought, a woman used to dealing with disappointments. It touched him unexpectedly.

"Better the hat than your head," he said. His voice was more brusque than he intended.

"I suppose so." She put it on and tied the bow .firmly beneath her chin. "We must not keep the carriage waiting."

He held out his arm. "If you are ready, Miss Templar?"

Grace took his arm more for confidence than support, and they went down to the lobby and out the front door. She was glad of his strength, for her legs were still a bit wobbly.

As luck would have it, there was an unusual amount of traffic for the time of day. The street outside his hotel was crowded with hackneys and carriages and mounted riders, backed up by a tradesman's cart with a lost wheel sitting haphazardly in the middle of it all.

McLean was chagrined. He'd hoped to get her safely away without attracting undue attention. He could only imagine what a spectacle they presented to the interested observers. At least her old-fashioned bonnet helped to hide her face.

"I am quite steady enough," she said when they reached the curb, and pulled away.

He let go of her at once. Her balance was still off. For a horrible moment she thought she was going to pitch into the gutter. He caught her and swung her into his arms in one lithe movement. Grace clutched wildly at his neck for security.

"I'm sorry," she whispered fiercely. "My legs seem to have turned to suet."

"Just as long as they are firm enough to support you once we reach your destination," he replied, and lifted her up into the carriage.

The handsome young man in the cart with the lost wheel laughed and gave a catcall when he saw Grace's exposed ankles as McLean jostled her onto the carriage seat.

McLean could only imagine what a spectacle they presented to the interested observers. It was apparent to him that most of the onlookers thought Miss Templar was drunk as a lord.

"Is she drugged or perhaps ill?" someone asked.

"Neither. She has been at the jug," an old woman said emphatically. She raised her hand to her mouth as if gulping from a bottle of *grappa*.

Grace spoke Italian fluently, but their dialect defeated her. Evidently Mr. McLean's talents extended further than hers. He said something unintelligible but definitely rude in tone.

The young man grinned cheekily and the old woman uttered another string of syllables. Grace caught only a single word. Her cheeks flamed but she kept her gaze straight ahead. "You can understand what they said."

"It is nothing that bears repeating, Miss Templar." He took his place beside her and they set off from the hotel.

She was too distressed to pay attention to their route. The scenes she'd "seen" in the Forum had been so real that she could still feel the horror of it. The sudden blackness, the utter terror as that last brick was set into place!

The very first incident she'd experienced had been mild in retrospect. She'd been walking through an old church, examining the medieval tombs with their marble effigies of lords and ladies and armored knights. One had particularly intrigued her. It belonged to a young woman who had died of plague.

The stone carvers had rendered her hair so faithfully that it looked almost real. Grace reached out her hand to touch it—and recoiled in shock. Instead of cold marble, her fingers had touched soft tendrils of golden hair and a cheek still warm with ebbing life. And then the closed eyelids flew open. She had found herself staring into light gray eyes filled with pain and accusation. A sudden certainty had filled her then: the woman had not died of plague, but of poison.

The entire incident was over in a split second. Once again the effigy was cool white stone. Later Grace had put it down to a dozen things: heat, hunger, tiredness. An optical and tactile illusion brought on by her always vivid imagination.

She shivered, remembering, then realized that McLean had turned off from the thoroughfare and was heading down the backstreets of Rome. The worn buildings were so tall and closely built that sunlight barely penetrated.

Grace was alarmed. "Are you certain this is the right way?"

McLean nodded. "It is, if we wish to avoid being seen by English tourists. And much quicker, as well. I recall it as being an old neighborhood in need of extensive repair and refurbishment, and thus thinly inhabited."

"Forgive me! I didn't mean to sound as if I doubted you."

"No offense taken." By her smooth response, he guessed that she was used to placating her employer. He wondered what her life was like. "Tell me about your young charge,

Miss Templar. Is Miss Bingley an apt pupil?"

"Perhaps I gave a misleading impression. Miss Bingley is sixteen, and has made her come out in American society. I am merely employed to help her in . . . ah, polishing her social skills and . . . and to assist her in other ways."

"In other words, you act as a combination teacher, chaperone and maid!"

Grace flushed. "I did not say that, sir!"

He took a corner a bit more smartly than caution would allow. "You didn't need to. I've known others in exactly the same awkward, untenable position."

"No one compelled me to take employment with Mrs. Bingley," she replied with dignity. "I have always wanted to see the world but circumstances denied me that pleasure. My placement with the Bingleys enables me to earn a living and fulfill my wish for travel at the same time. There is a possibility that we may visit Egypt during the winter months."

"You will be disappointed."

"Why do you say that?"

"Egypt is not as romantic a place as you might imagine. And you, Miss Templar, are a romantic at heart."

His comments irked Grace. She sat up a little straighter. "You cannot know what is in my heart or mind, sir!"

He cast a glance her way and smiled. "Not yet, at any rate."

They passed beneath an archway and came out into a large square while she was still wondering what he'd meant by that cryptic remark. Suddenly a carriage came around the corner and Grace gasped aloud when she saw its occupant. The timing couldn't have been more unfortunate.

"Quick, you must turn around before Mrs. Foxworth sees me!" She averted her face. "She is an acquaintance of Mrs. Bingley, and a terrible gossip."

"I cannot." McLean's jaw set and he urged the horse

forward. "There is no turning around in such tight quarters."

The carriage lurched over a section of broken pavement and Grace pitched forward against the front of the carriage before she could prevent it. Holding the ribbons with one hand, McLean caught her around the waist and pulled her back. His strength and quickness surprised her, as did her reaction to it. She felt as giddy and breathless as she had on the stairs; but this time it wasn't from the blow to her head.

The two carriages pulled abreast and passed one another. Grace held on to her bonnet and prayed that her raised arm had sufficiently hidden her face from Mrs. Foxworth's keen eyes.

A jolt over an ancient rut, and they shot out beneath another arched gate, turned left at a five-story block of apartments, and came out into an area of larger homes set in their own grounds.

"One of the things I like most about Rome," he said, "is its surprises. Apartments with laundry strung between them like flags at a regatta, then a lovely jewel of a church set in their midst. A blaze of scarlet geraniums against peeling yellow walls. Brown-cowled monks processing along garden paths that had been the private domain of emperors. At times," he said casually, "one can almost imagine that the streets are filled with the ghosts of ancient Rome."

He glanced at Grace, hoping for a reaction. Her gaze was focused on her hands clasped tightly in her lap and her cheeks were pale. She didn't reply.

They took another turn and the road was empty, lined by brick and stone walls fringed with trees. "We'll make good time now," he announced.

Grace lifted her head and looked down the deserted road. Her hand caught his sleeve. "Stop the carriage! At once."

"This isn't an abduction, Miss Templar. You needn't be alarmed."

"Sir, I am about to be vilely ill!"

McLean took one look at her face and reined in, hard.

Grace leaned over the side of the carriage, too wretched to even dismount. When she was done, he handed her a clean linen handkerchief and a flask of water.

McLean saw her dismay, and had the good sense not to comment. She sat in embarrassed silence, absently shredding his monogrammed handkerchief between her fingers.

Once they were under way again he took the road more gently. When they turned off toward their destination she was pale as a lily. She looked so ill it amazed him that she could still sit erect.

Suddenly he regretted the impulse that had made him take this route. He even regretted going to visit the Forum earlier. By God, he was almost beginning to regret coming to Rome at all.

No, that isn't true. I must have come, if not for my sake, then for Janet's.

The thought of his daughter gave him a pang of homesickness. He missed her dreadfully. McLean wished he could snap his fingers and transport himself and this carriage from the dust and heat of Rome at day's end, to the crisp clear air of his Highland home, with shadows stealing softly across the glen.

But fate had sent him to Rome instead. Now that he was here, he must see it out. For Janet's sake.

Chapter Four

"There is the house," Grace murmured. A brick wall surrounded the Villa Fortuna, hiding it from view. Once past the iron gates the graveled drive curved away through vegetation badly in need of pruning. Eventually it led to a rambling two-storied structure of brick and ocher stucco.

As they approached, Grace rallied. McLean glanced from the corners of his eyes as her spine stiffened, her chin lifted. Even her mouth, so soft and pretty, took on a certain crisp primness of line. She was once again—except for the crumpled hat—the poised Englishwoman he'd first seen strolling through the Forum. He imagined, from the set of her jaw, that she accomplished the transformation by sheer force of will.

He urged the horse up the graveled drive, past an ancient shrine to the goddess of fortune. The villa was more recent, built upon the foundations of the original place by some wealthy Renaissance merchant. He glimpsed a wide portico overlooking the uncontrolled gardens before they reached the cobbled court.

He reined in beneath the wide canopy of a cedar, whose dusty needles perfumed the warm sunset air. A tousle-haired boy with ebony eyes ran out to grasp the horse's bridle. McLean looped the reins and turned to assist his companion down from the carriage.

As he took her hand their eyes met. Grace hid the momentary confusion that came over her with difficulty. When she was safely on the ground she spoke the words she'd been rehearsing.

"I am very aware of the great inconvenience I have caused you, Mr. McLean, and most grateful for your many kindnesses."

He looked down at her intently. "I don't require gratitude, Miss Templar. I only hope you will recover from today's mishap without incident. May I call upon you tomorrow to inquire after your health?"

She was still wondering what to say, when the front door was flung wide. McLean saw a buxom woman framed on the threshold in an expensive abomination of magenta silk trimmed with quantities of ribbons, lace, and a good deal of unattractive ruching. She didn't see him because of the way the door stood open.

"So you have returned at last, Miss Templar!"

Mrs. Bingley's voice had a peculiarly unpleasant edge. It made McLean think of a grinding wheel grating against rusted steel. She glanced at the gold watch pinned to her massive bosom.

"Five hours late on your first free afternoon! And you wonder why I have not given you more time to your own devices. I am scandalized that you should take such advantage of my kindness. I cannot tell you what a state my poor nerves are in! And do not expect me to pay off the carriage driver. That expense must come out of your own purse."

McLean narrowed his eyes. He pegged the outraged matron as the ambitious widow of a man who had made his fortune in industry, and who had now set out to climb the ladder of society by tooth and claw and the judicious application of her lavish fortune.

She is doomed to disappointment, he thought with grim satisfaction.

Grace maintained her cool dignity. "I am very sorry,

Mrs. Bingley, to have irritated your nerves—"

"Well, that you have done—but won't do much longer, I'll be bound. This is a respectable household, and I won't have such goings-on, do you hear me?"

"Yes," Grace said. "Quite well, in fact!"

"Oh! Ungrateful girl! After all I have done for you, letting you take meals with us when we have no guests, and accompany us on drives. I should have known where such kindness on my part would lead. Well, I refuse to let you take advantage of my good nature any longer."

Mrs. Bingley drew herself up. "In fact, you needn't have even bothered to get down from the carriage. I have half a mind to dismiss you from your position without a character!"

McLean spoke from his place in the shadows. "You are precipitate, madam. I am sure that upon reflection, you will reconsider."

Mrs. Bingley was disconcerted, but not in the least cowed. "And who might you be?"

He stepped forward into the red-gold light of the setting sun and presented the indignant woman his most formal bow. "My name is McLean. McLean of Rossmor at your service, madam."

Mrs. Bingley was brought up short by his cultured voice and elegant appearance. He looked the sort of gentleman who mingled naturally with the very class of people she aspired to meet. That put an altogether different complexion on the matter.

Her face altered abruptly. "McLean? There is a Scotsman of that name who created a patented steam engine much used in the cotton and woolen mills. Would you be any relation to him, sir?"

He bowed again. "I am the nephew of the late scientist and inventor Randall McLean."

That deepened Mrs. Bingley's quandary. The inventor of the McLean steam engine that powered her husband's factories had not only been immensely wealthy, he had also been raised to the peerage. Either one was sufficient to insure her hospitality. After all, she was the fond mama of a daughter who had made her come out in the States, but alas! had not "taken."

An entire season and the most expensive gowns that money can buy, and not a single proposal of marriage to show for it, she thought with a familiar flare of annoyance. *Oh, if only the silly chit didn't sulk and whine so, how different her prospects for marriage might be!*

She eyed McLean shrewdly. Here might be a potential suitor for her daughter. And, come to think of it, there were not so many years separating herself in age from Mr. McLean. She favored him with a very warm smile and gave him her hand.

"Perhaps I *was* a bit hasty," she said. "So overset I was these past hours, and suffering palpitations . . . you cannot know!"

McLean hid his cynicism behind a charming smile. "You were naturally concerned when Miss Templar failed to return—and justifiably so, madam. I happened to be present when Miss Templar fell and sustained an injury this afternoon. She was forced to seek the attentions of a physician.

"I am returning her to you with his stern instructions that she rest a day or two before resuming her obligations. I am sure you will see that she follows them to the letter."

Mrs. Bingley beamed. "But of course. If you would care to step into the drawing room, Mr. McLean, I will ring for refreshments. Although I am sure," she added with a meaningful look at Grace, "that Miss Templar will wish to go up to her room at once after so strenuous a day."

He looked at Grace. There were dark circles of exhaustion beneath her eyes. "Perhaps it would be well if Miss Templar recruited her strength with a cup of tea before attempting to mount the stairs."

Mrs. Bingley swallowed her protests and led them in through the portico to the drawing room. McLean could tell by the matron's dissatisfied glance at the furnishings that she was not impressed by the graceful restraint in the decorating. Quantities of fringe and stuffed birds, and wax flowers under glass domes, would be far more to her liking.

She waved him to a seat, then arranged herself upon the divan, while Grace sank into a tapestry-covered chair. "Is it affairs of business that bring you to Italy, Mr. McLean?" Mrs. Bingley asked archly. "Or are you perhaps taking a tour of the Continent with your wife?"

"I am a widower, madam," he said, answering first the question that was foremost in Mrs. Bingley's mind. "I was invited to Rome to take part in a scientific symposium, and shall be leaving Italy and returning to Scotland within a fortnight."

Grace flushed at her employer's clumsy means of extracting his marital status. *Next she will be asking him the extent of his fortune and whether or not he is in the market for a wife!*

Then her eye caught his, and she realized his thoughts were running on the same track. He appeared to be more amused than offended. She was the first to look away.

"Indeed, I am very sorry to hear you will be leaving so soon," Mrs. Bingley said. "There is nothing a busy man of the world needs more than a good wife to see to the smooth running of his household."

As was the case for women with too many servants and too much time on their hands, Mrs. Bingley's thoughts revolved primarily around gossip, fashion, and marriage. She had suffered a pang of regret once they were in the lamplit drawing room and she realized that McLean was younger than she'd first thought. He still had all the qualifications for the open position of son-in-law, however.

A pretty, dark-eyed maid answered the tug she gave on the embroidered bellpull almost immediately. She ordered refreshments. "And see if Miss Bingley has returned from her walk in the garden."

She turned back to McLean. "My dear daughter Liza is a most accomplished young lady, if I do say so myself. She speaks the French and Italian tongues quite prettily. Miss Templar will tell you that Liza sings like an angel."

From Grace's expression it was apparent to McLean that she would be perjuring herself if she said any such thing. He sent Grace another one of those glances that seemed to tie the two of them into a special intimacy.

"And Liza is a very skilled needlewoman. She can darn a stocking as prettily as a bishop's wife can embroider an altar cloth. Not," Mrs. Bingley went on hastily, "that she has any need to darn a stocking, you understand. Or would if she did."

She seemed to understand that she had erred in mentioning an item of clothing so intimate as a stocking, but couldn't find a way out of the morass. McLean took pity on her.

"You are indeed the most fortunate of mothers. Delighted as I would be to meet such a paragon, I cannot linger. I have an appointment this evening that I must keep; however, I hope that I may call upon you tomorrow, to inquire how Miss Templar is getting on after today's ordeal."

"You may," she said graciously. "We have an outing with Mrs. Oliphant and her friends later in the afternoon— she is a relation of Lord Wollingham, you know. I had considered taking Miss Templar with us," she confided, "but one never knows how many others one might be obliged to take up in the carriage. There are sure to be several important guests in Mrs. Oliphant's party."

"No doubt you are right," he said. Grace saw the spark within his eyes and knew he was no longer amused by her employer's pretensions.

McLean bowed. "Your servant, Mrs. Bingley. Miss

Templar." His gaze met Grace's once more, and he smiled. "Until tomorrow, then."

It sounded, she thought, as much a threat as a promise. She watched him until the drawing room door closed. She wondered if he would really pay a return visit, or if he was merely being kind.

McLean went out to the court where his carriage was waiting. His face was no longer masked with his social smile, and his mouth formed a hard line. *The woman is insufferable! How the devil can someone as refined as Miss Templar stand sharing a house with such a crass vulgarian?*

As he mounted, voices carried to him from the open drawing room windows.

"Mama!" a shrill voice exclaimed. "I passed Miss Templar by the stairs and she said she was going up to bed. Why, you vowed that you would box her ears if she dared to show up, and turn her out of the house!"

"Hush, you stupid girl, or I shall box yours!"

"But Miss Templar—"

"Never mind her, she is of no account. Oh, if only you had come in a few minutes earlier. So vexing! Well, and Mr. McLean will be back tomorrow. You must wear your best blue dress and . . ."

The rest of her words faded as McLean snapped the reins and drove away.

Grace watched him from her window. *There is more to him than dark good looks and keen blue eyes. And there is something unusual behind his charming smile and polished manners.*

She was grateful for his kindness and wary at the same time. He was unlike anyone she had ever met before, and she sensed a dangerous intelligence beneath his suave façade.

After McLean drove away, Grace took down her hair and brushed it out before the spotted mirror. In ordinary circumstances she and Mr. McLean would never have met. Their paths had crossed for only one reason—her reaction to the terrifying scene of the past that she'd witnessed earlier at the Forum Romanum. Even now it made her shiver.

She sincerely hoped that she would never catch a glimpse of the past again; but for the second time that day, she wished that she could see at least a *little* way into the future.

McLean was still thinking of Grace as he arrived at his appointment half an hour later. He would have liked to have brought her with him tonight just to see her reaction.

The first joint meeting of the International Society of Experimental Psychology and the Society for Psychical Research was being held at the grand Renaissance Palazzo Borromini. Although the fractured countryside had finally been united in the new Republic of Italy only a few years earlier, the wealth and influence of the old Roman families remained unchanged. His friend Count Lorenzo Borromini lived in the princely splendor of his forebears.

Lamps lit the wide avenue that led to his palatial home, turning the spray of myriad fountains that divided it into sequins of glittering gold.

The faced-marble façade was aglow with light and two men in evening dress were just entering as McLean pulled up. As a groom drove his carriage off to the stableyard, he tucked a leather portfolio under his arm and ascended the wide fan of marble stairs. He gave his hat and cane to a footman in burgundy livery and was directed down the corridor.

Two more footmen opened the doors of a spacious crimson salon hung with Renaissance masterpieces in gilt frames to a group of some thirty people assembled there, only eight of whom were women. Their host came forward when he saw the new arrival. He was a dapper man with dark eyes filled with lively intelligence.

He extended his hands in greeting. The emerald ring on his right hand had once belonged to Cesare Borgia; the gold signet on his left had been a gift to a pope from his mistress.

"Ah, there you are, Alistair! I was beginning to fear that something had happened and that you would not come this evening after all."

"I was detained," McLean said, "but nothing would have kept me away from tonight's meeting. Thank you for inviting me, Lorenzo."

The count clapped a hand on McLean's shoulder. "You are too modest. It is interest in you and your research into the powers of the human mind that have lured my guests here tonight. How was your journey?"

"Blessedly uneventful."

"Excellent. By the by," Count Borromini said in a lowered voice, "Tonio, my scapegrace of a younger brother, told me how you came to his assistance when he fell in with thieves recently. I am most grateful."

"He'd gotten himself in well over his head with that crowd." McLean's face was grave. "I hope he'll learn to choose his companions more wisely in future. It was fortunate I saw him leave with them, and followed. They would have plucked his wallet clean, then taken him for his watch and stickpin, and as like as not thrown him into the Tiber for dead."

"He has learned his lesson, I promise you. Meanwhile, we are deeply in your debt. If there is ever anything I or my brother can do for you in return, you have only to ask."

He led the way to the far end of the room, where gilt chairs were arranged in rows before a lectern. The count nodded at the portfolio McLean carried. "You have brought the case studies to present?"

"Yes. I saw Max Wundt in Leipzig and he showed me the results of his research, which he'll present for publication in the new journal of experimental psychology. He gave me permission to read from it here tonight. Also, Alexander Bain was kind enough to send a report of one of his cases to discuss at our meeting."

Borromini was impressed. "I have read his book on the theory of the relation between mind and body. Most thought-provoking."

"You may be less pleased with another case, which I investigated myself. The young, uneducated French girl who claimed to converse with angels. It didn't take long to clear the mystery up."

McLean smiled wryly. "The poor simpleminded creature was merely the butt of a joke by two local lads, who whispered to her through a knothole in her bedroom wall. When the prank got out of hand and attracted investigation they were too afraid to own up to it."

The other man sighed. "It is such foolery that casts a shadow on our research. What of the German woman who claims to foretell the future when she falls into a trance state?" Count Borromini asked.

"Another sham."

"Are you certain?"

"My dear Lorenzo, there are four categories of people who fall into what is termed a trance, among them, those who suffer from illness or trauma of the brain and nervous system, which can be distinguished by other symptoms; those who are wishful of gaining attention and notoriety for themselves; and those who wish to defraud others."

"How can you tell among them which is which?"

McLean shrugged. "It is easy enough. The frauds and attentionmongers can be distinguished from persons in true trance states by the way they react to a certain stimulus."

The nobleman was intrigued. "And what may that be?"

This time the laughter in McLean's eyes was unmistakable. "The unexpected and forceful application of a sharp pin to a soft body part!"

Borromini joined in the laughter. "A direct approach! But those are only three. What is the fourth category?"

There was a short pause. McLean rubbed his chin. "Those trances that are genuine."

His thoughts circled back to Grace Templar. He'd give a good deal to know what she'd experienced earlier that day in the Forum. There was a good possibility he'd never know, as things stood. She was cool, collected, and wary of revealing too much. It would be difficult to win her trust.

The count was startled. "You are such a skeptic, I never expected to hear those words from your lips."

McLean set his portfolio down upon the lectern. "In fact, I've found several that are unexplainable by science—as yet. Among them, a woman who is consulted by both the London police and private parties in cases of lost or missing children, with extraordinary success."

"Ah, perhaps I can meet this woman when I visit England."

"She has, unfortunately, emigrated to Australia. However, I have all the testimonials on the cases."

"Excellent."

"I've also come across several cases of spontaneous healing," McLean added. "Most dramatically, the apparent cure of a gentleman with advanced consumption, who rose from his death bed after he dreamed that he was healed."

"Ah! You have affidavits?"

"Yes, from reputable doctors who treated him both before and after the event, and the testimony of the local cleric, who witnessed the event, as well."

Excitement shone in Borromini's eyes. "I know of a similar case. A man in his prime was thrown from a horse and suffered a grave injury. He was bedridden for many years, unable to stand. A relic of Saint Cecilia was brought to him—she was strangled in the vapor baths in her own home here in Rome, you will recall. Then one night he dreamed that Saint Cecilia appeared and bade him rise up with the sun.

"In the early morning he called his servants and family and told them of his dream. With the assistance of his sons, the man rose from his bed and walked. Not well at first, you understand, but with increasing strength and vigor over several weeks. He lived another twenty years in perfect health."

McLean was interested. "I should like to know more about this intriguing incident. Are there any living witnesses?"

"Yes." Borromini looked a bit uncomfortable. "Laugh if you like. The man was my own grandfather. I was only a boy, but I was there. I remember it well."

"That's fascinating! I should like you to write down your recollections for me, if you will."

"Of course." The count was gratified. He rubbed his jaw thoughtfully. "Do you know, the oddest aspect of the entire thing was that my grandfather was not a religious man. He claimed that religion was a sop for fools and old women— and yet this man who did not believe in miracles or saintly relics was cured!"

McLean shrugged. "Whether it was a miracle brought about by the power of the saint's relic, or the power of the human mind, is the question that science cannot answer at this time." He eyed his friend. "You've known of my interest in such matters, yet you never mentioned this before."

The count laughed. "I did not wish you to think me a fool. Or worse, gullible."

"I know you too well, Lorenzo. And after all, my family home has supposedly been haunted by a ghost for generations. She is known as the Gray Lady of Rossmor."

Borromini raised his eyebrows. "So you have secrets, too!"

McLean's smile was ironic. "More than you can guess."

"But tell me more! Have you seen this phantom yourself?"

"No, nor would I expect to do so. Others claim to have felt her presence, but she apparently appears only to the mistress of Rossmor." His handsome face grew grim. "A visit from her is considered an ill omen."

A woman in sapphire silk had come up beside them, eagerly waiting for a chance to join their conversation. "Ah, but you are a man of science, Mr. McLean." She tilted her golden head beguilingly. "Surely you would not let either fear or superstition keep you from seeking out the truth of a restless spirit beneath your own roof?"

McLean frowned. "No, I would not, Mrs. Dearing."

Mrs. Dearing was English, a self-proclaimed medium, whose special talent was supposedly relaying messages from the spirits of young children who had died to their bereaved parents. The count was convinced she was an unscrupulous fraud, but McLean wasn't yet convinced either way.

When he'd first met her a year earlier, she'd been living on the fringes of society, simply dressed with jewelry appropriate to her station in life. Of late she'd been gowned in fashions from the most exclusive houses and draped in extravagantly expensive gems—gifts no doubt from her clients, or purchased with their "donations."

McLean's eyes narrowed. Charlatans muddied the waters of research into psychic phenomena. If Mrs. Dearing was a spider feasting on the pain of others, it would give him great satisfaction to expose her. And if she were not, she might be of use to him.

She fluttered her fan. "I understand you are conducting an experiment at Rossmor in October, Mr. McLean?"

He shrugged. "It is merely a small house party of friends."

"How disappointing." She beamed at the count. "But I understand that you will be there, Count?"

Borromini bowed. "Yes, indeed. And Lord Peltersham," he added as the handsome young peer joined them.

"Two men with such an interest in exploring those things beyond our ordinary senses in a haunted manor house?" Her thin brows rose. "Indeed, I am sure you will not be able to resist attempting an experiment. I am filled with envy!"

McLean knew she was angling for an invitation, and he wasn't the least inclined to give in to her. "Envy is one of the seven deadly sins, madam."

A spark of anger flared in her light blue eyes, but her face remained unchanged. "Perhaps I chose the word unwisely. However, I have recently been in communication with a spirit guide from the other side," she added, fingering the diamond and sapphire lavaliere at her throat. "He instructed me to return home and travel far north before the year is out. 'There are great discoveries to be made,' he said."

"Perhaps your spirit is directing you to Scotland, Mrs. Dearing." McLean watched her face light with eagerness. "Although he might just as well have been urging you to a cross-polar expedition."

His joke provoked general laughter. Mrs. Dearing joined in, but hers was forced. McLean rubbed his jaw. *Why not?* Her presence at Rossmor might entertain his guests. "Your idea of conducting an experiment intrigues me. Perhaps, if you are free, you would care to join us at Rossmor?"

"I am delighted to say that I have made no plans for October as yet. I accept your kind invitation. How I shall look forward to seeing Rossmor. Perhaps we might even hold a séance."

McLean shrugged. "Yes, it would be easy enough to arrange. I am sure the other guests would find it entertaining."

"And yet," she said, tapping him lightly with her fan, "I

have the strong feeling that you do not believe in my powers."

"I am very open to the possibility that things exist beyond our five senses. Indeed, I believe that I witnessed a startling example of it earlier today. No," he added, "I shall not say anything more of it just yet."

Count Borromini wagged his finger. "If you intend to keep secrets from us, McLean, we shall have our chance to pry them out of you at Rossmor. Mrs. Dearing will conduct a séance and attempt to summon up the Gray Lady. Should she succeed, I intend to ask the phantom to reveal all!"

Mrs. Dearing smiled. "I shall not only try, I shall succeed."

"And I will bring along my cameras," the count announced with a sly look in his friend's direction. "In hopes that I may capture a portrait of this ghost."

"An excellent suggestion." McLean found the consternation on Mrs. Dearing's features disappointing. *So she has reasons to fear closer scrutiny.* Well, if she were a fraud it would be a good deed to expose her. "I will send particulars to you at your hotel tomorrow, Mrs. Dearing."

He favored her with a bow and she left them, well satisfied with her evening's work. The count raised his eyebrows. "What an encroaching, pitiful woman!"

"Yes," McLean said. "But by the time she leaves Rossmor she will find fewer lost sheep to fleece."

"Then I am right: you mean to expose Mrs. Dearing as a fake!"

"Of course. And what better place to do it than at Rossmor, where I can control the situation. Annoying as her presence may be, she will be useful to my research. I will be interested in observing how the temperament and expectations of the other guests color what they believe they actually see and hear during her little performance." He took his seat and the count opened the meeting.

The evening was lively, filled with discussion and controversy. Before McLean spoke, Mrs. Dearing decried the folly of scientists trying to explain the unexplainable. She went on and on about "the girl in France who speaks with angels. She is a pure soul, in tune with a higher plane of existence than the one upon which we mortals dwell."

"She is a girl of low intelligence, victimized by two village pranksters," McLean said, and brought out his proof. Mrs. Dearing turned crimson with embarrassment but held her tongue. There was no way she would jeopardize her invitation to Rossmor. She brooded through the reports and left the moment the meeting was adjourned.

McLean left soon after. He was glad to leave the glittering Palazzo Borromini behind and return to the quiet of his hotel. Grace Templar's scent of lavander and violets lingered in his suite. It unsettled him. He opened the balcony doors and went out.

He lit a cigar and glanced over to where the great dome of St. Peter's was only a black silhouette blotting out the stars. The church had arisen over the apostle's tomb, which had been built on the site of his crucifixion. A place of death had been transmuted by imagination and human effort into a beautiful embodiment of faith.

McLean watched a veil of smoke thin out over the Eternal City. *Rome,* he mused. *The city of saints and sinners, of Christ and Caligula, hope and skepticism. Miracles and madmen.*

The atmosphere seemed alive, resonating with invisible energy and the ghosts of the past. It was no wonder that Miss Templar had succumbed to it. But had it been nothing more than some hysterical reaction or the actual attunement of a born "sensitive" to the aura of the place? His personal stance on most psychic matters was neither completely yea or nay, but "not proven."

Mrs. Dearing and her ilk might be opportunists intending to milk the gullible, but there were other people who did seem to have talents that were unexplained as yet by rational science. For instance, the ability to unravel time and transcend distances. To grasp the past, intuit the present, or view the future.

Grace Templar, he believed, was one of them.

She had been on his mind all evening. He wondered what misfortune had befallen her that had left her to make her way in the world alone. She was intelligent and cultured. A woman of inner strength and resourcefulness. And quite lovely, despite her outmoded garments and the severe way she dressed her hair. In the ordinary course of events, she would have been married by now with a hopeful family of her own.

But then our paths would likely never have crossed.

She intrigued him greatly. He played the scene in the Forum over in his mind. He had no doubts that she'd glimpsed something there. Something that was invisible to him, but was terrifyingly real to her. It was more than a careful reexamination of the incident or his finely honed instincts for the unusual. More, even, than his ability to read the faintest of flickering expressions or the slightest rigidity.

He'd seen a similar look of mingled astonishment and horror upon his dead wife's face half a dozen times. It had been frozen on Finnula's features when her cold body had washed up upon the rocks—her eyes open, dull as stones. Accusing. It haunted him waking and sleeping.

Scenes of the happier past flashed suddenly before his eyes. Red-haired Finnula, dancing at their engagement party, all laughing mouth and sparkling blue eyes. He had known her most of his life. *Lovely, doomed Finnula.* He'd loved her so long he couldn't remember when it first began. That she cared for him too had seemed a miracle. On the day of their wedding he'd considered himself the luckiest man in the world.

She had always been changeable as the moon, laughing one moment and cool the next. It was only after they married that he saw her dark side. Her fragile temperament began to swing like a pendulum from wild gaiety to black despair. Had her fears and nightmares been born of something real as she had claimed, or were they the product of an increasingly disordered brain? That was the riddle that kept him going. He would find the answer to it one day.

Perhaps it would be at Rossmor, back where it had all started.

And ended.

He heard a woman's voice from the terrace and a man's response. Soft laughter floated on the air. *Lovers walking through the moonlit garden.* For some reason his thoughts circled yet again to Grace Templar. Had she ever been in love? Had a lover? Did she, beneath her cool, pragmatic façade, dream passionate, romantic dreams?

McLean wondered what would happen to her over the years ahead. Most gentlewomen condemned to the same fate would wither to resentful shadows, fetching and carrying for ungrateful domestic tyrants, until they were cast aside as unfit to work. It seemed too cruel a fate for anyone, much less a woman of her caliber.

Was there anyone of his acquaintance in need of a governess? He ran through a list of likely candidates, but their children were either still in leading strings or away at school. He'd find no position for Miss Templar among them. His own daughter took her lessons at the vicarage with his nephews and had no need of a governess yet. Certainly his cousin Elspeth and his sister Meg were set against one at this time.

He also doubted that Miss Templar would be willing to give up her proposed excursion to Egypt with the Bingleys, in exchange for an isolated manor in the wilds of Scotland. That made it even more difficult.

Miss Templar's position and the lectures in Rome were only two items on his agenda. The first and foremost was his daughter. Janet would be ten in December. She had his own blue eyes and her late mother's beauty, but her personality was very much her own. She was the brightest light in his heaven.

He touched the inner breast pocket of his jacket, where he carried her miniature portrait and a lock of her auburn hair in a thin leather case. *I will not fail you, Janet, as I failed your mother. I swear it.*

The few remaining lights of the city winked out as he struggled to find a solution to the problems that faced him. By the time he'd finished his cigar, he had come to a decision. His conscience pricked him only slightly. *I am a selfish man, perhaps a ruthless one—but I am not without pity.*

He went inside and closed the doors behind him. He knew exactly what he must do—and he intended to do it.

Chapter Five

Grace picked up the darning egg and slipped one of Liza Bingley's stockings over it. Because her stitches were so fine, she'd been graciously granted the honor of repairing them. Her silver needle flashed in and out in the light from the window beside her, as she focused on her task.

Her young charge sat on one of the brocade sofas, wearing an expensive outfit of lilac and white muslin and an increasingly sulky expression. She'd been alternately sighing and impatiently scuffing her heels against the sofa for the last quarter hour.

Grace worked hard at ignoring her. It was, she'd learned, the only way to handle Liza when she was out of sorts. Attentive concern only made the spoiled girl become more sullen.

She was in no mood for Liza's crotchets. Grace had spent the first half of the restless night thinking of Alistair McLean, and the remainder caught up in disturbed dreams, none of which she could remember clearly. There had been a churchyard and a marble angel that wept real tears . . .

She was so focused on trying to recall the dream that she jumped when Mrs. Bingley swept into the room.

"Well, this is a fine to-do! Here are Liza and myself, all primped and primed for a visit from Mr. McLean, and to no avail! I would have never thought it of him. It was most ungentlemanly to encourage us to think he'd call today, only to disappoint."

She glanced at the clock on the mantelpiece. "There is nothing for it. We shall have to depart soon if we mean to meet Mrs. Oliphant. Another quarter hour and we must take our leave."

Liza was dismayed. "A quarter hour? Why, Mrs. Oliphant told me that of all things, her son most dislikes unpunctuality."

Her mother sincerely hoped that Mrs. Oliphant's young son would *not* be a member of their party. While she intended to curry favor with the lad's mother, Mrs. Bingley had no intention of bestowing her daughter upon a well-connected but impecunious young man. Mr. Oliphant was a fine-looking lad with pleasant manners, but no prospects whatsoever.

While she hoped to snag Liza a title, she wouldn't sneeze at an offer from a wealthy member of the aristocracy—and one McLean of Rossmor was worth a hundred William Oliphants.

Mrs. Bingley believed in being prepared. She never read anything but the court news in the papers, or picked up a novel or book of poems, but she had obtained the most recent volumes of *Debrett's Peerage* and the *Almanach de Gotha*, along with a new volume entitled *The Hereditary Landholders of Scotland and Ireland*. They were tools to enable her to determine exactly the right degree of deference to give to the wealthy and titled she might chance to meet in her travels. And to distinguish the highly eligible suitor from one not quite so worthy.

If she closed her eyes she could recite the entry she'd looked up the previous night, almost verbatim. *"It has been the seat of the Highland McLeans of Rossmor since the Year of Our Lord, 1245. The princely property is situated on the banks of beautiful Loch Ross, and the discerning visitor will find it hard to believe that the imposing house, with its elegant architecture and beautifully appointed chambers, began as a simple fortified tower . . ."*

"No title, but a 'princely property'!" Mrs. Bingley's eyes sparkled. "I wonder what he is worth?"

Picking up the book from the side table, she turned to the marked page and began to read aloud: " 'The long drawing room at Rossmor is noted for its coffered ceiling and exquisite paneling. Its tall windows command an expansive view of the loch and its rocky islands, where legend claims the heart of William Wallace is buried. The eerie apparition reputed to haunt the older parts of the manor, however, is that of a woman. The phantom is said to be an ancestress of the McLeans, and is known far and wide as the Gray Lady of Rossmor . . .' "

"A princely property with a *ghost!*" That last gave her a delicious shiver. To Mrs. Bingley's mind, it was the magical touch. "Only a well-established family such as the McLeans may lay claim to an ancestral ghost."

Grace listened with gritted teeth. *If I have to listen to Mrs. Bingley list Mr. McLean's material qualifications as a prize on the marriage mart one more time, I will run screaming from the room!*

Unless I throttle her first.

Liza ignored her mother. She was tired of waiting anxiously to see young Mr. Oliphant. *Scuff scuff.* William Oliphant was very handsome, and had eyes of the most melting shade of brown she'd ever seen. *Sigh.*

"Mama, we will be late if we don't leave soon," she said petulantly. "We have been waiting for *hours* and *hours* and Mr. McLean hasn't come. And," she added, "he sounds quite *old!*"

Grace was surprised into a laugh. There were many adjectives to describe her rescuer of the previous day, and none of them were "old." The current mode might be for fair men with rosy cheeks and exquisite airs, but no woman who had seen Mr. McLean would forget him. His dark hair, strong jaw, and deep blue eyes made a definite impression.

He is handsome in a way that defies convention, she mused. *Intelligent. Quick to think and act. Impatient, and yet kind.*

She wondered what he would think if he heard himself so described. *Not much,* she decided. *He is a man who knows his own worth, but I doubt vanity is one of his besetting sins.*

That, she felt sure, would be the inability to suffer fools gladly.

No doubt he'd had enough of both Grace and her employer the previous day. She couldn't blame him. Grace picked up the wooden darning egg once more and began to mend another of Liza's stockings.

The minutes ticked by with no sign of McLean, until the clock chimed the half hour. Mrs. Bingley swallowed her bitter disappointment. "There is nothing for it. We must set off now, or offend Mrs. Oliphant. And as she is the niece of Lord Wollingham, that would not do at all."

She rang the bell and ordered the carriage brought around. "Put on your bonnet, Liza. Oh, Miss Templar! My calling-card case is empty. Fetch me some from the table in my boudoir."

Grace rose. "Of course, Mrs. Bingley."

"And my crepe fan, and the tin of mints. Yes, and now that I think of it, the book of poetry I promised to lend Mrs. Oliphant. I don't recall the name of it or the author, but I'm sure you will."

She said the last darkly, as if knowing the names of popular poets bordered on the sinister.

Liza frowned and looked around. "Where *is* my bonnet? That lazy girl, she forgot to give it to me. Miss Templar, tell my maid to fetch it to me at once! The one with the yellow ribbons and pansies."

Grace went abovestairs and delivered Liza's message, then went to Mrs. Bingley's chamber to retrieve her employer's calling cards and mints and the volume of poetry.

As she headed swiftly down the corridor, a gnarled figure in rusted black entered it from the left. The woman eyed her sharply, then nodded. Grace smiled and paused to let the elderly servant pass. The woman glided across the polished floor and vanished through the solid wall.

Grace gasped as a spurt of hot fear erupted in her chest. She stood there trembling. *No, please, God! I won't let it start up again.*

But she knew it was too late. It was happening again, just as it had before: something in the Forum yesterday had activated her old sensitivities to atmosphere and place. And she had as little control over her strange visions as she had over the movements of the sun and moon.

She took a moment to catch her breath and slow her thundering heart, then started for the staircase again. As she passed Liza's room a shadow fell across the threshhold. Grace gave a small cry of alarm, then realized it was only Liza's young maid.

"I cannot find the hat with the pansies anywhere, signorina."

"I will help you look, Simonetta. Perhaps it was misplaced." They opened all the bandboxes and turned out the cupboards and wardrobe to no avail.

Grace sighed and went down to break the news to Miss Bingley. "I thought perhaps the bleached straw with the lilac ribbons?" she suggested.

"Stupid creature!" Liza wailed. "I don't *want* the one with the lilac ribbons. I want the one with the *pansies*!"

Mrs. Bingley's eyes narrowed. "Ring for Simonetta, at once! I believe that she has stolen it. Foreigners! Untrustworthy and lazy—every last one of them."

Grace flushed with anger and embarrassment for her employer's prejudices. It deepened when she spied the housekeeper standing in the doorway to the back parlor, her face stony with anger and dislike.

She glanced back at her young charge. A flash of yellow caught her eye. "What is that peeking out from beneath your skirts, Liza?" she asked.

The girl jumped to her feet. The pansy-strewn confection lay on the divan where she'd been sitting, crushed beyond hope. "Oh! Oh! My best hat, utterly ruined!"

The girl's strong fit of hysterics was only forestalled by her mother's sharp reproof. "Liza, stop your sniveling!"

Mrs. Bingley looked up and froze, then bustled forward to where Alistair McLean stood just inside the open drawing room door. "Good afternoon," he said, his voice as cool as his demeanor.

"Mr. McLean! Come in, come in. We'd quite given up hope of you!"

"I fear that I've timed my visit poorly."

"We had expected you earlier, sir. We are on the verge of an outing. I do hope you will come to call another time, Mr. McLean, when my daughter and I can entertain you properly."

She caught sight of the ruined bonnet. "Miss Templar, go at once and fetch the bonnet with the lilac ribbons. And take the other one away!"

Grace swept out of the room by the far door without meeting McLean's eyes, her face burning. She wondered just how much of that vulgar display he'd heard.

When she returned with the bonnet in hand, her cheeks were even more flushed from the exertion.

McLean was leaning negligently against the mantelpiece, but his eyes were hard as steel. "The doctor gave strict instructions for you to rest, Miss Templar. I trust the exertion of going up and down the stairs so quickly hasn't caused you any problems."

She smiled at him and handed Liza her hat. "None at all, sir. I assure you I am quite used to it."

"I have no difficulty in believing that," he answered curtly. McLean turned to Mrs. Bingley. "I am sorry that

I've called just as you are leaving. I was called to consult with my friend Count Borromini on a matter of great importance."

Mrs. Bingley positively beamed. "Ah, the count. So distinguished a lineage. So fine a figure of a man. Wealthy as Croesus! Not that I have made his acquaintance, you understand; however, we did see him driving in the park the second day of our arrival in Rome."

Grace was once again embarrassed by her employer's lack of manners, and she was a little surprised at Mr. McLean. She didn't imagine that he was the type to drop names in casual conversation.

Her eyes met his, and she recognized the gleam in them. *So that is it. He has taken Mrs. Bingley's measure, and calculated the quickest route to winning her esteem.*

"I'll not detain you further, madam. Perhaps Miss Templar would accompany me for a drive? I am sure you cannot have the slightest objection to it, Mrs. Bingley. You may be certain that I will see to her every care and comfort."

For the first time she could recall, Grace saw Mrs. Bingley at a loss for words. Her mouth flopped open like a landed fish.

Which is entirely appropriate, Grace thought, *since she is a trophy of Mr. McLean's skillful angling.* He'd used Mrs. Bingley's own snobbery and the bait of his friendship with Count Borromini to reel her in.

"It might indeed be that Miss Templar would benefit from a drive," her employer conceded. "However, Miss Templar has the headache."

"There is nothing for a headache like a drive in the cool of the country," he said, favoring her with a bow. "Or perhaps Miss Templar might prefer a stroll around your gardens. They're quite lovely."

Mrs. Bingley was in a quandary. She'd agreed that Grace could drive out alone with Mr. McLean, and now she couldn't very well refuse to let him stay and visit with her. After all, Miss Templar was long past the days of youthful indiscretion, and the house was full of servants. After a brief inner struggle, she gave in, and swept out with Liza in tow.

In a few minutes Grace saw the carriage drive off past the drawing room window. She felt unaccountably nervous.

"We had quite given up on you," she said. "Mrs. Bingley kept the carriage waiting for some time, in hopes you'd arrive before they were forced to depart."

"Yes. I know." His eyes sparkled with laughter. "I've been waiting this past half hour in a grove of trees down the road, wondering if they'd leave before I lost patience."

She lifted a startled face toward him. "What a strange thing to do."

"Spare me your polite comments. I'm sure there are times you would like to escape their company."

Grace bit her lip to keep from agreeing.

"Why do you put up with them?" he asked abruptly. "You are an educated and cultured woman. Surely you could find a position more to your liking, than waiting hand and foot on that formidable tyrant and her spoiled daughter."

Her color rose. "You are very vehement, sir. I assure you that I am quite . . . quite *happy* with my position as governess to Miss Bingley."

"Yes," he pointed out. "Just as you assured me yesterday that you were quite all right, mere seconds before you fainted in my arms."

"A momentary weakness."

"I don't imagine that you indulge in many of them," he said, scrutinizing her closely. "And even if you were so inclined, I doubt your employer would take kindly to them. Your position here must be extremely trying to a woman of your sensibilities."

Her green eyes went cool and aloof. He was either too outspoken for civility or trying to learn more of her background through flattery. She had no intention of indulging either. This was dangerous territory.

Through no fault of her own, she had been dismissed from her previous position without a reference. Just thinking of it now made her feel ill.

Mrs. Abernethy's diamond brooch had vanished, and her maid been accused of taking it. But Grace, hearing of it from the hysterical girl, had known instantly where to find it. She'd seen it in her mind's eye so clearly, that she told her employer and her family that she could find the brooch—and it had been found exactly where she'd visualized it would be, hidden behind a book on one of the shelves beside the fireplace.

The moment her hand had touched the brooch, Grace had realized the truth: it was Mrs. Abernethy herself who had put it there. Her employer had been afraid to disclose her gambling debts to her husband, and had meant to give up the brooch in order to settle them. Mrs. Abernethy had then accused Grace of taking it. Instead of being a heroine, she was called a thief and thrown out of the house with her pitiful belongings.

Alone and friendless in London. She shuddered to remember it.

She'd been fortunate to find a position with Mrs. Bingley, using an old reference that Mrs. Bingley hadn't bothered to pursue. No matter how difficult the lady might be, Grace could only be thankful for her position—and the warm bed and food that came with it.

Folding her hands, she fixed him with a level glance. "While I'm grateful for your assistance, Mr. McLean, and it is kind of you to be so concerned for my welfare, I am forced to point out that neither my background nor the terms of my employment are any of your business."

"Well done!" His quick smile flashed out. "I see that I have misjudged the situation. A woman with so sharp a tongue as yours has little need of my misguided chivalry."

Grace laughed. "Unless she has collapsed in a public place! Forgive me. I do owe you something for your kindness to me. I am most sincerely grateful. However, I cannot oblige you by going for a drive." She held out her hand. "Thank you for calling, Mr. McLean."

"Cannot—or will not?"

"Whichever you choose, sir." She put a hand to her head, which was beginning to ache in earnest.

He was instantly contrite. "I apologize, Miss Templar, and hope you will let me make amends. Fresh air is my prescription for what ails you," he said. "There is a pleasant breeze and the countryside is pretty. Will you drive out with me?"

She wrestled with her conscience. Half a dozen excuses ran through her head, none of them completely convincing.

McLean saw her wavering. "Come, Miss Templar. What harm do you expect to come to you? After all, you spent several hours alone in my company at the hotel yesterday and managed to retain your virtue."

Grace was horrified. "Hush! The servants will hear."

"I will raise my voice louder, then, if that's what it requires to get you to agree." The laughter in his eyes took the sting from the threat. "And I have brought along a picnic luncheon in a wicker hamper in the strong hopes that you will."

Grace knew she should protest, but she was tempted. She knew that she would be away from the Villa Fortuna far longer than she should; but the Bingleys would be away for hours also. *Had the course of my life run differently, this is exactly how I would be spending a beautiful day.*

The afternoon beckoned beyond the closed windows of the parlor. So did the opportunity of spending a pleasant hour or two in the company of a charming and intelligent gentleman. The temptation proved overwhelming.

"Far be it from me to dash your hopes, Mr. McLean. I'll fetch my hat."

She returned in a few minutes with a shawl and a furled parasol over one arm and a wide straw hat with blue ribbons tied beneath her chin. It was not in the current mode of fashion, but he thought it suited her perfectly.

Grace saw the admiration in his eyes and her color rose. *I am like a giddy schoolgirl,* she thought, *blushing because a handsome man looks my way. And he is indeed handsome.*

As he handed her up into the carriage McLean's beautifully tailored coat set off his muscular width of shoulder, and the sunlight sparked red highlights in the depths of his dark hair. She tried not to think of it: she had learned as a child that it wasn't worth eyeing the candy in the confectioner's window, when all it did was leave her wanting.

McLean took the Via Tiburtina out of Rome. Once they were away from the city, he snapped the whip and they set out down the ancient road at a spanking pace. He seemed perfectly ready to drive in silence, and Grace felt it was up to her to initiate a conversation.

"You were in the Forum when I . . . uh, when I fainted. Are you particularly interested in antiquities?"

"You might say it is a combination of both business and private matters that brought me to Italy." He sent her a blinding smile. "However, at the moment I am more interested in enjoying so lovely a day in your company, Miss Templar."

Grace sent him a quelling look. "I am not accustomed to flattery, sir, so you must forgive me if I do not respond as you expect."

"Ah, my dear girl, but you have responded almost exactly as I would have expected—had I given the matter any thought."

Her laugh was spontaneous and full of rue. "Well, that was the perfect set-down. It has certainly cleared up any misconceptions I might have harbored as to your motives."

"But none at all where my manners are concerned." He

turned to smile again at her. She was blushing, and her heightened color brought out the delicacy of her features, the magnificent color of her eyes. "Have I offended you with my blunt speech, Miss Templar?"

"Not at all." Grace was delighted with his quick wit and sense of humor. "It has been a long time since I crossed conversational swords with a worthy opponent."

"No," he replied. "I don't imagine you get any practice with Mrs. Bingley or her daughter. They would come to the fray unarmed."

"Now you are being cruel, as well as blunt."

He shrugged. "I am a man of science. I describe things as they are, not as how I should like them to be."

"I see. You mentioned that you are here to attend a symposium of some kind?"

"Yes. I studied medicine in Edinburgh, and gradually shifted my focus from the purely physical to the metaphysical—the interrelationship of the mind, the soul, and the body. Now, like my friend and colleague, Jean-Martin Charcot, I am particularly interested in disorders of the mind, and whether their basis is physical or mental."

"Your work must require a great deal of dedication."

McLean smiled. "No, merely a great deal of curiosity! I don't work at treating the disorders directly. My purpose is to study the research and propound theories based on the information I gather. It is a subject that has fascinated me since I read of the experiments with hypnosis by a fellow Scot, James Braid.

"For instance—why do we dream? Why is one person happy and optimistic by nature and another suspicious and pessimistic? Why are some born with great gifts and others are born utterly lacking? Why," he continued, "do some stay sane despite the most terrible of trials—and others, who seemingly have everything life can offer, become so morose that they cannot find the will to continue living?"

Grace was impressed. "A worthy field of interest. Most

gentlemen of my acquaintance live on their expectations. They spend their time visiting their clubs when they are not racing, shooting, or playing at games of chance. Had I been born a man with such resources at my command, I hope I would have followed a more purposeful goal as you have, sir."

McLean raised an eyebrow. "You have educated and formed young minds. That is the most noble calling of all, Miss Templar. And had you been born a man, it would have been a very great shame. I prefer you exactly as you are."

She blushed and fell silent.

"Are you wishing you had not come out with me today?" he asked.

"If I said yes, I would be lying. And . . . and it is so cool and pleasant here after the heat of the city."

"Small compliment to me," he said, laughing. "If ever I feel my vanity expanding, I have only to apply to you, Miss Templar. Your honesty would puncture my pretenses as if they were soap bubbles."

"I will try to be a little more conciliating," she said with false primness.

"Good."

"Yes." Her eyes sparkled. "It's never wise to alienate someone who has the ability to dispense favors—such as a drive in the country on a hot summer day."

"That was a settler," he said, grinning. They drove on in companionable silence.

The road angled and the sun shone in her eyes. She closed them against the brightness, taking pleasure in her other senses. The warm caress of the sun upon her skin; the rich bronze smell of warmed earth and the crisp green fragrance of the pine.

She became conscious of others, as well. Her own sachet of lavender and verbena mingled with McLean's subtle masculine scent. It made her intensely aware of him in a way she'd being trying to ignore. The shape and strength of his gloved hands upon the reins; the firm lines of his mouth and chin; the magnificent breadth of his chest and shoulders.

She opened her eyes quickly. He glanced over at her and his color heightened. He turned his attention back to the road without saying anything.

Her pulse sped up and her cheeks burned. *Does he know what I am thinking? Can he tell that I am so strongly attracted to him?*

She concentrated on the minute darn at the wrist of her pale blue gloves until her heart steadied. For many years she'd prided herself on her ability to hide her emotions. It wouldn't do to forget now.

"Are you enjoying your visit to Rome, Mr. McLean?"

"More so than you, if I judge correctly. Tell me how a lady of quality came to be in the employ of the likes of Mrs. Bingley. You did not start out in life on such a bleak path."

The warm sun and cool breeze affected Grace like a sparkling wine, and loosened her tongue. "No, I was raised in comfort in a rambling Elizabethan cottage outside London. A lovely place of mellow brick and half-timbering," she said, "with latticed windows and a wild tumble of gardens leading down to the river. I was the only child of a vague and doting mother addicted to poetry and her gardens, and a brilliant, distracted father who spent the majority of his time spying on the habits of insects."

He turned his head and gave her a startled look. "Good God! Do you mean that you are the daughter of Jonathan Templar, the great naturalist?"

Her face pinked with pleasure. "You know of his work?"

"Indeed! You might say my interest in science was fanned by him. When I was a boy my uncle took me to hear one of his lectures on spiders at the British Museum. He brought several glass display cases of live spiders with him, including a yellow and black striped tarantula from South America."

Grace couldn't help laughing. "Yes, and its case was knocked over. The glass broke and the tarantula escaped into the audience. What a to-do! Prominent men shrieking and scurrying away like schoolgirls! I shall never forget the looks on their faces." She shook her head. "Poor Papa. He was not invited back."

"You were there!" McLean exclaimed. He remembered a young, dark-haired girl in a white dress with a sailor collar. "You popped out from behind the packing cases, ran after the great hairy creature and threw a box over it!"

His amazement was no greater than hers. Grace cocked her head and stared at him. *Those eyes, so darkly blue and intense.* Now she knew why they were so familiar.

"You were the boy who helped me slide the lid under the box!"

"Yes." McLean was still astonished. "The whole thing is extraordinary. Do you believe in fate, Miss Templar?"

"After this, I would be a fool if I said I did not believe in coincidence." Grace shook her head in wonder.

"I thought you were incredibly brave," he told her, "although I doubt I said so at the time. In fact, I fear that I was insufferably superior."

"No more so than any other boy addressing a younger girl," she teased.

"You showed no fear of the tarantula. I was quite impressed."

She laughed again. "That is because it had lived in its glass case in our back parlor for some time. The maid refused to dust in there, so it became one of my duties. When it escaped, my main concern was to trap it safely before someone tried to kill the poor, frightened creature."

He flashed her a quick smile. "A most unusual response for a girl of—what, eight or nine years?"

"I was ten." Grace shrugged. "But you see, I often

helped my father trap insects, or observe their behavior."

"It sounds a strange and lonely life."

Grace smiled and shook her head. "It was the most wonderful, fascinating childhood any girl could have had!"

His eyebrows rose in surprise. "You astonish me, Miss Templar."

"No, only think of it! No governesses. A house filled with books and flowers, rioting gardens where I caught crickets and ladybirds and imagined that faeries might live amongst the roses and peonies. The river, all brown and gold, where I caught snails and water-skaters, and swam on warm summer days."

She remembered how it felt to dive down below the surface through pools of liquid light, as if she were one of the gold and silver fishes.

McClain saw the rosy flush that lit her skin, the glow of her eyes. This was no tale spun to amuse him. She had indeed been happy in her childhood home.

"What happened to end it?" he asked abruptly. "How did you come to be on your own?"

"The inevitable, I suppose." She smiled a little sadly. "Neither of my parents had a turn for economy. There were financial reverses after my father's sudden death from pneumonia when I was eleven, and the house was sold."

"Only a year after our chance first meeting," he said quietly. "I am sorry."

The rest of her tale was grim but familiar. Their decline in status had been rapid. Bit by bit, her mother had sold off everything of value, from the household furnishings to the books and even her personal jewelry.

Grace touched the elegant silver brooch at her throat. The flat oval cabochon stone was translucent white with a decided blue-gray tinge, like an overcast sky at twilight.

"She kept only this milk-opal brooch for me. It had been a wedding gift from my father."

She had difficulty still, remembering those terrible times.

Her secure world had been shattered irreparably. Shabby but familiar surroundings had given way to hired rooms that smelled of despair and boiled onions. The thin walls that allowed the shouts and cries and curses of their fellow roomers to penetrate.

"You must have felt you'd been plunged into a nightmare."

She nodded. "Worst of all was the sense of dislocation, the bewilderment of finding myself plucked up and hurled into a colorless, confining world, as unfamiliar to me as the dark side of the moon."

McLean saw that her wounds were still raw. Time had merely scabbed them over. He felt a deep tug of sympathy. "And your mother? Is she still living?"

Her slender fingers twisted together. "No. Unable to cope with the loss of my father, she slipped into a state of melancholy so profound that she took to her bed and never rose from it. They were both gone within three months of each other."

He put his hand over hers. "She must have loved him very much."

Angry tears stung her eyes. Grace blinked and looked away. "She should have loved *me* enough to *stay!*"

It was wrung from deep within her soul, the frightened cry of an abandoned child. Grace was appalled. "I'm sorry! I . . . I don't know why I said that. You must think me quite hard-hearted."

"It is I who must ask *your* forgiveness. My lack of sensitivity caused you distress."

McLean fought a sudden impulse to put his arm around her shoulder and draw her close for comfort. "Deep-rooted emotions are like the closed-up rooms of a house, Miss Templar: there are times when they must be opened up and aired. I am privileged that you felt free enough to express yourself so frankly with me."

"You are very kind. I don't feel like that now, of course;

however, I didn't realize her death had affected me in that way. She was an unworldly woman, totally devoted to my father. Many times since I've imagined how very frightened and desperate she must have been, suddenly left to fend for us and without a clue as to how to do so."

"Yes, you've moved past the childish—and very normal—resentment at being orphaned. You see her now through the eyes of an adult."

"You have an extraordinary depth of understanding, Mr. McLean."

"I am sorry to have brought up sad memories, Miss Templar." He'd slowed the carriage and turned off a branching road. "And so you were packed off to stay with relatives?"

"No. There were none that I knew of left in England. Mother had made arrangements for me in her final days. I was accepted as a boarder at Miss Cranmer's Academy near Oxford, where I received my formal education and training."

McLean was again astonished. "Another link between us, Miss Templar. My sister Margaret was a boarder at Miss Cranmer's Academy, also. Perhaps you knew her?"

Grace was startled. "How odd that our paths keep entwining!"

"Not really. It's evident that members of our families shared an interest in science and education. Most select seminaries are nothing more than finishing schools to prepare young ladies of quality for marriage. Miss Cranmer, however, is a woman with great force of character, and holds very progressive ideas on the education of females. What more natural than that both you and my sister should be educated there?"

"Yes. That makes sense when you explain it."

She realized that there was a family resemblance between Mr. McLean and his sister.

"I knew Miss McLean by name and sight, of course, but we did not move in the same circles." Grace lifted her chin. "I was a scholarship student, my fees waived by the academy in return for the guarantee of my teaching services for five years after my schooling was finished. It would have set me apart from the other girls, even if my unorthodox upbringing had not."

McClain heard the taut cord of distress woven through her neutral tones. To go from complete freedom to regimentation, from being the darling daughter of the family to a charity girl, must have been a plunge into ice water.

"I imagine everything about Miss Cranmer's came as a great shock to you."

"It was," Grace said crisply, "much better than what I had recently become accustomed to. There was food on the table and there were no bailiffs at the door."

"You are a remarkable woman, Miss Templar!"

"No, I am not. There are hundreds of young women all over England who have found themselves in the same circumstance. I, Mr. McLean, am very fortunate! I was armed with a proper education, which enabled me to make my way in the world. I have no bitterness toward fate."

This time he couldn't resist. He reached over and covered her hands with one of his. "I say again, Miss Templar: You are a remarkable woman."

The approval in his voice, the depth of his sympathy, warmed Grace. Or perhaps it was his gentle strength, the heat of his hand through her thin cotton gloves that created the glow inside her. She wanted to pull her own away.

She wanted to stay like this forever.

Her fingers trembled in his grasp, and he relinquished her at once. "Forgive me. I meant no disrespect."

She didn't reply. She couldn't. His sympathy unnerved her.

The olive groves gave way to meadows. Gradually the road began to rise, and she saw green hills ahead, hazy with distance. She realized it had been some time since they'd passed any signs of habitation.

"Surely we should have reached our destination by now? Where are we headed?" she demanded.

"One of the loveliest spots on earth: Hadrian's Villa, outside Tivoli."

"Good heavens. That's at least twenty miles from Rome! We've already made a late start. We will never return in time."

"I assure you we will, Miss Templar. Although I admit our tour of the ruins will be a bit rushed. Perhaps you would rather visit someplace closer?"

"Hadrian's Villa is tempting, but I think it would be wiser not to venture so far."

McLean glanced over at her, his eyes bluer than the sky. "Then I know just the place."

He pulled off the Via Tiburtina onto a road that was little more than a track. The carriage bounced over dried ruts. They passed olive terraces and once she saw a hill town in the distance, the dome of a church gleaming on the summit, and ocher houses spilling down the wooded sides. It looked ancient and enchanting, and she had the impression that it might vanish like a mirage before her very eyes.

Grace grew concerned after another good half hour had passed. "Perhaps you have taken the wrong turn."

"No. There it is. Can you see that square tower rising from the side of the hill? It's what is left of an old chapel."

She strained her eyes against the sunlight. The trees screened it partially from view, but she could just make it out amid the slanting shadows. She sat back, relieved. "It is not so very far."

A smile played over McLean's lips. Distances were quite deceiving in the clear golden air. The tower was a good deal farther away than it appeared.

His smile grew.

Chapter Six

McLean reined in beneath the branches of a grove of gnarled pines and secured the horses. Birds sang in the warm, pine-scented air as he came around to help Grace down from the carriage. For a fleeting second she was poised at his level and their eyes met. Something hummed in the air between them. It set her pulse hammering again, until she felt so light-headed that she had to look away.

He sensed it, too, she knew. She could tell by the tension of his hand and the quick way he stood back and released her once she was safely on the ground.

McLean stepped away, unsettled. The bright spark that had leapt and flared between them had left him less in command than usual. He'd been almost overpowered by the urge to pull her into his arms and kiss her soundly. *Then the cat would have been among the pigeons,* he thought.

It had been a long time since he'd found himself so drawn to a woman. He was intrigued by the possibilities that she might have certain unique powers of perception, and he was strongly attracted by her wit and character. Her beauty was an unexpected bonus.

He turned away to tend to the team and Grace tried to convince herself the moment had never happened. *I am unused to a gentleman's company, and merely read more into his expression than was there.*

She looked around. The air was cool and fresh, the ground sprinkled with wildflowers and the scraggling descendants of cultivated plants that had once graced a garden. A small spring trickled down the mossy stones of the hillside to pool in a hollowed stone at their base. She was charmed by it all.

Strolling past a stand of trees, she came upon the old tower silhouetted against a blue sky filled with puffy clouds. The area just before it had hummocks of grass, marking the outlines of an ancient foundation. She perched atop the stone with a view of both the tower and McLean. *Those strong thighs, that long line of back and width of shoulder!* A sudden warmth came over her and she snapped open her parasol; but she was very aware that the sun wasn't responsible.

Grace was glad to have a few moments to compose herself. She was no fool. She knew that he admired her. That road ran both ways: he was exactly the kind of man she had dreamed of meeting in her days as an instructor at Miss Cranmer's Academy: *charming and handsome and kind—yet with a hint of passion—or perhaps ruthlessness—just below the surface.*

It seemed very odd that just when she'd given up all hope of ever knowing someone like him, he'd come into her life—and so dramatically.

She was equally certain that they lived in separate spheres which were touching only briefly. Their paths would part ways again, leaving her with a pleasant memory of a drive in the country. Nothing more.

It filled her with infinite regret. *If my life had gone differently we might have met somewhere . . . a dinner party or a ball. We might have laughed and danced together . . .*

But it was no use daydreaming. He would return to Scotland and she would spend the next several months in Rome and Cairo, at the Bingleys' beck and call.

McLean joined her. "This looks a likely spot."

Grace agreed, and he set down the picnic hamper and carriage rug in a patch of dappled sunlight. Her calm features and voice were a disappointment to McLean. He'd hoped that the atmosphere would affect her, although not as strongly as the Forum had.

Perhaps there is nothing here that speaks to her, he thought. *Either that, or I was completely wrong in my conjectures, and the occurrence in the Forum was a fluke.*

"I wonder what this part of the ruin was? Perhaps the chapel?" he remarked.

"No, this was the stable," she murmured, without thinking. He looked up at her sharply. "Why do you say that, Miss Templar?"

Her face paled and she hesitated. "Why, the . . . the scent of hay and horses is still very strong."

McLean smiled. The only scent he could identify was the light fragrance of her lavender-verbena sachet and the cool aroma of the pines. *So, this place speaks to her after all.*

"Sit here," he advised, putting down a cushion for her. "The view is best appreciated from that direction."

Grace hung back just a little. She was afraid of glimpsing some unpleasantness from the past. But there was nothing at all to frighten her.

She sat on the cushion while McLean opened the hamper. He brought out dishes of cold ham and chicken, cheese and apricots ripe with the bloom of summer, and flaky pastries dripping with a syrup of honey and ground almonds.

"Are you thirsty, Miss Templar?" McLean removed a bottle of wine and two glasses from the basket.

"If you have water or lemonade that will be sufficient."

"Alas, this is all we have," he said, pouring out a pale, sparkling wine into two crystal goblets. "I believe it is quite mild." He handed her one. "To your health, Miss Templar."

She eyed it dubiously, then took a sip. It was tart and refreshing, with a lingering taste of pears. Before she realized it she'd finished the entire glass. McLean was quick to refill it.

Grace was famished, and made a substantial meal of it all. "There is still enough to feed a regiment," she said when she was done.

He handed her another pastry on a china plate with a smile. "I believe you overlooked this one."

She eyed him quizzically. "You must think me a glutton."

"I think you're a woman with healthy appetites," he answered. "But I don't know enough about you to form an opinion. At least, not yet."

She didn't know quite how to respond to the implication that he intended to see more of her. Certainly it pleased her. But life had held too many disappointments for Grace to get her hopes up. He seemed a consummate gentleman, and she doubted he had dishonorable motives; but it was unusual for a man of wealth and position to pay so much attention to a woman in her circumstances.

She saw that McLean was watching her closely. Too closely. She tried to divert his attention. "Tell me about this place. What is that building?"

"The local people call it 'the dovecote.' "

"A *columbarium,* you mean?" The Latin word for "dovecote" was also used to describe places filled with little niches to hold the ashes of the dead.

"No, it was a rest stop for pilgrims on the way to Rome," he said, "as well as a place of healing. As penance for his sins, a nobleman gave up his privileged life and built this tower where he lived the rest of his days in prayer, caring for the travelers. Those who were ill or injured stayed on till they were well enough to travel. Eventually others joined him in caring for them." He gave her his most charming smile. "Shall we explore it?"

She hesitated just a moment. The place seemed peaceful enough. "Very well."

"I'll set the picnic basket inside the door so the wild creatures don't make off with the food."

McLean held open the heavy door and Grace stepped through. Although she was a little hesitant to go inside, there seemed nothing to alarm her here. No sense of human strife, of past joys and sorrows. No stirring of ancient shades. The place was devoid of menace, as tranquil as a meadow.

A shaft of light from the open door illuminated a small table along the back wall. There was a wooden cross set upon it, and fresh wildflowers in a stone jar. It touched her.

"Someone has been here recently."

"There is an elderly priest who takes care of the site," McLean responded. "Sprightly, but deaf as a post. He opens and closes the place each day, sweeps the steps and empties the alms box, where coins are still collected to care for the poor. He might have put them there."

Grace didn't think so. She had the impression of a young girl, desperately in love. Then it faded away.

The lower area had been used mainly for storage, and the next opened up to a kitchen with a huge hearth and a door at the far end. It opened to a plot of ground that had once been a garden, backed by the sheer stone of the hill rising straight up some thirty feet.

"They can't have grown much here," she said. "There isn't enough light. How on earth did they feed everyone?"

McLean laughed. "What a practical woman you are, Miss Templar! According to the guidebook, it was used for the growing of healing herbs which required shade. Food was donated by the neighboring farms."

The last room on the ground floor was a common room, with a long refectory table and wooden benches. A series of square holes in the top of the walls brought light and air into the windowless room. The walls were decorated with faded frescoes rendered with the charming simplicity of a child's drawing.

She examined the nearest one. A woolly, rather cross-

eyed lamb, was draped across the shoulders of a strapping
man with a shepherd's crook and a twinkle in his painted
eye.

"Christ as the Good Shepherd is one of the oldest sym-
bols of Christianity," McLean remarked. "Images of the
Crucifixion were not used in the early days of the Church."

Grace was drawn to it. "How delightful. He looks like
a real person, not some pale plaster saint!"

They admired the fresco of the Wedding at Cana with
the blessing of the wine, and another of the Miracle of the
Loaves and Fishes. Grace smiled up at McLean. "I'm glad
we came here."

His blue eyes lit with pleasure. "Then so am I, Miss
Templar. Do you feel up to exploring the upper rooms?
There are several frescoes above."

"I should like to, very much."

As they came through to the entry the outer door swung
shut behind them, plunging the first floor into twilight
gloom.

Winding steps led up to the next level. One tiny chamber
was a garderobe, another a sort of bathing place, with stone
basins, where water from the hillside spring was diverted.
"All the amenities," McLean said dryly.

The rest of the second floor was divided into identical
cells with arched openings and tiny slits for windows. The
washed-out frescoes here were scenes from nature apparently done by the hand of the same artist.

"These were the rooms where the holy men stayed and
weary pilgrims and the ill were given refuge. Perhaps it is
the small chambers that gave this place its familiar name."

The thought came into Grace's mind, fully formed: *He
called them his little doves.*

McLean looked down at her. "Really?"

Grace flushed. She hadn't realized that she'd spoken
aloud. "I am guessing," she said hurriedly and went on to
the next chamber. She entered and stopped short.

A man in a dark cowled robe knelt in the center of the little room, telling his beads. The polished brown wood slipped between his fingers with a faint snicking sound. He looked up and saw Grace, and his dark eyes were filled with kindness and inquiry.

"Oh, I am so sorry, *padre*!" she exclaimed in Italian. "We didn't mean to intrude upon your devotions. We thought the place unoccupied."

The man rose and came toward her with a gentle smile— and vanished before he reached the doorway.

She stared at the tiny cell with a raised pallet, small table, and crucifix on the wall. Where the man dressed in a friar's robes had stood, there was only a patch of sunlight on the worn floorboards. Grace felt her pulse speed up until she thought her heart would burst with its efforts.

McLean came up behind her. "I heard you speaking. I thought there was someone in the room with you, Miss Templar."

"No. I . . . I was merely thinking aloud." Her thoughts were racing as furiously as her heart. The man had looked so real! As real as the stones that formed the tower. As real and solid as her own flesh.

In the past, she'd always felt herself being drawn into the past as if she were watching a play, and had suddenly found herself onstage among the costumed actors. Yesterday in the Forum she'd become, for a few terrifying seconds, the principal figure in the play.

Today there had been no separation between the past and present. It had been a seamless whole. Either she and the robed man had existed in this chamber at the same time—or else she was going mad.

"It's getting late," she said. "Perhaps we should go back."

He heard the panic beneath her quiet tones and his excitement heightened. She'd seen something. He was sure of it. "Nonsense. We've at least an hour before we must start back, and there is still a good bit of the place to explore."

"I really think we should leave," Grace said.

He took her gloved hand in his. "What is wrong, Miss Templar? You seem distressed."

"Nothing is wrong," she replied. "I am only concerned with reaching the Villa Fortuna before Mrs. Bingley and Liza return."

"I think it is something more," McLean said. "Some people are sensitive to atmosphere. I believe you are one of them."

"Yes, there is a good deal of atmosphere here. I'm sure you feel it, as well."

His dark blue eyes held hers. "I do indeed, Miss Templar. There are some people who claim they can do more than experience the aura of such a place—to perhaps attune themselves to events which occurred in the past in such surroundings."

Grace smiled coolly and turned her head. "You are a man of science, Mr. McLean. I would be very surprised to learn that you believed in such mystical powers."

"Would you, indeed? Somehow I thought you to be a woman of more imagination."

She felt a flutter in the pit of her stomach. "You imagine a good deal, Mr. McLean."

"I wish you would trust me a little," he said softly, and cursed himself when she withdrew into chilly dignity.

"If I did not trust you, you may be certain I would never have driven out with you today." Grace gathered her skirts and swept out of the chamber.

Since he blocked the stairs down, she had no place to go but up. He followed her, still cursing himself for speaking too soon. She was frightened by her experiences and had been used to keeping her own counsel. She wouldn't admit him to her confidence without good reason.

He intended to provide her with one.

Grace hurried up the uneven steps, wondering what was

going on in his mind. She did not want him to see her as a freak of nature. A curiosity for scientific study. Her ability to view the past had brought her nothing but grief. And less than a hundred years ago, people had been put to death for it . . .

Nor, she thought, blinking back angry tears, *am I a specimen, to be dissected and examined under a magnifying lens, like a microbe in Mr. Pasteur's laboratory!*

At the top of the stairs there were more chambers, and a wide arch leading out to a platform of living rock. She stepped out upon it warily. They were much higher than she'd realized, and the view ahead was nothing but endless sky. McLean went to the edge and looked down.

"It's safe enough," he called to her. "Come. The view is fantastic."

Grace realized the back of the tower was actually formed from the sheer limestone walls of a cliff. Far below the land stretched away, its color changing from the brassy green of the hills to the dry, washed-out tones of the distant plain. There was nothing at all of the present to stamp itself on the landscape.

I could be standing here on this rocky ledge at any point in time since this tower was built.

The thought slipped out before she could stop it. The moment it came into her consciousness she knew it was a mistake. The light took on a subtle change. The transparent air seemed to grow solid, to fold about her and enclose her in crystal. The scents came first, as always . . .

. . . rosemary . . . citrus . . . myrrh. The sublime strains of Gregorian chant rose softly all around her, rising and falling in a benediction. She was aware of shapes forming out of the air. A wooden railing. A low table. Pallets set out in the warm sunshine for the ill and injured . . . men in the humble brown robes of monks moving among them, offering water and prayer and words of comfort . . .

Grace was vaguely aware of McLean moving toward

her, as she struggled to free herself from the coalescing images of the past.

"No!" she exclaimed beneath her breath. "Not here! Not now!"

The images wavered, like reflections on a wind-ruffled pond. Gathering her inner strength, she willed them away. They dissolved abruptly, and she snapped back to the present with such force that she almost lost her balance.

McLean was at her side in an instant. "What is it, Miss Templar? Are you taken ill?"

"No! Merely a . . . a brief touch of vertigo."

"Here, let me help you." He put his arm around her waist for support and led her to the wooden bench. "Sit down. No, don't close your eyes. It will only make it worse."

Grace didn't know how long she sat there, gulping air and grasping at reason. It didn't seem as if much time had passed; but when her head cleared she gasped in dismay. A luminous blue dusk was gathering over the hillside, and a single star shone in the cloudless sky.

"Oh! What is the time? We must go back," she cried.

"You needn't be unduly concerned. Evening falls early on this side of the hills. Once we're out of their shadow, there is at least another hour of daylight."

Grace shook her head. "That will get us back with little time to spare."

"You are forgetting it is all downhill. The return journey will be much quicker."

His soft words calmed her. "I cannot believe it is so late," she said.

"The day has flown by," he agreed. "I must admit I hate to see it come to a close. I have enjoyed our outing immensely, Miss Templar."

Something in the timbre of his voice made her look up. She found McLean smiling warmly down at her. The blood rushed to her cheeks and her breath hitched in her throat.

I am acting like a giddy schoolgirl, she thought and wrenched her gaze away.

After a few minutes she composed herself and rose. "I am quite recovered now."

"Good. We'll set out at once. Everything will be all right," he told her as they headed down the stairs. Grace held that thought to her like a bouquet of roses—right up to the time that McLean tried to open the door at the base of the tower, and found it locked.

Chapter Seven

"What the devil!" McLean pulled against the door. It wouldn't budge.

Grace ran to the narrow window slit. Through the three-inch gap, she could just make out the figure of a bent old man in a priest's cassock disappearing down the path opposite to the way they'd come.

"He has locked us in!" She called after the cleric, and McLean raised his voice as well. The deaf priest continued on his way and vanished from view.

"You'll have to force the door," she said.

McLean raised his eyebrows. "Your confidence in me is touching but misplaced, my dear. In the first place, that door is six inches thick and was made to withstand battering by the bandits that roamed these hills. In the second place, it opens inward. There is no way to force it from inside the tower."

Grace pressed her hands to her cheeks. "What shall we do? How can we return to the Villa Fortuna tonight?"

"I don't believe we can. I am very much afraid we will have to spend the night here."

"No!" Grace ran back up the stairs, desperately searching for another exit. Although she could still catch glimpses of the sunlit valley floor, the light had faded to a dull orange. As she stood there, almost weeping with vexation, the sun dropped behind the rim of a hill, plunging the tower into violet shadows.

McLean had climbed up beside her, very much aware of Grace's distress. He was sorry for it, but it couldn't be helped.

"There must be a way down from here," she said.

"Only if we were eagles, Miss Templar. Or angels."

"Mrs. Bingley will be furious. She will dismiss me without a character."

He watched her, wondering when she would throw her thoughts ahead further than the immediate problem. If he judged her correctly, she wasn't a woman given to hysterics. *In any case, I'll soon know.*

"I saw a lantern in one of the rooms," he said. "I'll find it and light it. Perhaps the priest will see it and return to investigate."

"So we must wait." Grace sighed. She couldn't let herself believe that he was wrong, that they were stranded in an isolated tower in the hills.

He came back with the lantern lit. It revealed a niche she hadn't noticed earlier, containing a small table, a rude stool, and a long wooden chest.

He opened the lid and found an old blanket and a fur lap rug, which he handed to her. "No doubt we're in for a long wait. We might as well be comfortable as we try to pass the time."

Grace paced restlessly and he tried to distract her. "Tell me more of your history, Miss Templar. Did you enjoy your teaching duties?"

Grace was in no mood to talk of herself. "You have heard enough of my life story, Mr. McLean, yet I know little of yours."

"My home is in Scotland, along the shore of Loch Rossmor. It's a sea loch, running deep into the land, flanked by moors and mountains. Some consider it a harsh setting, but to me it is a place of great beauty."

His tactics worked. He described his home so well that Grace could almost see it. The dark waters of the loch glinting in the sun, the tidy stone village tucked at the foot of the heather-clad moors, and the steep rise of the crumpled mountains beyond.

"You have a great love for it," she commented.

McLean smiled. "I would rather be at Rossmor than anywhere else on the face of the earth."

Grace sent him an appraising look. "And yet you are far away in Italy at this highly unseasonable time of year."

"I travel for many reasons, both business and personal. Until the death of my wife four years ago, I was content enough at Rossmor."

She flushed and murmured her sympathy. "I am sorry to hear of your loss. She must have been quite young."

"Certainly too young to die," he said.

"Are there children of your marriage?"

"Yes. A daughter. Her name is Janet. She is not quite ten years old."

He hesitated, then withdrew something from within his jacket almost reluctantly. It was a piece of slim leather that opened like a book to reveal the portrait of a pretty girl, all glossy curls and smiling dimples and dark-fringed eyes.

"She's lovely," Grace said.

"Yes. The very image of her late mother."

"That must be a source of great comfort to you."

"It is a source of greater pain!" He closed the leather folder abruptly and put it away.

Grace sat very still, struggling to hold her tongue. She couldn't do it. "You must forgive me for speaking my mind, sir, but I cannot be silent. If that is the reason you avoid your home, you are doing her a great disservice. Yes, and yourself as well. Since she has lost one parent, it seems harsh to deprive her of the other."

His jaw set. "You know nothing of the situation!"

"I do not. But I do know the pain and bewilderment of

a bereft child longing for her family." Her face, so white a moment earlier, now flushed with deep emotion. "Poor little thing! My heart goes out to her."

She expected harsh words from him for her impertinence. Instead McLean stared at her. "As does mine, Miss Templar. As does mine."

The light from the lantern outlined his fine physique and made his strong cheekbones stand out in high relief. He looked handsome, she thought, and very remote. She watched him, considering what he'd said from every angle. There had been something in his voice . . .

Sorrow, she decided. *Sorrow and concealed anger.* But whether the latter was at fate or at herself she didn't know.

"Where is your daughter now?"

"She is at Rossmor, in the care of my cousin Elspeth Lachlan. She is the widow of a retired army officer with no children of her own."

Complete darkness had fallen while they talked. The lantern light did little to dispel it. Time passed and no miracles occurred. Grace couldn't pretend any longer. "There is no use hoping for an easy way out of our predicament. The priest won't return until morning."

"Yes. It makes for a very awkward situation, Miss Templar."

She put her hands to her cheeks. "Then my fate is sealed. Mrs. Bingley will send me packing."

His eyes reflected the flames in pinpoints of light. "Would that truly be so hard a fate?"

"Unlike more fortunate individuals, I must work for my bread, Mr. McLean. No genteel family will employ me if word of this escapade gets out!"

"I certainly have no intention of trumpeting it about," he said, "and I'm sure you will not do so. It is Mrs. Bingley who must be persuaded to remain silent."

Her breath came out in a little sigh. "You'd have more luck holding back the tide than stilling her tongue."

"Her scruples may be outraged—but her sense of self-preservation will quiet them. Think! The scandal within her household would blight her social ambitions, as well as Liza's prospects of landing herself an eligible husband."

"I sincerely hope you're right. But however discreet she is, Mrs. Bingley will still throw me out of the house. I will have to find a new position. Perhaps one of the hotels has openings for a chambermaid."

"Good God!" McLean scowled. "You cannot hold a high opinion of my character, if you think I would abandon you to such a fate."

She stared at him. "What other choice have I?"

"One that apparently has not occurred to you." He took her hands in his. "I would be a villain of the worst sort, if I abandoned you. Although I am solely to blame, we are in this tangle together. You needn't bother seeking employment, my dear. I will take care of everything."

Her eyes were wary. "What exactly are you suggesting, Mr. McLean? And why?"

"I am not suggesting anything," he said with a careless smile. "I am proposing to you. I sincerely hope that you will accept my offer of marriage, Miss Templar?"

"Marriage! But that is absurd."

"There is no alternative. The protection of my name will erase this sorry episode and put to rest any wagging tongues. Perhaps it is not what you wish—but it is the only way I see for both of us to come out of this damnable coil with our reputations intact."

She was sure he could hear the thundering of her heart through her bodice. It was so loud in her own ears that she thought it would deafen her. "No. I cannot accept."

"Why not?" His grip tightened on her hands. "You are intelligent enough to see the advantages of such a union on either side."

"Why, we are almost strangers," she stammered.

"We will get to know one another better after we are married."

Married. Grace was shaken. "You cannot mean it. Our stations in life are not equal. Such a union would benefit me alone. I have no fortune or family connections to recommend me as your wife in a marriage of convenience."

He gave a short laugh. "Are you thinking it would be a marriage of *in*convenience on my part? I assure you that wouldn't be the case. You are an educated woman of superior intelligence and impeccable breeding. Rossmor is a large house in need of a mistress with those very traits." McLean played his trump card. "And my daughter needs a mother."

"Unfair!" she exclaimed and pulled away.

"But true. Janet is growing up. She needs a woman to steady and guide her."

"What of your cousin?"

"Elspeth and Janet are frequently at loggerheads because their natures are too different. Where my cousin is cool and collected, my daughter is all passion and feeling. I believe your intelligence and warm heart would bridge the gap." He lowered his voice. "You accused me earlier of neglecting my daughter. I love Janet very much. She and Rossmor are everything to me."

He saw her wavering. "There is another factor, as well. You may condemn me for my part in bringing us to point nonplus—and well I deserve it! But I am a gentleman and my reputation is also at stake here. I don't wish to figure in gossip here and at home as the despoiler of your virtue, Miss Templar!"

"No. I can quite see that . . ."

"Then you accept my offer?"

She held up a hand. "Please. I must think a moment. My head is whirling."

Grace tried to see her way clear. There was so much to think over—and so very few options open to her. She was in a foreign country, friendless and surely unemployed. The chances of finding another genteel position were as remote as the stars: she had no references, no friends or family to turn to for aid.

And once word got out that she'd spent the night alone in Mr. McLean's company, no proper matron would let her set foot inside her door. Despite her brave words earlier about scrubbing floors, she dreaded sinking down from her current position. *To be forever exiled from my own kind! I do not think I could bear it!*

Mr. McLean, out of guilt and a valid concern for both their reputations, was offering her the quickest and safest escape from this ridiculous predicament. Mentally she ticked off the other benefits. The arrangement would give her far, far more than she could ever have dreamed of as a governess, suspended in that bleak shadow world that lay between the glittering universe abovestairs and that of the servants below.

As she pondered his proposal, McLean watched her intently, reading her thoughts as they flickered over her lovely face.

It is a great temptation, Grace admitted to herself. Marriage to Alistair McLean would give her immediate status and stop any gossip. She would oversee the running of Rossmor and live in ease, free of the tyranny of the Mrs. Bingleys of the world, and without the slightest worry for her future.

She would also see to the raising of young Janet McLean. It was equally difficult to turn her back on that. The motherless girl's portrait and her sad history had already touched Grace deeply.

And each time Mr. McLean had mentioned his daughter, a vision flashed before her mind's eye: a young girl in a nightgown, her face blanched, her blue eyes wide with emotion. It was accompanied by an intense sense of loneliness and longing. The scene was so brief, the background so dark that Grace couldn't make out the details, but she had no doubt that the child she "saw" was Janet McLean.

A girl who had been orphaned young, just as she herself had been.

Grace tried to reconcile herself to accepting McLean's proposal. *It is clear that the marriage he offers would be one in name only. A business contract, no more and no less: his name and protection, in return for my services to his home and his daughter. It seems a fair bargain.*

Despite the obvious benefits, Grace still found herself oddly reluctant. She paced the chamber in agitation, while he lounged against the wall, waiting for her acceptance of the inevitable. Even in repose he radiated an aura of barely contained power that drew the eye.

I am no foolish young girl, she told herself sternly. *Why should I recoil from his most gentlemanly offer to rescue me?*

A shiver ran through her. She knew. She knew.

His ring would be on her finger, his name on her calling cards; she would have all the rights and privileges granted to any respectable married woman. But in reality, she would be nothing more than a combination of housekeeper and governess, acting the role of Alistair McLean's wife before the world, yet living as chastely as a nun.

Grace wondered if she had the fortitude to carry it off. Her nature was deeply ardent. She'd always imagined that somehow, someday, she would meet a man whose passions of mind and soul and body equaled hers. That they would marry in love and trust, and one day she would conceive and bear children as fruit of their union.

She ached to be held and loved, longed for a relationship that would satisfy her needs, body and soul. Grace was a woman who honored her vows. Entering into a loveless marriage of convenience with him would mean forever denying her deepest desires. Burying her dreams.

Alistair McLean might enjoy her company, but his marriage vows to her would be no more than an act of charity. Could she play her assigned role? Could she hold up her head, knowing he'd married her out of pity and a sense of honor? For a moment the thought was unbearable.

She drew a deep, shaky breath. There was no other way out. *Dear God, what else can I do?*

Grace watched as stars lit the sky overhead. There was no magical sign from the heavens to help her come to a decision.

"I am very tired, Mr. McLean. I am going to try and sleep. I will give you my decision in the morning."

"Very well. I'll keep watch while you sleep."

She was alone, under the most compromising of circumstances, with a man she scarcely knew, and should be in near hysterics. But Grace had no fear of him, and felt safe enough with him. There was nothing to be done until daybreak. In the meantime, she would curl up in a blanket on the bench and ponder the pros and cons of his offer.

As Mr. McLean's wife, her troubles would be over. She would never have to worry again about her future. When she grew old there would still be a warm roof over her head and food on the table, instead of the room in a boardinghouse she'd imagined at the end of her working days, and nothing but weak tea and gruel cooked over a spirit lamp. The weight of that terrible fear would be lifted forever.

She would be mistress of Rossmor.

On the other hand, what kind of relationship could be forged out of such base metal? In time, he would surely come to resent the circumstances of their sham marriage— and to resent her. She knew nothing of him other than what he'd told her and what she had observed herself. He was handsome with excellent address. He'd come to her rescue when she'd fainted in the Forum, and was willing to do so again. Surely that showed that he was generous and kind and responsible.

A man she could trust.

But he was also a keen, scientific observer. A man who had studied abnormalities of the human mind. Would he discover her secret? Would he fear she was touched by madness, or could he accept her strange abilities without condemnation? Or would she become one of his experimental subjects? The thought was chilling.

Her nerves were terribly on edge. She could only imagine the commotion her absence must have caused at the Villa Fortuna. There was no hope of returning to Mrs. Bingley now. She accepted that. Grace realized that she would have to accompany McLean to Rome and set her new course from there. But what that might be was still unclear to her.

Although she expected sleep would elude her, she drifted into the deep slumber of emotional exhaustion . . .

. . . *She was walking beside the water at sunset. The slanting light turned the stones to gold nuggets. The wind gusted up without warning. She saw it dancing toward her from the far side of the loch. The dark blue of the water turned silver and white as the wind sped over it, and she pulled her cloak around her in anticipation of its keen breath.*

"I suppose it's time we turned back," she said to her companion.

He slipped his arm about her shoulders. "There is no turning back now," he said. "We'll go on together."

She buried her face against his wide chest and as he drew her close she smiled . . .

McLean turned away from the fire he'd built in the open hearth pit. He hoped the priest wouldn't mind his sacrificing a battered footstool in a good cause. She was sleeping, with a faint smile on her lips. She looked tender and tempting and vulnerable. "I'll make it all up to you," he said beneath his breath. "I promise you that."

He rolled up his jacket for a pillow, and made himself as comfortable as possible on the floor. He could understand her initial reaction to his proposal—after all, she didn't know him from Adam.

Then a thought occurred that hadn't struck him before: perhaps her reluctance was because she already had an understanding with another man. Someone she hoped would trust her enough to believe in her innocence despite the damning circumstances.

I should like to meet such a paragon if he exists, McLean thought cynically. *But on the whole, I would rather that he didn't exist at all.*

He lay awake all night, listening to her soft breathing, and waiting for morning to decide his fate.

Chapter Eight

It was the whisk of a broom on stone that awakened Grace. McLean put his fingers to his lips. "It is the elderly priest. No need to scandalize the poor man. We'll slip away when we can do so without being seen."

They were afraid he'd climb the stairs and discover them but perhaps his rheumatism was bothering him, for the old man hobbled out of the tower shortly afterward, leaving the door unlocked.

McLean had retrieved the picnic hamper. They broke their fast on stale rolls, the remainder of the cheese, and fruit. It was scarcely light but they set out the moment McLean could get the carriage hitched. Neither of them spoke until they were well away.

He reined in beneath a line of pines. "You've had time to come to a decision. Will you accept my proposal, Miss Templar?"

Grace closed her eyes. It would be so easy to say yes. To put the struggles and fears of poverty behind her. To assume a role in the world that should have been hers by birth.

I could make myself useful to him. See to his comfort and the smooth running of his household. Help to guide and educate his daughter.

And she realized that she wanted to do it. Wanted it desperately.

"Very well, Mr. McLean," she said. "I am ready to meet my fate. If you are still willing, I accept your proposal of marriage."

If he was surprised by the curtness of her reply, it didn't seem to matter. McLean lifted her gloved hand to his lips. "I am honored, Miss Templar. You will not regret your decision."

Her smile went a little awry. "I only hope, sir, that you will not regret yours."

She pulled away, too aware of his nearness, the subtle scent of his cologne. Now that the die was cast, she wanted it all safely over and done with. "When can you arrange it?"

"As soon as may be." He frowned slightly. "There are some difficulties attendant on the marriage of Protestants in this country. Please believe that I will take every step to guard your reputation from further damage, until we've exchanged our vows."

She nodded. "Forgive me. I wasn't thinking clearly. I will leave it all in your good hands. I am conscious of what I owe you and—"

He touched her mouth with his finger, stilling her words. Her heart gave a jolt of pleasure. "It was through my doings that this situation arose. You owe me nothing, Miss Templar! Nothing. Remember that."

She was taken aback by his vehemence. "I cannot hold you entirely to blame."

McLean collected himself. "You are very generous. It is my fervent wish that your sentiments remain unchanged after we are married. I am afraid it may take a day or two to arrange."

"What?" She held her hands to her burning cheeks. "But . . . it must be at once!"

"It might be difficult to find a Protestant minister to

marry us in Rome, or some alternate arrangement. Be assured that I will do so with all due speed."

Grace knew he was right. "What . . . what will we do in the meantime?"

"I've given it some thought. We'll return to my hotel first. Then, while I seek out someone to witness our vows, you must see to your trousseau."

"There are more urgent matters than providing me with a trousseau!" she said.

"You must be dressed as befits your new station. Anything else would draw comment," he explained. "We want no hint of haste. There is an elegant dressmaker's shop not far from the hotel where my cousin Elspeth shopped while in Rome. I'll deliver you to their doorstep and leave you in Signorina Martino's hands. She'll know exactly what you require as a young matron of fashion."

Grace blinked in surprise. "All this planned out on the spur of the moment! I am impressed!"

McLean flushed. "I spent most of the night laying our plans."

She seemed to accept that, but he was uneasy. *My soon-to-be wife is nobody's fool.* He didn't know if that would work for him, or against him, in the long run. One thing he knew for sure: he'd have to watch his step—and his tongue—very carefully, until his ring was firmly on her finger.

The bedchamber was dark, when Grace was awakened from a troubled dream. She heard voices in the other room, the sound of a door closing. She thought that she was back at Mrs. Bingley's, and wondered what was wrong to wake her employer at such an ungodly hour.

A moment later there was a rap on the door of the bedchamber. It opened, spilling lamplight into the room. McLean came in bearing a tray.

"Good, you're awake. It's time."

Grace remembered everything. She was in his bed in his hotel room. It was like a splash of cold water in her face. She sat up, pulling the covers up to her chin. "But . . . what time is it?"

"An hour before dawn. I received the message after you'd gone to bed, and didn't want to awaken you." He set the tray down on a table, keeping his eyes carefully averted to spare her modesty. "It isn't much. Tea and bread, fresh from the baker's oven. You have half an hour to make ready."

Grace pushed the hair back from her eyes while he lit the tapers on the mantelpiece. When he was gone and the door closed again, she swung her legs over the side of the bed and climbed down.

She was still groggy and detached. Nothing seemed quite real. For a few moments Grace wondered whether it was all part of a bizarre and continuing dream. But no, the yeasty fragrance and heat of the crusty bread rolls were as real as the pungent perfume of the tea.

She poured out a cup of steaming brew, added a large spoonful of sugar, and sipped it cautiously. The heat of it warmed her while she watched thin gray light leak around the edges of the shutters.

So, this was it. Her wedding day.

She couldn't imagine anything less romantic.

After bathing her face and pinning up her hair, she donned her wedding ensemble. It was of cream silk inset with cobweb lace, and finer than anything she'd ever owned or hoped to own.

Grace pinned her mother's milk opal beneath her collar. *Something old.* It comforted her in the midst of so much change, although the inexpensive trinket was at odds with the splendor of her outfit.

Certainly her husband-to-be was a very generous man. If she'd had the slightest doubts, the packages and bandboxes that filled the dressing area were there to refute them. She'd spent half the previous afternoon selecting the items, the rest being fitted. It had taken only a tuck or two to tailor the garments to her slender form.

The contents would take her from dawn to midnight, changing with the hours. Breakfast robes. Day dresses and walking dresses. Tea gowns and evening gowns and night-gowns. Fine linens and embroidered shawls, gloves in sev-eral lengths, lace scarves and cloaks and bonnets and parasols. Slippers and sandals and half-boots, including the ones she was wearing to match her outfit.

So much for something new.

She was about to put in her pearl earrings, when McLean knocked again. This time he brought her a small velvet box. "A wedding gift," he said.

She opened it to reveal a set of lovely earrings. Lover's knots of gold wire hung below square-cut sapphires set on their points. The effect was elegant and stunning.

"They're exquisite!"

"A mere bauble. I'll find you something more suitable for a bride gift when there is more time. 'Something blue,' " he said. "Isn't that right?"

She gave a shaky laugh. "Yes. Thank you! Now if you have 'something borrowed' and 'a silver sixpence for my shoe,' everything in the old rhyme will be covered."

"Here is one of my handkerchiefs to tuck inside your reticule." He produced a folded square of fine linen with his monogram, and handed it to her with a flourish. "As to the sixpence, I'm at a loss. But four out of five are surely good odds."

She took the handkerchief. "Are you a gambler?"

His mouth firmed. "Only where matters of great impor-tance are concerned. Hurry, now. We mustn't be late."

Grace leaned in toward the mirror and put the earrings on, surprised that her hands didn't shake. Her yearly salary as governess would not have paid for even one of them.

There was no time to think of that now. Taking up a fetching bonnet trimmed in the same lace as her outfit, she settled it carefully over her hair and tied a jaunty bow beneath one ear.

"Charming!" He held out his arm to her. "Come, the carriage is waiting."

Grace slipped her hand in its cream-colored glove through the crook of his arm. As they descended to the ornate lobby, she glanced at him through her lashes. He'd thought of everything so far. But what did he think of *her*?

She hadn't a clue. And, she realized, she wanted desperately to know.

He smiled when they reached the carriage. "You look lovely, my dear!" Grace's heart lifted in response.

McLean handed her up and they set off through the empty streets. It was not quite dawn. The air was cool, the gray sky streaked with clouds the color of the milk opal at her throat. Soon the world would stir; but for now the very breath of time seemed suspended.

They wound their way past monuments to emperors long dead, and tenements, museums, churches, and palazzos. The neighborhood changed abruptly as they left a piazza and entered a narrow street.

The structures that overhung the worn cobblestones were an odd mixture of style and centuries. One side was pale stone, severe and masculine, pitted with age. Across the way were a jumble of apartment buildings in patched yellow stucco. Their rows of tiny, arched windows were closed against the morning chill. In the distance the dome of St. Peter's rose against clouds faintly tinged with gold and pink.

"This is the Borgo," McLean told her. "It was settled by foreigners to Rome."

They came out through a square where a large fountain plashed, the drops of its myriad sprays like gleaming gray pearls in the luminous haze.

Grace was caught up in the unreality of it. When they stopped abruptly before a worn marble façade she jerked upright, like someone rudely awakened from a dream. The building was high and narrow, with two arched windows and the hint of a dome just visible above the peaked roof. Three worn steps led up to a great wooden door. Her heart turned over.

It was real. In a very short time she would no longer be Grace Templar, disgraced governess, but Mrs. Alistair McLean of Rossmor. Tiny shivers of fear and excitement raced up and down her spine.

He helped her dismount as the morning sun rose in a suddenly lurid sky. The air seemed on fire. Even the pale stone of the buildings turned rosy in the burnished light. Grace hoped it was a good omen.

"What is the name of this church?" she asked.

"San Marcello al Corso." McLean escorted her up the steps and opened the ancient door. The spicy odor of beeswax, incense, and old wood wafted around them as they entered. The scents reminded her of the parish church where she'd spent so many hours at Sunday services and evensong. Once her eyes adjusted to the dimness, Grace discovered that was the only resemblance.

She found herself in a small vestibule, guarded by angels of carved and gilded wood in marble niches. It opened to a vaulted nave half-filled with scaffolding. The smell of paint and varnish was everywhere. What was visible of the walls was covered with swirling frescoes. Every square inch was ornamented: saints and prophets floated on sunset clouds surrounded by gamboling cherubs and, oddly, what appeared to be several gleaming gold fish.

Stained-glass windows pierced the domed ceiling, glowing like dark jewels, and a brass lamp with a ruby shade cast its glow over the sanctuary. The altar was a marvel of the woodcarver's art, all covered in heavy gilt. Its candles were lit, and their steady flames highlighted the stunning bronze depicting the Assumption of the Virgin Mary into Heaven.

Grace's fascination turned to concern. "But this is surely a Roman Catholic church! We are not of that faith—how can we be married here?"

McLean frowned. "I hope you do not have strenuous objections to it. This was the best I could do on such short notice. The embassy said it could take a week or more if we wished to wait and seek out an English priest. I didn't think you would want to put it off our union that long."

"N-no, of course not. I am just surprised. I hadn't thought . . ."

"Then let us get on with it." He eased her forward by the gentle pressure of his hand against her shoulder. "Brother Antonio has agreed to perform the ceremony and sign the necessary documents before the daily mass."

Grace looked over to where he'd indicated. A man in a monk's robe and cowl had stepped out of the sanctuary, clasping a large prayer book in his hands. He smiled encouragingly at them.

She didn't know what to say. "I suppose it doesn't matter, as long as we are wed."

"Good girl." McLean smiled down at her and took her hand in his. "I am sorry that this affair is so rushed and unorthodox. I have an idea. My brother-in-law is a minister and has the living at Rossmor. If it would make you easier in your mind, we can repeat our vows before him once we are settled at Rossmor, and receive the blessing of the Anglican Church."

That settled all her qualms. "I should like that."

He led her up the aisle and introduced her to the cleric. He was a tall man with thin aristocratic features, sparkling dark eyes, and a merry smile. Greetings were hurriedly exchanged. "Two impatient lovers," he said with a little chuckle. "I am happy to oblige you."

Grace felt herself blushing. If he knew the real reason

for their hasty marriage, she doubted he'd go through with the ceremony.

It was over more quickly than she had imagined. A few words, the sign of the cross made in the air over their joined hands. A gold wedding band set with a rose-cut emerald slipped upon her left ring finger as they recited their vows. Then it was done.

Brother Antonio blessed the air before them again. *"In Nomine Patris, et Filius, et Spiritu Sanctus. Amen."* He cleared his throat and spoke in lightly accented English. "By the powers invested in me, I now pronounce you husband and wife. Go forth and multiply!"

Grace turned a shocked face to him. Surely that last wasn't part of the ceremony? But then, this was not the church in which she'd been raised, and she knew nothing at all of Romish customs. She glanced at her new husband to see his response.

McLean looked grim. He signed the register and handed the pen to Grace. She took it with shaking fingers, but managed not to blot the book. The cleric signed last, with a small smile and a rather extravagant flourish.

When the formalities were done, McLean took the papers that were handed to him, and pressed something into Brother Antonio's hand. "A gift toward the restoration of the frescoes. Or perhaps another worthy cause. I shall leave the decision to you."

Brother Antonio's eyes twinkled and his smile widened. *"Grazie.* I wish you the best of good health and good fortune, Signor McLean, Signora. Perhaps you will name the little *bambino* after me."

Grace was horrified. Hot color suffused her cheeks. "There isn't any . . . I am not . . . You mustn't think . . . !"

McLean sent the friar a darkling look and drew her away. "It isn't Brother Antonio's province to *think*," he said acidly. "He has done his part, and we have what we came for. Let's be on our way."

He escorted her down the aisle so swiftly her feet scarcely touched the floor. Grace thought she heard the echo of laughter follow them, as they stepped out into the clear morning light.

Chapter Nine

They didn't return to McLean's hotel from the church. "I've booked a suite at another hotel," he told her. "Our luggage is already awaiting us there."

Grace was appalled. "Good heavens, what possessed you to do that?"

"It's always best to start as you mean to go on. The hotel was once a private villa and has extensive grounds. There will be several acquaintances of mine there, no doubt. You'll make your official debut as my bride with me at your side. By the time we return to Scotland, the marriage will no longer be a seven-day wonder, and you will be accepted by society."

"You seem to have thought of everything," Grace exclaimed.

His blue eyes looked calmly down into hers. "I certainly hope you are right, my dear."

The carriage stopped at the entry to the elegant hotel that had once been a palace. McLean escorted Grace inside, and immediately stopped short. "Fortune is with us."

She followed his glance over to an elderly woman in an old-fashioned gown of purple silk, complete with hoop skirts. She spoke sharply to her companion, then looked across the lobby with a querulous expression. It changed to a smile when she saw McLean.

She raised her hand imperiously, and he went up to her at once, with Grace on his arm. "*The Countess of Andringham,*" he said in her ear as they approached the dowager. "If you win her approval, you will be set in society."

"Ah, Lady Andringham." He bowed low over her hand. "I had heard you were visiting Rome and hoped our paths would cross."

"You are a charming rogue, Mr. McLean," the dowager said. "I doubt if you knew a thing about it until your eyes alighted upon me."

"Do you doubt me? Count Borromini told me so himself."

"Dear Lorenzo. I am to dine with him this evening. Now. Who is this young woman you're parading about on your arm?"

"Allow me to present my wife, madam. We were married very recently, here in Rome."

Grace almost choked. Very recently! She prayed that Lady Andringham would not inquire more deeply into the matter.

The countess eyed Grace through her lorgnette in silence for what seemed like an eternity, but she kept her composure.

Lady Andringham cleared her throat. "A very pretty gel, with a look of good breeding. Go away, Alistair, and let me speak with your wife."

McLean laughed and did as she said. Grace was horrified, but managed not to show it. The duchess focused all her attention on the new bride. "Sit down, gel. Rome is thin of company, and you have a lively and intelligent look about you. Heaven knows, I have little enough conversation out of my stolid lump of a companion."

The faded lady beside the countess blinked, but otherwise showed no reaction. Grace felt immensely sorry for the woman. "You are severe, Lady Andringham."

"I am frank-spoken, rather. And you," she said with a hard glitter in her eye, "are impertinent."

"I am sorry for it," Grace said calmly.

"No, you are not." The shrewd eyes examined her. "I like you for it. Better than I did the first Mrs. McLean. A lovely creature, but flighty." She turned to her companion. "Hermione! Fetch me my silk shawl."

"Of course. The puce-colored one?"

"Do you think I would wear puce with a purple gown, you silly fool?"

The other woman bolted for the staircase without a backward glance. "Don't feel bad for her," the countess said. "I suffer more for her companionship than she does from mine. But she is a relation of sorts, and she likes to feel useful—as well as live high at my expense."

Grace didn't know quite how to reply. Her silence didn't bother the dowager in the least.

"You look to be a lady of good sense, Mrs. McLean. Your husband is a lusty man. I can tell. In my days we didn't pretend that such things didn't exist. Take my advice, then. Keep him well fed at the dinner table, well entertained in the drawing room—and well pleasured in bed. That's my advice to you."

Grace felt a hot blush sweep up to mantle her face. "I will do my best to follow it," she said quietly.

The dowager folded her fan with a snap. "Your generation doesn't know a thing about men! There are books, you know. French, mostly. We read them all in my day. But your generation is too namby-pamby to take that route. If you're wise, you'll follow his lead. A man doesn't get to be the age of Alistair McLean without having some experience of the world. One good lover makes another, I always say."

Grace's chin lifted. "I will take your word for that, also."

Lady Andringham gave a cackle of laughter. "I hope so—for your sake. One other word of advice. Keep him guessing as to whether your heart is entirely his." She gave a bawdy wink. "The juicy peach just out of reach is always the most tempting."

A shadow fell over them and both looked up. McLean stood beside them. "May I reclaim my wife, madam?"

"Yes, you handsome rogue. She is a credit to you. Treat her well."

To Grace's surprise, he flushed like a schoolboy. "You may be sure of it."

Taking her arm, he led Grace away. "Our chambers are ready. I thought you might wish to retire and rest."

She was grateful for his consideration. Their suite was on the third floor. The sitting room was lovely, more like a proper drawing room. It had a floral carpet and exquisite tapestries, and furniture upholstered in rose silk. Comfortable chairs were interspersed with inlaid tables and fine cabinets. Sofas flanked the fireplace and the windows opposite the door opened to a balcony overlooking a formal garden ringed by a high wall.

"Your luggage is already here and unpacked," he told her. "I'm afraid that I have several calls to make this afternoon and must be off. Ring for the maid to help you undress."

"I assure you that I can do so without the help of a servant. I don't require the maid's assistance."

"Perhaps not—but gossip concerning the honeymooning English couple would not spread half so quickly."

She laughed. "You have a devious mind."

His smile was not reflected in his cool blue eyes. "Rest well. We'll dine here at the hotel and make an early night of it. Which," he added, "will also fuel the gossip."

Grace blushed. "Need we always be so concerned with what others say, Mr. McLean?

"You must learn to call me Alistair," he said. "Remember that at present you are unknown in society. Once your credit is firmly established we can disregard the conventions."

He went out, and she rang for the maid, which resulted in taking three times as long to get out of her garments and lie down upon the silk counterpane. *How silly, to go through all this for an hour's rest*, she thought. But when she awakened it was hours later and the room was in half-light. She'd slept most of the day away.

Grace found a note in the parlor from McLean, stating he didn't wish to disturb her, and telling her when they would dine. She realized there wasn't much time, and rang for the maid again.

The girl was eager to assist her. She opened the wardrobe. "Such lovely gowns! Which does Madame wish to wear this evening?"

There was only a brief moment of panic while Grace made her choice. *I am not a girl out of school*, she reminded herself. *I know what is appropriate for the time and place.*

She slipped into a sophisticated and shockingly expensive gown of rustling black taffeta with a wide ruffle of ivory lace framing her bare shoulders as if she'd done so every day of her adult life. The past twenty-four hours had seemed like a dream. While the maid set out various hair ornaments, Grace studied the wedding ring on her finger. It was real enough.

"Perhaps the diamond and pearl hair clips?" the girl suggested.

"What?" Grace glanced at the velvet box the maid held open. "Oh. Yes. The diamond clips." She stared at them. There was no mistaking the rich, creamy depth of the lustrous pearls or the winking brilliance of the blue-white stones. *God in heaven, they are real!*

And so were the necklace, the brooch, the bracelet, and the matching ear clips the girl had set out on the dressing table. There was also another parure of aquamarines set in rose gold and a delicate set of garnets fashioned in the shape of stars. So this was the mysterious errand that her husband had gone out to do earlier.

Grace sat at the dressing table, hiding her growing anxiety at the role she'd stepped into with so little preparation, while the maid finished turning her into a fashion plate. When the girl stepped back, an elegant stranger regarded Grace from the looking glass.

So this is Mrs. Alistair McLean, she thought in surprise. *Perhaps I shall be able to pull it off, after all.*

"The signore will be pleased," the girl said when she was done. Not ten seconds later the door opened and McLean walked in.

He was not only pleased, he was stunned. The diamonds that shone in her dark hair were no brighter than her eyes. The tight-fitting bodice and waist of the gown displayed her figure admirably, and the skirts with their swept-back sides showed off the feminine curve of her hips to advantage. He felt the heat of arousal pool in the pit of his stomach. Taking her hand, he kissed it and then held it captive in his own.

"My dear, I shall be the envy of every man in Rome."

Her cheeks flushed with pleasure but she accepted the compliment as if she were accustomed to hearing such praise on a daily basis. *So,* he thought, *you have something of the actress in you.* That could work to their mutual advantage.

They went down to dinner, which was served beneath lanterns on the terrace, while a string quartet played softly in the background. Grace held back a bit at the doorway, struck by a horrid possibility. "What if we should meet up with Mrs. Bingley?"

"You needn't concern yourself with her. I paid a visit to the Villa Fortuna earlier while you were resting, and proffered profound apologies for swooping you up into our runaway marriage."

"I am surprised that Mrs. Bingley let you in the door, much less listen to your explanations! Was she dreadfully outraged?"

McLean smiled. "Rest assured that Mrs. Bingley will have nothing but good to say of you."

"How on earth did you manage that?" She eyed him warily. "You constantly amaze me, Mr. McLean!"

"Alistair," he corrected her. "You must call me by my given name. It wasn't a difficult task. A mention of house parties at Rossmor was all it took to win the lady over." He saw the look of consternation on her face. "However, I stopped short of issuing an invitation."

They were seated at their table and had an excellent meal of poached turbot followed by veal braised with vegetables and mushrooms in wine sauce, and an iced gâteau. Through it all, McLean managed to keep Grace amused with clever anecdotes, while gently extracting more information on her earlier life. When dessert was cleared, a new bottle of wine was broached.

"Is this champagne?" she asked, watching minute bubbles rise up through her goblet of pale, golden liquid.

"It is."

"I don't believe I will try it."

"Why not?"

She wrinkled her nose. "I don't believe I should like it."

McLean threw back his head and laughed. "My dear girl! You won't know if you don't try."

Grace lifted her thin goblet and took a sip, then another. She sighed and set it down. "I was right. I shouldn't have tried it."

"You don't like it?"

"Oh, I do. It makes me feel worldly and wicked."

McLean smiled at her across the rim of his glass. "Good. That was exactly my intention."

He signaled the waiter to refill their glasses. Halfway through the second, Grace realized it was a mistake and set the glass down. Her head felt light and effervescent.

"Any more and I shall not be responsible for my actions."

"Time to retire for the night," he said. "Although I predict it will take us a while to reach our suite if we leave through the lobby. I can see that every man to whom I've ever been introduced in Rome is hoping to meet the new Mrs. McLean."

He whisked her out through the garden and around to a side door. When they finally escaped to the sanctuary of their suite she was breathless. He unlocked the door and held it open. Only a few candles had been lit, giving the room an intimate appeal. "Thank you," she said. "It was a lovely evening."

"Only the first of many."

His smile melted her bones. Grace turned unsteadily and hurried to the open door of the bedchamber, and paused to look back on the threshold. Her alabaster skin was bathed in rosy light from the small boudoir lamps. McLean's resolve scattered like leaves in the wind.

As he stepped forward she glanced at the clock. "Oh! So late. I must ring for the maid to undress me."

She reached for the bell cord but McLean forestalled her. "There is no need to bother the girl when I am here."

Grace was startled. *I misheard him,* she decided. *The champagne has addled my hearing.*

But he closed the door and came to her side. Grace took a step back. "What are you doing?"

His eyebrows rose. "I am helping you undress."

Something in his tone sent bright little sparks through her veins. "I can manage well enough," she replied breathlessly. "No doubt you wish to retire to your own bedchamber."

He flashed her a smile. "You are under a misapprehension, my dear. This *is* my bedchamber."

She felt something hard behind her knees, and sat down abruptly on the edge of the settee. "But . . . you can't expect to share the room with me."

Blue devils danced in his eyes. "My dear girl, I expect to share the *bed* with you. We are married. You are my wife."

"But . . . it is a marriage of convenience!"

"If you'll think back, that was your term, not mine." His dark blue gaze caressed her face. "I assure you that I would find it exceedingly inconvenient to have all the obligations of marriage, and none of its pleasures."

"There is . . . there *must* be some misunderstanding," Grace said breathlessly. "I thought . . . I am to be your hostess and act as mother to your daughter."

"Yes. And," he said firmly, "as wife to me."

Grace bolted up from the settee. "You cannot mean to force me."

"No." He crossed the carpet toward her. "I mean to seduce you."

The timbre of his voice sent shivers up her spine. She lifted her chin. "I don't suppose you can do so without my cooperation!"

"It would defeat the purpose," he agreed in a teasing manner. "The goal of any seduction is to achieve the complete willingness of the other party."

"You are making a jest. We scarcely know one another."

"It is not so unusual a situation. Marriages are arranged every day."

He was so close Grace could feel the heat radiating from his body. She moved away but McLean had anticipated her reaction. A subtle shift of his lean body and he was between Grace and the door. "Perhaps I was too precipitate. You need time to adjust to the idea."

He cupped her cheek in his hand. "We can have a good

life together, Grace. I am a passionate man, and you are a passionate woman." She didn't deny it. How could she, when her blood was afire? His thumb caressed her trembling mouth. "We have entered this marriage without knowing one another well. That will come over time. Meanwhile, we needn't deny one another the pleasures of the marriage bed."

She couldn't think when he stood so near. The touch of his skin against her mouth rendered her speechless.

McLean regarded her in silence a moment. "Perhaps," he said slowly, "it is something more. Do you find me unattractive?"

"No! Of course not."

"Is there anything in my manners or person that has given you a disgust of me?"

"No!" Grace shook her head. "You have shown me every kindness and consideration—until now."

His eyes locked with hers and he brushed his fingertips lightly over her lips. "Then we are at a standstill. Unless . . ."

His nearness made her jumpy. Her mouth burned where his fingers had touched it. She couldn't tear her gaze away from his. She realized that she was trembling violently. "Unless . . . ?"

"Making love is like drinking champagne," McLean said softly. "You might like it if you try it."

She knew he was laughing at her and tried to smile. "I suppose it makes one feel 'worldly and wicked,' too?"

"All that, my dear, and much, much more. I shall delight in showing you."

His fingers tangled in her hair and he lowered his mouth to hers. His lips skimmed lightly over hers. Grace couldn't move. Couldn't breathe. She was stunned, embarrassed— and yes, aroused. She thought her heart would stop. It only skipped a beat, and then began to race in earnest.

He lifted his head. "Was that so very bad?"

"N-no. It was very *good*."

"Then I'll do it again."

He claimed her mouth with more ardor. Without thinking, she let herself respond. Her body curved toward his. She felt as if she were dissolving against him, the softness of her limbs flowing into the hard strength of his.

It frightened her so much that she pulled back. He released her instantly. Reluctantly. "I suppose the idea of a husband is something a woman must get used to gradually, over time."

McLean's gaze roved over her face and there were dark lights in the depths of his eyes. She thought he might kiss her again. Instead he lifted her hand and kissed her fingertips. "Good night, my dear. Sleep well."

He turned and went out of the room. Grace stared after him, then hurried to the door of the bedchamber. He had his hand on the knob of the door leading out of the parlor to the corridor.

"Where are you going?"

"To lose my disappointment in a glass of brandy." His wry smile took any sting from his words. "You needn't wait up. I have the key." He bowed and went out. The door clicked in place and she heard the lock turn.

She couldn't believe he'd left her alone. *Well, I can't very well protest that it is our wedding night!*

It was late when she rang for the maid, much later before she finally went to bed. It was a very large bed, with fine linen sheets and sensuously soft feather pillows. She rolled on her side. *How could he possibly have expected me to let him share this bed? We are almost strangers to one another.*

Her indignation ebbed, leaving conflict in its wake. She tossed and turned, remembering that she owed the salvaging of her reputation to his kindness. Remembering the touch of his lips on hers, the warmth of his arm around her. Remembering the spark of desire that had leapt between them, hot and bright.

How could I have been such a silly fool as to think he wouldn't wish to claim the rights of a husband?

That was the problem. She hadn't thought. She'd jumped to an embarrassingly wrong conclusion.

I have made such a sorry botch of it. Everything he said is right. I am his wife and he my husband. There is no reason this strange marriage of ours should not become a marriage in truth. Except that I am not ready to take such a giant step as yet. I have been alone too long to let down my barriers.

Even for him.

Again she tossed and turned on the cool linen sheets. When she fell asleep she dreamed that she stood on the edge of the sea, with warm blue waters glistening all the way to the horizon. She wanted to race into the lace-crested waves and let them carry her away from the deserted shore: but try as she might, she could not force herself to do it.

Sometime in the early hours she awakened and heard the grate of the key in the lock of the parlor door. She stretched out beneath the blankets, wondering what to do. His footsteps crossed the parlor floor, passing by the bedroom door. Her limbs froze but her blood ran hot. She wanted him to hold her. Kiss her. Touch her and teach her what it meant to be a woman in the arms of a virile man.

The light in the parlor was extinguished. She held her breath and waited for him to come to her. There was only silence on the other side of the door.

Grace spent the rest of her wedding night alone with her thoughts, which were cold comfort.

Grace awakened to the sound of a door closing. For a moment she was confused and disoriented. Her small, spartan room at the Villa Fortuna had metamorphosed into an ivory and gold bedchamber with elegant furnishings and curtains of rose brocade.

It all came crashing back on her. The carriage ride and disastrous visit to the dovecote. The strange wedding in the beautiful old church. The husband she'd rebuffed the night before.

Her cheeks grew hot at the thought of it. How on earth would she face him this morning?

The light, masculine scent of his cologne lingered in the air. She suddenly realized he'd been in the bedchamber earlier while she slept. He'd left his razor case on the shaving stand, a crumpled shirt over the back of a chair, and a pair of silver cuff links on the dressing table beside her hair combs.

The thought of him seeing her in bed, sleep-tousled, was unsettling. She tiptoed to the door and found it cracked an inch. Grace peered through it warily. She was alone in the suite.

An envelope with her name was propped up on the mantelpiece in the parlor. She went through in her nightgown and retrieved it. Taking the letter opener from the desk, she broke the wafer. His penmanship was very like him. Bold, efficient, and very male. She scanned the lines of black ink that slanted across the page.

> *My Dear Wife,*
> *I was called away on a matter of business. We dine with Count Borromini and Lady Helena Ainsely at the Palazzo Borromini this evening. She is an old friend of mine and has left her card for you. Perhaps you might care to have luncheon with her tomorrow as she suggests.*
>
> *Alistair*

There was a hastily scrawled postscript:

The gold gown would be most suitable.

                                                    A.

She crumpled it in her hand. *Does he think me so so-
cially inept that I wouldn't have known to select the proper
ensemble?* The salutation annoyed her as well. *"My Dear
Wife." What does that mean? Is he reminding me of my
obligations?*

Grace sighed and sat down on the bed. The answer to
both questions was yes. Left to her own devices, she would
have been in a quandary over which one of several gowns
to wear for such an occasion.

As for the other, he was well within his rights to do so.

She took the heavy cream card he'd tucked beneath the
envelope. *Lady Helena Ainsley.* Grace knew who she was,
of course. The court news, to which Mrs. Bingley was addicted, often carried accounts of the glamorous socialite,
dubbed "Helena of Troy" by her admirers. Although she
was not much over the age of twenty-five, gossip said that
her lovers were legion. She had already sent two wealthy,
elderly, and doting husbands on to their graves.

No doubt, Grace thought wryly, *with smiles upon their
faces.* She set the card and note aside.

After dressing, she took a solitary stroll through the hotel
gardens, and came back to find several congratulatory notes
that had been sent round to their hotel. Word of their marriage had spread quickly. It was with mixed emotions that
she answered each one, dipping her pen into the crystal and
gilt inkstand to sign her new name: *Mrs. Alistair McLean.*

The last of the notes was from Mrs. Bingley. It was
excessively cordial, and ended with the hopes that Grace
would not "forget your old and affectionate friends" once
she was installed as the mistress of Rossmor.

Grace's reply was more restrained and stated her regret
that she could not accept Mrs. Bingley's invitation to dine
at the Villa Fortuna on the following Tuesday, as she and
her husband had already accepted an engagement. She

added that they would be departing for Scotland by the end of the month.

The moment she'd written it, the reality sank in. *My husband. The Highlands of Scotland. Rossmor.* A chill ran up her spine.

Except for Alistair McLean himself, Grace would be far away from anyone and everything she knew. Then she remembered her new stepdaughter, little Janet McLean. The thought of the lonely, motherless child gave her courage to face the changes that were rapidly transforming her life.

Taking out another sheet of paper, she began a letter to Janet. It was difficult to know what to write. Three attempts later, she managed a brief, warm note to the girl and left it at that. Words were well and good, but any normal child of ten years would be more speedily won over by a thoughtful gift. She would surely find just the right thing at one of the exclusive shops nearby.

"I have never had anyone to buy things for before!" Grace was excited. She decided she would find something for her husband's cousin, Elspeth Lachlan, who was looking after Janet during Alistair's absence from home.

She spent the afternoon happily exploring the elegant shops near the hotel, where she purchased several gifts for her stepdaughter.

"I also need a gift for an older woman whose tastes I do not really know," she told the owner of a little jewelry shop.

"I would suggest one of these, perhaps?" The woman brought out a round gilt brooch studded with garnets, and a gold locket in the form of a book, set with a spray of seed pearls.

"The locket is perfect."

Grace went back to the hotel in a more confident frame of mind. She felt her care in choosing the gifts for Janet and Elspeth would be realized, and that her effort would help lay the foundations for good relationships.

The moment she entered their suite she knew her husband hadn't returned. The place felt empty and lifeless. She was both relieved and disappointed. After she put her purchases away, Grace went to the wardrobe and opened the door. A spirit of contrariness had taken hold of her. She eyed the gold frock with disfavor. It was the most exquisite—and expensive—of all, the kind of gown that would make a scullery girl feel like a queen. Grace pushed it aside.

She considered the lace-trimmed azure, the audacious scarlet, and the low-cut bronze. Anything but the gold that her husband had recommended.

The deep-green emerald in her wedding ring sparkled as it caught the light. That decided it. She gave the bellpull a determined tug.

The girl hurried in and curtsied. "You rang, signora?"

"Yes. I will be dining out this evening." A faint smile touched Grace's lips. "I shall wear the emerald green gown."

As he escorted Grace through the lobby on their way to the Palazzo Borromini that evening, McLean was gratified. He noted the wary looks of the women, the appreciative glances of the men as she rustled past in her gown of green crepe de chine and a light cloud of French *parfum*. His new bride was creating quite a sensation.

"That gown suits you admirably," he said. "It brings out the same color in your eyes."

"You wanted me to wear the gold," she reminded him. "Did I?"

She saw the hint of amusement on his face. "You *knew* I would choose something else if you suggested it!"

He smiled and took her gloved hand in his as they went out to the waiting carriage. "You weren't in charity with me when I left, and I suspect you have a pronounced independent streak. I thought you'd enjoy asserting it."

She let him hand her in and settled back against the squabs. "Do you always manipulate people with such subtlety?"

McLean laughed. "Only, my dear, when there is no other way to achieve my ends."

Grace was very quiet for the rest of the short ride.

Grace's first sight of the Palazzo Borromini was intimidating, but the count soon put her at ease. "I am enchanted to meet you, Mrs. McLean." The house was fabulous, the painted ceilings and works of art extraordinary, the food delectable, and the conversation as sparkling as the gilt and crystal chandeliers.

To her surprise, Lady Helena Ainsley was not the "Embodiment of Loveliness" that she'd been proclaimed by the arbiters of society. Her face was too narrow at the chin, too broad at the cheekbones, her nose too long to fit the popular notions of perfection. Despite this, her features came together in a way that pleased and intrigued; but it was her charm of manner that dazzled.

Lady Helena had a way of gazing at each person who addressed her as if they held every atom of her attention. *She is like a bright ray of sunshine, dispensing her warmth and light. And,* Grace judged, *perhaps as impersonal. It is too early to tell.*

With only four of them dining in an intimate salon, there was no rigid structure to the evening. They discussed art, music, and the current political issues as well as their travels. Grace felt invigorated by their wit and insight. It had been far too long since she'd been in company who showed interest in anything but themselves, their wardrobes, and their social conquests. Despite her feelings of caution, she was soon caught up in the sparkling net of charm and sophistication with which Lady Helena captured and held her admirers.

McLean watched Grace without appearing to do so. She was not at any disadvantage in the present company. Like a jewel that has finally been placed in the proper setting, she glowed with inner radiance. He was pleased that she was so well informed, and that she could hold her own with the clever—and very much admiring—Borromini.

He realized that Lady Helena was watching him, in turn. Their eyes met and she gave him a little nod.

"You have done well for yourself, Alistair," she said in a low aside. "I approve of your choice."

"I am glad of it. She'll need your support—and Elspeth's."

Lady Helena raised her elegantly arched eyebrows. "You have mine. I cannot vouch for your cousin."

"Nonsense. Elspeth must surely be lonely for the company of another female. There is no one but my sister in the immediate neighborhood who moves in the same circles. She and Grace will become good friends. I haven't the least doubt of it."

Lady Helena simply smiled and turned away to answer a question the count had posed. When the last course was removed the two ladies retired to an intimate parlor overlooking the lantern-lit gardens, leaving the men to linger briefly over their brandy. Lady Helena took a place on a gold brocade settee.

"Mrs. McLean," she said, "I must confess I am delighted with this turn of events: I had given up hope that Alistair would ever remarry. But I admit to great surprise. He never breathed a word of it to me beforehand."

Grace flushed. This was the first test, and she'd been dreading it. "Our acquaintance is not one of long duration."

Those light blue eyes regarded her shrewdly. "So I would imagine. Otherwise you and I must have met one another sooner."

"You and I have not moved in the same circles, Lady Helena."

"Touché!" The other woman laughed merrily. "That was a most polite set-down, Mrs. McLean, and I admit that I deserved it. You are right in your conjecture: I was indeed trying to learn more about your sudden marriage. How you met, for instance. Was it through mutual friends?"

Grace hadn't been prepared for such an outright question. "We were both touring the Forum Romanum at the same time," she responded coolly. "You might say that Alistair swept me off my feet."

"How very romantic. Where did you exchange vows?"

"An exquisite little church—San Marcello al Corso. It is in the Borgo, near the Plazza San Pietro. Do you know it?"

"I've never been inside. In fact, I thought it was in the Quirinal." Lady Helena shrugged. "There are so many churches in Rome I daresay there may be any number of them with similar names." She leaned forward and touched Grace's arm. "No doubt you think me far too inquisitive about your affairs. You must forgive me, for Alistair and I are old friends. My grandfather has an estate near Rossmor. He used to go up every year for the grouse."

Grace nodded. "Alistair told me that you have known one another since childhood."

"Oh, yes." Lady Helena smiled and shook her head. "If not for Finnula, I suppose we might have made a match of it—although we would not have suited. Alistair is too wrapped up in his work. And I," she laughed, "am too wrapped up in myself."

That mention of Finnula opened a conversational door. Grace ventured through it with care. "You knew them both, then?"

"We more or less grew up together, the three of us, racing our ponies across the moors."

"What was she like? Alistair does not speak of her."

Lady Helena thought a moment. "Very beautiful, of course. But fragile. Not physically, although she was dainty and thin. There was something magical about her. I should call her a quicksilver girl, all moonbeams and shadows. Never holding any one form for long."

She sent Grace a long, assessing look. "She was nothing like you, if that is what you are asking."

Grace flushed. "I can see that. No one would ever describe me as quicksilver."

"No. I should imagine that there is steel in you, Mrs. McLean. That is not a bad thing," Lady Helena added reflectively. "Have you ever seen a drop of quicksilver? It is intriguing and frustrating—if you try to pick it up, it turns into a dozen pieces and scatters everywhere. It cannot be held, only contained."

Grace gathered her courage. "She was very young when she died."

"Yes." Lady Helena sighed. "A tragic affair. It doesn't do to listen to the rumors, though. Most of them are vicious lies! Alistair's blunt tongue has made enemies."

Her answer made no sense to Grace. It still chilled her blood. There were secrets here, and for a moment she almost backed away from them. "Will you . . . will you tell me how she died?"

"I can only tell you what I know." She took Grace's hand in hers. "There are many rumors. One is that Finnula was insane at the time. I don't know if the rumors are true, but I am certain of one thing: Alistair did *not* murder her!"

The door opened as the men joined them in the salon, and there was no time for Grace to ask any of the questions that Lady Helena's comment provoked.

Chapter Ten

"Your husband and I were discussing the house party at Rossmor this coming October," Count Borromini said when the men joined them. "I have not yet visited Scotland, and look forward to enjoying your hospitality, Mrs. McLean."

Grace was still in shock from Lady Helena's statement. Her mind was reeling but she hid her consternation. She hadn't known that she would be playing the role of hostess to high-ranking guests, much less than in six weeks' time.

You might have warned me, her startled glance said to McLean.

"We will be very pleased to welcome you to our home," she told the count smoothly.

McLean sent her a look of approval. Despite the awkwardness of their situation, she was able to keep up outward appearances with the skill of a duchess—or a born actress.

He smiled at his host. "Some find the Highlands austere and rather formidable. To me, they are a place of haunting beauty. I hope you will share my opinion."

"We share so many others," Borromini said smoothly, "that I am sure I shall feel the same. It is to be a large house party?"

Relief surged through Grace. His question to Alistair had

saved her the embarrassment of not knowing the answer.

"Professor Rosenthal and Miss Rosenthal have accepted," McLean replied. "Perhaps Dr. Hayes, whom you met in London last year. I am hopeful that Lady Trent will be able to spare the time away from her writing. The rest are members of my family: my sister Meg and her husband, the Reverend Hugh Kinsale. He has the living at Rossmor and is very interested in my research. If my uncle is returned from Canada in time, he will come over from Gorse Manor. Last, but not least, my cousin Elspeth Lachlan, who makes her home with us. I don't believe you've met her."

"No, I have not had that pleasure."

"She is the widow of a retired military man. A most superior woman! Charming and well informed. I don't know how I would have managed without her these past few years."

While the two men talked, Grace's mind chuffed along like a steam engine. A house party arranged for Rossmor in October! That was very soon. She was out of her depth, and she knew it. She had no idea what such a house party entailed, and what her role as hostess would be in seeing to the planning of it. Menus and assigning bedchambers and airing linens. Special menus to please her guests. And then they would need to be entertained, as well.

Then there were the servants—not just those already employed at Rossmor but any extra help needed to be hired in: Count Borromini would surely bring his valet and perhaps his secretary with him, and Lady Helena would have her dresser along. The servants would also have to be housed and fed, but that wasn't the problem she dreaded most.

It was one thing to pretend that everything was normal between herself and her husband for a few hours of dinner and conversation with his friends, but how on earth would they hide the truth in close quarters with guests and relatives and—oh, God!—a great houseful of servants? Gossip inevitably flew back and forth, abovestairs and below. Servants always knew more that went on in a household than their employers did.

They knew, for instance, the faces that people wore behind their polite society masks. Their great joys and sorrows. And if a husband and wife were sharing the same bed.

But it was what Lady Helena knew that rampaged around the back of Grace's mind, setting her brain awhirl. *Why did she say that Alistair had not murdered Finnula?*

If Lady Helena's disclaimer was intended to reassure her, it had had the opposite effect. There had been something odd in her tone—and a hard little glitter in her magnificent eyes—that put Grace on the alert.

What had she meant by it? She made it sound as if Alistair stood accused—at least in popular opinion—of murdering his late wife!

She tuned into the conversation again, realizing it had taken another tack. Count Borromini was asking something and the words "camera" and "séance" leapt out at her. The subject was dropped when their carriage was announced. The evening ended with promises to meet for a drive out to the Castello in two days' time.

As they pulled away from the palazzo and down the lighted drive, McLean scrutinized Grace carefully. She was amazingly beautiful and had pulled off her first major social engagement with well-bred ease. He had no doubt that she would be an asset to Rossmor, as well as to himself.

She sat very rigidly as the carriage swayed around the corner, looking out the window. Something had occurred to upset her. *Most likely Helena. She does like to stir things up!*

"Are you tired, my dear?"

She gave a start but recovered quickly. "Only a little."

"I was afraid that Lady Helena might have worn you out

with her chatter. Her energy can be exhausting to one unused to it."

"She is rather overwhelming. But I liked her very
much."

"Yes. She has extraordinary charm and a lively mind.
Too lively at times. And she likes to poke sticks into hor-
net's nests: when I was twelve she created an uproar by
telling my father that there was no reason for him to think
that I had taken one of the guns out of the gunroom. I
hadn't, of course. Which, as she pointed out later, was exactly what she'd said."

McLean laughed ruefully. "But by the time she was
through, my father was utterly convinced that I had somehow spirited one out of the locked guncase and then spirited
it back. It got me in a deuced lot of trouble!"

"I can imagine so!" Grace was thoughtful. "Yes, I can
see that she might imbue things with a certain drama."

He smiled. "I have always said that if Helena hadn't
been born a lady, she would have found her place upon the
stage."

"She said as much to me!"

Grace was surprised and embarrassed at the relief she
felt. Lady Helena's comment about Alistair not murdering
his wife was nothing more than one of her verbal games.

*How could I have been such a fool as to read anything
at all into her remark? I will not fall for another so easily.
Nor,* she thought with real regret, *will I be as open to her
friendship.*

Perhaps she and Alistair's cousin Elspeth would strike
up a cordial relationship. Grace hoped the older woman
would welcome her and be willing to take her under her
wing. It would be nice to have a friend and ally at Rossmor.

Later, when Grace and McLean were back in the suite,
she brought up the other matter that was on her mind. "The
count mentioned séances. Are you planning to hold one at
Rossmor?"

"Yes. One of our guests is a medium. Mrs. Dearing is her name."

"I have heard of her. Mrs. Bingley had considered consulting her regarding some sort of investments, but did not want to pay her fees. 'Donations,' as she calls them."

Grace removed her bracelet and rings and set them in her jewel case. "I know that Theosophism is all the rage these days, but I didn't imagine that you might be interested in such things."

McLean had already taken out his pocket watch and chain, shucked off his jacket and hung it in the wardrobe. He looked up from removing his shirt studs. "Spirit guides and table-rappings, you mean?" He shook his head.

"My dear Grace, do you really picture me mesmerized by trumpets sailing about a darkened room and ghostly manifestations of glowing ectoplasm coming from the mouths of entranced mediums? Let me assure you that my interest in such things goes beyond parlor tricks to fool the gullible! However, I believe that some mediums have a talent which cannot be explained by ordinary means."

She stared at him. "Do you mean . . . communicating with the spirits of the dead?"

"It is an area of interest to me."

She was startled, and waited in vain for him to elaborate. He removed his stickpin in front of the looking glass and put it aside, then opened his collar. His tanned throat stood out against the white shirt. Her mouth went a little dry. How handsome he was, this stranger who was her husband. He took her breath away.

His eyes met hers in the mirror. There was such an intensity in his glance that it unnerved her. A ripple of heat slid through her from head to toe. She turned her head.

Grace removed her earrings with trembling hands and fumbled with the clasp of her necklace. It was caught in the hair at her nape. The more she tried to free it the worse it became ensnarled.

"Would you be so kind as to undo my necklace, Alistair?"

He turned slowly. She rarely called him by his given name. That was encouraging. "Of course, my dear."

She went to him and presented her back. It took a while to untangle her from the necklace. His fingers were warm against her skin as he freed her hair and unclasped the necklace. His touch sent delicious shivers along her spine.

McLean felt a throb of heat as his hands moved against the silken skin of her nape, but his voice was cool. "There you are," he said, putting the necklace into her hands.

She wanted him to touch her again. "If you would please be so kind as to undo the buttons of my frock?"

"Of course." He started at the top and moved slowly down, undoing the tiny fabric-covered buttons. "You are the most beautiful woman in Rome," he said casually as he finished the last button. "There you are. If there is nothing more . . . ?"

There is everything more. She couldn't say it aloud. "Do you mean to go out again?"

"No." His hands rested lightly on her bare shoulders. "I intend to read over some papers Borromini sent to me, and then stretch out on the sofa for a good night's sleep."

"Perhaps you would prefer the bed," she said a little breathlessly. "It is exceedingly comfortable."

There. It was out. Surely he would understand what she meant, without her having to put it into words.

His brows rose. "How wifely of you to offer. However, I am perfectly comfortable on the couch."

But as he spoke his hands slid down her arms, and his lips pressed softly against her nape. Sensation flooded her. She sighed and tilted her neck as his mouth roved to her ear. She felt his breath stirring her hair. His nearness stirring her blood. He released her abruptly. "Good night, my dear."

"You've forgotten something."

McLean spun her around to face him. Her hands splayed out against his chest. "A good-night kiss?" he said with a wry smile. "I would be happy to comply."

"Your pocket watch," she said.

"My hopes are dashed. I see that I am doomed to disappointment. A shame, really." He cupped her cheek in his hand. His thumb caressed her skin, outlined the soft fullness of her mouth.

Her breath hitched. "You are mocking me."

"Not at all." He slid his arms around her and held her close. "But I believe I am entitled to a kiss to dream on."

His voice was low, his eyes focused on her mouth. She couldn't have moved away if she'd wanted to. His strong fingers tangled in her hair, tilting her head up for his kiss. His mouth touched hers, softly, softly. She felt as if she stood on the edge of a precipice, and the slightest pressure would send her hurtling over.

McLean had only meant to tease her, to tempt her. He was caught in his own trap. His arms wound round her shoulders and he crushed her against his chest in a powerful embrace.

She was lost in the moment. She didn't care when he pulled the clips from her hair and scattered the long pins upon the carpet. It tumbled over her shoulders in shining waves.

The scent of her hair, the warmth of her body, the pliant way she curved against his length sent McLean's blood pounding with need. She was beautiful and she was his, and he wanted her with a sudden fierceness that shook him.

His lips skimmed along her cheek and down the graceful curve of her throat. Her head was thrown back, her body arched against his, and he felt her trembling in his arms.

The need was in her, too. She felt it rising like a flame inside her. She kissed him back with the same fervor, sighed against his mouth with pleasure as he took the kiss deeper.

It was McLean who stopped. He wouldn't jeopardize everything for a few moments of gratification. He must bide his time, woo her gently. Make her ache for him the way he ached for her.

Grace's head was still swimming when he released her. She clutched at his shirt but he pried her fingers away. "Go to bed, Grace," he said with more coolness than he thought. "Lock the door."

He went out of the bedroom, leaving her aroused and bewildered and stunningly angry. Grace went to the door and snapped the bolt home. She turned and leaned against the painted panel. She tried to calm herself, but her whole body ached with longings she'd never known before. Desire and disappointment were compounded by frustration. He'd made a fool of her.

Without thinking, she picked up her hairbrush from the dressing table and threw it across the room. It hit the wall with a thud.

McLean stood on the other side of the door, laughing softly.

Chapter Eleven

Over the next seven days Grace felt herself caught up in a world she'd never known. Although the ranks of society were still thin, there were enough visitors and permanent residents in Rome to fill her days. She was rapidly finding her footing amid McLean's circle of acquaintances.

They seemed eager to meet his new bride. Invitations poured in for luncheons and dinner engagements and excursions to various points of interest. By the end of a whirlwind week, floral offerings, boxes of candy, and books of poetry filled their hotel suite.

"You have taken Rome by storm," McLean told Grace. "If this keeps up, we shall have to take a second suite to hold the gifts from your smitten admirers."

"I don't encourage it," she said, looking up from her task of opening more notes of invitation. "In fact, I am rather overwhelmed by all this unsought attention. As of now we have only one evening free before we take our leave of Rome."

"I am amazed that we have any," he replied.

She slit the letter opener beneath the seal of the last envelope.

"If we accept this, there will be none. It is an invitation from Mrs. Dearing to join 'a select company for an evening of discussion on topics of mutual interest.' Shall I decline?"

He pondered the invitation. "On the whole, I believe it would be better to do so." He had no doubt that one of Mrs. Dearing's cronies would manage to "convince" her to hold a séance during the course of the evening. He didn't want to become involved in one, in a setting that Mrs. Dearing controlled.

"We should have one night to ourselves, without your eager conquests fluttering around us like moths." McLean hated to admit it, but he was becoming irked by it.

Young Lord Peltersham, who was to be one of the house party at Rossmor, was clearly the most smitten of all. They had met him by chance one afternoon at the foot of the Spanish Steps.

Peltersham bowed his golden head over Grace's hand as if she were a queen. "My dear Mrs. McLean, I am totally enchanted! Count Borromini's description did not do you justice. Does your husband realize that he is the most fortunate man in Rome?"

"You will have to ask him that yourself," Grace replied, "as any answer I give will leave me open to accusations of conceit."

Peltersham's pale eyes danced with appreciation. "As witty as you are beautiful. Can I convince you to abandon your husband and run away with me?"

"That," McLean said smoothly, "is something you had best not put to the test, Charles."

The young nobleman quirked an eyebrow. "Playing the jealous husband already! Are you threatening to call me out?"

"No," McLean drawled. "I am warning you."

Although the two men were friends, Peltersham heard an undertone of steel in the other man's voice. "The lovely lady has eyes only for you, Alistair. You needn't fear."

McLean laughed. "My only fear, Charles, is that I will have to throw you into one of the fountains and ruin your elegant suit."

They invited him to join them on their visit to the church at the top of the steps and he agreed readily. Like her husband, Lord Peltersham had come to Rome for the first joint meeting of the Society for Psychical Research and the society of Experimental Psychology at the Palazzo Borromini. While she found the fulsome compliments that tripped off the viscount's tongue an embarrassment, Grace thought he was delightful company. He was clever, handsome, well-informed and good-natured in the extreme.

He also proved a good distraction, arranging excursions to places of interest to her. In fact, he would have kept her social schedule filled with outings from dusk to dawn. At first she had been afraid that visiting some of the old sites in Rome might trigger another episode like the one she'd experienced in the forum, and Grace had been leery of accepting.

Fortunately there had been no recurrence. She'd toured temples and tombs, tossed coins into ancient fountains, and clambered up the steep stone rows of amphitheaters without any problems. The only time she'd felt ill at ease had been outside the Colosseum. Then Alistair had appeared at her side, and her uneasiness had been banished by relief.

"You needn't go traipsing all over the huge structure if the heat is overmuch for you," he'd said. "You're looking overly flushed."

"It is a bit warm," she'd responded—and that had been that. While the others scrambled over the tiered seats, she and Alistair had gone off to a little place nearby that sold fruit ices instead.

The days and nights were busy with engagements: carriage rides and walks in the Borghese Gardens by day gave way to sparkling conversation and elegant dinners, plays and midnight suppers.

Grace liked Lord Peltersham and was charmed by Count Borromini. She was increasingly wary, though, of Lady Helena. The two women had had little chance to converse privately together, but Grace was uncomfortably aware of some silent exchanges between her husband and the merry widow across the dinner table or on the dance floor of the hotel ballroom. Their degree of easy intimacy bothered her more than she cared to admit.

They have known each other all their lives, she reminded herself frequently. *And even if there has been something more between them, well, that is their business! It is not as if our marriage were a love match, and I a jealous wife.* But the feeling roused in her breast certainly fit every definition of the word.

The more she tried to convince herself that his dealings with other women were no business of hers the more she wondered about his relationship with Lady Helena.

McLean was aware of her doubts and fostered them by flirting discreetly with Lady Helena at every opportunity. There was nothing like the presence of another charming female, he knew, to make any self-respecting woman sit up and take notice.

Grace was increasingly restless, without being able to put her finger on the pulse of her emotions. She found her new husband an entertaining companion, an excellent partner in the waltz, and an elegant host to his friends. It was only when they reached their own suite that the laughter and chatter died down. Their conversations were those of polite strangers, belying the silent and increasing tensions.

On their last night in Rome, she decided to confront the problem head-on. Increasingly, Grace suspected he realized that he'd made a terrible mistake, and waited for him to say so.

Tonight they were dining alone at their hotel, and she was exceedingly nervous. Alistair hadn't said a single word to her since he'd returned from an afternoon engagement. At the moment he was perusing a newspaper. While she finished dressing her hair atop her head, Grace regarded him in the mirror. She realized, as she placed the last pin in her chignon, that he hadn't turned the page in some time. He was watching her.

The moment she rose from the dressing table, he looked down at the newsprint.

"Are you pretending to read so you needn't speak to me?"

McLean set aside the newspaper and looked her over with frank admiration. Her eyes sparkled like the aquamarine necklace draped around her throat. The matching brooch winked at her corsage, and the long earrings brushed her white shoulders. "You look charming, my dear." He picked up the newspaper again.

"If you are angry with me," she said, twisting her hands together, "I cannot blame you for it. You have given me all the rights of a wife, and none of the obligations."

"I am not angry with you." He didn't look up.

Grace crossed over to him. "This cannot go on! The situation is intolerable."

"I am surprised. You seemed to be enjoying yourself." His blue eyes regarded her thoughtfully. "I suppose that Mrs. Bingley may be persuaded to take you back if she has not already found a replacement for your former position. On the whole, I wouldn't recommend it. You'll be much happier married to me."

"How can you possibly say so?"

"Do you find marriage to me so distasteful?"

"You know that is not what I meant," she answered. "This is what I feared from the beginning. You regret your hasty impulse."

"You are putting words in my mouth. Perhaps they would be more honest coming from yours."

"No." Grace felt her face flood with color. She pressed her hands to her cheeks. "You have been everything that is good and kind and generous to me."

His expression hardened. "If that is true, then you should

have no complaints. I assure you that I have none."

"How can you say that?" she asked in a low tone. "After I have struggled for years to make my way in the world, every obstacle has been removed by this ring upon my finger. A few simple words and I suddenly have all the elegancies of life at my command. It is one-sided arrangement. You have taken on a wife who is no wife to you. You have gotten the worst side of the bargain."

"I do not agree in the least," he replied. "I am happy with my 'bargain,' as you call it. Therefore there is no reason for you to be so overwrought."

"I am not overwrought," she said, resisting the urge to negate her words by stamping her foot.

He checked the mantel clock and rose. "If you are ready we'll go down to dinner."

Grace bit her lip. "How can I argue my point, when you refuse to believe there is a point at all?"

"Exactly," McLean answered.

There was nothing more to be said. Grace found that maddening.

Her dissatisfaction grew. She had taken everything and given nothing in return. Her husband refused to acknowledge it.

She let him slip her silk shawl over her shoulders, and felt the accidental brush of his fingertips against her skin. A wave of sensation ran along her spine, followed by a quick rush of heat. He felt it, too. She knew it by his quick intake of breath, and the electric air around them.

Looking up beneath her lashes, Grace saw raw desire in his eyes, knew it was mirrored in her own. She thought for a moment that he would pull her into his arms and kiss her. The moment spun out endlessly. She stood frozen in time, waiting for his next move.

It was toward the door.

McLean had used all his willpower to resist crushing her in his arms. There were times in the dead of night when

he lay awake, thinking about the past few weeks and wondering what the devil had possessed him to marry her.

He'd never intended to marry again in the first place.

In the second, he'd thought that he was the one in charge
of ushering their relationship in the proper direction. There
were times—like the present moment—when she almost
won the upper hand, without even knowing the rules of the
game he was playing. Or that there was a game at all. His
pawn had metamorphosed into the white queen. If he
wasn't careful he'd find himself in check.

Grace rustled past him as if nothing had happened. Inside she was furious. He was playing a game to which she
herself had set the rules—and using them against her. At
the moment it was stalemate.

Just before they reached the dining room, a lady in a
striking crimson ensemble accosted them. "My dear Mr.
McLean, I hope you will introduce me to your lovely wife.
I wish you both happy."

McLean made the introductions. "I had heard that you'd
gone to Venice, Mrs. Dearing."

"My visit was canceled rather abruptly," she said. "Our
plans fell through and I decided to stay on in Rome. I hope
you have not changed your mind about our forthcoming
experiment?" This last was accompanied by an arch look.

"Not at all. Your invitation to Rossmor still stands."

Mrs. Dearing looked gratified. "It will more than meet
your expectations, I assure you."

"And yours," he said cryptically.

"Tell me more of Mrs. Dearing," Grace said in a quiet
tone as the woman swept away. "You said she is a medium.
You must have a strong belief in her abilities."

"She is either a woman of great psychic powers—or a
leech upon society, posing as a gracious benefactor," he
responded, and guided her into the dining room. "And
when she visits us at Rossmor. I intend to discover the
truth."

The elegant dining room was crowded, but their regular table awaited them. It was a choice position at a pair of windows open to the terrace, and a stunning view of the lights of Rome.

Grace was too preoccupied with their problems to dwell on Mrs. Dearing. Tonight was the first time the two of them would dine alone since their farce of a wedding. There would be no one else present to provide a buffer between them.

Grace was aware of people watching them. She smiled brightly and carried on with the breeding of a true lady, throwing out topics of conversation that might interest her husband. It was hard going. His responses were confined to a word or two, and he ventured no topics of his own.

As the courses were removed, she found herself at a standstill. *I will serve him up the same cold shoulder*, she thought with a tinge of annoyance. *Let him be the one to speak next. I won't utter another word.*

It was a promise she couldn't keep. She noticed several of their fellow diners watching them, and making asides to one another. *Alistair and I are clearly the topic of their discussions.*

She fixed a smile on her face. It felt as if it were pinned there at the corners of her mouth, stiff as a papier-maché mask.

"I suppose we shall have to say something from time to time," she said, "or people will think we have quarreled."

McLean smiled across the snowy linen and crystal goblets. "As you will come to realize, I don't particularly care what construction others project upon my behavior. As for talking—my dear wife, I would very much prefer to simply look at you." He lowered his voice. "You are very beautiful, you know. You take a man's breath away."

His gaze was as warm and intimate as a caress. She realized what he was doing then. He *was* seducing her. But why? She could think of several reasons: from need or want

. . . to prove his mastery . . . the masculine drive for possession.

Again and again her thoughts wound back to that brief touch of his fingers on her flesh, the sudden spark that leapt the gap between them. She lifted her wine glass and saw her reflection multiplied in its sparkling facets. A dozen tiny Graces looked back at her from the shining crystal, and not a one of them had the slightest clue as to what would happen next. When—and how—this interminable evening would end was beyond the powers of her imagination.

"It's a fine night," he said when she set her glass down. "I suggest a walk through the gardens before we retire."

"I . . . I thought that you were invited to play at cards this evening with Mr. Pierce and his friend?"

He steered her out through the terrace and down into the formal garden. "With those two fine young bucks? I have no desire to join them. They're a pair of wolves looking for a fat sheep to fleece."

They strolled past a jetting fountain. Its spray cascaded back in the moonlight, looking like a rain of small silver balls. "I can see that a wife is a good thing to have while traveling," he added conversationally. "It keeps one from falling into bad company."

Grace stopped and turned to him. "You're making light of the matter, but you can't go on ignoring the situation. I . . . I should never have accepted your offer. What we have is no marriage, but a sham!"

He was suddenly wary. "What are you trying to say, Grace?"

She pretended a calm she did not feel. "We have been like fencers with blunted foils, darting in and dancing back, circling around and never coming close to settling anything. It is time to take the buttons off."

McLean stood back, arms out from his sides. "Strike, then. I am at your mercy."

"You needn't mock me."

"My dear, that is the least of my intentions."

Grace looked out across the lantern-lit gardens. "Out of the goodness of your heart, you offered me the protection of your name. I misunderstood the rest of it—no doubt, as your publications on the science of psychology point out, through an unwillingness to face the facts."

"Which are?"

She heard the sharpness in his tone and her stomach sank. "You are a man of strong desires. Surely you must regret the impulse that has put us in this tangle. I will understand if you want to rid yourself of me."

He went very still. Light from the windows cast his face in sharp relief. "Is that what you think I want?"

"Yes. No. Oh, I don't *know* what you want!"

He put his hands on her shoulders. The air between them hummed with urgency. "Don't you, my dear? I thought I'd made myself quite clear. I want you in my arms. In my bed. But I will not make love to you unless you are willing."

There was such power in his voice, such sudden ferocity, that her blood thrilled with it. Grace felt her heart lift with excitement. "If we could start anew—take our time to know one another—I would be very grateful."

His eyes were dark with desire and frustration. Was she using his own psychology upon him? If so it was working.

"Damn it to hell! I don't want your gratitude," he said harshly. "I want your passion! And, by God, I won't settle for anything less."

Her voice was only a whisper. "That is what frightens me. What if I have none to give?"

"Little fool," he said softly, pulling her into his arms. "You are ripe and bursting with it."

As she sighed and swayed nearer, McLean drew her to him in a surge of triumph. The purgatory of waiting was over. The moment to act had come at last. He lowered his mouth to hers and claimed it. She was soft and yielding in his embrace.

His first kiss was tender. It drew Grace in, lured her with gentle sweetness. The next was different. His mouth was hungry and possessive. It took and demanded and set her brain reeling. His lips grazed the angle of her jaw, moving down to the soft hollow at the base of her throat.

Champagne is nothing to this, she thought. Heat and cold mingled in her. She drew in a ragged breath and twined her arms around him.

His mouth moved lower, skimming the top of her breasts. Grace sighed with heedless pleasure. Her head was thrown back, her eyes closed. She wanted more. Now.

He sensed it. "Let me love you, Grace. Tell me you want me too."

"I do. I do want you, Alistair."

Her response had his blood singing. He hadn't expected her surrender to be so unconditional. Beneath that collected exterior, passion burned in her like a white-hot flame. She was his, and he wanted to carry her into the deeper shadows of the garden, make love to her beneath the shimmering stars.

But recklessness would ruin everything. Tonight it must be on soft linen sheets, with candlelight gilding her body. He would lead her slowly up to the wild heights of arousal and lay the world at her slender feet.

There was no need to go back through the dining room. They went hand in hand up the stairs to the balcony like forbidden lovers, and entered the upper lobby. He kissed her again in the shadow of an alcove. Her innocence touched him, her ardor excited him. He felt eager as a boy with his first love, heart pounding with anticipation.

They found their suite almost by chance. She laughed softly when he fumbled the key in his impatience to open the door. Then they were inside with it closed behind them, locking out the rest of the world.

He pulled her hard against his chest and ravished her mouth with wild, deep kisses. She trembled in his arms as her silk gown was whisked away to pool on the floor at her feet. His jacket and shirt followed. He gathered her hard against him, his hands as demanding as his mouth. His pulse was pounding in every cell of his body. Never in his life had he wanted anything the way he wanted her. He tried to rein himself in. He was a scientist. A scholar. A rational human being. She'd turned him into a madman.

In the back of her mind a stray thought fluttered like a moth at a lamp. This wasn't how she'd expected to give up her virginity, her sovereignty. Not in this fierce, sweaty, glorious haste. She'd envisioned herself in a white peignoir, her hair arranged like a fan on the pillow . . . a few tender kisses. A tentative touch followed by a quick joining. A brief pang of ecstasy before it was over, leaving her to hastily rearrange her disordered gown.

She sighed against his mouth. This was so different. So right.

She was filled with a deepsure knowledge of what she wanted. He seemed to know as well. His kisses kept hers in thrall as his strong hands stripped the rest of her garments away. The heat of his mouth upon her breast was so exquisite she felt faint.

Triumph surged through him. She was eager and greedy for love. This would be no slow seduction. He swept her up in his arms and carried her to the bed. The past weeks of restraint had been a challenge to his self-discipline, because he'd guessed at the degree of passion in her, and was impatient to awaken it. The restraint had been worth it. They were both at fever pitch.

Stretching out beside her, he caressed her curves with the touch of an experienced lover. Sensed exactly when to hold back and when to lead her further down the path. She was ready now.

His hand slid over the soft swell of her belly and down.

She froze a moment until trust and her own need won out. She felt the dampness between her thighs, welcomed his skillful touch. The intimacy deepened and she let him lead her where he willed.

She was hot and slick and ready, but he drew out the pleasure for her, whispering soft words as her body tremored and arched beside him. He knew she was reaching the crest before she did. At the precise moment he leaned down and took the tip of her breast into his mouth.

She was beyond thought, immersed in a world of touch and scent that was completely new to her. Suddenly she was flung into an unknown universe of pure sensation. Her body arched up against him wildly. He kissed her mouth, smoothed her hair, whispered hushed endearments as he sheltered her in his arms.

He cupped her in his hand, began again before she'd recovered. When the moment was right, when she was hot and aching for him, he moved with swift sureness. She gasped in surprise and clung to him as he took her back up to the edge of consciousness. She felt the rush of blood begin somewhere deep inside. It expanded until it filled her with its dark, hurtling glory. They rode it together, locked in each other's arms.

She fell asleep with her head on his shoulder. For the first time since she was a young orphan, Grace felt secure and protected. Loved.

She woke up toward morning, and found him watching her gravely. They made love again, starting more slowly, vowing restraint and then throwing it away to the winds in the heat of their passion. Afterward he held her so hard she thought her ribs would break, covered her face with kisses. Said all the right words except the three she longed to hear.

I am being foolish, she thought later, as she lay in his arms. *This was nothing more than the result of natural desire, for either one of us. We have not known each other long enough for love to bloom. But it will come in time.*

No matter how she tried to convince herself of this, in her heart Grace knew she wasn't being completely honest. Alistair admired her and desired her. All well and good. But they were very tame emotions compared to what she felt for him.

For many years now, she had steered a course by her own stars. In a few short weeks, Alistair McLean had become her sun and moon, eclipsing everything else.

It amazed and delighted and rather frightened her. She, who had guarded her heart so well and for so long, had fallen deeply, recklessly, head-over-heels in love with the handsome stranger who was her husband.

Chapter Twelve

SCOTLAND

The train rushed through the Highlands, its clacketing rhythm like a mechanical heartbeat. From the comfort of a private compartment, Grace watched as they rounded a long curve. A veil of steam streamed back from the engine's funnel, blending with drifts of low cloud in the clear morning light.

Grace's relief at approaching journey's end was equaled by her increasing anxiety: the deeper they had gone into the Highlands, the more withdrawn her husband had become. Instead of the passionate lover she'd known, Alistair seemed more like a chance-met stranger, somehow put into her private car by error.

He sat across from her, his face stern in profile. He'd been staring out the window for hours, remote as the mountains. From time to time she fancied that she caught glimpses of his thoughts. They were like images seen through her father's microscope when she was a girl—incredibly clear, yet unreal. Close-up views that revealed minute detail but baffled more than they enlightened:

Sunlight dancing on steel-blue waters. Moonlight on cool, gray stone. Dark waterweeds washing against rainlashed rocks.

Grace shivered, although the interior of the car was warm. *I am imagining things. Since leaving Rome, I have not had a single episode like those I experienced in the Forum, and later in the dovecote. Perhaps our marriage has conferred immunity on me: my love for Alistair keeps me tethered so strongly in the present that visions of the past cannot intrude.*

McLean turned and caught her staring. "Was I off wool-gathering?"

"For the past two hours and more."

He reached over and took her hand in his. "Poor Grace! I've neglected you shamefully. I swear I shall make it all up to you tonight, once we reach Rossmor."

She gave him a cool smile. "I should rather have a little of your attention now. It will be quite late when we arrive, and all I'll be wishing for will be a hot bath and a soft bed!"

He laughed and kissed her hand. "Well, now you have put me in my place! Not wed a month and I have been replaced in your affections by—"

The conductor knocked on the door and looked in. "Ten minutes to arrival at Inverness," he announced in a thick Scots burr. McLean relinquished her hand and sat back. The conductor ducked out again quickly, but the playful mood was shattered.

Grace watched her husband turn back to the window. His face settled almost immediately into the same stern lines as before. *No*, she realized suddenly. *They are lines of pain. What an insensitive fool I am! Alistair made this same journey with Finnula more than once.*

"I am very sorry," she said as the train slowed. "I was forgetting that your homecoming must stir up many memories . . ."

He gave a little shake of his head, like someone waking from a dream. He regarded her with a strange gravity. "It is not the past that has absorbed me, my dear, but the future. I only hope I have done the right thing in bringing you to Rossmor."

A flush rose up her cheeks. "I know that I am very ignorant about my duties as mistress of such an historic place—and especially as Janet's new mother. I assure you I will endeavor to learn them quickly and well."

He reached out and pulled her onto his lap with a strength and ease that surprised Grace. Her book thudded to the floor of the railway car, unnoticed. He cupped her chin, tilting her face up to his. "It is you I am thinking of, my dear. I most sincerely hope that you will never come to regret marrying me."

There was such fierce protectiveness in his gaze that it quelled all her doubts. "I won't," she told him, sliding her arms around his neck. "How could I?"

He crushed her to his chest and kissed her breathless. When the conductor came back along the corridor at Inverness, he was surprised to find the compartment locked. As he was lifting his hand to knock, he heard a soft sigh of pleasure from beyond the closed door.

He shook his head, wondering what the world was coming to; but he went on down the aisle, smiling.

Grace was lost in her own thoughts as their traveling carriage bowled along the moor road. There had been a delay in Inverness, and although the sun still shone in the west, the long northern twilight was closing in rapidly. Suddenly McLean knocked on the carriage roof, signaling the coachman to stop. His put his hand on her arm.

"There it is, my dear. Rossmor!"

She peered out her window, eager for a first glimpse of her new home. It was a daunting sight: gray clouds smoking down between rumpled mountains, the waters of the loch gleaming like a sword of hammered silver piercing deep into their heart.

She'd expected an imposing manor: Rossmor was all

that and more. It stood alone on its own peninsula, outlined against the dark waters of the loch and the mountains beyond. On the far side, the bulk of an ancient fortified tower rose like a defiant fist against the massing storm. Odd little turrets sprouted halfway up the corners of the tower, each with only a single arrow slit to break their bleak façades. This was the oldest portion of Rossmor, a stern monument to the fierce raids that had once bloodied the glen.

She hadn't realized it was so large. So old. *Proud and fierce,* she thought. *And a little frightening.*

McLean was watching her closely. "You are very quiet. Perhaps you were expecting something grander?"

"No, indeed! It is far grander than I expected." Despite hunting desperately for just the right words, Grace fell short. "It is . . . ah . . . quite atmospheric," she said at last.

He laughed. "It is a little overwhelming, I suppose, when seen for the first time. I grew up here, however, so it has always been home to me."

She gave him a rueful smile. "McLeans have lived and died here for over half a millennium, while my dowry consists of a silver locket, and my mother's milk opal brooch. I feel the veriest imposter!"

He squeezed her gloved hand. "You will be an ornament in Rossmor's crown."

The square tower drew her eyes like a lodestone. A scene trembled in her mind, like a reflection in rippled water: *a staircase winding up into darkness . . . blue sky and crenellated battlements hewn from gray stone . . . far below, dark rocks edged with lichen rose from water black as night.* Now she knew that these scenes were not the products of her mind. They existed here at Rossmor.

"Is the tower still in use?" she said, in a voice as dry as ash.

His grip on her hand grew tighter. "It isn't safe. You must promise me, Grace, that you won't go there alone."

"How mysterious you are." She shot him a look. "Is it haunted?"

McLean's eyebrows rose. "If so, *I* have seen no evidence of it. But it was built in 1242 and is in disrepair. It's closed off from the rest of the house while renovations are being undertaken."

She hid her relief with light banter. "It looks so Gothic that I'd hoped to find dank dungeons and oubliettes filled with shackled skeletons."

He shook his head. "The ancestral McLeans were not so subtle as that. A good broadsword or Highland dirk dispatched the unlucky foe."

"Now I am disappointed. Lady Helena assured me I should find it very wonderfully romantic."

McLean shook his head. "Helena would! If by romantic she means drafty, uncomfortable, and inconvenient, it certainly meets the criteria."

Grace laughed. "I don't believe that's what she had in mind. Is it still in use?"

"Yes. A good portion is employed for storage of furniture and household inventory, but the rest is kept very much as it has always been. When we have a large house party the rooms are pressed into service as extra bedchambers, and the Great Hall becomes the ballroom. The carved beams and woodworking are exquisite, and there are several fine Flemish tapestries. To me the old tower is—and will always be—the heart of the manor."

Grace was eager to see it. "You love Rossmor very much," she said.

"Yes. Not just the house and history but the loch and glen and moors. I hope that in time you will come to love it as I do."

Looking at the grim outline of the tower, Grace felt a few reservations, but kept them to herself.

He signaled the driver to start up again. "I don't believe

the storm will hold off until we reach the house." But his eyes shone as he settled back beside her. She realized that he was looking forward to the coming storm. Was it something in the inherent wildness of the weather that called to its like within him? *How little I really know Alistair,* she thought, with a little pang.

As their carriage descended into the glen the light changed. Broad rays of sun poured through a gap in the gathering clouds, transforming everything. The hills were touched with purple and rose and the land fell in broad sweeps of emerald velvet down to the shining loch. Now the middle section of the house was revealed, its slate gables bristling with chimneypots.

"You'll see the new wing when the road curves," Alistair said. "It consists of the Long Drawing Room, the Dining Salon, Breakfast Parlor, and estate offices, with bedchambers above."

Grace had a glimpse of an elegant façade and gardens tumbling down to the loch, but wraiths of mist moved in, veiling the landscape in swathes of white tulle. As she strained her eyes for a better look, the westering sun sank behind the highest mountain crag, plunging the glen into indigo night. It was as sudden as the snuffing of a lantern.

A gust of wind rattled the carriage. "Now we're in for it," McLean said, and put up the window. Spatters of rain whispered against the glass, tapped impatiently on the roof. Grace smoothed her leather-gloved fingers against the condensation on the glass and peered out as a flash of lightning lit the sky. The thickening fog created a strange illusion: Rossmor seemed to float upon the air, half real and half something out of legend.

Very atmospheric! All it needs, she told herself, *is a wailing banshee, or a phantom on the battlements!*

That was when she saw it, revealed in the next lightning flash—a swirl of diaphanous gray draperies atop the tallest turret, the merest suggestion of a face. Grace shrank back in alarm. The shape altered, thinned out into vanishing tendrils of rain and mist.

It was only an illusion, she told herself, trying to calm the erratic pounding of her heart. *Nothing more.*

But it reminded her of something she hadn't wanted to confront: in the haste of their marriage and the passionate discovery of their honeymoon, she hadn't dared let herself dwell on Rossmor and its long history. A place so old must be filled with echoes of its long and violent past. The possibility that she might suffer another "incident" within Rossmor's ancient walls was very real. She tried to convince herself otherwise.

Grace glanced over at her husband's profile. It was almost as if the fact of their marriage had conferred some sort of immunity upon her. *Perhaps it is my love for Alistair. It keeps me tethered so strongly in the present that the past cannot intrude.*

She took great comfort in the thought.

Lights sprang on in two of the windows of the sprawling structure, glowing like squares of topaz against the tarnished pewter stones. Curtains closed, shutting the one from view. The other remained open, and she thought someone was standing there. *Janet, watching for her father's return?*

The heavens split open with the roar of a hundred cannons. The rain thundered down on the carriage roof in time to the rapid beating of her heart.

"Not a pleasant welcome for you," McLean said. "But I must admit I love a good storm. It clears the air."

"I am so nervous." Grace touched his hand. "I hope your daughter will grow to like me."

"How can she not?" He kissed her gloved fingers. "And in time, I am certain that she will grow to love you."

. . . As I do, she hoped he would say.

But in all the hours they'd spent together in the past few

weeks and all the times they'd made love, he hadn't said it once. *Perhaps it is still too soon,* she reminded herself. *He has been in love before and suffered through the loss of his first marriage. Perhaps once we are settled here it will be different.*

Alistair McLean was everything she'd ever dreamed of in a man. He had character and integrity, and the same passion for life that burned within her. He was well educated and intelligent, with a wry sense of humor that matched her own. And he was so handsome that there were times she had to force herself not to simply sit and stare at him.

He is, she thought for the hundredth time, *almost too good to be true.*

The carriage plunged down a steep incline and the house vanished from view behind the woods that lined the drive. He kept his hand over hers, but Grace felt him withdraw into himself. She glanced at his face as another sheet of lightning ripped the sky. He looked aloof and rather stern.

No doubt he is remembering the first time he brought a bride here, she thought.

Thunder cracked like rifle shot, and the horses shied in alarm. Another clap sounded even closer at hand and Grace was thrown against her side of the carriage, then back the other way.

"What the devil!" McLean clung to the strap with one hand and held her fast with the other. There was a moment of confusion as the coachman fought the team for control. The coach slewed sideways, then bumped and shuddered to a halt.

McLean rolled down the window and shouted into the lashing rain. "What's wrong, Dougal?"

The man's accent was so thick Grace had to strain to make out his meaning. " 'Tis a great rock rolled down from the moors across the road, sir. The woods are so mortal thick along the way, I dinna ken if I can go round her."

McLean swore. He pressed Grace's hand. "I had better check out the situation."

Cold air swirled inside the carriage as he opened the door and jumped lithely down. Grace waited anxiously in the dark interior. She could hear him conferring with the groom, although the steady rain muffled their words.

"It will take more than a day to clear this all away." At least the rain was slackening. The swift-moving storm was already rolling away, revealing clear snatches of starry sky. He examined the off-wheeler, and patted the beast's head. "A nasty graze, that. Give me that lantern, Dougal."

The coachman complied, and McLean strode back toward the carriage. His jaw tightened. The wheel was cracked.

Grace waited apprehensively. It was several minutes before McLean returned. In the light of the carriage lamps his eyes looked black as jet, and rain dripped from his cape and hat.

"A boulder has broken loose from the escarpment on the moor and fallen onto the road. It's a miracle Dougal was able to avoid it! I'm afraid both horses have sustained injuries. They'll have to be unhitched and led to the stables."

"Oh, dear! What shall we do?"

"Dougal will stay with the horses while I go for help, but it will take some time before it arrives. You have two choices, my dear. Wait here with Dougal, or set off on foot with me. The rain has almost stopped, and there's a path through the woods that leads straight to the house. I can have you safe at Rossmor in less than a quarter hour, if you're game for it."

"I'll chance the woods with you," she answered. "It will be my first adventure at Rossmor."

"Good girl! I salute your courage. You'll arrive wet and muddy, but I promise you tea with a dram of whisky and the hot bath and cozy bed which you longed for earlier."

Grace tied her bonnet on more firmly. "At the moment that is all the lure I require."

McLean lifted her down. He spoke to Dougal, then lifted the lantern and led the way up the bank and into the woods. Ribbons of fog wove a pattern around them until she was totally confused as to direction.

"How can you tell where we're going, Alistair?"

"I know these woods. I spent my youth playing in them. In fact, I've often left the coach after a long journey and taken this shortcut through the woods to the house. It brings back good memories."

God knows, he thought, *I need them.*

Grace gave a little cry of alarm. "I'm caught on something."

"Only a bramble bush." He set the lantern down and helped untangle her. The glow lit the wet black trunks and turned the thin branches of wild bramble to gold. "The path narrows here. We'd best go single file."

It was more of a rude track than a path, but at first the way was clear and easy. Gradually it became harder going and the ground squelched unpleasantly beneath Grace's feet. She felt cold liquid seep inside her boots and hoped they weren't ruined beyond repair.

"Watch where you tread," McLean announced. "There is bogland on either side of us. Take care you don't stray off the path."

"There *is* no path," she exclaimed in rising panic. "Nothing but briars and branches grabbing at me. And my feet are sinking deeper by the moment!"

"We're almost through the woods. I can see the lights of the house ahead through the trees."

"Thank God!" The fog was so thick she could see no more than two or three feet ahead. Moisture beaded her eyelashes as she hurried on, with mud sucking at her boots. She gasped and glanced down as something supple and furry scurried across her instep and fled away into the darkness. When she looked up Alistair had vanished as well. The woods were dark and silent except for the dripping of rain from the leaves overhead and the sound of her own harsh breathing.

There was a faint sound of shattering glass, and she thought that she heard him mutter a curse. "Alistair? Where are you? I can't see an inch!"

"A branch swung back and broke the lantern. Don't move! Stay where you are and keep talking. I'll find you."

She didn't know how he possibly could. In the distorting fog, his voice seemed to come from everywhere and nowhere. Grace tried to free one foot but the ooze held it like an iron fist. She heard a stealthy sound somewhere . . . behind her? Then the twigs snapping. Something was moving nearer. Closing in . . .

"Alistair?"

He didn't answer.

It must be an animal. She wondered what kind of creature ventured out in such filthy weather. *A hungry one!* On the heels of her thought there came a violent thrashing through the brush. Grace wondered if there were still wolves in Scotland.

She grabbed at the nearest briar bush and felt the thorns pierce her gloves. The stinging pain didn't matter. She was able to pull herself free of the muck and force her way through the brush. It was so thick she made little headway. A sudden gusting wind rushed through the treetops, shaking loose the clinging drops of rain. They stung her face like shards of glass.

"Alistair?" Her voice quavered just a little.

She was shaking with cold and her feet were numb. Then his voice drifted to her ears. "Grace? Can you hear me?"

"Yes! Over here!"

"I see you. Come toward me slowly. You're on the path." She turned toward the welcome sound of his voice and started forward, then went sprawling as she tripped over something in her way.

Her breath was knocked out of her. Grace lay where she had fallen, stunned by the impact. There was a series of ominous creaks and groans from overhead, then a loud crack followed by the terrible sound of limbs snapping all around her. A great tree crashed to the ground with astounding force. The earth shook with it, sending up showers of mud and debris. Grace braced herself, expecting to feel the tree smash down, tearing her flesh and splintering bone.

Numbing blows to her shoulder and hip were the worst of it. She lifted her face, gasping for air; but when she tried to struggle up, she couldn't move. Grace turned her head. She was beneath the crown of the fallen tree, held down by the weight of the interlocking branches.

Alistair broke through the mist like an apparition. *"Grace!"* He scrambled nimbly over a broken branch and knelt at her side. "You're injured. Don't move, for the love of God."

"No. I am not hurt at all. I stumbled and fell before the tree came down. Sheer clumsiness saved my life."

"You've had a very narrow escape," he said.

It was only when he'd freed her from the tangled mass of leaves that she realized he wasn't exaggerating. A massive limb had missed her by less than a foot. Reaction set in and her teeth chattered like castanets.

McLean helped her climb out of the debris and held her close. "Not a very pleasant welcome for you, my dear. But you'll soon be tucked into bed, safe and sound."

"The sooner it is the happier I will be," she said with feeling.

"This time stay close. Better yet, take the edge of my cloak and hold on to it for dear life."

McLean forced a way through the broken branches. In less than five minutes they came out onto a sloping lawn. Grace could have wept with joy when she saw the windows of Rossmor glowing through the swirling fog. He held out his hand and led her across the lawn and down to the graveled drive.

She really couldn't see the house, but Grace had the impression of a massive stone wall towering over them. A surge of emotion rushed through her, but whether it was from irrational fear or garden-variety nervousness, she couldn't decide.

"I hope Braedon hasn't bolted the door against the night," McLean said when they reached the front door. He pressed the latch and pushed it open. Then he swooped Grace up in his arms and carried her across the threshold.

"We're home," he said softly as he set her down upon her feet.

For a moment she thought he meant to kiss her. Grace was disappointed when he stepped away. She would have liked the reassurance of a kiss.

She glanced around quickly while water puddled about her on the stone-flagged floor. They were in a large hall paneled in gleaming dark wood. Candles still burned in the heavy brass chandelier that hung above an ancient table, casting their light on several pastoral landscapes in heavy gilt frames, and a suit of armor guarding the foot of the handsome staircase. The empty eye slits looked back at her in a way she found unnerving.

While Grace examined her surroundings McLean reached for a tapestry bellpull beside an enormous sideboard of ebonized wood. Every inch of it was carved with figures of animals, real and imaginary. The wall above was crowded with racks of antlers rising all the way up to the coffered ceiling.

Grace turned her head and saw a butler emerge from the

shadows at the back of the hall. Although there was no silver in his hair, his craggy face showed his age—and, at the moment, a good deal of astonishment. The man glanced from McLean to Grace and back again before he schooled his features.

"Welcome home, sir."

"Ah, there you are, Braedon. It is good to be home at last." McLean stripped off his gloves. "This is your new mistress. We must get her out of her wet garments before she takes a chill."

The butler's jaw dropped. He recovered himself quickly and bowed. "Welcome to Rossmor, madam."

"There." McLean smiled down at Grace. "Now you are official, my dear. Mistress of Rossmor!"

"I am afraid I am making a bad first impression, bedraggled as I am," Grace said as she let the butler take her cloak. The man made a strangled sound of acknowledgment.

McLean shrugged. "Given that you've tramped cross-country in the rain and mud and were nearly crushed by a falling tree, you look respectable enough."

He turned back to the butler. "A great rock has fallen onto the road at the head of the glen. Dougal is stranded there with the coach and team. The off-wheeler has a badly strained hock and the other has grazed his knees. Please notify Davies. He'll know what to do."

He glanced around for his housekeeper and raised his eyebrows at her absence. "I expected to see Mrs. Finley."

The butler shook his head. "I regret to say that Mrs. Finley is not in residence at the moment. She left to visit her sister yesterday, just before the arrival of the telegram announcing your return."

"Well, it can't be helped," McLean said. "I'm sure we'll manage somehow. Where is my cousin? Has she already retired for the evening?"

"No, sir. Mrs. Lachlan went up to Miss Janet, who was upset by the storm. She asked to be informed upon your arrival."

"Please do so. Meanwhile, we'll go into the library and warm ourselves at the fire. Have Cook make us up a tray of refreshments."

"Mrs. Lachlan has ordered that hot soup and a cold platter be kept at the ready."

The butler bowed and vanished behind the baize door at the end of the hall. McLean turned to Grace. "Elspeth is a wonder. I should have known that she would arrange it beforehand." He held out his arm to her.

Grace hesitated. "Perhaps I should make myself a little more presentable before meeting the household."

"Come along and warm yourself before the library fire while I pour you a cordial. You are half-frozen."

It was too tempting to resist. She tucked her hand in the crook of his arm and McLean steered her down the hall and past the foot of the staircase. Movement in the shadows above caught Grace's eye. She looked up and her heart tumbled over in her chest. A pale, insubstantial shape materialized out of the darkness on the landing and drifted to the rail. She gave an audible gasp before realizing that it was only a young girl in a long white nightgown.

"Papa!" The small figure hurtled down the stairs. "Oh, Papa! I have missed you so much!"

McLean turned and knelt to welcome the radiant, dark-haired girl who dashed into his arms. "Janet! How can you have grown so much in two months' time?"

He closed his eyes a moment, inhaling the fresh, flowery scent of her hair that he remembered so well. Then he caught her up and whirled her around and around until the hall rang with his deep laughter and her bright squeals of delight.

"My precious girl! I've missed you terribly."

The unbounded happiness of their reunion touched Grace. This was a new facet of her husband revealed, and she liked it very much. Janet looked like a sprite in her nightdress, and was far prettier than the portrait her father carried with him. In the wildness of her joyous outpourings, Grace sensed loneliness and a need for reassurance that echoed her own past. Her heart immediately went out to the motherless girl.

"Janet!" A sharp female voice cried out from the top of the stairway. "The storm is over, and it is long past your bedtime. You should be fast asleep!"

"But it is Papa!" the girl protested. "He has come home from Italy!"

"Oh! *Alistair!*"

Quick footsteps headed for the other side of the staircase. A woman dressed in rustling black silk swept down them. She was tall and graceful, with dark eyes and red-gold hair braided into a coronet atop her head.

McLean smiled and released his daughter. "Elspeth!" he said, holding out his hands to the newcomer.

Grace stared. *So this is Alistair's cousin!* This striking woman was nothing like the mental image she'd formed of Elspeth Lachlan. *Why, she cannot be many years older than I.*

Although the widow's only ornaments were a large cairngorm brooch and a pair of gold *taille de epergne* earrings, Grace noticed that she was dressed rather formally for a country evening. Candlelight winked enticingly from the black beadwork that adorned the low bodice of her gown and gauzy lace shawl. The stylish ensemble had the unmistakable stamp of Paris in every line.

McLean leaned down to kiss the cheek his cousin offered him. "Is that one of your new gowns? It's very becoming. How well you look!"

"I wish I could return the compliment to you, Alistair."

Elspeth looked him over from head to toe. "You are covered in mud and look as if you'd slept beneath a hedge!"

"The road was blocked by rockfall. We took the old footpath through the woods."

Elspeth smiled warmly. "I had given up hope of your arriving tonight. When you weren't here by sunset, I was sure that you'd been delayed by storms along the way. I told Braedon I didn't expect to see you until sometime early tomorrow!"

"You *knew*?" Janet exclaimed. "You knew that Papa was returning home, and didn't tell me?"

"I had only your best interests at heart." Color flamed in Elspeth's pale cheeks. "I didn't wish you to be disappointed if your father was detained yet again."

McLean relinquished her hands and drew Grace forward. "And here is the cause of my tardiness." Elspeth stared at Grace as if she were a chimney sweep let in by the wrong door. Her arched brows rose even higher.

"Good heavens! Now, who is this?"

Grace flushed. A glimpse in a mirror on the paneled wall showed her damp hair hanging loose from her chignon, and her face daubed with mud. She felt like a half-fledged chicken suddenly come face to face with a beautiful black swan.

Elspeth eyed Grace. "Ah, no! Do not tell me that you have brought a governess for Janet, after all. Why, I thought we had already settled the matter. There is no reason she cannot continue taking her lessons with Meg's boys at the vicarage. Really, Alistair, I wish you had not sprung it on me like this."

She shook her head as the butler took Grace's sodden cloak from her shoulders. "I'm afraid there isn't a bedchamber made up for you. Perhaps we might set up the old truckle bed in Janet's room for the night . . ."

McLean frowned. "You didn't get my letters from Rome? Or my telegrams?"

"A telegram arrived last evening asking to have the carriage meet your train; but I have received nothing from you these past five weeks or more, since the letter from France." Elspeth sighed. "Well, the first thing is to get you both warm and dry, I suppose. Janet, it's long past your bedtime. Go along up to the nursery . . ."

"But Papa has only just come home!" The girl looked on the verge of tears.

"No arguing, Janet. And take this young lady with you . . . ah, Miss . . . ? I'm sorry, I don't know your name."

Grace was stunned. Something had gone very much awry, if no one in this house knew of her coming.

McLean went to her side, his face filled with chagrin. "This is a devil of a coil," he said in a low tone, and gripped her hand. "My letter to my sister was in that same packet. I am afraid our news will be a great shock to everyone."

Elspeth turned her attention to Grace again. "You must be weary. I only hope you have not made the long journey for nothing. If you will accompany Miss McLean up to her room, I'm sure one of the maids can loan you a nightgown until your own trunks are brought in—"

"Elspeth!" McLean said curtly.

She whirled gracefully around at the sound of his voice. "What is it, Alistair?"

"You are under a misapprehension," McLean said firmly. "The letters which I wrote would have explained everything. To put it baldly—I have not brought a governess to Rossmor. I have brought home my bride!"

His cousin turned startled, dark eyes on him. Her face was white as stone. "Your . . . *your bride*?"

"This is my wife, Grace. Formerly Miss Templar. My dear, this is my cousin Elspeth Lachlan, who makes her home here with us and has acted as my hostess these past few years."

Janet looked confused. "I don't understand," she whispered. She stood uncertainly on the bottom step, twisting a strand of dark hair around her finger.

McLean reached out to his daughter and brought her to his side. "I'm afraid that I have made a botch of it! My darling Janet, I know how much you miss your mother, and how you have longed for a mother's care. This is your new mother. I know she will make you as happy as she has made me."

The girl's blue eyes were wide with shock and anger. "A mother? I don't *want* a mother. I *have* a mother—only she is *dead*!"

Pulling violently away, Janet fled up the stairs and vanished into the dimness of the upper floor.

Elspeth was clearly upset. "Had I known of your marriage, I would have carefully prepared her to receive this momentous news. How *could* you spring it upon us like this, Alistair! Poor, poor child. I'm afraid Janet will never forgive you for this!"

And neither will you, Grace thought. She sensed that perhaps the relationship between her husband and his cousin had been heading in a romantic direction—at least on Elspeth's side.

"Go to Janet," she said softly. "I am sure that Braedon will see to our comfort."

Elspeth blinked in astonishment, to hear someone else directing the flow of the household. She collected herself rapidly. "Yes. I will go to Janet." She gathered her skirts and started up, then paused. "Welcome to Rossmor," she said stiffly. "I wish you both happy."

There was something in her tone which told Grace that Elspeth sincerely doubted her wish would be fulfilled.

Chapter Thirteen

Grace was still shivering with fatigue and reaction almost an hour later when McLean took her upstairs to their bedchamber. She stood before the flames in the hearth while his valet and a chambermaid unpacked their trunks, feeling as if she would never be warm again.

McLean crossed the high-ceilinged room to where draperies patterned in navy and claret were drawn across the tall windows. He pulled them aside with one hand and looked out, then let them fall back in place.

"What a shame the rain has started up once more," he said. "There is a full moon tonight, and I was hoping to show you the view out over the loch."

Grace was glad of the downpour. Even with the curtains closed she was aware of night pressing in upon the panes.

She jumped as lightning flared through the gap in the draperies, followed by echoing cannon booms of thunder. McLean signaled the servants to withdraw. The maid whisked away into the dressing room, the valet through the door to the sitting room leading off the opposite side of the bedchamber.

When they were alone he strode across the carpet to her side. "Poor darling! Don't be so cast down."

He looked so concerned, so handsome with the firelight bringing out the red tones in his dark hair. She tried to smile, and failed. In this vast house in the forbidding shadow of mountains and moor, only he was safe and familiar.

"Things have gotten off on the wrong foot; however, I have no doubt that you will win Janet over," he told her, taking her hands in his. He pulled her into his arms.

She leaned her head against his broad shoulder. "I'm not so sure the damage can be undone. Oh, if only the letters had arrived to at least prepare the way! Poor child—to have a stepmother thrust upon her without the slightest warning! I fear your cousin is only half-right. Janet may forgive you, but she may never forgive me."

"Nonsense. Janet is young. She will learn to love you. Everything will be all right, in time. It is nature's great healer."

Grace tilted her face up to his. "Do you truly think so?"

"I promise you it will." He kissed her soundly. "Meanwhile, a good night's sleep will do you a deal of good. I must go down and see what is happening with Dougal and the team. You needn't wait up for me."

"I wish you need not!" Grace felt suddenly that she couldn't bear to have him leave her.

He touched her cheek. "I'll be back as soon as possible. Don't worry, I'll keep you safe." Then he was gone, leaving her alone.

The door didn't shut entirely, and she went to close it. She was surprised to see her husband going down the far corridor, instead of toward the main staircase. There must be another set of stairs at the end. *God knows a place this size must have half a dozen of them.*

The maid returned and dipped a curtsy. "The hot water is not yet ready for your bath, madam. I will go down and check on it."

After she left, Grace wandered about examining their suite. The curtains of the high tester bed were done in the same navy and claret as the draperies at the windows, and the spread was fashioned from the same navy silk that covered the walls. *A masculine room,* she thought, *with no sign of a woman's touch. Not so much as a vase on the mantelpiece.* It was as if it had been wiped clean of every trace of Finnula McLean.

Two lamps burned in the sitting room and she entered it. The colors were reversed here, with the walls a deep burgundy and windows swathed in navy fabric. The furnishings consisted of a small table and two straight chairs, a leather armchair by the fireplace, and a small sofa. The painting over the mantel was old, and showed Rossmor in high summer, before this new wing was built.

Grace turned away, suddenly aware of a growing unease. Her neck prickled unpleasantly and she whirled around, certain she was no longer alone. The bedchamber beyond was empty when she returned—but the sensation grew stronger moment by moment. She faced the darkest shadows on the far side where the door to the dressing room stood half-open.

"Is someone there?" She crossed the room boldly.

The dressing room was also empty. A fire had been lit in the grate but a draft swirled through the room. It felt as if she were wading through an icy pond. *I am tired and imagining things again,* she scolded herself. But the feeling of another, invisible, presence did not abate. She prayed it wasn't a precursor to one of her strange visions: if she saw anything in this room, it was bound to be something she surely didn't want to see!

Please, God! Not here. Not now!

A rap on the door made her jump in alarm. The maid had returned, followed by two sturdy footmen, carrying large cans of steaming water.

"I'm Cait, mistress," she said, with only the hint of a burr to her words. "Mrs. Lachlan has sent me to see to your needs. The hot bath will be ready for you in no time."

"Thank you, Cait."

The footmen left, touching their forelocks to Grace. She wondered if she would ever become used to so many servants coming and going. It was certainly a change from being at Mrs. Bingley's beck and call.

She let the maid help her undress beside the copper tub. The water steamed, filling the air with a faint floral essence. "What is it you've put in the bath?" Grace asked. "The fragrance is wonderful."

The girl looked at her in surprise. "Nothing, mistress. Water is all."

Grace dismissed her, then stepped into the tub. The aroma of flowers grew stronger. *No matter what the girl said, there is something in the water.* Rose geranium and lavender, she decided. Perhaps the faintest trace of bergamot.

Whatever it was, it had a soothing effect. Gradually the travel weariness and tension seeped away. Her limbs grew rosy and her optimism resurfaced. The world would surely look a little brighter in the morning. *Rossmor will not seem so overwhelming once I know my way about.*

She pondered the situation with Janet. Grace reassured herself that she had always had a way with children. Her training at Miss Cranmer's would stand her in good stead. Children of Janet's age took strange fancies, but their affections were pliable. While the unfortunate circumstances of their introduction would slow things down, she hoped they could establish a fond relationship.

As for Elspeth Lachlan, it was far too soon to say.

Grace could hear someone moving about in the bedchamber. "Alistair?" There was no reply. She rose from her bath and dried off, then donned her nightshift and dressing gown. The maid was gathering up her traveling clothes in the bedroom. She dipped a curtsy. "Is there anything else you'll be needing this night, madam?"

"No, thank you. I'm sure you are as eager for your bed as I am for mine."

Grace climbed into the bed beneath a down comforter, intending to remain awake until her husband returned. She drifted off to sleep and awakened sometime later, startled to find herself in a strange room. Recognition dawned.

I am at Rossmor, she thought groggily. She turned and was disappointed to find the other side of the bed still empty. The candle on the night table had guttered out, and the banked fire had burned down to ash limned by a ribbon of glowing crimson. Silvery light outlined the tall wardrobe with its heavily carved doors and the two tapestry chairs drawn up by the fireplace.

The rain has stopped and Alistair has opened the curtains.

"*Grace?*" She heard the soft whisper, felt the brush of cool fingers against her cheek, and smiled contentedly.

"What o'clock is it?" she asked.

He didn't answer, and she thought he'd gone through into the dressing room. But a moment later she heard his footsteps pass by the foot of the bed and cross over toward the door. "You are not leaving me, again?"

Still he didn't reply.

She sat up, expecting to see her husband in the dim glow. The room was empty, the door to the sitting room closed. Moonbeams gleamed from its polished surface, struck blue fire from the faceted crystal knob.

A faint aroma filled the air, growing stronger with every tick of the clock: rose geranium, lavender, and bergamot. She was filled with the sudden, heart-stopping knowledge that she was not alone in the room. "Who is there?"

There was no response and the urge to flee was strong. Grace swung her legs over the side of the bed and froze in place. The curtains were still drawn and it wasn't moonlight that illuminated the room so brightly. It wasn't like any light she'd ever seen before. The cold fist of fear gripped her.

Grace.

The urgent whisper sent a thrill of terror racing through her veins. Her heart thudded painfully. She was afraid to look across to the far side of the room to see who—or *what*—it was that called her name.

She had to force herself to turn her head. When she did, time and her heart stood still. A luminous light filled one corner of the bedchamber. Its source was a nebulous mist floating above the polished floorboards.

Grace!

She was too frightened to cry out, too stunned to pray. While she stared in horror, the apparition coalesced into a vaguely human shape. A woman's shape. It grew more solid and began to drift toward her.

Grace shook off her paralysis and shot off the far side of the bed. She stumbled across the room in a blind panic, groping for the door handle. It was like a knob of ice. She yanked it open, expecting to feel the skin of her palm tear like exposed flesh frozen to bare metal.

A touch, light as a caress, fell upon her shoulder. Cold flowed from it into her, filling her chest, numbing her mind, as she scrabbled to escape like a woman possessed.

Chapter Fourteen

It was well after midnight when McLean sought his bed. The flame of his candle flickered in a draft as he went up the staircase and along the corridor. Grace must surely be asleep. It was a damnable thing that his letters should have gone astray, and that she'd had such a traumatic introduction to the house.

Janet, he was sure, would come about once she got to know her new stepmother. Elspeth was another matter. Despite his assurances to Grace, he knew his cousin was very much upset. *It will take a good deal of work to smooth her ruffled feathers now!*

Elspeth was a proud woman, and had been acting mistress of the house for several years now. His bringing home a bride affected both her status and authority. It would not be easy for her to hand over the reins to a woman who was a complete stranger.

I will speak to Elspeth in the morning and assure her that her place at Rossmor is secure, and that Grace's arrival will make no difference to our close relationship.

As he turned into the upper corridor, a pale figure drifted out of the shadows to block his path. His heart slowed in his chest, then sped up in reaction.

"What the devil?" He held the candle higher.

"Alistair . . ."

"*Grace!* What in God's name are you doing roaming around without a candle at this time of night? You could injure yourself!"

She didn't answer. He stepped closer and saw her face contorted. "What's wrong? Are you ill?"

As he came toward her, she flung herself at him, babbling. "Oh, thank God it is only you! I am frightened half out of my wits!"

"Did you have a nightmare?" He put his arm around her. "Come. Let's get out of this drafty corridor before you catch your death." He tried to steer her to the bedroom.

"No!" She pulled back. "I . . . I can't go back there. I won't! There was someone . . . *something* in the room with me just now. A figure . . . a woman in a long gray dress."

"You were dreaming."

Fear made her indiscreet. "I know what I saw!"

"Do you?" He took his candle and lit a branch that stood inside the door. The wicks caught and wavering light chased the gloom back.

He turned toward the window. "See. It is only the lace curtains behind the draperies. The window has blown open."

He set his candle down on a side table and went to the casement, pulling it shut. She shook her head. "That's not where I saw it. When I woke up I thought that you had just come in. I thought I heard the door. Oh, Alistair! It was there in the room with me. *It touched my face!*"

"As I said, you were dreaming." His voice was curt; but when he saw the state she was in, his expression softened. Her teeth were chattering, her pupils so widely dilated her irises looked black.

"Poor girl! You look absolutely terrified."

"I was! I am! It wasn't a dream."

He pulled her into the shelter of his embrace. The solid warmth of him comforted her. "The human mind is complex. It plays tricks on us all, you know. The shadow on the wall that resembles a specter. The ghostly yowls in the dead of night that turn out to be nothing but the screeching of a cat in heat."

She wanted to believe him. God forbid it should turn out to be one of her waking visions! Certainly it had been nothing like them in any way.

Grace sighed. Perhaps it *had* been just another nightmare, like the recurring ones of the churchyard and the black obelisk. "I suppose you are right. In any case, I will be all right, now that you are here with me."

Her confidence touched him. "I'll search the entire room if it makes you feel better." He made a great show of checking the dressing room, of looking under the bed and behind every door.

"There," he said. "You see? Not so much as a bogeyman lurking in the wardrobe."

She felt foolish now. There was no sense of "otherness" in the room with them. It was merely an elegant and very comfortable bedchamber in the long hours of the night.

"You're shivering, my dear. Come, I'll warm you."

McLean set the candle down and lifted her in his arms. "You're cold as ice, poor darling." He carried her to the bed and slipped beneath the covers with her. His hand covered her breast, and a sudden heat spread out from the pit of her stomach.

"Your heart is racing," he said. "Are you still so frightened?"

"No." Her voice was husky with desire. "I've already forgotten it. You have that effect on me."

McLean smiled. "I'm glad." Leaning down, he kissed her mouth. "You taste like honey."

"It came with the tea."

"No. It's you." His mouth was on hers, this time with a flare of urgency. "My delicious Grace," he whispered. "I can never have enough of you . . ."

Her arms wound round his neck boldly. Fiercely. "Take me, then."

She wanted him to hold her, kiss her, fill her. To prove to her that he was real and her fears were not. Indeed, as his hands stroked lightly over her, the last of them melted away. The world followed. There was nothing but the two of them, alone in the mellow candlelight.

His mouth followed where his hands had been, skimming over the thin nightshift. She thought the heat of his breath had fused the fabric to her. Then she realized that he'd undone the tiny pearl buttons, exposing her breasts to his lips and tongue. He took one straining tip in his mouth. The light scrape of his teeth sent a shock of desire rippling through her. She cried out and arched against him and her hunger for him grew.

She responded to his lightest touch with such delight and passion it reverberated through him. Every sigh, every quiver echoed back a hundredfold. Her skin was fragrant and soft as a ripe peach beneath his mouth. He wanted to devour every luscious inch of her.

His hand slid over the curve of her ribs, down to her neat waist and beyond. She moved beneath his questing hand, offering herself up to his touch. His nimble fingers slipped between her legs, seeking to pleasure her. Her scent rose up to tantalize him, her nails made sharp little crescents in the muscles of his shoulders, while her teeth nipped at his chest.

He teased her, touching and retreating, until she was wild with desire for him, with the need to give and to take. Her body strained hungrily against him. "So greedy?" he asked. "Shall I feed your cravings?"

She was too far gone to bother with words. She let her mouth and hands speak for her, touching him intimately, until heat poured through him and he knew he couldn't resist much longer. But first he meant to make her needs meet his. Again his fingers touched and stroked, and he watched her back arch in erotic pleasure. He kissed her breasts, worked them with mouth and tongue while his hands urged her on.

Grace was wild for the culmination, pulling at him, urging him to take her. Instead he brought his mouth curving down between her breasts, down the soft swell of her belly and then farther still.

The knowledge that she trusted him completely was a drug in his blood. It hummed and sang through every cell in his body. He lifted her hips and pressed an intimate kiss against her, waiting. Watching for the slightest resistance. Swearing he would pull back at the first sign of it, yet unsure if he had the strength to keep his vow.

She felt the roughness of his cheeks against her thighs, the pressure of his mouth in a place it had never gone before. The brief flash of surprise was drowned in a wave of heat so fierce she felt faint with it. When he drew back, she startled them both by grasping his hair, urging him back again. It was all the encouragement he needed. Their bodies glistened in the candlelight, slick with sweat and need. Her breasts were tipped with gold as she arched up toward him.

This was the moment. *Now,* he thought. *Now, when the need is on her.*

While her heart shattered against her ribs, his tongue touched and probed and flickered against her. He lifted her hips higher, drank in the taste of her, plundered every last bit of honey.

She was lost in bliss, and followed him blindly, eagerly, down a road whose existence she had never known before. She had no idea of where they were going or where it would end. With every step her body shivered and shook. He went deeper. She felt as if she were sinking slowly into a warm, enfolding darkness, a sensual quicksand pulling her down and down. She gave in to it, let herself go deep into sensation, gave up all pretense of control or will. The moment she surrendered it, she was filled with primitive elation, bursting with a bright, hot glory. Her body bowed and she twisted away from an ecstasy that was almost too great to bear.

He took her at the crest, sliding inside her just as she was coming down. One thrust and she arched again, wrapping her legs around him. He plunged deep, rode her through the wild, aching joy of it, claimed her with boldness and every atom of passion he possessed. Then he was overwhelmed with the fury and gave himself up to it. They reached the summit together, and went soaring over the edge.

Later, when they lay gasping together, their hearts in rhythm, their tangled thoughts ran along similar lines.

She is mine. She will never leave me now. She is mine. I will never let her go. The exultant refrain ran through his head like the steady beat of his heart.

I am his and he is mine, she thought.

She no longer needed tender phrases of love to let her know it. He had shown her in a way that proved it more than any words. She fell asleep praying that it would always be like this—the hunger and the rapture, the deep satisfaction that left them exhausted and triumphant in each other's arms.

It was near dawn when Grace slipped into her recurring dream:

Fog ... a lonely churchyard in the shadow of the moor ... leaning headstones covered with lichen ... a marble angel weeping marble tears.

The setting shifted. She was climbing up winding stairs in the dim light from the window slits. Up and up and up until it seemed she would never reach the top of the tower. At last—there was the landing and the iron-studded door! She opened it and stepped through.

There was nothing on the other side. Nothing but a cold, clinging mist and the knowledge of the terrible rocks waiting below.

A hand grasped her shoulder from behind and pushed.
Then she was falling, falling. Spinning down into the
heart of darkness, with the cry of a hawk overhead, and
the sound of laughter echoing in her ears . . .

Chapter Fifteen

Grace awakened with her mouth dry and her heart pounding. She opened her eyes and found Alistair at her side, his arm wrapped around her protectively. The fragments of dream faded as he gazed down at her.

"You look so very serious," she said.

He caressed her cheek. "I am seriously bewitched by you."

"And I am glad of it." She ran her fingers through his tousled hair. "Just think. If we hadn't been forced to spend the night together, you would be here alone. And I," she laughed, "would be sitting in a hired drawing room with Mrs. Bingley and Liza, wondering if I could murder them and get away with it."

His hand cupped her chin. A few months ago he didn't know of her existence. Now she was so much a part of his life, he couldn't imagine it without her.

"I would have found you," he told her fiercely, and followed his words with a kiss.

She smiled up at him. "I believe it is your fate to rescue me from awkward situations. First in the Forum, then from the Bingleys, and last night from my fright."

"Poor Grace! You were in a shocking state."

She looked around the pleasing room with its gilded sconces and navy blue silk wallpaper patterned with delicate gold traceries. "It seems silly of me to have been so frightened now in the daylight—but at the time I assure you it seemed all too real."

"That is the nature of dreams," McLean said. He added without thinking: "In any case, there have been no alleged sightings of the Gray Lady in this wing of the house."

The moment the words were out of his mouth, he wished them back. She blinked up at him solemnly in the morning light. "Who," she asked, "is this mysterious ghost? Mrs. Bingley had a book of great houses. It claimed that Rossmor was haunted by a Gray Lady."

McLean cursed inwardly. He hadn't meant for her to find out about the legend just yet. His wayward letters to Elspeth had been full of admonitions not to alarm Grace with such tales, and instructing his cousin to make sure the servants held their tongues. Now he'd been the one to blurt it out. He'd have to divert her interest.

"Didn't I tell you of her?" He shrugged. "One of my ancestral legends. Like the treasure that was said to be buried on the moor by the first McLean, when the Norsemen came a-viking. Great golden plates and cups studded with emerald and rock crystal, and rubies redder than blood."

His tactic worked. She leaned on her elbow. "Buried treasure! Is it true?"

"The story has been handed down for generations. One afternoon I'll take you up on the moors and show you the runes inscribed upon the rocks. Supposedly they tell where the treasure can be found. I suspect they really mark the burial site of some ancient chieftain."

Grace was disappointed. "Then no one has actually found any signs of it?"

"From time to time something turns up to whet our interest. Last year when one of my hounds dug out a badger's burrow, I found an old bronze brooch of a dragon swallowing its own tail. I'll show it to you. It's under lock and key in the library."

"I should like to see it!"

"There are other items which will capture your interest as well. Among them, letters from the Queen of Scots, enlisting support for her marriage to Lord Darnley."

"From the Queen of Scots!" Grace was thrilled.

"There is a second one written by her to my ancestor—urging the same for her marriage to the Earl of Bothwell, after Darnley was murdered."

Grace was intrigued. "I suppose any place this old must have its legends as well as its mementos."

McLean was relieved that the awkward moment had passed. He would issue orders to the servants that no one was to discuss the Gray Lady of Rossmor with his new bride.

Cait brought in Grace's morning chocolate. Alistair's valet was setting out his master's clothes in the dressing room. After the servants were dismissed, Grace took her cup of chocolate and perched on a slipper chair watching her husband at his shaving stand. She loved to listen to the slick-slick of the straight razor against the leather strop, the rasp of the blade over his chin, the splash of the water in the basin. Homely and comforting sounds to which she had become accustomed over the past few weeks.

"Shall I come down to breakfast with you, Alistair?"

"Stay abed as long as you like. I must go out and check on the damage from yesterday's storm. I'll pay Meg a call on my way back. It will perhaps be better if she hears the news of our marriage from my own lips."

Grace agreed. She secretly wondered how his sister would take the news. "Then, since Mrs. Finley is away, I will ask Braedon to show me over the house while you are away," she said, thinking aloud.

"You would do far better to ask Elspeth to give you a tour this afternoon," he said shortly. "She has acted as mistress here for several years, and will prove invaluable to you in learning to oversee the running of the household."

Much as she dreaded it, he was right. "Of course."

Grace set the cup aside and rose from the chair to hunt for a striped bandbox containing her gifts for Janet and Elspeth. They might help to break the ice. She discovered it on the top shelf of the mirrored wardrobe, and laid the wrapped items out on the counterpane.

There was a necklace of glass beads from Venice, as deeply blue as the loch shining beyond the windowpanes, a clever little jewel box from Florence that opened up only if one knew the proper place to press the gilded wood, and an ivory brush and comb from Rome, carved and enameled with forget-me-nots. Grace had selected them in hopes of pleasing her new stepdaughter.

She unwrapped the brooch she'd selected for Alistair's cousin. The book-shaped locket with the coral insert was a pretty trifle, but not at all the sort of thing that would suit a woman of Elspeth Lachlan's style—or red hair. It might suit Meg, however. She was a great reader.

Everyone at the academy had expected that Meg would marry well, possibly into the peerage. Her sparkling debut in society was followed through the newspapers with interest and a good deal of envy. It was difficult now for Grace to imagine the aristocratic beauty married to a country parson.

"How did Meg meet her husband?" she asked. "Is he from Glen Ross?"

"He was born and raised in London, where we met at a lecture at the British Museum. I invited him to visit us at Rossmor. While he was here, the incumbent of St. Declan's fell ill, and I arranged that Hugh would stay on as his assistant."

McLean rinsed his razor in the basin. "I was so preoccupied with . . . other matters at the time, that I didn't realize a romance was blooming. Hugh was hesitant to put himself forward. As the youngest son, he hadn't two shillings to rub together, and they were both afraid I wouldn't favor his suit. When the Reverend O'Dowd retired due to his ill health, I immediately offered the living to Hugh. And not many weeks later, he asked for Meg's hand in marriage."

"A romantic story." Grace smiled. "It must be very pleasant for you to have Meg and her family nearby."

He turned to her with a wry smile. "If you think so, it is only because you haven't met my twin nephews. They're a rambunctious pair, and lead her a merry chase. If Angus doesn't think of some form of lighthearted mischief, Geordie is sure to do so."

"I shall look forward to meeting them." She went back to unwrapping the gifts.

McLean rinsed off his face and blotted it with a towel. In the past weeks he'd become used to thinking of Grace as his wife, yet it was strange to see her in his bedroom at Rossmor, perched upon his bed. It made their marriage seem more real.

She looked up and their eyes met. There was something in his that disturbed her. Grace hesitated as a new thought struck her. "Does it . . . does it bother you to see me here in Finnula's place?"

He froze, then threw the towel down on his shaving stand and went to her side. "You are not in her place, my dear. She never slept in this room."

"I didn't know," she said softly. "I am relieved to hear it."

Pulling her into his arms, he kissed her thoroughly. She leaned against him, her arms wound around his neck while he stroked her hair. "You must never compare yourself to Finnula," he murmured. "Promise me that."

"I cannot help it," she said softly, "but I *will* try."

McLean released her with a kiss on the forehead. "Good girl. I'd best get dressed. There's a lot of business to which I must attend this morning." He returned a short time later, handsome in his hacking coat and breeches and highly polished boots. He pulled on a pair of riding gloves, his gaze abstracted.

She sighed. "I'd hoped we could spend our first morning at Rossmor together."

"It is unfortunate, but cannot be helped. Perhaps you might spend time getting to know my daughter."

Grace hesitated. "It may take a while for her to warm to me. Girls of Janet's age are very prone to taking sharp likes or dislikes, which can prove difficult to overcome."

"I trust that your kind heart will make the difference." McLean sat down on the edge of the bed and took her hand. "I had better tell you the truth, as you will learn it anyway. My valet brought me a note earlier, sad news. One of the crofters has been found dead out on the moor, and foul play is suspected. As the local magistrate, I am obliged to investigate the matter. I will stop to pay a condolence call upon his widow and children, after viewing the scene."

"Oh, poor man! I am sorry to hear of it." She hesitated, unsure of her new role. "Should I not accompany you?"

"It is not necessary. I would be grateful if instead you kept Janet occupied. Elspeth and I should return in two or three hours at most."

"Elspeth?" Grace was stunned. "But surely as your wife it must be my duty to do so."

His dark brows rose. "Of course; however, our circumstances are awkward. Since our letters never reached Rossmor, no one here knows of our marriage. But the local people do know Elspeth, and she will be a comfort to the bereaved family."

Grace couldn't refute his logic, and had no inclination to thrust herself into a situation for which she had neither experience nor training. "When will you return?"

"Elspeth and I will be back in time to sit down to luncheon with you and Janet. I promise." He leaned down, kissed her cheek, and quickly left the room.

*   *   *

Grace was at the elegant dressing table brushing out her long hair, when the maid called Cait entered and dipped a curtsy. "If it pleases you, mistress, Mrs. Lachlan said I was to wait upon you this morning. I've a good hand at dressing hair."

"That was very thoughtful of Mrs. Lachlan," Grace said, surrendering the brush to the girl. This promising sign of conciliation heartened her.

"All agog everyone is, to learn that a new bride has been brought home to Rossmor," Cait remarked as she plied the hairbrush. With a deft twist of her wrist, she caught Grace's hair into a loose knot atop her head and held it in place with a tortoiseshell comb. It was a simple arrangement and very becoming.

"Thank you, Cait." Grace rose from the dressing table. "Is my stepdaughter awake?"

"Aye. She's an early riser. At this time of day, like as not she's in the old solar."

"That is in the medieval section of the manor, isn't it?" Grace asked casually. "I suppose it is there that the Gray Lady walks?"

" 'Tis the old tower and battlements she haunts, so they say." Cait stopped and put a hand to her mouth. "Och! We're not to be talking of her to you!"

"And why not?"

Cait shrugged. "Master's orders. Braedon will have my head!" She was eager to escape further questions. "If there's naught else you'll be requiring, mistress?"

There was no more to be got out of her, Grace was sure. "No. You may go."

She left her gifts, now all done up in silver paper and blue ribbons, on her dressing table and went down to the drawing room.

As she reached the landing, she saw two menservants

carrying what appeared to be a large rectangle of wood. They were gone when she reached the last step and there was no one else about. After hesitating, she selected the door to her left, and found she'd chosen correctly.

The drawing room was a large and handsomely appointed chamber with a coffered ceiling and walls papered in burgundy and green above dark wainscoting. The walls were hung with family portraits: men and women in powdered wigs and old-fashioned garments, and smiling, rosy-cheeked children. Directly opposite the door, draperies of heavy burgundy damask framed tall windows leading out to the stone-flagged terrace.

Grace liked the room. It was elegant yet cozy, filled with comfortable chairs and settees and a pianoforte at one end. She could imagine warm days with the windows open to the scent of heather and the sweeping view of the loch. Winter nights with a great fire roaring in the hearth and falling snow beyond the frosted windowpanes.

This will be the heart of our home at Rossmor, she thought happily. An image rose in her mind: Alistair reading by the fire while she worked at her embroidery, Janet curled up with a kitten in the wing chair.

At the moment, however, there was no sign of Janet at all.

Grace was about to pull the bell cord and ask Braedon if he knew her stepdaughter's whereabouts when one of the paintings caught her eye.

It hung alone between two glass cases holding a display of fine porcelain and crystal. It was an exquisite rendering of a young woman by moonlight. She was costumed as the goddess Artemis, with a thin crescent moon upon her wide white brow, and stood atop a stone parapet. A silver bow and quiver of arrows lay at her sandaled feet.

Grace's heart tumbled in her chest. She knew beyond reason or doubt that this was Finnula McLean, Alistair's late wife.

She is stunningly beautiful, and she will never age,
Grace thought. *Ten years from now, or twenty or thirty,
when the years weigh down upon me, she will still be young
and beautiful in this portrait—and in Alistair's memory.*

At first glance the painting seemed calm and serene; but
despite the slight smile on those sweetly painted lips, there
was something wrong, something deeply unsettling about
Finnula's portrait. She stepped closer.

It is the shadows, Grace realized. At first it had appeared
to her that Finnula was stepping out of the darkness. Now
she had the impression that it was the reverse, that the shadows were enfolding Finnula into the blackness. Absorbing
her.

Although her feet stayed planted on the ground, Grace
felt as if she were being pulled, gently but inexorably, out
of her body and into the painted scene. A wave of fragrance
enveloped her: rose geranium, lavender, and bergamot . . .

. . . *Her entire world had been distilled into this single
moment: moonlight glazing the ancient stones like hoar-
frost, the night air filled with the poignancy of summer's
ripe scents fading into smoky autumn.*

*Regret welled up inside her along with a terrible longing
. . . a primal ache for things that never were—and now
would never be . . .*

"Is something wrong, madam? Are you taken ill?"

Grace blinked at the sound of the butler's voice. For a
moment she didn't know where she was. *Who* she was.

"Madam?" Braedon touched her arm and she was instantly jerked back into the present, as if her soul had been
stretched to the limits of its tether, then snapped back inside
her body like a band of India rubber. Her pulses hammered
and her insides vibrated with the recoil.

She shook her head to clear it. "I was just . . . just admiring the portrait."

Braedon's face was carefully blank. "Which portrait
would that be, madam?"

Grace turned back and felt the blood drain from her face. There was no painting there at all: only a darker rectangle of burgundy silk to show where one had been recently removed.

Chapter Sixteen

Grace gathered her wits and her courage. "I should say, rather, that I had come to admire the portrait of the first Mrs. McLean that was hung here. What have you done with it?"

Braedon blinked. "Mr. McLean asked me to remove it to the music room and put another in its place."

"To spare my feelings, no doubt." She took a deep breath and issued her first order as mistress of the house. "It was kindly meant, but I am sure it would cause Miss Janet grief to find her mother's portrait gone. Please replace it, Braedon. If my husband should inquire, you will tell him that I directed you to do so."

His faint smile was the only hint of his approval. "As you wish, madam."

"Have you seen my stepdaughter this morning?"

"Yes, madam. Miss Janet has gone to the solar, as she does every morning after breakfast."

Following Braedon's directions, Grace cut across the terrace to the courtyard formed by the three wings of the house. The medieval section was in the center, linking the old with the new. The old casement windows reflected a blue and cloudless sky. The September sun was warm on her face as she crossed the flagstoned court, but Grace felt chilled.

She glanced over at the ancient tower off to her left. At its foot the loch gleamed like a mirror of dark blue glass, until a fish leaped up, shattering it into ever-expanding circles of shimmering silver light. The green hills on the opposite shore stood out sharply against the misted mountains in the distance.

Finnulla always loved this view, Grace thought. She was instantly aghast. Where had it come from, this strange knowledge that had embedded itself in her mind, as if the memory of it were her own?

This sudden and startling connection to Finnula frightened her.

She hesitated outside the oak door to the medieval wing, wondering if it was wise to enter. A terrible sense of dread clung to her, wrapped itself around her like a shroud. Glancing back the way she'd come, she saw Braedon hovering by the open drawing room windows. *I must not let him know that anything is wrong!*

She opened the door and stepped inside. Her brain was alert, her nerves on edge as she let the aura of the place fill her. Nothing occurred to disturb her. The only scents were beeswax polish and wood and a faint touch of something exotic she couldn't name. She sighed in relief. *It is just a lovely old hall in the morning sun.*

The heavy door swung shut behind her. It was a large room, with high windows on both sides, and a fine hammerbeam ceiling. The stone chimney breast above the enormous hearth was carved with the McLean coat of arms and flanked by two standing candelabra filled with fat candles. She could see that it would make a fine ballroom for the masquerade that Alistair had told her would be held during the coming house party.

Taking the stairs to the next floor, she found the solar at the top, just as the butler had described it. The door stood open. Janet was sitting at a narrow table, building a house from a deck of cards. She didn't look up when Grace entered. Tongue between her even white teeth, she took the last card and carefully placed it to roof in the third level of the pasteboard structure. It wobbled, but held.

Janet lifted her head and smiled at Grace. "There! I did it!"

For a moment she looked happy and very young. Then her pretty features twisted. With a sudden sweep of her arm, she brushed the cards aside. The little house collapsed in a heap; but one card went spinning across the ancient boards to land at Grace's feet.

She stooped down and picked it up. "The ace of spades," she commented, returning it to the table.

"The death card," Janet said, with a good deal of solemn pleasure.

There, Grace thought, *the gauntlet has been laid down.* She smiled back at the girl. "If you are trying to frighten me," she said, "it won't work. And if I wish to have my cards read, I can do it myself."

Janet stared at her. "Can you? Read the cards?" She was obviously impressed. "Cook can, and Mrs. Finley, too. But neither of them will show me. They say I'm too young." Her voice was filled with indignation. "I know geography and mathematics and all the kings and queens of England in order! I am sure I can recall the meanings of the cards."

"Perhaps," Grace said gently, "what they really mean is that you are not yet ready to know your future."

Janet cocked her head. "Perhaps I am not. But you can do *your* future." She took the deck and handed it to Grace.

Grace took the chair beside her. It had been many years since one of the other junior teachers at Miss Cranmer's Academy had shown her how, but she still remembered.

"I learned on a deck with many pictures, but it's easy enough to do with any set of standard cards. I will take three." She picked up the ace of clubs. "Aces are beginnings and clubs are the same as Wands. They stand for opportunities. So it means the beginning of a new enterprise. In this case, it means my marriage to your father, and the new relationships that will grow from it."

Janet looked at her. "That's one meaning. But Wands also mean strife and discord."

"Well, I see you know more about it than I realized." Grace smiled. "But it is all in how one looks at things, isn't it? If you choose to look for strife, that is your business. I prefer to look on my coming here as the start of a new life for all of us. Now I shall take another card."

She picked one up and turned it over. "There, you see? The nine of hearts. The 'wish card.' All good things come true."

The girl laughed. "You're clever. I like that. Cousin Elspeth is not very clever, you know."

"She seems quite intelligent to me. Why do you say such a thing?"

Janet eyed her with a peculiar expression. "If Cousin Elspeth were as clever as she thinks, then she would be my new stepmama. She always meant to be, you know. Indeed, I think she would have succeeded—if not for you."

"I am sorry if her hopes may have been disappointed, but you shouldn't say such things. You cannot know if you are right."

"Elspeth is in love with my father. She believes that you have stolen her rightful place at Rossmor."

Grace was startled out of discretion. "I'm sorry if that is how she chooses to think of it!"

The girl stared at her. "I don't think one can choose about such things. You love someone, or you don't."

"Yes. Yes, I suppose that is true."

"I have tried to love Cousin Elspeth most sincerely," Janet said, curling a strand of hair around her finger. "But I cannot. Except, you know, in a dutiful way." The blue eyes, so like Alistair's, regarded Grace intently. "Do you love my father very much?"

The change of pace caught Grace off guard. She felt her cheeks grow hot. "Yes. I do."

"Perhaps I should be glad you've come, then. Because I love him very much, too. I want him to be happy. When I was little he was always happy," she said wistfully. "Or so it seemed. But now I wonder . . ."

"Don't look to the past, Janet, but to the present and the future. I will do my best to make you both happy," Grace said. "If I fail, it will not be for lack of trying."

The girl cocked her head. "Yes, you're clever. I didn't think I would like you, but now I am not so sure that I won't." She stacked the cards into a neat rectangle as she spoke. "And I have just realized something wonderful— now that you are here at Rossmor, I am no longer in any danger."

Her words were like a cold splash of water. Grace blinked. "What do you mean? What kind of danger? From whom?"

"From the Gray Lady." Janet slipped the cards into her pocket. "Cousin Elspeth has always been safe, of course. She was never really the mistress here, she only pretended to be. And although she is a cousin, she's not a McLean by either blood or marriage. So the ghost never appeared to her. The Gray Lady only appears to the mistress of Rossmor."

Grace sat very still. "I have heard there is a ghost. Do you mean to say that you really believe in her existence?"

Janet's eyes grew overlarge in her pale face. "I don't 'believe'—I *know*." Her voice dropped to a whisper. "I have been so afraid!"

Grace saw that her stepdaughter was trembling. She leaned forward and covered the girl's hand with her own. "Of what are you afraid, Janet?"

"Why, that the Gray Lady will come for *me*."

"Who has been filling your head with such nonsense?"

"It is not nonsense!" Janet pushed back her chair and

rose. "You don't believe now, but one day you will." She cocked her head again, and her mouth curved up in an odd little smile. She looked far older than her years.

"And now that you have married my father, I needn't worry any longer. *You* have become the mistress of Rossmor—and when the Gray Lady comes, she will come for *you*!"

She fled the room laughing.

By the time Grace reached the top of the stairs Janet had vanished. She decided to explore her new home. The first door beside the solar was locked. The next door led to a small anteroom and the library beyond. It was wonderfully preserved. The ceiling was covered with ornamental plaster in high relief and the paneling was exquisitely carved.

Except for the oriel window in the middle, the opposite wall was row upon row of leather-bound books caged behind slender bars of ornamental brass. Some of the volumes looked very old, but there were newer shelves holding modern books, including several novels Grace had been longing to read.

Two massive high-backed settles flanked the hearth on the left and two matching chairs and a round table of ebonized wood dominated the center of the room. A chess set stood on it, the red and white pieces placed about the board as if a game were in progress. Grace paused to examine it. The red queen held the white king in check.

Two comfortable armchairs of more modern design were pulled up close to the second fireplace, where the claymore of some McLean ancestor was hung upon the chimney breast.

Grace crossed over to it, amazed by its great size. Its pommel was set with polished bloodstone the size of a hen's egg and the time-darkened blade was as long as she was tall. *What was he like, the warrior who wielded such a mighty sword?* she wondered.

She saw him then, standing beside the table, staring down at the chessboard. A red-haired giant with the Mc-Lean plaid draped over his shoulder and held in place with a silver badge studded with polished agate. For all the detail, he was insubstantial, like a painting on the air.

As she watched he became as solid and real as the floor beneath her feet. Leaning down, he moved the white queen across the board and smiled in triumph. *Checkmate.*

Grace stumbled back and bumped into a chair. The man was instantly alert, his blue eyes calculating the danger. "Who are ye?" he demanded, rising to his full height. "Why do ye haunt this chamber?"

"I am not the ghost," Grace cried out in fear. "It is you! You!"

He reached out to catch her sleeve, staring at his hands in wonder as they passed through it. She saw the startlement in his face before he dissolved into dust motes dancing on the air. Glancing down at the chessboard again, she saw that it had been no illusion. The white queen had indeed been moved.

Turning on her heel, she fled the room and ran blindly down the corridor. Grace didn't stop until she reached a dead end and was forced to retrace her steps. She'd lost her sense of direction completely. Was the staircase to the right or left? Her breath came in great gasping sobs and her only rational thought was to put as much distance between herself and the apparition in the library as possible.

She took another wrong turn somewhere, and came to a stairway going up. Rather than go back past the library, she hurried up them.

Braedon said there is a connecting door on each floor between this section and the new wing. I will find it. I must find it!

The narrow stairs led up to a series of small rooms used

for storage. Old furniture and trunks filled most. The one on the end had a small window with a dusty casement of thick glass rondels. There was no way to look out without opening it. The catch was difficult but she managed at last.

She leaned out as far as she could, dirtying her hands and the front of her dress in the process. Her hopes of getting her bearings were dashed. There was nothing to see but gables and chimney pots and the moor rising up beyond them.

Her panic increased as she went along the narrow corridor looking for the door to the new wing. *There it is!* Grace hurried toward it and lifted the latch. Instead of the new wing, she found a stone staircase with steps winding down into gloomy shadows on her left hand, and up toward a diffused light on her right. She realized that she had stumbled on the original fortified tower. The glow from above must be light from one of the window slits cut into the thick stone walls.

Grace laughed in relief and stepped onto the landing. It would be easy to find her way back from the foot of the tower. All she had to do was reach the bottom and let herself out to the terraced courtyard.

She went out to the landing. A simple rope strung from circles of iron set into the wall served as the only handrail. It seemed pitifully inadequate, given the steep pitch of the stairs, but there was nothing for it. Lifting her skirts with one hand and grasping the rope with the other, she began to descend.

She felt it before she reached the third step: a terrible grief, a deep, numbing cold that pierced her to the bone. Her teeth chattered as the heat drained from her body and her limbs grew clumsy and stiff.

Grace stopped in her tracks, afraid to move. Glancing up, she saw that the glow at the top of the stairs had grown brighter. It was flowing down the steep steps, like a luminous fog. Fear gave her wings. She flew down the stairs to the lowest level, grasped the door handle and pulled. The door wouldn't open. She yanked again with both hands, but still it didn't budge. *It's locked! Oh, God! Oh, God!*

Despite her terror, she became aware of the darkness receding around her. The eerie light had followed her. Found her.

She raced back to the upper floor, heart pounding fit to burst her ribs. The fear that struck her was beyond reason and she cried out and pounded on the ancient wood until her fists were sore.

The door jerked inward suddenly and she fell forward with it. It hadn't been locked at all: in her panic she'd tried to open it the wrong way.

McLean caught her as she stumbled over the threshhold. "Grace! What the devil? You're white as a ghost!"

She went into his arms and clung to him, warming her chilled body against the heat of his. "I . . . I was lost. I . . . I couldn't open the door!"

He lifted her chin and scrutinized her face. "And that had you beating upon it and screaming like a madwoman? Why didn't you just go down to the ground level and out to the courtyard?"

"I . . . I did! It was locked!" She shuddered and buried her face against his jacket.

He shook his head. "There is no lock on it," he said slowly.

Chapter Seventeen

The sun was high in the sky the following morning, but Grace was still abed. Alistair had spent the night reading with the sitting room door ajar. She had been comforted by the light but would have felt better with him beside her in their big bed. He sat on the edge of the mattress. "I hope you will remain here until I return."

"Really, Alistair, you must not treat me like an invalid! I was lost and got a little rattled yesterday. I am perfectly well."

"Humor me a little longer," he said, leaning down to brush his lips against her temple. "The inquest won't take long. It will be adjourned as foul play by person or persons unknown."

"You haven't told me what Meg said when she heard the news of our marriage."

"I was too shaken when I found you." His smile was rueful. He reached inside his coat pocket and pulled out an envelope. "She sends you this."

Grace took it and broke the seal eagerly. Her smile grew as she scanned the lines of perfect copperplate. "Dear, dear Meg! She is delighted with the news and welcomes me into the family as her sister. Well, I must say I am gratified she took it so well."

McLean laughed. "If she were not so elegant, you might

say that she squealed like a happy piglet when she learned of our marriage. She instantly forgave me the letters that went astray, and promised to call upon you today. I'll stop by and tell her to postpone her call until tomorrow."

"Oh, but I so want to see her!"

Grace argued but lost. "I am adamant," McLean said, taking her hand in his. He saw the stubborn set of her chin. "Give me this small concession, my dear. One day of rest. Think of it: we've been traveling for weeks, we arrive to a household knowing nothing of our marriage, and then you become lost in the tower your first morning here. It's no wonder you became overwrought."

She had to admit it sounded logical. "Tomorrow," he added, "Meg may descend upon you with those two hellcats of hers with my blessing. But today you must rest and recruit your strength."

"Very well. But I will not remain abed any longer."

"Promise me you won't do any more exploring of the house on your own as yet."

Grace shuddered. "You have my word."

He kissed her cheek and went off to the inquest.

Grace dressed and went down to the drawing room, and was disappointed to learn that Janet had gone into the village with Elspeth to purchase some ribbon. She wished they had invited her to go along. She picked up a book of poems from a side table and leafed through a few pages, then set it down. Suddenly she couldn't bear to stay inside the walls of Rossmor another minute.

Alistair can have no objections to a stroll through the gardens.

She rang for her hat and shawl, intending to enjoy what was left of the late-booming flowers inside the sheltered garden; but when the brick walkway divided she chose the way that wound down to the sparkling loch instead.

The water was a deep delphinium blue, reflecting the hills and clouds, and a path wound along beside it. It lured her on. As she crossed the lawn a young collie bounded down to greet her, wolfing and prancing with joy.

"Are you wanting to accompany me?" Grace leaned down and scratched its ears. The dog grinned up at her and wagged its tail. "Very well," she said with mock severity. "But I refuse to toss sticks for you to chase. It is beneath my dignity."

The dog wagged its plumed tail faster. "All right," Grace said, laughing. "But only when we are out of sight of the house."

Grace was soothed by the dog's uncritical companionship. They started down toward the water and the farther they got from Rossmor the higher her spirits grew. She eyed the path. "Come," she said to the dog. "Let's go exploring."

White swans graced the shallows. They ignored the playful yips of the dog and turned back, gliding silently toward the deeper water. Disappointed, the collie had no choice but to follow Grace. From time to time he nosed an interesting scent and took off over the meadows, but he always came frisking back again.

After a brisk walk, she came past a stand of trees and saw a huddle of buildings in the far distance. The village of Rossmor had looked small and unprepossessing from her bedroom window. From this vantage point, however, she could see that it continued on along the shores of the loch. Beyond the shops and houses flanking the main road, the hillside boasted a straggle of small stone houses with flowers in window boxes and gardens in the rear. The moors rose up steeply behind them.

She strained her eyes and made out a large house of elegant proportions below the crest of the moors. That would be Gorse Manor, which belonged to Alistair's uncle.

Suddenly the dog took off like a cannonball. A rabbit bounded up out of the tall grass and the chase was on. "Come back!" Grace called. "Oh, bad dog!"

Rabbit and dog vanished over a rise and she decided to turn back.

A man on horseback was coming up along the loch. For just an instant she thought it was Alistair, but he proved to be a stranger. Although his hair was white, his face deeply tanned and lined with age, his eyes were the same startling color as her husband's. He reined in and doffed his hat as he came abreast of her.

"Good morning. Was that True I saw bounding off through the grass?"

"I am afraid that I don't know. I am new here."

"Yes. You must be my nephew Alistair's new wife," he exclaimed warmly. "I am his uncle, Gordon McLean."

"My husband has spoken fondly of you, sir. You live at Gorse Manor."

"Yes." His eyes twinkled. "I hope that young rascal hasn't been filling your head with stories of my adventures?"

Grace smiled. "No, indeed. Are they very bad?"

"I have never thought so. But then I wouldn't, would I?" He swung down from the saddle to walk beside her.

"I only know that you are a widower, sir, and have spent most of your life sailing the seven seas. In fact, Alistair thought you were visiting your son in Canada."

"So I was." His face creased in a wide smile. "Expensive young rascal! Compared to him I was an angel in my youth. I returned home only yesterday, and found Alistair's letter waiting for me. I rode over to pay my respects, but Braedon informed me that you were out. I am glad now that I took this way home."

"And so am I, sir. It is pleasant to have company on my explorations."

"You've come quite a distance."

"Have I?" Grace stopped and glanced back in surprise. With its crenellated battlements, Rossmor looked like a toy castle in the distance. "Good heavens!"

"Don't worry, I'll show you a shortcut back."

"I don't mind the exercise. Not when the view is so spectacular."

Gordon McLean made a sound of contentment. "Magnificent country, isn't it? Although I imagine in the winter months you will find it isolated and dreary. We do not have the attractions and gay social life that London can offer a young lady such as yourself."

Grace tried not to smile. "I have not been about much in society of late," she told him. "Indeed, I think I will have more than enough to occupy me here."

"Yes. Janet will keep you on your toes," he replied. "She has led Elspeth a merry dance these past three months while Alistair was gone, so I hear. She needs a firm hand. The girl is too much like her mother."

The opportunity to learn something about Finnula McLean was too good to pass up. "What *was* her mother like?" Grace asked.

"Finnula? Moody and morbidly overimaginative. To put it baldly, she made Alistair the very devil of a wife, if you'll pardon me saying it." He smiled kindly at her. "Is that what you wanted to know?"

Grace felt her face burn. "Perhaps it was not a very tactful question to put to you on our first meeting. But you see, Alistair never speaks of her."

"You need not guard your tongue around me. I am a blunt man. I like to see the cards all laid out upon the table, myself. And it is only natural that you should be curious about your predecessor. What else would you like me to tell you?"

She was rather embarrassed and hunted for the right words. "I don't wish you to think that I am prying. It is only that, not knowing anything of her, I am afraid of . . . of perhaps doing the wrong thing and stirring up painful memories."

"I see. You are a woman of exquisite sensibilities. Have

you been wondering how you would fill Finnula's place at Rossmor?"

She nodded.

Those eyes, so very like Alistair's, regarded her thoughtfully. "You can't. Nor should you even try. She was Alistair's first love, and a man never forgets that. But it was a most unsuitable match. Everyone else could see that the marriage was headed for disaster from the start." He rubbed his jaw. "It's no wonder it ended as badly as it did."

She lifted her eyes to his face. "How *did* it end?"

Gordon McLean looked taken aback. "No one has told you?"

"I know very little. Only what Lady Helena has related to me."

"Oh, so you've already met her?" He walked along in silence for a few yards. "Helena is a fascinating creature. At one time I thought perhaps she and Alistair would make a match of it. But their temperaments are too much alike. Both of them stubbornly single-minded and persistent in pursuing their private goals."

She sent him an inquiring look. "You make that sound more vice than virtue, sir."

"Not at all! Certainly I don't mean to criticize your husband. He is my only nephew and I am very fond of him. But I don't believe that partiality should blind one to another's flaws. When Alistair wants something he leaves no stone unturned until he achieves it. Anything that stands in his way will be removed."

Grace stopped and turned to him, her green eyes wary. "Are you trying to warn me of something?"

He looked very uncomfortable. "No. I shouldn't go so far as that. But there is one thing you should know: despite the rumors, and whatever it is that Lady Helena told you, my faith in Alistair has never wavered. I have known him, boy and man, these thirty-some years and I will say it to your head—he had nothing to do with Finnula's unfortunate death."

Grace schooled her features but her heart lurched. "Lady Helena said the same."

"There, you see? It does no good to listen to rumors and speculation." He indicated a path leading up from the water's edge. "This will take us to a point halfway between Gorse Manor and Rossmor. Tell me, what do you think of the old place?"

She wanted to ask more about Finnula—how she died—and why anyone would possibly hold Alistair responsible. But the constraints of good manners prevented it.

"It's extraordinary. I am afraid that—until now—my life has been rather ordinary. I am new to Rossmor and to my role as chatelaine of the manor. I would be grateful, sir, for any advice you may have that will help me in finding my way."

"I expect that Elspeth Lachlan will be your best guide in such matters. I also suspect that she will have some difficulty in handing over the reins to you. I don't imagine she ever expected to do so, in any case. An awkward situation!"

"Indeed it is. You are very astute, sir."

"Well, you may count on me to help smooth things over." They walked along in silence a while. "You married my nephew in Rome, eh? At the embassy, was it?"

"No. Alistair and I were married at a lovely old church in the Borgo."

He looked surprised. "Ah. I didn't realize that you were a member of the Church of Rome."

"I am not, sir. I was baptized and confirmed in the Church of England. But you see, Alistair was due to leave Rome and there was no time to arrange for a Protestant marriage in a country so profoundly Roman Catholic."

Gordon's eyebrows rose even higher, but he didn't comment. They had come to a narrow track intersecting the path. "I'll leave you here," he told her. "Follow it through the copse and you'll come out near the stable block. You'll be able to find your way to the main house from there."

She gave him her hand. "I hope to see you soon at Rossmor, Mr. McLean. Perhaps you might come to dinner one evening this week? Tomorrow, if your plans allow?"

"I should like that. But you must not stand on such formal terms with me. I hope you will call me by my given name as Alistair does—and give me leave to do the same now that we are family."

"Of course I do."

Gordon regarded her steadily. "Meanwhile, my dear girl, do not worry about either Finnula or Elspeth. You are the mistress of Rossmor now. It is *you* who will set the tone for the future."

She smiled. "You are very kind and encouraging. I thank you for it."

"It is my pleasure to be of any assistance that I can." He kissed her hand. "And tell that young nephew of mine that I approve of his choice."

He mounted his horse and rode away, with a wave of his hat. Grace went on along the way he'd shown her, feeling more settled than she had since her arrival. In Alistair's uncle, she had found a friend and ally.

Turning their conversation over in her mind, she was halfway to the copse when she heard her name called softly. *"Grace . . ."*

She looked around, thinking it was Gordon McLean who spoke; but she could see him in the distance, cantering along the track to Gorse Manor. There wasn't another soul in sight. Somehow, in the next few minutes, she lost her bearings. The path had given way to stony ground studded with hardy weeds. She would have to climb the hill ahead to spy out the lay of the land.

After cresting the hill she stopped to rest in the shade of the copse. It gave a fine view of Glen Ross and the

wooded valley that widened on the outskirts of the village.
She spied a church steeple among the thick trees, and the
gabled roofs of a large house. *The vicarage where Meg
lives with her family*. And off to one side, a churchyard
with lines of tilted headstones like a well-bred matron with
a mouthful of crooked teeth.

She recognized it instantly and totally: this was the place
of her haunting dreams.

Grace tried to convince herself otherwise. She remembered Alistair and Count Borromini speaking one evening
of the experiments of Max Wundt in Leipzig, and of how
the mind played tricks, blending memories of past experiences with the present, to produce the phenomenon known
as *déjà vu*. Perhaps the details of the dream in her memory
were being overlaid by details of the similar scene before
her.

But there was the black obelisk, an exclamation point of
grief against the blue sky. She stood frozen for a long time,
fighting the urge to walk to the churchyard and examine
the obelisk at close hand. It was so strong it frightened
Grace.

She had to know . . .

She descended the hill to the lych-gate. The cold iron
with its the cracking paint and gritty rust, felt real enough
beneath her gloved fingers. She pushed it open and entered
the churchyard. There were the rows of staggered stones,
just as she remembered. The graveled path that led past the
dark yews.

Grace approached the obelisk. The black stone pierced
the sky, bleak and ominous. She looked for an inscription
but the side facing her was blank. Stepping around the monument, she stopped short with a startled cry.

There was the angel, wings outswept and its inhumanly
beautiful face turned toward her. Marble tears glistened like
tiny pearls upon its smooth white cheek.

Grace felt as if she were caught up in a nightmare. The

air seemed to thicken and her limbs grew heavy as stone. She forced herself to walk around the obelisk and read the inscription chiseled into its square base:

Finnula McLean, Beloved Wife and Mother

Elspeth was crossing the hall when Grace entered. She paused, then came forward. "These are yours now," she said, withdrawing a silver chatelaine from her pocket. She undid the fleur-de-lis pin that kept the chain and dangling keys pinned inside and held it out to Grace. "I hope you will prove worthy of the honor."

Grace recoiled as if she'd been slapped. It took only a moment, however, to collect her thoughts. Her experience teaching had taught her to deal with would-be bullies quickly and decisively.

"My husband is fond of you, Mrs. Lachlan, and so I had hoped we would be friends," she said. "However, it is plain that you have decided to dislike me. I am sorry for it, but I will not let your attitude intimidate me. Nor, may I add, will I permit you to undermine my position. There can only be one mistress here."

The other woman's mouth dropped open. "Well," she said after a moment. "You are very blunt. I will be equally so. Do you wish me to leave Rossmor?"

"No. If you are thinking that I wish to be rid of you, you are wrong. Rossmor has been your home for several years. I hope it may continue to be so. But if we cannot regard one another in friendship, let us at least act with outward respect."

Elspeth flushed. "You are generous. Very well. I will try my utmost to make the transition as easy as possible—for both our sakes."

"I cannot ask for more," Grace said. "And I shall do the same. I met Gordon McLean while out walking and invited him to sup with us tomorrow. I hope you do not object?"

"How can I?" Elspeth replied wryly. "You are mistress here and must do as you think best."

"Where is Janet?"

"Gone up to her room to fetch a book."

Grace excused herself and went up to seek the girl out. She stopped by her own room first and picked up the packages she'd purchased for her. She found her stepdaughter curled up in a window seat, staring out at the loch.

"Are those for me?" Janet asked eagerly.

"Every one of them. I chose them especially for you." She handed her the first package, and was pleased to see that Janet was thrilled with the blue glass beads. "To match your eyes," Grace told her.

The comb and brush were a great success, but the clever little box was clearly the favorite gift of all. She showed Janet how to open and close the secret drawer. "To hide all your treasures and secrets," she told the girl.

Janet colored and set the box down on the window seat. "You went to a good deal of trouble to find gifts to please me—and they do. Very much so." She looked up at Grace anxiously. "I am sincerely sorry that I was so horrid to you earlier."

"We'll start afresh and say no more about it, then." Grace kissed Janet's cheek, and left the girl to enjoy her gifts, encouraged by the way things had gone between them.

Now that she'd begun to make peace with Elspeth and Janet, the future looked brighter. *How foolish I've been these last two days. Anyone might suffer from a nightmare or mistakenly try to make a door swing the wrong way. As to the obelisk, why, there might be one in every churchyard in Scotland, for all I know.*

It was only later, as she was making her way down to the drawing room, that she remembered the blank space where the portrait of Finnula McLean had hung. She saw Braedon hovering at the foot of the stairs.

"The picture that was taken down in the drawing room this morning—where is it now?"

The butler sighed. "It has been restored to its proper place, madam." Grace thanked him and went in search of it, aware that he was watching her. The painting was exactly as she'd envisioned it, down to the ominous shadows and the crescent moon upon Finnula's white brow. And no matter how much she rationalized the other strange events, there was no explaining that.

Chapter Eighteen

Grace sat at her writing table in her upstairs sitting room, penning a note to Lady Helena, while Janet worked on her assigned studies. Since this consisted of curling up in a comfortable armchair with an engrossing book, the girl had no complaints.

"Elspeth had me read the dullest things—mostly books of sermons," she told Grace. "This is ever so much more interesting."

Grace looked up and smiled. "I'm glad of that. I wouldn't want you to take reading in dislike!"

"You're clever," the girl said, smiling back. "And you're giving two lessons in one, because I'm learning Shakespeare's stories at the same time."

Braedon entered. "Mrs. Kinsale has come to call, madam. I have put her in the drawing room."

"I'll go down to her at once." Checking her reflection in the mirror, Grace smoothed her hair in place and hurried down to the drawing room.

A young woman rose from a settee. "Miss Templar! Oh, how good it is to see you again."

Grace recognized Alistair's sister immediately. Meg had changed very little since her school days. She smiled and held out her hands. "Dear Meg! How wonderful you look. Fairly blooming! I am so happy you came to call."

Meg wrinkled her dainty nose. "Alistair will be very cross with me. He tried to persuade me not to come today. I promise I will not tire you out."

"My dear girl, I have just tramped halfway to the village and back out of sheer boredom, and am not the least fatigued. I hope you will stay as long as you may. There is so much news to exchange."

They sat side by side on a settee and talked of school days and of Meg's two sons, whom she'd left behind at the vicarage, in charge of their nurse. "They wanted very much to accompany me, but I thought it would be too much. And to be perfectly truthful, I wanted to have this first visit with you all to myself."

"Perhaps you might bring them tomorrow then, if you are free? We could have a picnic luncheon by the loch with Janet."

Alistair's sister beamed. "How comfortable it is to have you here at Rossmor. And how merry we shall all be this winter, while Alistair and my husband are closeted with their experiments!" Meg gave a little sigh. "He is away in Devon now, at the deathbed of his aunt. Poor thing, she is lingering long past her accounted days."

"He has been gone a while, I take it?"

"Four weeks, and bidding to be longer. Not that I begrudge Aunt Maude every day on earth to which the Good Lord has entitled her." Meg's eyes grew bright with tears. "Only it is the first time we have been separated since our marriage. I miss him terribly!"

"I can understand that," Grace told her.

Meg relaxed. "How nice it is to have another married woman to talk with. And it will be like old times, having a house party at Rossmor. Lady Helena wrote to me that she will be one of the party gathering at Rossmor next month."

"Don't remind me!" Grace said with a look of mock horror. "I am dreading it more with each passing day."

Meg's eyes danced. "I had thought that it would be a stuffy scientific group, but if Helena is coming the company must surely be quite lively. I believe Alistair has some sort of surprise up his sleeve. He is being very mysterious about it all."

"The guest list is quite small; however, this is the first time I will play hostess to so large and distinguished a group. Except for those few I met in Rome, they are all strangers to me. I will have to rely upon you—and Elspeth, of course—to help me keep them entertained."

"I should like nothing better!" Meg rose. "Come to the vicarage one afternoon when Janet takes her lessons with my sons, and we will put our heads together on how to do so. And now I must be going, or Alistair will give me a blistering scold!"

"No fear of that. He's tied up with his account books today."

Meg laughed. "It would be wise to stay out of the way until he's through." She departed with promises to return with her twin sons the following day.

Grace knew that Meg was right: no man wanted to be disturbed while he was going through the estate ledgers. But after a while she grew restive. She wandered over to the estate room in the central portion of the house.

She found him with his elbows on the desk, staring blankly out the window. There were open ledgers and stacks of papers everywhere. "Are you dreaming of escaping by that window?" she teased.

McLean looked up. "Would that I could escape my problems so easily. I've just been informed that there is worm in the beams of the tower, and damage to the south gable of the new wing from a series of unusually strong summer storms. I'm trying to juggle expenses about so I can have the place in fair shape before winter."

"It will be quite costly, then?"

"Very. And dangerous. I don't want you or Janet wan-

dering about when the workmen are there. They will be
tearing out railings and replacing treads in the staircases.
But you haven't come here to be told of dry rot and beetles
in the woodwork."

Taking her hand, he pulled her down on his lap. "At
least I hope that is not why you're here." He tilted her face
up to his and kissed her until she was breathless.

Does he know how he affects me? she wondered as her
arms wound round his neck. *I cannot think clearly when
he is too near.* She pulled away.

McLean tangled his fingers in her hair and dragged her
to face him for another kiss. It was a calculated move on
his part, a subtle statement of possession. He released her,
noticing how her cheeks were flushed, her pupils dilated
with pleasure.

"Much better than going over columns of figures," he
said.

"Yes." She leaned her head on his shoulder and nuzzled
his neck. "It's such a lovely day! Do you think you could
escape your obligations for a little while? Elspeth is writing
letters, and Cook has promised Janet that she might help
baking tarts for our afternoon tea. I thought it would be a
good opportunity to have some time alone with you."

He trailed a finger down her cheek and along her jaw.
"So greedy, my dear? So soon?" He glanced at his watch.
"Not three hours since we made love."

He was laughing, but it irritated her. She pulled away.
"I don't mean that way. I was hoping we could talk."

McLean's eyes grew wary. "What about? The house
party? You had better let Elspeth be your guide. She has
handled the details before."

Grace stood up and went to the window. The loch was
a deep and transparent topaz in the shadow of the moor.
The rest of it shone bright as gold. She leaned against the
sill.

"Since we arrived at Rossmor you've spent more time with Elspeth than you have with me."

"That's not true . . . if you'll think back to last night, my dear. And this morning." He went to her, his voice soft and cajoling. "If you don't remember, then it is quite a blow to my pride!"

She hadn't quite placed the source of her discontent until he said that. "I remember quite vividly. However, I should like to spend time with you engaged in other ways. We can't always be making love."

"Good God, woman. We're on our honeymoon still!" He lifted her chin with his fingertip and smiled. "We're supposed to be making love as much as possible."

He saw his joke hadn't had the effect he'd wanted. "Would you like to take a walk through the garden? Or, better yet, let's take the sailboat out on the loch. Cook will prepare a hamper of food. It's a perfect day for it. There won't be many more like it in the Highlands this time of year."

"A sailboat! Yes, if you promise that you won't overturn it and dump me into the loch. I cannot swim an inch."

"I will swear an oath not to let you tumble overboard. And to give you my undivided attention for the rest of the afternoon."

"A tempting offer. I see that I really have no other choice."

Half an hour later they were out on the loch, sailing a ribbon of light across water as reflective as a mirror. Grace had never experienced anything like it in her life. The sail was a white swan's wing, carrying them out in glinting arcs, until the battlements and towers of Rossmor were almost lost to view.

"How long is the loch?" she asked as the bow cleaved the bright waters.

"Eighteen miles from end to end, and five at its greatest width."

She looked down into depths as dark as peat. "How deep?"

"No one knows."

He altered the sail and their speed dropped rapidly.

McLean took her north, toward the dark masses of oak and birch and evergreen that rose from rocky isles. "The five sisters," he told her.

"That sounds as if there is a story behind the name."

"Indeed. There were six to start, each one more beautiful and haughty than the last. A ragged stranger came to their father, claiming to be a great wizard set upon by thieves. No one believed him. He begged for the hand of each girl in turn, but every one of them spurned him as too poor and humble—except the last. So he married her and carried her away, but not before he turned her sisters into islands and their hair into the moss and trees you see."

"What of the sixth sister whom he wed?"

His blue eyes were filled with laughter. "I suppose she lived happily ever after. Isn't that the way of fairy tales?"

"It wasn't very loyal of her," Grace said.

His face grew serious. "Perhaps not to her sisters—but she was loyal to her husband."

"It was cruel of him to make her choose."

"Times were different then. You cannot judge them by our moral standards. I wonder if you will agree with my family motto? 'Loyalty before all.' "

She shook her head. "Not before honor."

"Sometimes they are inextricable."

"The right thing is sometimes done for the wrong reason. But a wrong thing done for the right reason must always be wrong."

He smiled down at her, but there was sadness in the unfathomable depths of his eyes. "The people of Glen Ross fought and died for a lost cause, because they had sworn an oath of loyalty. For that, many of them lost their lands in the clearances, and the right to speak their own language or wear the McLean tartan. A way of life was forever destroyed."

Grace searched his face. "Their loyalty was to a principle, not to a person."

McLean brought the sailboat to one of the islands, where the water lapped against an ancient wooden dock. He made it fast and held out his hand to her. Once they were safely on shore, he took her arm and led her over the rocks until they stood beneath the leafy branches of the trees.

Despite the shelter of their arching limbs, there was a peculiar sense of desolation to the place. Grace was extraordinarily sensitive to it. "This is as good a place as any," he said, setting down their picnic hamper.

Grace took out the bread and sliced ham and cold chicken while he opened the wine. In any other place, she would have been glad to linger on such a lovely afternoon; but there was something about this island that got under her skin, leaving her edgy and anxious to be done.

After she'd repacked the basket, he rose and held out his hand. "Come, there is something I wish to show you."

He led her into the midst of the trees. A massive rock stood alone in the clearing, black as the haunting McLean obelisk in the churchyard, a crude symbol of a bird and a jagged lightning bolt etched upon it.

Her uneasiness grew. "What is this place? I don't think I like it much."

McLean put his hand at her nape and steadied her. "This is the burial site of the man reviled as the Black Laird. He was the husband of Freya, the daughter of the Fair Maid of Ross. The rock was brought down from the mountains at great labor. It was placed there in the belief that it would prevent him from rising up from the grave to seek vengeance."

"Ah. He was murdered?"

"That depends on which way you view the matter. Some say he was justly executed. The McLeans had fought at

Bannockburn with Robert the Bruce, and later at Flodden field for the Stuarts. During the '45, the Black Laird led the men of Rossmor at Culloden, in support of the Jacobite cause. They trusted him. But at the decisive moment he betrayed them and their cause, so that he might keep Rossmor and its vast lands. The men of Glen Ross were led into a trap and slaughtered like helpless sheep."

Grace shivered. "A terrible story!"

"Are you cold?"

He pulled her into the circle of his arms, and she felt the heat of his nearness enfold her like a warm cloak. Her heart quickened. Nothing—not even that fearsome cairn of stone—had the power to frighten her as long as he was there beside her.

She leaned her cheek against his shoulder. "How did the traitorous Black Laird meet his own end?"

"Not in the agony of battle. He returned to Rossmor and died in his bed—at the hand of his own wife, while their young children slept in the room below."

"His wife! How shocking." She pulled back.

McLean's face hardened. His voice rang through the cool, clear air like steel. "Freya was the daughter of a Norse warrior and Frida, the Fair Maid of Ross. Until this century the estate passed down through the female line, and she was captain of this branch of the clan by hereditary right. The protection of the clan and dispensing of stern and swift justice were among her sworn duties. Was it murder, therefore—or an execution? Where should her loyalties have lain, with her slain people or her husband?"

"That is a question only a Solomon or God Himself could answer. I don't pretend to have such wisdom."

His gaze was intense. "Then tell me this: what would you have done in her place? Right or wrong—here would *you* have placed your loyalty?"

Grace pulled her warm shawl more tightly around her shoulders against the chill breeze off the loch. Her voice came soft as a sigh. "With those innocents whose welfare was entrusted to me."

"Yes," he said. "There was no other choice."

Her answer had pleased him and yet Grace felt him distancing himself even further from her. How very different Alistair seemed here. As if a stranger had put on the mask of a familiar face. She tried to shake off the fantasy.

"What happened to Freya afterward?"

"She went to her children and kissed them tenderly and told them she must go away." A muscle ticked in his jaw. "Leaving them in the care of her old nurse, Freya went up to the battlements on the old tower, and threw herself over onto the rocks below. She died instantly."

Grace was stricken. "But what of her children? How could she have left them?"

McLean's face was somber. "Some say she never did."

It took a moment for his words to sink in. Her eyes went wide. "I understand you now. This is a ghost story. And Freya is the Gray Lady of Rossmor."

He looked out across the water. "So it is said. It was then that the legends of the Gray Lady was born. Some say she stays on as guardian of the place to expiate her sins, warning those who come after her of impending disaster. Others say she will walk until the McLeans wipe away the stain of the Black Laird's betrayal. It is our great and enduring shame."

"You cannot take the blame for one man's actions, Alistair! Certainly not one who has been dead almost a hundred and fifty years!"

He shook his head. "I am the McLean of Rossmor. It is my responsibility to see to my clansmen and women. Many of those who survived the massacre were removed from the land during the clearances. Some emigrated to America, others to Africa. Every farthing that I can wring from the estate—yes, and my father before me—has gone to buy up their land that was confiscated, in an attempt to bring the scattered families back."

"I see." Grace put her hand on his sleeve. "It is a noble endeavor, Alistair. I promise I will no longer begrudge the time you spend working to right this wrong."

He felt as if a weight had been lifted from him. His face softened and he lifted a hand to touch her cheek. "I should have known that you would understand."

"I will always try my best to do so," she said.

He looked at her strangely then, she thought. As if he wanted to say more and then thought better of it. A cool breeze gusted in off the water and she drew her shawl closer.

"It's time we headed back," he said. They went back to the boat in silence and he handed her in. She was glad when he cast off the line and raised the sail. *There is a darkness to this place.* And she knew that she would never come back to this particular island willingly.

"Did you bring Finnula here?" she asked.

The question caught them both by surprise. McLean adjusted the canvas and took his time answering. "Finnula came here with me frequently when she was a girl. She and Helena liked to frighten themselves, as children do. Later she developed an aversion to the place. Meg was always less imaginative and more sensible than either of them. She said that once was enough, and after her first visit she refused to go back."

Grace realized that Finnula had sat in this very boat, on the seat where she sat now. It gave her a jolt. She was so in love with Alistair that she had willfully blinded herself to the actuality of his first marriage. Everything at Rossmor must remind him of Finnula. It was a few seconds before she identified the odd feeling that swept over her as jealousy.

Her conscience shamed her. Finnula was dead while she was achingly alive. She had Finnula's husband and the care of Finnula's daughter. *She* was mistress of Rossmor.

She looked out across the loch, sapphire and silver in the bright light, and realized that Finnula had known it in every mood.

Just as she had known Alistair.

She watched him, admiring the strength of his body as he maneuvered the boat with easy grace. The sun brought out the red highlights in his dark hair, the intense blue of his eyes. He was so splendidly masculine, so vital and vibrant, that he made every man she'd ever known seem pale and insubstantial in comparison. Her breath caught in her throat. She wanted them to sail on and on in that clear, golden moment.

Because when they reached Rossmor she would have to come to terms with the truth that was lodged like a festering splinter in her heart: Alistair had chosen Finnula to be his wife, while his marriage to her was the result of an absurd misadventure.

In the depths of her heart she couldn't believe that he would purposely have chosen an obscure governess whom he scarcely knew from Eve, with neither family nor fortune to recommend her, as his wife.

All the pluses were on her side of the ledger. He was everything she had ever looked for in a man. A charming companion. A considerate husband. A passionate lover. Given the choice, she would wed him again in a minute.

But what would he do, if given that same choice?

There. It is out.

As the bow sliced through the water, she held her breath, as if in doing so she could magically suspend time between the tragic past and veiled future.

They reached the dock too soon. McLean made the boat fast and helped Grace out. Her face was pale, her body taut as a bowstring. He thought he understood: she found herself wearing another woman's shoes, and they were pinching her at every step.

She started to move away, but his arms closed tight around her. "Grace. Bide a moment." He took her chin in his fist and raised it until she had to look at him. Her eyes were darkly green and filled with doubts.

"You've been very quiet since we left the island. You are thinking that I see Finnula in every place we go—am I right?"

She shivered. "How can I not? She was a part of your life, and is Janet's mother. I can never take her place."

His mouth tightened. "Finnula is gone. You must make your own place here."

"I will sort it out in time." Her voice shook. "But it is not easy for me."

McLean was touched and exasperated and filled with guilt. There was so much he wanted to say, but couldn't. Not yet.

"I realize it is a trial, and I am sorry for it. I had hoped you would be happy at Rossmor."

"I am. But it is very difficult just now." Grace bit her lip to keep it from quivering. "I confess that I feel like an imposter."

McLean's brow cleared. "That is no doubt the result of our hurried and unorthodox wedding. Exchanging vows in a strange church at the crack of dawn lent the entire proceedings a sense of unreality. That is easy enough to remedy. As soon as Hugh Kinsale returns home, we'll have an official blessing of our marriage—better yet, we will renew our vows before him in the parish church. What do you say to that?"

Grace gathered her courage. "I should like it. But that is not the root of my insecurities: you married Finnula for love, and me out of kindness. I understand that, and must try to deal with it. But it weighs upon my conscience."

"Devil take it! My marriage with Finnula has nothing to do with my relationship with you." His fingers closed over her shoulders. "I was a mere boy when we fell in love, and she was only a girl. Even after we wed and she gave birth to Janet, she remained a girl at heart."

He drew her closer and his voice grew low and urgent. "But I am a man of flesh and blood, Grace—and a man wants a woman. I want *you*."

Her heart sank. Not love, but want. Perhaps she expected too much, too soon.

His mouth hovered near hers. "I want you desperately. Now. Come up to our bedchamber, Grace, and I'll prove it to you again."

Want. Need. Never once "love." Grace hid her dismay.

"You forget," she said breathlessly. "Your uncle is due here at any moment. Yes, you see, there he is riding up the drive."

"Damn and blast! Well, there is no help for it."

McLean relinquished her and Grace hurried up the path to the house, preternaturally aware that Finnula had trod this way a hundred times before her.

McLean watched her go and cursed beneath his breath. Finnula was dead and in her grave—and yet she still had the power to ruin his life.

Chapter Nineteen

Grace and Elspeth sat in the drawing room, waiting for McLean and his uncle to finish their after-dinner port and join them. While the older woman plied her needle on a chair cover she was working in the McLean coat of arms, Grace idly turned the pages of a book. The two women had yet to find common ground, other than Alistair and Rossmor, on which to base any friendship.

The door opened and Alistair and Gordon joined them. The four soon fell to discussing the coming house party. "It will be good to see Lady Helena again," Gordon commented. "She used to be a frequent visitor to Rossmor before—" He broke off as if he'd been about to say something indiscreet.

"Alistair has invited a medium to enliven things," Elspeth announced into the awkward silence that fell. "A Mrs. Dearing."

Gordon turned to his nephew. "I have heard of her through friends. But I am surprised that you would want her at Rossmor."

"She is an acquaintance of Count Borromini. I suspect she is a charlatan," McLean said. "If so, I shall expose her during the séance."

"Up to your old tricks, nephew?"

"I don't know what you mean."

Gordon wasn't intimidated. "It is evident that Mrs. Dearing believes she is to participate in a joint experiment—while the true experiment will be your attempt to expose her."

The discussion was interrupted by Braedon's sudden appearance. He coughed discreetly. "You are wanted in Miss Janet's room, Mrs. Lachlan."

Elspeth set down her embroidery and rose. Grace was concerned. "She went up to bed hours ago. She is not ill, I hope?"

"She occasionally has difficulty sleeping," McLean said. "Elspeth is always able to settle her down."

He was proved wrong when Braedon returned in less than ten minutes. "Your pardon, Mr. McLean. Mrs. Lachlan has asked for you to join her."

"I'll come at once." He put his hand on Grace's shoulder. "It is nothing, my dear. From time to time my daughter suffers from nightmares. I will go up to her now, if you will both excuse me?"

"Of course you must go to her," Gordon replied. He bowed to Grace. "Meanwhile, I shall spend the time making better acquaintance with your delightful bride."

After the door closed behind McLean, Gordon went to a side table. "I almost forgot: I borrowed this book on West Indian customs from Alistair and intended to return it before I went to Canada."

Grace recognized the title. "There is a second volume to this subject. I saw it in the library only today."

"Is there, by Jove? Excellent. I'm afraid this one did not contain all the information I required."

"Come along to the library, then, and I'll find it for you." She led the way to the older section of the house and True followed faithfully at her heels.

"The dog has taken quite a shine to you, Grace."

"He's my shadow. Except when Janet is about. Then he

is false to his name: he abandons me the moment she rubs his head and practically grovels at her feet."

She kept up a stream of conversation all the way to the library. It was the first time she had been this way after sundown. The servants had lit the lamps in their glass sconces along the way. It seemed a great waste of oil to have so many lamps burning; but the farther they went from the new wing, the more her opinion changed. There was something eerie about the place, and the lonely echoes of their footsteps. She would not willingly come here alone after darkness fell.

While she rummaged among the titles on the shelves, Gordon strolled over to a glass case. "Ah, the Peiping Bowl. It is my favorite of all my grandfather's collection."

Her heart stopped and skipped a beat when he opened the case and took out the fragile item. The bowl was twelve inches across, carved from precious jade of gray and white. The sides were intricately pierced around the rim, the rest so delicate and fine that light shone through as if it were stained glass. She was afraid he might drop it.

"Perhaps you should put it back before True leaps on you," she suggested gently. "I don't trust him to behave himself."

"Nonsense. He's a good dog." Gordon turned the bowl toward the light. "As for myself, I'm in the habit of dealing with fine jade and porcelain wares. At one time I was involved in the import trade. I've quite a collection up at Gorse Manor. You remind me to show it to you when you visit."

"I should love to see it," she said, and heaved a sigh when he replaced the bowl as lightly as if it were formed of the cloud it resembled.

He examined a butterfat jade snuff bottle with a carnelian cap. "This is new." His fingers caressed the smooth sides with the appreciation of a connoisseur. "I must say that Alistair has as exquisite taste in Chinese artifacts as he does in wives."

"Heavens! You make him sound like Bluebeard."

"Good God! My unfortunate tongue." He set the snuff bottle back inside and closed the door. "What I meant, my dear, is that you do him proud. Rossmor has never looked better."

"I cannot claim credit for that. It is due to Mrs. Finley's ministrations and to Elspeth's care. Indeed, I am struggling to fill her shoes."

"How do the two of you march along these days? Is her nose still out of joint?"

"I can answer for myself, Gordon." Elspeth stood in the doorway, her face as flaming as her hair. "My nose, as you can see, is perfectly in line. However, my temper is drawn rather fine at the moment."

"So I see." He bowed to her. "You know my blunt ways, Elspeth. I spent too many years at sea to bother with the formalities. I say what is on my mind and in my heart."

"Do you, Gordon?"

He lifted his head and looked at her. Grace watched the strange byplay between them and felt the tension in the air.

The moment passed. Elspeth brushed past Gordon and pushed against the door of the glass case. It clicked shut. "You hadn't closed it properly," she admonished him. "Alistair must see that the broken lock is replaced."

"Grace said you took excellent care of Rossmor. I wish I had someone to look after Gorse Manor even half so well."

Elspeth flushed. "I would suggest that you place an advertisement in the Inverness newspapers!"

She swept out, and Gordon took his leave shortly afterward. Grace wondered if there had been some sort of romantic attachment between Alistair's uncle and cousin at one time. It wasn't an unreasonable assumption. There was no blood relationship, for Elspeth was related to Alistair through his mother, and Gordon was a fine figure of a man, still in his prime.

Perhaps they will make a match of it, she thought. She liked the idea. If Elspeth were happily married and mistress of Gorse Manor, she would forget her grudge against Grace. Perhaps, in time, they might become friends.

After seeing Gordon off, she went upstairs. Alistair wasn't in their bedchamber, so Grace went along the corridor to Janet's room.

The girl sat upright in the bed beneath her coverlet of white and blue. Her eyes were wide, her skin pale as wax, but she seemed calm. Every lamp and candle in the room was lit, and a hearty fire leapt in the hearth. Not a single shadow lurked in the corners of the room.

"May I come in?"

"Janet was just asking for you," McLean said. "I have given her a mild sedative."

"Is that wise? She is just a child."

A faint frown formed between his brows. "A short time ago she was a very hysterical child in acute distress! And I, need I remind you, have a degree in medicine."

"Of course. How foolish of me." Grace sat on the other side of the bed and took the girl's hand in hers. "I understand you had a bad dream?"

"Oh, yes. I was so frightened, I cannot tell you! I was in the tower, climbing the stairs, and I heard someone coming up behind me." Her voice quavered as she relived it in her mind. "Then I awakened—and she was here in the room with me!"

McLean's face was hard but his hands were gentle as he brushed a loose tendril of hair from her face. "It was only a dream, darling."

Janet leaned forward. "No. It was not a dream, Papa. I swear it."

Grace picked up the book on the nightstand beside the lamp. "Shall I read to you until you grow sleepy?"

"I should like that," Janet said with a faint smile.

"Very well. 'Once upon a time there was a Selfish Giant . . .' "

McLean waited until Janet's eyes closed and her breathing deepened. Grace smiled and nodded for him to leave, thinking the girl was almost asleep. She read on for several minutes, then let her voice drift away. She placed her hand on Janet's forehead and brushed back her hair.

The girl's eyes opened sleepily. "Oh! I thought it was *her*!"

"Were you having another dream?"

"It wasn't a dream," Janet whispered. "She was really here. I could smell her perfume."

Grace's heart gave a sickening lurch. "That is surely unusual. I have never heard of a ghost that wore perfume."

Janet turned on her side with her back to the light. Grace had to lean down to hear her reply: "Mother always wore perfume," she murmured. "Lavender and roses and something else . . ." A few minutes later she was sound asleep.

One of the maids had been assigned to sleep on the truckle bed in case Janet awakened in the night, and Grace left to seek her own bed. She hurried down the corridor and didn't pause till she was safe in her own bedchamber.

McLean came out from his study in a dressing gown. "How is she?"

"Sleeping soundly."

She wanted to ask him about Janet's strange words, and why she feared her mother's ghost; but he pulled her into his arms. Her face was already angled for his kiss. Her breasts ached with yearning.

"This is the time of day I like best," he murmured into her ear. "When we are alone together and the world does not intrude."

"I, too. I've missed you these past few days, Alistair, when you have been so preoccupied with the estate."

"Is that what it is?" He lifted up her chin and kissed her.

"You feel ignored? Well, my dear, I intend to devote a good deal more attention—beginning here and now . . ."

His lips were warm against the angle of her jaw, his hands caressing as they ran lightly over her curves. One cupped her breast as his thumbnail traced intricate patterns over its tip. Grace sighed with pleasure. The intimacy of the gesture, the low pitch of his voice stirred her with sensations. With images of his naked body gleaming in candlelight as they lay entwined amid the embroidered sheets. With fevered memories of his touch upon her flesh and her own, wanton response to it.

He undid the blue ribbons that tied her gown together and slipped it from her shoulders to pool at her feet. His hands reached out to take the ribbon from her plaited hair, and tugged it all loose. It fell down her back like a silk curtain.

"Beautiful Grace," he said softly. "Do you know what you do to me with a touch, a glance, the gentle swaying of your body against me? You drive me mad! I want to devour you."

His mouth skimmed over her shoulder and down her breast. He suckled gently, then pulled and tugged and nipped with his strong teeth until she moaned with need. He was alert to every sensation that shuddered through her. She was burning with desire.

A fever of need shook Grace. Heat rose from her belly, licking over her skin like tongues of flame. Her questions and worries went up in smoke. Ghosts, secrets and rumors all receded from her mind. There was nothing but the hard, lean length of him against her, and the fire that leapt between them.

Her body felt liquid and as insubstantial as the moonbeams that fell across the floor. McClean swept her up and carried her to the bed. She curled against his chest, weightless in his arms. He felt every tremor that went through her body. Knew that she wanted him with primitive urgency that matched his own, and he exulted in it.

He placed her on the bed and blew out the candle. Moonlight illuminated her, silvered her rounded shoulders, the sweet globes of her breasts, the graceful line of hip and thigh.

She watched him strip off his dressing gown, and her mouth went dry with desire.

How magnificent he is! She imagined the crisp dark hairs of his chest brushing across her breasts, the strength of his arms about her, the way his hands stroked and teased and incited. She moved against the soft sheets, arched her back, raising her arms above her head.

His breath caught in his throat. Her witchy hair was spread out on the pillow like a veil. He fisted handfuls of it, slid his fingers through it, reveled in its sensual texture, its deep, arousing scent. "I think you have cast a spell upon me."

McLean stretched out beside her and cupped her breast in his palm. He could feel the quivering of her body, the wild beating of her heart. There would be no languorous foreplay this time. There was no need of it. She was as impatient for the consummation as he.

Grace wanted him with such fierce hunger that nothing else mattered. If they were still downstairs in the drawing room, she would have felt no different. Instead of the moonlit bed, she would have let him take her on the carpet in the glow from the hearth.

Want built to need, need to such wild desire she had no control over it. Over herself. She reached up eagerly as he straddled her and lowered himself over her. Welcomed him with all the passion that welled up from the deepest reaches of her soul.

Their joining was fierce and free, a dark rapture that caught them up and whirled them, slick and gasping, into its fiery heart.

Later, when they were cast up on the still shore of contentment, she lay with her back to him, within the warm circle of his arms, drowsy and replete.

It was only later, as she drifted to sleep with her body curved into his, that she remembered there was something she had wanted to ask him. Something about . . . It slipped away as softly as the moonlight on the floor.

Grace awakened in the night, groggy and shrouded in the echoes of fading dreams. She sighed and rolled over on her back, then realized the other side of the bed was empty.

The light of the moon poured through the uncovered window. The shadows of the mullions lay across them in dark contrast like the bars of a jail cell. Grace got up to close the curtains and gasped. An apparition hovered on the far side of the room: a disembodied face with a mouth like a gaping wound. She froze in place, too terrified to move.

The door from the corridor opened and candlelight filled the room with wavering shadows. "Alistair!" she exclaimed.

He went to her side, setting the lit taper down on the bedstand. "I went to peek in at Janet. She's still sound asleep."

"Look! Over there in the corner."

He laughed. "You are as foolish as my daughter. It is only your own face reflected in the looking glass."

She laughed, too, but with embarrassment. "That is twice since we've arrived here that I've made a fool of myself."

"It's only natural. I've learned that expectations color observations. Even the most objective scientist can be tricked by them. You've heard rumors that Rossmor is haunted, and Janet imagined earlier that she'd seen a ghost. Your sleeping mind combined the incidents into the dream from which you've only just awakened, and it projected the expectations of that dream onto your waking interpretation of reality."

"It sounds perfectly logical when you explain it," she said, trying to quiet the rapid pummeling of her heart against her ribs.

He got into bed beside her and pulled the blanket up. "I'll hold you until you fall asleep."

Grace snuggled against him, letting the warmth of his body seep into hers. With his strong arms around her, she felt protected, even from the power of dreams. As she drifted into slumber, she was vaguely aware of a familiar fragrance: rose and lavender and bergamot. Of a light, gusty exhalation.

It sounded very like a woman's sigh.

Grace awakened from a dream near dawn. It seemed urgent that she recall it, but the details faded away like mist. Rolling on her side, she discovered that her husband was awake, as well. He stood by the bed looking down at her. "What is it? Has Janet had another nightmare?"

"No. She hasn't stirred, the maid said when last I checked. I thought I heard you cry out in your sleep." He removed his dressing robe and slipped beneath the covers. "I wondered if you were having a bad dream."

"I don't remember any of it—but I don't know if I can fall back asleep again."

"Well," he said, pulling her against his chest, "I have the cure for that. Since we are both awake and in bed . . ."

He kissed her and she reciprocated with all the passion he could want. When he touched her all doubts vanished and there was nothing but the two of them, alone in the indigo shadows of the bed.

His hands slid down and covered her breasts. His palms

brushed lightly, and he felt the quick, quivering response. He'd never expected such ardor from her. Each time he was amazed. He rolled over, pinning her beneath his weight. "Beautiful, beautiful Grace."

He nipped at her shoulder, moved lower, and she curved up in delight for more. As his hands caressed and roused, she wound her arms around him. Her breathing quickened and her body arched up, eager for his touch. He teased her with his tongue, taunted her with deliberate prolonging of every movement.

She was dizzy with desire. He told her that she was beautiful, that she drove him to the edge of madness and beyond. Grace prayed for something more. *Tell me that you love me, Alistair. Tell me that what we have between us is more than physical need.*

His lips skimmed from the hollow at her throat to the curve of her breast, while his hands smoothed over the sweep of her hips to the tender, silken skin of her thighs. But he never spoke the words she longed to hear.

The heat of his mouth, the stroke of his fingers, drove everything else from her mind. There was nothing but the glow of the banked fire, the slow, intensely sensual rhythm of their lovemaking. The growing urgency and pounding need. The sudden, spangling flight that shattered her with its brightness.

They slept and wakened, kissed and slept again. Just past dawn they made love a second time, this time hot and hard. She wrapped her legs around him, raked her nails down his back, dared him to take her faster and higher than before. Sweat-slicked and wild, they reached the crest together, their deep cries muffled by their breathless wonder.

A chambermaid, hurrying silently past their room, smiled and shook her head. They were a lusty pair, the master and mistress. She'd never heard the like!

Chapter Twenty

Grace sat before her mirrored dressing table while Cait combed through her damp hair. Her thoughts were not on the reflection in the looking glass, but on her predecessor. No one seemed to have the same image of Finnula McLean.

Lady Helena Ainsley had called her lively and charming, Gordon McLean had hinted that she was moody and morbidly over-imaginative, and Meg had spoken of her as gracious and beautiful and beloved by all. The Finnula that Elspeth had known was quiet and fragile, and she kept any other opinions of Alistair's late wife to herself. Mrs. Finley, the housekeeper, clearly had adored her, and, as for Braedon, trying to pry a morsel of information out of the old butler had been as fruitful as milking a rock.

Grace sighed. Which Finnula was the real one?

The facts she'd gathered were few. She had been the only daughter of an aristocratic union and had grown up in a grand house, although nothing on so large a scale as Rossmor.

While Grace had been teaching at Miss Cranmer's, Finnula had been the toast of London. "Books of sonnets were dedicated to her, and artists vied for the opportunity of painting her," Meg had said with a wistful sort of pride.

Grace smiled wryly. *I am not exactly an antidote, but I can't imagine anyone writing sonnets to me.*

Cait saw her grimace. "Did I tug too hard on your hair, mistress?"

"No, I was off woolgathering."

The maid nodded. "So much to be done yet for the house party, what with fixing up the old tower. Och, but it will be good to see the house filled with guests again." She set down the comb. "There. Not a tangle left. Shall I plait it for you, madam?"

"Thank you, no. I cannot stand to have it put up wet. I'll sit here by the open window with my book and read a while."

"You'll catch your death, you will," the maid scolded, "and what would I tell the master then?"

"I've been doing it all my life, Cait, with no harm to me yet."

"There is always a first time!"

It had taken Grace and Cait a few weeks to become used to each other's ways. What Grace had first thought was slyness and surliness on the girl's part turned out to be a bluff goodwill hidden behind a naturally pessimistic and anxious nature.

"I'll fetch you up a pot of tea to keep you warm," she said.

As the maid went out, Elspeth entered, looking elegant in navy faille with pearl and enameled buttons. She came bearing a parcel. "This has just arrived for you. It's from Lady Helena Ainsley."

Grace undid the twine and gummed labels. "From Mssrs. Langan and Robertson," she said, removing the contents from the box. There were three books bound in calfskin with gold stampings, and one large but thin volume tucked inside an unmarked red leather slipcase. Setting the latter aside, she looked at the titles on the others.

"*Portrait of a Lady*," she read from one binding. "Oh, it is Mr. James's new publication. And one from Mr. Ibsen. How thoughtful of Lady Helena." She examined the third.

"And a philosophical work of some sort by a woman named Eddy."

"Alistair and I have discussed her writings," Elspeth said. "Mrs. Eddy believes that the doctors are unnecessary, and that faith in God's healing powers can cure all ills of the body and mind."

"An interesting concept," Grace told her, "but one I wouldn't wish to try with a sick infant—or a broken leg."

Elspeth sat down on the edge of the bed. "You are a skeptic."

"More a pragmatist," Grace replied, and set the books aside. "While I believe faith can move mountains, I wouldn't wish to try and lecture a child suffering from the chicken pox."

"Nor I," Elspeth admitted. "But Alistair says the powers of the human mind are more incredible than any force of nature. Perhaps there is something to Mrs. Eddy's beliefs." She set an envelope down on the quilt. "Here is the receipt for my honied-brandy tonic, which I promised to Meg, if you'll be kind enough to deliver it for me when you take Janet to the vicarage today. She is afraid that Angus and Geordie are looking a little peaked. Personally, I think they are missing their father."

Grace saw an opening. "Would you like to accompany us? It's a lovely day for a drive."

"I must regretfully decline," Elspeth said dryly. "I like Meg's boys very much, but the truth is they are a little too full of high spirits for my sanity. Only last week while I was there, Geordie had gotten his head caught in the wrought-iron trim of the garden fence. And then there was Angus and the affair of the pewter tray!"

Grace laughed. She'd heard that the younger of the twins had attempted to ride a serving tray down the vicarage staircase, resulting in damage to the tray, the stair treads, and his lower lip. "It must be difficult for her to manage with her husband away for so long."

Elspeth shrugged. "It will be worth it in the end. His aunt is quite wealthy—and though Hugh is sincerely attached to her, I cannot help but think that his devotion has been enhanced by the possibility of being named her heir. He has no other income, and is dependent entirely upon the living of St. Declan's. Which is to say, Alistair's generosity."

"I imagine it will come in quite handy with two boys to educate and set up in the world," Grace replied.

Elspeth checked the monogrammed gold watch pinned to her bosom. "Well, I must leave you to your toilette. There are matters which I must discuss with Alistair. Have you and Mrs. Finley gone over the arrangements in the tower for Count Borromini yet?"

"I am meeting her in a half-hour's time to do so. Although why anyone would want to sleep in a haunted chamber where a murder was committed, is beyond me."

Elspeth gave a short laugh. "When you get to know Alistair and his friends better, nothing will surprise you. They will go to outlandish ends to further their experiements in occult phenomena. We are none of us safe from them!"

She left with a graceful swing of her skirts. Elspeth was a very attractive woman. Grace frowned at her reflection. It seemed that three or four times a week Elspeth and Alistair closeted themselves away in his study, to "discuss something." It made her feel very much an outsider in her own home. *What business could they possibly have together that requires them to spend so much time alone?*

She was amazed by the wave of sudden jealousy, and a little ashamed. But Alistair brought out such strong feelings in her that at times they were a little frightening.

Janet came in and sat down on one of the chairs, swinging her legs. "I'm bored. I wish it was time to go to the vicarage."

"If wishes were jewels, we all would be decked out like queens."

"Yes." Janet swung her heels. "My mother and I used to play a wishing game. If you could have your dearest wish, Stepmama, what would it be?"

"I don't know. I cannot think of anything I lack."

"There must be something."

A husband who loves me . . .

But she shook her head. "I am the most fortunate of women. The only things I've ever truly desired were a home and family of my own, and the leisure to indulge my vice for reading. And I have those now, you see."

Janet's eyes met hers, and then her lids came down to hide their expression. "Mama used to wish for all sorts of things."

"And what were they?"

"Once it was for a singing nightingale made out of gold and jewels, like in Mr. Andersen's story. Another time it was to have wings to fly like a bird. I remember that she used to go up to the tower when it was warm like today, and let the wind blow through her hair to dry it. She said it made her feel as if she were flying."

The girl picked up a porcelain trinket box from the table and examined it. "Mostly it was to live in London in a fine house and go to balls every night, like she did when she made her come-out. She said she would go mad if she had to spend another winter snowed in at Rossmor."

She set the box down. "Will you go mad?"

Grace shook her head. "I am sure I'll find enough to keep me occupied. And that reminds me: After we return from the vicarage, I thought you might like to help me with the sachets for the guests' rooms. I finished sewing the last of the satin sacques for them yesterday evening."

Janet looked surprised but pleased. "I would like to— only I don't know how."

Grace smiled. "Then you will learn. I've noticed that you are very quick when we play at jackstraws. Perhaps you might pick out the lavender stems from the blossoms."

She saw the beginnings of a sulky look on the girl's face. "Then as a reward I'll give you even more work—if you like, I'll let you sort the rose petals."

"Really? Elspeth never lets me help." Janet's eyes sparkled and all sullenness was banished. "May I help stuff the sachet sacques?"

"And tie them with ribbons too, if you like."

Janet thought a moment. "I suppose I have nothing better to do."

Grace tried not to laugh. The girl was so transparent, so eager to be liked—and so quick to rebuff any overtures. "If anything more entertaining should present itself, I won't hold you to it," she said.

She expected Janet to leave then, but the girl sat on the edge of the bed, absently stroking True's head. She seemed lost in thought.

"Is there anything wrong?" Grace asked. "You've seemed preoccupied of late."

Janet met her gaze solemnly. "I had another nightmare. But it was different this time. I dreamed about the churchyard. We were going there to put flowers on my mother's grave."

"Would you like to do that? We could stop on our way to the vicarage."

"I don't know." She lifted her head and Grace saw the strain in her face. "There is a marble angel near it. In my dream, when I passed by the angel frightened me. There were tears like milk sliding down its cheeks." Her voice dropped. "And it spoke to me!"

Grace was stunned. The resemblance to her own recurring nightmare was uncanny. The comb fell from her suddenly nerveless fingers, knocking over a small cut-glass scent bottle. She retrieved it clumsily from among her lotions and perfumes. "What did it say?"

"I don't know. I can't remember . . . but my mother had the same dream, I think. I heard her tell Papa that she went to the churchyard and the angel spoke to her. I am not supposed to know of it." Janet glanced up anxiously. "You won't tell, will you?"

"No, my dear. It will be our secret."

"Thank you!" The girl jumped off the bed. "I am so glad I told you about the dreams. I . . . I don't know why, but I feel better now."

"I'm very glad that you do."

Relieved of the burden of her nightmare, Janet kissed Grace lightly on the cheek. "I will be in the garden with True when you are ready to leave."

Grace watched her in the mirror until the door closed behind her. *Here is a mystery!* She and Janet and Finnula had all dreamed the same dream. *It is impossible. Unless . . . somehow, Alistair is the link between us! But what does it all mean?*

She rubbed her temples. The whole thing was too disturbing. She didn't want to think about it.

In the past weeks she'd learned her way around the old house. The door at the end of the corridor was a shortcut, opening to the upper gallery of the old hall. She slipped through it. The panelling and the ceiling beams had been waxed and buffed to a soft glow. She passed the gallery where the crimson curtains had been beaten of their dust, and opened the door on the far end.

She was in the tower, on the second landing. Her heart beat a little faster at her daring. She hadn't ventured here alone since her first day at Rossmor. Grace waited with the door open, to see if any remnants of the past lingered. There was no stir of memories, not a single echo or strange glow. The tower felt empty and safe, and she started up.

Scant light fell through the window slits, but she could see how the center of the steps were worn from the generations of feet that had trod upon them. The first slit gave a view across the meadows to the sudden rise of moorland. There was the vicarage, and just beyond it the churchyard where Finnula was buried. She could even make out the gables of Gorse Manor through the trees. Gordon McLean's home was large and comfortable, and filled with wonderful treasures from his travels.

Another circle of the tower brought her to a window with a view of the loch. It was as still and smooth as polished silver. Another turn, another door. Grace paused. This was where the infamous Black Laird had met his end. She'd never been this high up before alone. She decided not to venture inside until she had Mrs. Finley's company.

The door opened suddenly and she gave a stifled shriek of surprise. Mrs. Finley peered out. "Ah, there you are, madame. All is in readiness."

Grace smiled. "Rossmor could have no finer housekeeper than you, Mrs. Finley."

"And a joy it is to have the caring of it. I fell headlong in love with the old place the first time I set eyes on it when Finley—God rest his soul—brought me here as a young bride. He was head gardener, you know. 'You'll never get me out of here again except feet first,' I told him."

"Let us hope that day is far off," Grace said. The housekeeper chuckled.

"I've no plans of going anytime soon, be sure of that!"

Grace became aware of a scent: rose and lavender and bergamot. A chill rippled through her. "What is that lovely fragrance?"

"That would be the potpourri. Miss Finnula made it every summer from an old receipt she found in the still-room."

Grace examined the chamber's only furnishings: a carved-wood bed with a high brocade canopy, a small night-table, two low chests and a table and two chairs of ebonized wood. *Certainly Spartan, compared to the splendors of the Palazzo Borromini,* Grace thought. But the count had insisted that nothing be changed from the original. Once Grace gave her stamp of approval, the housekeeper whisked off to her appointment with Braedon.

Instead of following her, Grace was emboldened to go up. She opened the low door that led to the battlements and stepped out, leaving it ajar. A brown bird gave a startled cry, flapped its wings and flew away. The sun was warm, the wind soft and sensual as a lover's touch.

She went to the parapet and stood in awe. The view commanded the entire glen, from the rolling moors and distant mountains, to the toy village sprawled along the loch. A sudden gust of wind snatched her lace cap away. Her hair tumbled loose, dark locks streaming back behind her like wings. If she stretched her arms out, she would take flight, soar out over the silver-blue water with the sun warm on her back. She lifted her arms to the wind, tipped her head back and closed her eyes. A wild surge of elation poured through her. It *was* almost as if she were flying.

And then suddenly she *was*. A hard blow struck her between the shoulder blades, pitching her forward and into the gap between the walls of the rampart.

She fell against the stone and the force of it knocked the breath from her lungs. She lay there on the edge of nothing, terrified and fighting for breath. Below her was seventy feet of dizzying nothing—and there at the bottom, sharp-toothed rocks rising up through the dark water at the tower's base.

There were footsteps behind her.. Her heart pounded so loudly she couldn't tell if they were running toward her or away. The next instant rough hands seized her shoulders. She was yanked up and lifted completely off her feet.

Grace screamed and kicked out. Her lashing foot connected with something solid. There was a grunt of pain, but an arm like steel wrapped around her waist. She seemed to hang in the air for eternity, waiting to be hurled helplessly over the parapet and dashed down upon the rocks.

She was jolted to her feet, pinned against a hard, muscular frame. Surrounded by a familiar scent. "Alistair!"

He spun her around to face him. He was livid with fury. "What the devil were you trying to do?"

"I might ask the same of you! You almost sent me over the edge."

"I pulled you back, you little fool! Mrs. Finley told me you'd come up here. I found you hanging halfway over the parapet."

Grace was trembling violently. She scanned his face. His anger and fear seemed as real as her own. "Oh, Alistair! I was so frightened. Someone hit me hard between the shoulders, and I lost my footing."

He glanced around. "You must have tripped. There is no one here but the two of us."

Her shivering grew stronger. "I know what I felt! Someone shoved me. Hard!" She burst into tears of fear and anger. "Who would do such a thing?"

"Calm down," he said, smoothing his hand across her back. "You're safe." And he pulled her into his embrace.

She felt the thud of his heartbeat as if it were her own, the sheltering strength of his arms. He smoothed her hair and she thought for a moment that he meant to kiss her. Instead he smiled stiffly and released her.

There was a great flap of wings overhead, and McLean looked up. "There is your answer. It must have been one of the birds that nest up here," he said. "It swooped in so swiftly to land, that it flew right into you."

Grace shook her head and held on to him tightly. "It didn't feel like a bird. It felt like a hand!"

"I've seen birds shatter windows from the force of their speed. Come," he said. "We'll go down and I'll fix you a cordial to restore your spirits. Perhaps it would be best if you say nothing of this to anyone."

She was stunned. "You don't believe me, do you, Alistair?"

"My dear, you must see that it would cause a good deal of comment. You say you were pushed—and I tell you that there was no one else up on the battlements."

Grace fought her rising anger. "Are you saying that people will think I am making up bizarre stories merely to be interesting?"

"They are just as likely to say that it was I who pushed you," he told her. He eyed her coolly. "Is that what you believe?"

"No! Of course not." Nor did she want to start any more unfair rumors about her husband.

McLean's jaw tightened. "Servants gossip—and Janet is young and very impressionable. I don't wish her to be frightened again, now that she is just beginning to sleep well."

Grace softened immediately. "I understand. I will say nothing of it to anyone."

He tipped her face up to his. "It isn't safe up here, my dear. You must promise me that you will never come up here alone again."

Grace shivered in the chill October breeze. "You have it willingly!"

He released her, smiling. "Look! There are two feathers where you were standing. I imagine the bird suffered as great a shock as you when the two of you collided."

She turned and saw the glossy gray and white feathers, and a little fluff of down at their bases. Relief left her light-headed. What had she been thinking, to doubt Alistair even for a moment?

As he held the door open for her, she took a last glance over her shoulder, and caught a glimpse of something moving against the stone, just beyond the edge of her vision. Gray on gray, like layers of mist.

She blinked and it was gone.

Grace put the incident in the back of her mind as she and Janet rode up to the vicarage. "You're right," she told her stepdaughter. "The pony will soon be too small for you, and you are a good enough rider to have a horse on which to hack about. I'll speak to your father."

She couldn't have said anything that would have brought a brighter smile to the girl's face. Then the door to the ivy-covered stone house opened and two red-haired boys came running out onto the wide side porch. "Janet! Janet! You must come see the clever toy Father sent us from London! It does all manner of clever things."

They stopped shyly when they saw Grace, and sketched her quick bows. She was a prime favorite with the twins. "But first," she said, "let me guess which of you is which." She spied the tell-tale scab on one's lip. "You are Angus, of course—and you are Geordie."

Meg's boys were awed. "No one can tell us apart except Mother and Father!"

"Well, now you know that you cannot fool me either," Grace told them. "So you must not waste your efforts in trying."

"We wouldn't do that," Angus declared. "You are a great gun!"

"May we take Janet up to the nursery and show her our new toy?" Geordie asked. "It is a hand-powered engine, and can spin tops or make sparks on a friction wheel or . . . or, well, a great lot of other things besides."

"Of course. And I have brought a fresh batch of scones from Cook to have with your tea."

Meg ushered Grace inside. "You must tell me what you think of the new curtains and slipcovers. I do so hope that Hugh will like them."

The cozy parlor had been done up in William Morris fabric of subtle gold and black scrolls on a royal blue background. The two armchairs beside the fireplace were re-covered in blue velvet and the windows hung with gold. "My dear Meg, it is enchanting! And I like the piano where you've moved it over by the bookcases."

She noticed that some photographs had been arranged along the top of the piano and went to admire them. There was a lovely daguerreotype of Meg and a smiling young man who must be her husband, Hugh. A silver frame held one of Lady Helena in full court dress—and its twin one of Alistair with his first wife. They looked young and happy, and she wondered if it had been taken for their wedding.

"I hope you do not mind," Meg said anxiously when she saw that Grace had noticed it. "I had thought of putting it away . . ."

"You needn't do so on my behalf. I am sure it is a comfort to Janet to see it there."

While the children played abovestairs, the two women discussed plans for the coming house party at Rossmor. Meg was eager for any change from her domestic routine, and immersed herself in details. Grace, however, found her attention wandering. She was increasingly distracted by the view from the bow window, dominated by the square tower of the church and the graveyard beyond. Once Finnula had sat here, making plans with Meg. Now she lay beneath the black granite obelisk.

I cannot escape from her, she thought anxiously, and remembered her dreams of the gravestone and the weeping angel. Grace threw caution to the winds. "When I passed the churchyard I couldn't help but notice a tall black monument set off by itself."

Meg smiled and shook her head. "That is one of the McLean markers. Vulgar, isn't it? Grandfather was enamored of all things Egyptian."

"It seems somehow familiar to me. Amazingly so, in fact."

"As well it should. There is an engraving of it that has been much reproduced. There was even a popular song that featured the monument on the sheet music. One of those overly sentimental ones, verging on the morbid: 'My true love sleeps upon the moor,' " Meg sang, " 'beneath a heather quilt.' Quite dreadful!"

Grace was astonished. "I have heard the words and melody somewhere, but cannot place it."

Meg crossed over to the pianoforte. "I believe that there may be a copy of it in the music cabinet. The engraving was used as the cover. Yes, here it is," she said after riffling through a few sheets.

Suddenly she stopped and frowned down at it. Grace rose and went to her side. The engraving of the black obelisk stood out starkly upon the pale lavender paper.

"Of course!" Relief welled up giddily. "I must have seen a copy of this piece of music at least a dozen times. One of the young ladies at Miss Cranmer's Academy sang it for the spring musicale."

Meg hesitated. "I had quite forgotten: it is dedicated to Finnula."

Grace could have laughed out loud with relief. For weeks she'd been haunted by dreams, which she'd taken to be some sort of unexplained and frightening phenomenon, like her vision in the Forum. And all the time the explanation was so simple!

She remembered Alistair and Count Borromini speaking of the experiments of Max Wundt in Leipzig, and of how the mind played tricks, blending memories of past experiences with the present, to produce the phenomenon known as déjà vu.

At some level not accessible to conscious thought, she had connected the dedication with Finnula and the engraving of the obelisk upon its cover. Since she didn't recall any of it in her waking state, her mind had woven it throughout her dreams.

"Meg, perhaps it is very wrong of me to ask—and I will ask you this only once, I swear it. Please forgive me if it distresses you—but I should like to know how Finnula died. Alistair never discusses it."

"Oh! I thought Alistair would have told you." Meg looked away. "She fell from Freya's Tower during a storm."

"Ah. That explains why Alistair was so upset that I went there alone today. He said it was not in good repair."

"Y . . . yes." Meg drew the syllable out. "That is one reason, I am sure."

"But there are others?"

The other woman blushed. "You will think me foolish, no doubt, but I have always avoided it."

"Have you a fear of heights?"

Meg shook her head. "No. It is the Gray Lady. That is where she is said to begin her ghostly walk."

A little shiver slithered up Grace's spine. All the way back to Rossmor later, while Janet chattered of Angus and Geordie and their clever toys, she was aware of Freya's Tower looming above the roofs and gables. Remembering a brief glimpse in the storm that first night of what had looked like a spectral figure on the battlements. In her mind's eye the shape of it became more distinct, the form more solid even though she knew it had been nothing but layers of mist.

Alistair is right. Expectations do color observations and alter memories. I must train myself not to expect phantoms in every turn of the corridor, and ghosts popping out of the woodwork.

McLean poured out two fingers of whisky into a crystal glass and took it over to the window. Janet and Grace were out in the garden with a basket, selecting the last of the late flowers for the drawing room. They had a quantity of late purple asters and chrysanthemums in gold and cream. He watched as Grace added branches from a shrub covered with shiny berries mottled in dark red and wine and palest yellow.

Somehow she would manage to work them all together into a harmonious arrangement, just as she was doing with the household. Janet's initial jealousy was being replaced with growing affection, and Elspeth's dislike had mellowed into a grudging respect.

Not that my cousin will admit it to me, he acknowledged. *Or even to herself.*

He hoped he'd done the right thing. He'd been so sure of himself in Rome, so certain that he knew what he was doing and could handle the consequences. Could handle his own attraction to Grace and the inevitable complications. McLean cursed himself for being a complete and utter fool.

She came up the brick walk halfway toward the window where he stood, but with the sun reflecting from the panes she couldn't see him. It seemed a metaphor for their relationship: Grace, going blithely through the sunshine, while he stood in the shadows.

He downed the whisky neat. The warm, peaty taste of it filled his throat and the fire of it burned straight to his heart. Beyond the glass his wife leaned over and snipped some leafy green stems, her movements as delicate as her name.

This was how he'd always imagined his life would be: work and family and Rossmor. It was all illusion—but just for a moment he could pretend that it was real. That it could last.

The sounds of their voices carried, although he couldn't tell what they were saying. Janet laughed a little too shrilly, and he gripped his empty glass so hard his knuckles blanched. She'd been alternately overexcited or quiet and withdrawn the first few days of his return home. Her emotions had swung like a pendulum, and he wondered what would happen if they swung too far. Finulla had been so at the same age.

There were times when Janet reminded him so much of her mother that it wrung his heart. He remembered all too well how Finnula could be. In tears one minute, bubbling over with gaiety another. Every emotion magnified. Sometimes she had seemed to balance on a razor's edge, ready to fall either way.

A poor choice of words, he told himself, and poured out a little more of the water of life.

When the devil is Hugh Kinsale coming back? Without his brother-in-law, this little charade might not hold together much longer. He wondered what Grace would do if his schemes unraveled.

I should never have set foot on this twisting path, he thought, rubbing his hand over his jaw. *But now that I have . . . I must do whatever is in my power to see it through!*

For Janet's sake.

That night, as Cait was helping her undress for bed, Grace heard the girl gasp. "What is it?"

"Och, madam! You've a great walloping bruise on your back!"

"Yes. A bird struck me when I was up on the battlements this morning."

"A bird dinna cause that mark, madam! I'd swear it on the Good Book!"

Her vehemence made Grace uneasy. "Hand me the mirror, Cait, if you please."

She took the handmirror the maid gave her, and turned around to look over her shoulder at it in the large looking glass on her dressing table. A dark bruise covered a swath of skin in the center of her back and there were several smaller ones just below her shoulder blades.

A chill ran up her spine. Whatever had caused the purple discoloration, she had to admit it looked very like the imprint of a human hand.

Chapter Twenty-one

Grace sat at the inlaid desk in her bright sitting room, going over the household inventory of linens Elspeth had provided her. The house guests would begin to descend upon them at months' end, and there was still so much to do.

She glanced down at the paper covered in neat writing and read it again in bewilderment. Six tablecloths of fine damask, three of lace, four of embroidered linen. So many embroidered sheets, so many plain. Pillowcases of various lengths and descriptions. A goodly number of quilts and spreads and down coverlets.

"Four sheepskin blankets faced with cotton," she read aloud, "one bound in blue cord, one mended in right-hand corner. Sixteen lace and cotton sachets: rose; ten embroidered cotton sachets: lavender. Good God. What in heaven's name am I supposed to do with this?"

True lifted his head and thumped his tail against the carpet. She patted him. "You are fortunate to be a dog, True. All you have to worry about is whether you'll have a nice meaty bone for your dinner."

She consoled herself that even if she seemed to be making scant headway in mastering her duties as chatelaine of Rossmor, at least she was forging ahead in educating her stepdaughter. She was pleased with Janet's intelligence and eagerness to learn, and accompanied her to the vicarage for the lessons that were given there to Meg's twin sons by Mr. Murrah, a retired schoolmaster.

While the children recited their Latin verbs or scribbled away at figures on their slates, Meg and Grace came to know each other well. Their affection was deep and their friendship abiding. Elspeth, however, remained aloof.

Alistair breakfasted with them almost every morning, but after that he was so busy with estate matters and the repairs to the old part of the house that they didn't meet again until they sat down to dine in the evening. It irked Grace that he managed to spend so much time closeted with his cousin Elspeth, yet had so little time for her. It was only after they went upstairs for the night that she had his full attention. Then he was as passionate a lover as any woman could ever wish.

Her own relationship with Elspeth remained civilized but distant.

She hoped this coming house party would help to break the ice between them. On an impulse, she went along the corridor to Elspeth's sitting room. The door was ajar, and she was standing with one hand holding aside the yellow window draperies while she looked out through the panes. She turned slightly but kept her face averted when she heard Grace at the door.

"May I come in?"

The other woman shrugged.

"You are mistress of Rossmor, and may come and go anywhere you please."

"I am. However, this is your room. I won't trespass upon your privacy." She started to retreat, but Elspeth stopped her.

"What is it you wanted of me?"

"I wondered if you would care to go over the final preparations for the house party," Grace said. "You know Rossmor and most of the guests, and you have the expertise of hosting a large party, which I lack. I would be very grateful for your suggestions."

"You will learn as you go. As I did, and Finnula before me."

Grace ignored her rudeness. "I suppose I shall. But in the meantime, it might make things considerably uncomfortable for our guests. I am not asking for myself. I am asking because I wish to do credit to Alistair . . . and to Rossmor."

She saw that she'd selected the right lure. Elspeth wavered only a moment. "Very well. Tomorrow, if that suits you. Not for you or for Alistair, but for Rossmor."

She turned away, dismissing Grace, but that was a miscalculation. Grace had no intention of leaving now until she cleared the air. "I think it is time for the two of us to have a tête-à-tête. You are angry at Alistair for marrying me," she said, "and at me for usurping what you feel should be your role here."

Elspeth's fingers curled tightly about the drapery fabric. "No. Not for that. Perhaps for overturning our quiet little world. I thought we should go on as before when Alistair returned from Rome. Only everything is so changed . . ."

Grace shook her head. "Change is the very nature of life. Nothing can remain unaltered by time."

The other woman was silent and Grace realized that she held a crumpled handkerchief in her other hand. It appeared to be damp with tears.

Grace realized belatedly that what she'd interpreted as coldness in Elspeth's voice had been her efforts to control her emotions, to keep them from spilling over. "What is wrong, Elspeth?" she asked in alarm.

"It is nothing to do with you! I have been thinking of the past a good deal lately," she said. Elspeth gestured to one of the armchairs pulled up before the fireplace, where a low fire crackled against the chill. "Perhaps it would be best to clear the air. Sit down. Please."

Elspeth closed the door and leaned against it. Her eyes were red-rimmed from weeping. "I was married at sixteen and went out to India with my husband. Twenty years ago today. It was the greatest change imaginable, but I managed to survive. I learned to adapt and became a part of an exotic world that was totally alien to me."

"It must have been difficult," Grace murmured.

"It was fascinating and frightening. The houses were strange and servants spoke another tongue, and dressed in white tunics or gossamer silks dyed in a thousand colors. It was a country of paradoxes. There were cobras in the garden—and gorgeous flowers that might have come straight from paradise. One night we heard a tiger roar and in the morning we saw his pug marks in the road. Later that same day we attended a ceremony in honor of the queen's birthday."

Elspeth was totally caught up in her memories, and her voice grew soft and dreamy. "The afternoons were so hot when we arrived that everyone napped through the middle of the day, and the wax flowers melted on my best hat. In the monsoon season we were shut up in our houses while the wild rains lashed the trees and battered the roofs. But I was a young girl and madly in love with a dashing officer. I learned to shut myself away from the strangeness of my new life, and carry on as if I were still in England. I lived in a world that was largely make-believe."

Elspeth knotted her slender fingers tightly around her crumpled handkerchief. "Then Donald became ill. A recurrent tropical disease from which he never quite seemed to recover. He retired from the military on his pension. Gradually our friends returned to England or were posted elsewhere. And then one day, he was gone. So you see, everything changed again. It was a very lonely and distressing time."

"You must have been very young when you were widowed."

Elspeth looked up sharply. "I do not mean he died. I meant that he was gone, literally! Donald left me for a native woman. They lived together quite openly, although they were shunned by the English community. The humiliation of it staggered me. I could no longer remain in India. When Alistair learned of it, he invited me to stay at Rossmor, and I accepted gratefully. Janet was barely out of leading strings and Finnula had just suffered a miscarriage. There were several in the next few years."

Grace was startled. Here was a piece of information that no one had told her.

"When I first accepted Alistair's offer I thought I could make myself useful," Elspeth continued, "and I was looking forward in many ways to returning to my homeland. I was homesick for Scotland. But when I arrived, I discovered that it was no longer home. Instead of cool mountains and rolling moors, I pined for heat and bright colors. For spicy curry and rosewater ices, and the clamor of the bazaars. I struggled so hard to fit in . . ."

She collapsed in a chair, weeping. Grace rose and knelt beside Elspeth's chair. "I am so sorry for dredging up such painful memories. I didn't know . . . Alistair had told me only that you were widowed."

"And so I was," Elspeth said bitterly. "Donald died suddenly, leaving his doxy and son behind. I made no claim upon his estate—but I was so angry! She had a home and a child, while I had nothing that was my own. Nothing!"

Grace held her hand. "I begin to understand you. After Finnula died, you carved out your place here. And then I came along and snatched it away from you. Is that what you felt?"

Elspeth nodded. "But today I realized it wasn't your arrival, it was something more profound. I was not mourning the loss of my position here, but the loss of control over my own life. I had blinded myself to it, substituting Rossmor for husband and family. It was merely a symbol for all my life lacked, but I mistook it for substance. Today Alistair helped me understand that I didn't want Rossmor to belong to me, but for *me* to belong to Rossmor."

"I do understand," Grace said softly. "And you will always have a place here."

"No. I don't want a place *given* to me. I want to *make* a place that is mine. Oh, dear! I am explaining it so poorly." Elspeth dabbed her eyes. "You must think me an utter fool."

"No. I think you are a woman of great sensibility, who is strongly in need of a friend—and a cup of tea," Grace replied in a rallying tone. "Shall I ring for it? Or perhaps something stronger?"

Elspeth laughed weakly. "Something stronger would be in order. For both of us. There is a mead-and-honey cordial on the little table beside the sofa."

Grace found the cut-crystal decanter and poured rich amber liquid into two small stemmed glasses. Light flared from the facets and Elspeth's fingers closed convulsively around the stem. "I warn you, this is not for the faint of heart," she said. "Better to drink it down quickly, and get all the agony of it over at once. Then you can enjoy the aftereffects at leisure."

Grace perched on the edge of the armchair again and sipped from the other glass cautiously. It went down like flaming honey.

The older woman's color and spirits had revived with the cordial. "Perhaps you have wondered what Alistair and I talk about when we are alone," she said to Grace.

"Yes, I admit that I have."

"You know that his research concerns the workings of the human mind, and phenomena for which we have no rational explanation."

"Yes, he had told me that."

"Currently he is putting some of his theories into practice—he plans to eventually publish his research. For the last few weeks, Alistair has been helping me search for the true cause of my distress through the use of hypnotism. During the sessions he encourages me to become relaxed and look at my problems as if from a far distance. Hypnosis, it is called. It has helped me a good deal."

She blew her nose. "Today was what Alistair called my breakthrough. He helped me to see that I am jealous neither of your relationship with him, nor your position as mistress of Rossmor. It is myself I am looking for. My true purpose in life. I wept then as I did now—as if a floodgate had been opened. I feel . . . cleansed and renewed. As if all the debris of my loss and anger has been swept away."

Grace had her own admission to make. "I'm afraid that I misunderstood the situation entirely. I have been so overwhelmed with learning my new role as mistress of Rossmor that I failed to look beyond it."

But in losing Elspeth as a suspected rival, Grace had also lost her explanation as to why Alistair had distanced himself from her. It was difficult to reconcile the aloof, watchful and unfailingly polite stranger with the passionate lover of her honeymoon. Thank God she had Janet and Rossmor to keep her busy. And that was what Elspeth needed, too.

"Until you decide what you wish to do, I hope I may persuade you that I need your help desperately. I promised Mrs. Finley that I would write up a final designation of who is to stay where, but became hopelessly entangled in the protocol. I am hoping that you will take pity on me and help me through it."

Elspeth blew her nose. "If you like, I will come down when I have composed myself, and go over the proposed arrangements with you."

Grace smiled. "I should like that very much, indeed."

"You said once that you had hoped we could become friends . . ."

"Yes. And I still do, Elspeth." She held out her hand, and the other woman took it.

"As do I. You are good for Alistair, and making progress with Janet. She has warmed up to you," Elspeth said, "in a way she had never done with me."

"I can never take her mother's place, but I hope to fill a void in Janet's life. Perhaps, one day, in her heart as well. I am exceedingly fond of her."

Grace paused, then plunged into a topic she had never dared broach before. "No one ever speaks of Finnula but Janet—although Meg told me how she died. What a tragedy."

Elspeth eyed her with dismay. "You must not judge her harshly."

Grace's eyes widened. "I do not judge her at all."

The other woman turned her gold bangle bracelet around and around on her wrist without realizing what she was doing. The tiny rubies in the eyes of the gold lion head on it caught the light like little flames.

"Finnula . . . Finnula was under strain," she continued in a low voice. "She had been upset and out of sorts for some time. It was attributed to her miscarriages. There were several after my arrival, as I've said. She had dreams. Nightmares that preyed upon her mind.

I suppose I must be honest with you. She thought she was being haunted by the Gray Lady. In time she began to believe that the ghost was trying to lure her to her death. I tried to reassure her and Gordon sent over special cordials to help her failing appetite. Not even Mrs. Finley's cakes, which Finnula used to love, could tempt her to eat. We were frantic. Alistair sent for the best experts to heal her— although they were ostensibly at Rossmor as ordinary guests. They held sessions with Finnula, similar to those Alistair conducts with me."

"And did they help her overcome her troubles?"

"It seemed so. She suddenly snapped out of the doldrums. Finnula was almost herself again. Lighthearted and gay, almost to the point of hysteria. Fey, as we say in Scotland. Finnula climbed Freya's tower and leapt to her death. Out of respect for Alistair and the McLean name, the coroner ruled it death by misadventure."

Grace's heart thumped against her ribs. "You are saying that she committed suicide?"

"No one knows for sure what was in her mind except God." She bit her lip. "Alistair awakened in the morning to find her gone. The house and grounds were searched. It wasn't until later in the day that her body was spotted, cast up on the rocks below the old tower."

They were both silent a moment. Grace put out her hand to cover Elspeth's. "I am sorry to have put you through that. But I thank you most sincerely for telling me. Hopefully, the knowledge will prevent me from doing or saying anything to rake up the tragedy."

"Yes. It is best not to speak of it. Alistair blames himself for being too wrapped up in his research to see what was happening to her until too late. He'd thought she was well on her way to recovery. And I blame myself for being too wrapped up in my own misery to be the friend Finnula needed."

"You cannot know that it would have made any difference," Grace murmured gently.

"Perhaps you are right. Leave me now to compose myself," Elspeth said. "I shall come down within the hour and together we'll finish the plans for the house party."

"Thank you. I shall look forward to it."

Elspeth smiled. "So shall I."

True to her promise, Elspeth soon helped sort out the arrangements for the house party. By the time Grace had finished going over the sleeping arrangements for the houseguests and their servants—and the order of precedence at the dining table—her head was whirling.

"It must be so natural to you that you no longer have to think about it," Elspeth encouraged. Grace closed her eyes and recited aloud:

"Count Borromini at the top of the tower, his secretary on the floor below, and their valets in the two small rooms at the bottom. Lady Helena Ainsely in the Rose Bedchamber, Miss Rosenthal in the Blue, and Mrs. Dearing in the Gold Room in the new wing. Professor Rosenthal and Lord Peltersham in the suites above the Great Hall in the medieval wing, and their servants to be housed in the various rooms on the upper floor."

"Very good," Elspeth told her. "And now we must go over the dinner seating."

Grace groaned. "I am thankful this is a small party or I should lose my mind before the guests arrive."

Janet came bouncing into the drawing room. She was wearing a blue riding habit that matched her eyes.

"I'm ready," she announced. She saw the blank look on Grace's face. "You promised we would ride over to the vicarage today."

Grace laughed. "So I did. But you are early."

Janet's face went from sunshine to cloudy in the blink of an eye. Grace pretended not to notice. "I will go up and change into my riding habit as soon as we are finished here. While I am changing, perhaps you might wish to select one of the ginger cat's kittens for Angus and Geordie."

"I should love to! But will Aunt Meg mind?"

"It was her idea. She wanted to surprise them."

"I know just the one! It's yellow, with gray stripes. Or"—she cocked her head—"perhaps the funny little black one with the white paws. But the calico has the sweetest face. Oh, dear. I cannot make up my mind."

She skipped out the door to the corridor just as her father came in from the terrace. "I couldn't help overhearing," he said to Grace. "You have a remarkable way of handling her."

"I am not 'handling' her, Alistair. Janet isn't a pony to be trained."

"If you'd seen her galloping across the lawn not ten minutes past, all stockings and flying petticoats, you might think differently!" McLean's smile turned to a frown. "I was a little short with her, I'm afraid."

"I wish you would not be so hard on Janet! It is only the natural high spirits of youth. There's time enough for her to grow up."

He turned to his cousin, as if expecting her to side with him in the matter; but Elspeth had slipped discreetly away. "The two of you seem to have set aside your differences," he commented.

"We had a long talk earlier. About Elspeth's past—and about your hypnosis sessions. I have been wondering why you never discuss your scientific work with me."

McLean shifted uncomfortably. "I considered them to fall under the same protection as confidences between a physician and patient. There will be enough of that during the house party. As to my general research, I would prefer you to make your own observations and form your own judgments, independent of mine."

Grace laughed. "I have never had a problem with drawing my own conclusions or expressing my opinions. You need not fear I will begin now. In fact, I will tell you that I have been hurt that you have kept so much of your work a secret to me."

"I could not very well discuss Elspeth's problems, spoken to me in confidence as they were, with you. I hope you understand."

"I do now. But if there are other aspects of it you could share, I should enjoy learning about your research and experiments."

He took her hand. "My secretiveness has made you feel left out. I see that now, and apologize for it. You are very important to me, Grace." He lowered his voice. "More so than you can even guess."

"Oh, I do hope so, Alistair! I have been so afraid that you had tired of me, and regretted our hasty marriage."

McLean saw the sheen of tears in her eyes, the faint quiver of her soft lips. He forgot his resolve and pulled her into his arms.

His mouth covered hers, gently possessive, then with an increasing urgency that reverberated through her entire body. She wished for a moment that they were away from Rossmor, just the two of them. He seemed to read her mind.

"I must go to London in early December to address a congress on aspects of my research. Would you like to go with me? We could journey down a week ahead of time, and stay over afterward."

"I can think of nothing I'd like better," she said reluctantly. "But I don't think it would be wise to go away so soon again. For Janet's sake."

Her words shocked him out of their mood of sudden intimacy. McLean released her.

"Then we'll take her along. Yes, and Elspeth, too. I'll hire a house, and we'll return here in time for Christmas," he said briskly. "I'll send a letter to my London agent to find us a suitable place."

The moment was lost. Filled with regret, Grace left to go up and change into her riding habit. *Alistair must think I didn't want to be alone with him.* They were back in limbo. As she was crossing the hall, Braedon appeared at her side. "The post, madam."

Grace reached out and took three letters from the silver tray. The topmost one was from Lady Helena Ainsley, the second from Mrs. Bingley, and the third from Miss Rosenthal.

She took them up to her room and rang for Cait. Grace sat at her dressing table and opened the letters while Cait fetched the garnet riding habit, which she had just finished pressing. Mrs. Bingley's letter was crossed and recrossed, full of the news of her daughter's engagement to Mr. Oliphant, and glowing plans for a wedding in London during the Little Season.

> *Although the recent death of his great-aunt makes a large society wedding impossible, I am over the moon at seeing Liza so happily settled. To think my dear daughter will be marrying a young man so rich in prospects! (He is heir to his uncle, Admiral Leighton, if I have not told you so before.) Although I confess I cannot like their plans to reside in Africa, where the discomforts are myriad and there is no society life as we know it, my dear Mrs. McLean.*

A smile curved Grace's lips as she read on. It was good to know that Mr. Oliphant was no fool. Removing Liza from her mother's sphere of influence would do both Liza and the marriage a deal of good. The postscript jolted her.

> *There has been much talk among the English traveling abroad on your marriage to Mr. McLean. I assured those who spoke of it that he is most civil and gentlemanly, and that I place no conviction in the rumors regarding his first wife's untimely death.*

Grace crumpled the letter in her hand. There it was again, that monstrous scandal aimed at Alistair. And how vexing that Mrs. Bingley, who was usually the font of the most minute bits of gossip, had failed to be more specific. She wondered what circumstances there had been surrounding Finnula's death—whether by accident or suicide—to cast such a long shadow over her husband's reputation.

Grace watched Cait put away the bandbox that had held her smart riding hat with the dashing feather. "How long have you been at Rossmor, Cait?"

"Twelve years now, madam."

"Then you were here when the first Mrs. McLean fell to her death."

"Oh, yes, madam. I had just been promoted from scullery girl to nursery maid to Miss Janet."

Turning toward the mirror, Grace set the fetching hat atop her hair and adjusted the angle. But her eyes were on Cait's reflected image, not her own. She never listened to servants' gossip, but this was different.

"Tell me," she said casually. "Is it your belief that the first Mrs. McLean fell—or that she jumped?"

Cait's face went white. "There be some as say she was pushed, madam."

Grace twisted around on the bench. "Pushed! By whom?"

" 'Twas the Gray Lady. Cook says that she grew tired of guarding the house, and so chose another mistress of Rossmor to take her place."

"What utter nonsense!" Grace said. "It's no wonder that my stepdaughter has nightmares if these are the sorts of things she hears from the servants' hall!"

The maid eyed her stubbornly. "Miss Janet did not hear it from any of us, madam. 'Twas her mother herself who told her of it—aye, and any other body that would listen to her, poor raving, mad creature! And her so beautiful. 'Twas a terrible pity."

Cait recollected herself. "But I should not be nattering on about what is over and done with, and long past mending. Will there be aught else, madam?"

"No, thank you. You may go, Cait."

The girl whisked out of the room before her mistress could ask her any further awkward questions. Grace sat there thinking over what she'd said. The more she heard of Finnula's demise the more confused she became. Now she had three versions of the event and a couple of dramatic twists. Depending on who was relating the story, Finnula either fell, jumped in a fit of despondency, or was purposely pushed either by the malignant family ghost—

Or Alistair.

And if Finnula had truly been insane then suicide seemed the most likely option. Grace wondered if her condition had inspired Alistair to abandon physical medicine for research into the triumph and frailties of the human mind.

The mantel clock chimed softly, and she collected her thoughts enough to read through the other two letters she'd received. Lady Helena's note was short. It took Grace a moment to read it, as the writing was exactly like Lady Helena herself: a bit dashing, very elegant—and more complicated than was first apparent.

She wrote that she looked forward to seeing Grace again, sent her fond regards to Alistair, Elspeth, and Janet—and hoped it would not inconvenience them unduly if she arrived "a few days in advance of the other guests" as had been her frequent habit in the past, since she was already in Scotland and "it would be a great folly to travel all the way back to London only to turn right around again."

Grace stared at the date of her proposed arrival in shock. Lady Helena intended to come the following day, a full week before the other guests.

Good heavens, how will we manage to entertain her until the others arrive? There aren't enough people in the neighborhood to provide her with the kind of social stimulation to which a woman of her station is accustomed!

She broke the wafer on Miss Rosenthal's letter last, thinking as she did so that perhaps she might invite them to come in advance of the other guests as well. According to Alistair's accounts, Professor Rosenthal and his daughter were charming, well informed, and witty: exactly the kind of company Lady Helena would appreciate.

But as she scanned the flowing lines of writing, Grace's spirits sank. Miss Rosenthal sent her most sincere regrets; her father had been taken ill in Vienna quite suddenly, and while a complete recovery was almost assured, he would not be well enough to attempt the rigors of travel for several months.

Grace went into the sitting room and immediately dashed off a reply, sending good wishes for the professor's full recovery and hopes that they would be able to visit Rossmor at a future date.

As she was gathering up her things, she became aware of an overwhelming fragrance of rose, lavender, and bergamot. She looked around uneasily. A scratchy whisper made the fine hairs at her nape stand on end and sent spiky shivers up her spine:

Grace.

The heat was draining from the room as if an arctic wind blew through it. Her blood chilled. *Grace!*

"Who is it who calls me?" she cried out defiantly.

Finnula . . .

The sound of the dead woman's name in that breathy exhalation filled Grace with cold terror. "Why?" she demanded. "What is it that you want?"

A sigh echoed through the room. *To warn you . . . that you will be next . . .*

Grace didn't stay to hear more. She fled the room and almost collided with her husband.

He grasped her arms. "What's wrong?"

She held out Miss Rosenthal's letter still gripped tight in her hand. "I . . . I was coming to tell you. We have a change in plans. Lady Helena is arriving tomorrow, and Professor Rosenthal is too ill to travel, although expected to recover eventually."

"The devil you say! Poor Ernest!" McLean released her. "And I was coming to notify you of another defection: Lord Pettersham has been appointed to head a diplomatic post of extreme delicacy which he cannot in good conscience refuse. He regrets that he will be leaving for South America, and does not expect to return before the New Year."

Laughter bubbled up inside Grace. "That leaves only Lady Helena, the count, and Mrs. Dearing. Here I was dreading cutting my teeth as a society hostess—and now we will be woefully short of guests and my greatest feeling is disappointment. There is no pleasing me!"

She looked so disappointed that McLean drew her into his arms without thinking. "Isn't there?" His mouth was warm on hers, his hands exciting as they skimmed over her face, her throat, the soft rise of her breasts beneath her jacket. "You're wearing one of those new French corsets," he whispered against her ear. "The topless one. I like it very much."

"Do not like it too well," she laughed, fighting the temptation to surrender her plans. "Janet is waiting for me. We are expected at the vicarage at any moment."

His voice was low and teasing. "Then you must wait for tonight to see how well I intend to please you."

Another kiss and he released her. "Until this evening . . ."

Her cheeks were flushed when she came down the stairs, just thinking of it. But on the way to the garden where Janet was waiting, she glanced up at Freya's Tower. Something moved behind one of the arrow slits. Who would be up there at this time of day, now that the restorations were completed?

A shiver came over her as she remembered that eerie voice, and its icy warning. Grace cursed her unexplained abilities, wishing that she could see only what was tangible, touch and smell and taste only what existed in the here and now.

She hastened along the brick walkway, unaware that two undergardeners saw her pass. One of the men scratched his head. "Will ye look at the mistress there? Pale as tallow. Do ye ken as there might be a wee laird on his way?"

"Aye," the older of the two said thoughtfully. "It's possible. Or else the poor lass has seen a ghost."

Chapter Twenty-two

Grace and Janet rode toward the vicarage on a picture-perfect afternoon. Cream-colored sheep grazed on the golden moors above them and down below the loch was a gleaming smear of Prussian blue. On any other day it would have filled Grace with a sense of tranquility, but she was too disturbed to appreciate it.

Grace had a fair idea of how prevalent the rumors had been following Finnula's death. She wondered why they had started in the first place. Was it because Finnula was so young and lovely, and her death so tragic? Or had there been other reasons? Gordon McLean had hinted that his nephew's relationship with his first wife had not been perfect, yet among those closest to him Alistair's devotion to her was never doubted.

Grace realized that Janet was speaking to her. "I'm sorry. I was off woolgathering."

Those blue eyes, so like Alistair's, regarded her gravely. "Something is worrying you. Is it the house party? I can help, you know. Perhaps I could come up with anagrams, or titles for charades."

"An excellent idea," Grace said, "although I fear we will run out of guests long before we run out of ways to entertain them." She explained it all to Janet and saw the girl's keen disappointment. "At least Lady Helena will be with us, and she is coming tomorrow."

That news perked Janet up immensely. "I do like Lady Helena! She is like Uncle Gordon and never makes me feel as if I should be hidden away somewhere in the nursery."

"Elspeth's notions are a little old-fashioned, but she is coming round."

As they turned into the drive of the old vine-covered vicarage, they realized that a carriage was pulled up to the front door.

"It must be Uncle Hugh!" Janet slipped down from her pony and handed the reins to the stablelad. She managed to untie the basket from her saddle and was at the door before Grace had even dismounted.

Meg met them on the porch, her face flushed with joy. "Come in! My husband has only just returned."

"Perhaps this is not a good time for us to call," Grace protested.

"Oh, no. Hugh is most anxious to meet you."

She ushered them into the neat parlor where Angus and Geordie were wound around the legs of a tall man with fair hair and laughing brown eyes. He disentangled his sons, gave Janet a quick hug, and came forward to Grace with his hand extended.

"My dear Mrs. McLean, I am most happy to make your acquaintance at last."

"And I, to meet you, sir." He'd sent Grace a warm congratulatory note upon hearing of her marriage to Alistair and his presence radiated the same good nature.

"Now that you've had time to settle in, what do you think of Rossmor? Is it sufficiently old and haunted to please your notions of romance?"

"It is a unique and fascinating manor."

He must have heard something in her voice she hadn't intended. The dark eyes scrutinized her. "You sound unsure."

"Merely a catch in my throat," she said quickly.

"I'll see to the refreshments," Meg said. She smiled at Janet. "Now, what can it be that you've brought in that basket? More scones, perhaps, for our tea?"

Janet smiled shyly and set the basket down before her cousins. "Something even better." She lifted the lid and a gray tabby kitten peered over the rim, then tried to climb up and tumbled out onto the carpet. The two boys were ecstatic.

"A kitten! Can we keep her?" Geordie asked, picking up the ball of squirming fur. "What's her name?"

"Can we give her a saucer of milk?" Angus wanted to know.

"It is not a 'her,' but a *him*," Grace told them, "and you must decide between you what to call him. He is very fond of milk."

"Why don't the three of you come into the kitchen with me, and we'll find a dish of milk for the dear little creature."

The children went off eagerly, carrying the mewling kitten with them. After the commotion of their arrival, Grace found herself alone with Alistair's brother-in-law. He came to her side and spoke with odd intensity.

"Meg has written me a good deal about you, Mrs. McLean, telling of your many kindnesses. I feel I know you quite well."

"Then I hope you will not stand on ceremony, but call me by my given name."

"And you must call me Hugh." He gave her a conspiritorial smile. "After all, we are the outsiders here and must stick together. I noticed your hesitation earlier when I asked you about Rossmor. Has anything occurred on the premises to upset, or possibly to frighten, you?"

"Forgive me," Grace said, "but that is a peculiar thing to ask."

"Is it?" His gaze was shrewd. "A young bride should be

happy and content, not nervous and abstracted. And, given your special psychic abilities, it would be no surprise to learn that you have experienced some unnerving contacts with what is euphemistically called the 'other side.' Perhaps even a visitation from the Gray Lady herself."

She felt the color drain from her face. " 'Special psychic abilities . . .' "

"Should I not have mentioned your particular gifts? Forgive me if I have offended you. However, since such matters are the basis of Alistair's research, I thought you would have no objection. We discuss such matters quite openly among ourselves."

"I am at a disadvantage," she said, brazening it out, "since I am not sure how much Alistair has told you."

She was making it up as she went along, trying to pull information from Hugh without letting him know that she was very much in the dark. It worked.

"Alistair and I have long shared an interest in such phenomena," Hugh said. "I received a letter from him during his visit to Rome written the day after the society met at the Palazzo Borromini. In it he mentioned that he had met an interesting and intelligent young Englishwoman in the Forum that afternoon, and that he believed her to be one of the rare people blessed or cursed by the second sight. I admit that I was very excited to read it, for he had almost given up on his quest to find someone with the genuine talent to access the past."

His warm smile flashed again. "When Meg wrote to me that Alistair had fallen in love with a young Englishwoman he'd met in the Forum Romanum, I was certain the two were one and the same. Unless, of course, he had suddenly formed the habit of lurking about the place in hopes of meeting personable young Englishwomen."

Grace could have bitten her tongue. Hugh Kinsale hadn't known for sure, he'd merely been on a fishing expedition— and she had risen to the bait like a trout to a fly.

It was a moment before the rest of his words sank in. Alistair had *known*. He had always known.

She cast out a conversational lure of her own. "I see. Then this was something he had been searching for over some time."

"Oh, yes. The powers of the mind have always been an interest of his. He did not become obsessed with studying them, however, until after Finnula—" He broke off suddenly, two high spots of color in his cheeks.

"You needn't put on kid gloves with me," Grace said. "I am aware that my husband's late wife suffered under certain delusions. Although I have never exactly seen how my . . . special abilities, as you term them, have any bearing on her state of mind."

Hugh was taken aback. "Perhaps it is better if that information comes from Alistair himself. I am sure he has his reasons if he has not disclosed them to you."

"I see." She tried to appear calm although her spirits were extremely agitated. She couldn't get past the fact that all this time she had been trying to hide her unnerving abilities from her husband, and he already knew . . . No, it didn't make sense. Or did it? She had heard him speak several times, of how expectations colored observations. Of how volunteers in various experiments were often not informed—or misinformed—about the actual goals of those experiments.

She chose her words carefully. "What exactly did he tell you about me?"

"I am afraid that was the extent of it. And that he was due to leave Rome in a few days' time and regretted that there would not be sufficient time to persuade you to volunteer for his experiments in psychical research—he had something planned. I would not have been at all surprised to learn he had actually done so, however. Alistair is a very persuasive man. And an exceedingly determined one! I have never known him to fail in anything that really mattered to him. Obviously, he didn't expect your friendship to develop into a love match so rapidly at the time he wrote to me."

"No. Nor did I," she said slowly. She felt ill. As if she were smothering from the wild battering of her heart inside her chest. She had to get away somewhere to think.

The Reverend Kinsale didn't notice. His attention had been captured by the parlormaid standing in the open doorway. "Mr. McLean," she announced.

Grace looked up in a panic, expecting to see Alistair in the doorway. Wondering how she could meet his eyes without revealing her shock and outrage.

Instead it was Gordon McLean who strolled into the parlor. "Hugh! I saw the carriage and wondered if it could be you returned home. How good to have you back among us."

While they exchanged greetings, Grace took the opportunity to get a grip on her reactions. She still couldn't fathom all she'd just learned: Alistair had known from the very beginning that she had a strange talent to view the past. Why hadn't he said so?

She saw her happiness come tumbling down around her like one of Janet's houses built of cards. Alistair had not had the time to persuade her, so he had secured her interest in the only way possible: by marrying her.

She saw it all now with brutal clarity: the ride into the country, the visit to the dovecote. Their being locked in overnight. All of it engineered with one end—to ensure that she would have no choice but to put her trust into his hands.

To think I believed it was a kindly Fate that brought us together!

And that his interest in her had taken on more depth and meaning in recent weeks.

It was a bitter draught to swallow.

Gordon came to her side and took her hand. "How pale you are, my dear. I hope you are not coming down with the headache?"

She managed a wilted smile. "No. No. It is nothing, I assure you."

Both men scrutinized her, then looked away. Her face flamed as she realized what they were thinking: they suspected that she might be with child.

Good God! It was possible. She was several days overdue in her monthly cycle. *Not now,* she thought in perfect wretchedness. *Please, God, not now!*

Since Meg returned, followed by the maid with a tray of refreshments, there was no time for her to dwell on it. A quarter hour of agony passed by while the other three made pleasant conversation and she struggled to put in a comment from time to time. At the first moment politeness allowed, she rose.

"After Hugh's journey and your long separation, you cannot wish to entertain visitors," she said over Meg's protests. "Janet and I only intended to deliver the kitten. We must be on our way back to Rossmor."

"And I, as well. You will want to be alone with your family," Gordon added. "We will catch up on our news soon enough."

"At least let Janet stay a while," Meg pleaded. "She and the boys are having a great time, trailing a string for the kitten to chase. Let her sup with us and I'll have the groom take her back in the carriage later."

Meanwhile, Hugh and I can leave the three of them in care of the maid, and slip away to spend some time alone together.

Grace understood the unspoken words in Meg's eyes as clearly as though she'd said them aloud. She agreed to let Janet stay to dine with them, as much for her sake as anyone's. She couldn't decide if she wanted to confront Alistair without delay, or take some time to gather her shattered thoughts. Grace slipped on her cloak.

"I'll go out and tell her of your kind invitation."

Janet's cousins were delighted to learn she would take her supper with them. Grace was detained in the garden longer than she'd intended, as Angus and Geordie had to show her the gleaming wagon their father had brought home as a gift to them, and when she and Meg went back through the house, Hugh Kinsale was no longer in the parlor. Grace was relieved. She set off toward Rossmor in a state of agitation. All her niggling doubts regarding her marriage had crystalized into one dismaying truth: Alistair's reasons for marrying her had not been altruistic. He had served his own motives, although Grace wasn't sure what they might be.

As she rode through the wooded glen alone, she had the strong feeling that she was being watched. Grace glanced over her shoulder at the vicarage. The curtain had been pulled aside, and she wondered if it was Hugh standing there, looking after her. He was astute enough to know he'd said something to distress her; but of course he had no idea of what was actually—horribly—wrong.

She spurred her mount into a fast trot, and almost lost her hat when a sharp branch hit the crown with a snap. Grace straightened it, feeling the tight pull of her hairpins against her scalp. The headache she'd denied was fast becoming a reality. Her temple throbbed and burned.

Thunder echoed across the loch. She looked off to the mountains and saw swift dark clouds scudding in from the northeast. She kicked her horse into a gallop and raced the storm home, and she never once looked over to Freya's Tower.

As she reached the stables, Grace felt something brush her temple and the corner of her eye, like tiny wings. A freckle-faced young groom ran out to catch her reins. "Och, madam, what has happened? There's blood on your face!"

She touched a hand to her temple and looked at her tan glove. The fingertips were red with blood. She stared at it dully.

"It's nothing. I scraped my head against a branch cutting through the woods."

"You'd best have Mrs. Finley take a look at it."

"I will," she said, and let him help her dismount.

She went into the house and up the staircase without passing anyone. She had no desire to speak with Alistair until she thought out exactly what she intended to say. But when she pulled her hat off, a dark spot on the crown caught her eye. Grace touched it and her finger went through the neat bullethole. There was another on the opposite side, larger and slightly ragged.

She swayed as her vision dimmed, and crumpled to the floor.

When Grace came to, she was in her bedchamber with the curtains drawn. There was a sticking plaster at her temple and Alistair sat in the chair beside her, holding her hand. For several seconds she couldn't remember how she'd gotten from the vicarage parlor to Rossmor.

"How did I get here?"

His hand gripped hers. "You've had an accident, Grace. A poacher on the moors. You were exceedingly fortunate! His shot went wild but merely grazed your temple."

Grace closed her eyes as it all came back to her in a flood of pain and hurt and blazing white anger. She didn't trust herself to speak.

McLean lifted her hand and kissed her fingers. "If I find the villain responsible for this, I swear that I'll flay him alive with my own two hands!"

"Yes," she said, pulling away as her eyes flashed open again. "I can imagine you might. After all your careful plans and the deceit of luring me here to Rossmor, it would be a shame if death prevented me from my unwitting participation in your research experiments!"

He went very still. His eyes were alert and intense. "I won't pretend to misunderstand you," he said quietly.

Grace realized in that moment something she had always known on an instinctive level: her husband was a very dangerous man.

Chapter Twenty-three

Grace propped herself up against the pillows although her temple throbbed with the effort. It was nothing compared to the ache of her breaking heart. "You don't deny it, then. You brought me here for one reason only—because you believe that I may have abilities that reach beyond the normal human senses.

"I deny your implications," he said fiercely. "My interest in you was piqued by your unusual abilities—yes, I guessed something of them from the start—but the relationship that developed between us has nothing to do with that."

"Naturally, I see it quite otherwise. You took me to the dovecote planning that we would be forced to spend the night there." Her voice shook. "I was a fool to believe any of it."

He reached for her hand but she snatched it away.

"I swear on my soul that it was an accident—although I can see from the set of your face that you will never believe it now. I should like to know who has poisoned your mind against me."

She pushed her loose hair back from her face. "No one has 'poisoned' my mind. I can draw my own conclusions."

"What has this to do with anything, Grace? Devil take it, I married you to save your reputation, yes. But I must tell you I was not at all averse to the idea. I was attracted to you from the very start for reasons that had nothing at all to do with my research. And since that time, my feelings for you have grown so much stronger that I haven't dared admit to myself how deeply I care for you. Until now."

"How convenient that you should only just discover it," she said dryly. The effort of remaining calm had her fingernails digging deep into her palms. Inside she was bleeding.

His skin was flushed with anger. "You are being unfair. Would you have come away with me in Rome, if I had asked you to travel to Scotland in order to take part in my experiments? Because that was my original intention."

"Somehow you guessed that I am one of those people you have sought for your research."

"Yes. I will not lie to you. I realized in the Forum that you were in some sort of trance state—and that whatever you were experiencing affected you profoundly. I also realized that you saw things which I did not on our visit and unscheduled overnight stay at the dovecote. But don't you see that only enhanced my interest in you?"

Grace struggled to understand. "You brought me here hoping I would see something, either on my own or during the course of the séance. What was it, Alistair? At least tell me that. Tell me what was so important that you felt you had to dupe me?"

"I had several reasons—the first and foremost that I felt I had brought you to the brink of ruin through no fault of yours—or mine—and that it was my obligation as a gentleman to see you suffered no harm from it.

"Secondly, you are an intelligent and well-educated woman, with excellent powers of observation. I merely wanted any impression you received of Rossmor to be spontaneous and true. Untainted by expectations of what you might see or discover. It is the first rule of good science to conduct an experiment under controlled conditions, so that the conclusions drawn will not be colored by other factors."

His explanation made a lot of sense, which only made Grace angrier. "So you tricked me in the name of science? How noble!"

"What is the difference in my thinking you had a talent that might be useful to me, or in your thinking that a husband with private means and a large estate would make a marriage even more convenient?"

"How *dare* you!" Her hand arced out toward his cheek but he caught it and held both her hands firmly.

"You forget that we were almost strangers and that what we had initially was a contractual obligation to one another, not a love match. But I swear to God, Grace, I love you with more passion than I ever knew existed between a man and a woman!"

"This revelation has come upon you quite suddenly," she exclaimed.

"Don't be a little fool. I discovered it while we were on our honeymoon. But you gave me no hint that I had roused anything in you but your passions. If you think back over the course of the past two months, neither have you spoken words of love to me."

She couldn't refute his argument. Hot color rose in her cheeks. "It is difficult for a woman to be the first to speak out, especially given the circumstances. You are a gentleman and even if you felt trapped into marriage, you would not have shown it. As to myself, I imagined that you were well aware of my sentiments."

"How could I be, my dear, if you never spoke them?"

Her blush grew rosier. "I expected that my ardent responses to your lovemaking would be proof enough that my affections were deeply engaged."

McLean stared at her, and then began to laugh. "Oh, my delightful innocent!" He lifted her hand and kissed her fingers. "I forget that you have been sheltered from the world in many ways. I assure you that love and passion do not always go hand in hand. We, my darling, are two of the fortunate ones."

He leaned toward her and she breathed in his light cologne and the dearly familiar, masculine scent of him. But when he reached out to her, she held him back. "I believe there is something more to your story. I should like to hear it now."

"The experiment itself."

"Yes." She wrapped her arms around her knees. "Tell me everything."

He hesitated, frowning. "I must go back a considerable way. It is hard for me to say this. It has to do with Finnula, who is not here to defend herself."

"I understand you. Gordon hinted that the two of you were unsuited to one another, and that all had not been well between you at the time of her death."

"He was off the mark. It wasn't our marriage that was the problem, but her mental state. I loved Finnula and would have done anything I could to help her. She had always been . . . fey, I suppose is the best word. She was a girl of quicksilver moods. In the last year of her life there was more darkness in them than light.

"Finnula had a weakness of the mind, and had also suffered from headaches and nightmares for some time. She thought that she was going mad. She claimed to have seen the Gray Lady. That the ghost told her she would die and take its place. I feared her mind was deteriorating at a rapid rate."

Grace lifted her head. "I have heard voices, too. I have seen things. Do you think I am mad, also?"

"No." Alistair dragged his hand through his rumpled hair. "Neither do you smash every mirror in the house, or set fire to the curtains in your bedchamber. And slash your wrists and write vulgar words in blood upon the walls."

"Dear God!" Grace heard the flat hopelessness in his voice, and the hard ring of truth.

"I took her to Edinburgh to consult the finest doctors but her mind grew more anxious and less able to recognize reality. When we returned her condition worsened. For several weeks she was so bizarre and violent she had to be kept under lock and key. I tried every new cure or drug that offered hope. I brought experts in disorders of the brain and personality to visit her here. Finally, through the use of an Indian herb and Max Wundt's suggested treatment, she seemed to improve dramatically. I was encouraged enough to think the cure was permanent."

Grace's heart ached for him. "And it was not?"

"The lull before the storm. One winter afternoon I had estate business to attend to with my manager. Elspeth had gone out for a drive and Janet had been feverish earlier. Finnula promised to remain with her. When my business was concluded I went up to see how my daughter was faring. Her bed was empty and there was no sign of Finnula. I went below and Braedon told me they were in the drawing room."

His face grew grave. "The doors to the terrace stood open. There were fresh footsteps in the snow. Two sets of them. I found Janet lying outside the Old Hall. She was so cold and white that I thought she was dead. But when I lifted her in my arms she moaned and my heart lifted with hope. Another half hour and it would have been too late."

"How fortunate that you found her!"

"There were many anxious hours before we knew if she would recover without losing any fingers or toes due to frostbite. Days when her fever raged and I feared that lung fever would carry her off."

"But how did she get out there alone in the first place?"

"I believe that Finnula left her alone in the drawing room and went out into the snow. Janet followed her—that was apparent from their tracks—but she was wearing only a thin nightgown. She succumbed to the terrible cold before she reached the Old Hall."

"I see. But where was Finnula? Why had she gone and left Janet alone?"

He looked away. "I didn't know or care at the time. I didn't even look for her—and that is what I must live with now. At the time my anger was so white-hot I didn't dare face her with it, knowing how fragile her state of mind was."

"I cannot blame you for your anger. It was natural under the circumstances."

His eyes met hers. "It was more than anger. It was a black rage. I was afraid that I would throttle her with my bare hands! The next morning she was found lying dead among the rocks and ice at the foot of Freya's Tower out of remorse."

His mouth thinned. "Other people put a different interpretation on it. Some claimed that she was pushed over the parapet by the Gray Lady; others that it was I who sent her plunging to her doom."

Grace frowned. "A terrible tragedy. But what does this have to do with your research? Did you hope to contact Finnula's restless spirit?"

"No. It is Janet who concerns me now. You know of her dreams. But you don't know the rest of it. She believes that she is visited by a ghost, just as her mother claimed to be. The ghost of the Gray Lady of Rossmor."

"I still don't understand."

His eyes were stricken. "It was the need to uncover the truth that drove me. I had to find out—for Janet's sake. Has my daughter inherited her mother's hysterical personality—and potentially, her madness? Or could it be that Janet has the second-sight and 'sees' things in the same way that you do?"

"And if there is no ghost?" Grace asked softly.

"Then I would sell everything I have and travel to the

ends of the earth, until I found the cure to save her."

"I see. That is why you wanted to bring me here. To help you discover whether Janet's dreams and visions have a basis in madness or if she too has the power to look into the past."

"Yes. Will you help me, my love?"

Her answer was slow in coming. "Like you, Alistair, I will do anything I can. For Janet's sake."

"I knew I could count on your forgiveness, once you learned the truth." He reached out for her hand, but Grace pulled sharply away.

"You have my understanding," she said quietly, "but not my forgiveness. There should be no such secrets between man and wife. And I would have helped you willingly, as now, had I known the truth from the beginning. But this has placed a wedge between us. Trust is as fragile as a butterfly's wing. I will not give you mine again until I am more sure of you."

McLean's face went white. "I love you, Grace. You must believe me when I tell you that."

She shook her head. "How can I?"

He leaned forward, taking her face between his hands. "Then I shall woo you again, until I've won you." He leaned down as if to kiss her lips. Grace's hands splayed across his chest, pushing him away.

"You won't earn my trust by seducing me again, but by proving yourself worthy of it. Until that time," she told him, "I will sleep alone."

He rose, biting back the curse that rose to his lips. She was right. He had brought this down upon himself. "Very well. I'll have my valet move my things down the hall to my old suite of rooms. There will be talk among the servants, you realize."

"Yes. I'll tell Cait it is only until I'm recovered from

today's events." She looked away. "After a while they will become used to it."

McLean stopped and turned in the doorway. His eyes burned like dark blue flames in his strained face. "There will be no need. I'll win you back, Grace. I swear it!"

Chapter Twenty-four

Grace was luring a bright-eyed kitten across the drawing room with a length of red yarn, when the Reverend Hugh Kinsale was announced. He came into the room, his face furrowed with concern. When he saw her up and about, he looked taken aback.

"My dear! I am relieved to see you in such fine fettle," he said, striding across the room. "But should you be exerting yourself so soon after yesterday's mishap?"

"Between you and Alistair, you would have me wrapped up in cotton wool!" Grace smiled. "Even Elspeth is playing nursemaid today, plying me with possets and powders and cups of broth. I assure you—as I have them—that I am perfectly recovered, except for the slightest headache."

"Excellent news! Meg will be happy to hear it." He removed a folded square of paper, and a small stoppered vial from his pocket. "She sends her love in this note, and this headache potion that is guaranteed to banish all symptoms. A teaspoon of this in a bracing cordial or cup of hot tea, and you'll be right as rain."

"How kind of her! I wish she had come with you."

"We didn't know if you would be up to a visit. I have come by to consult your husband on a matter of business and promised to look in on you."

Grace thanked him. "I would enjoy her company greatly.

Please ask her to bring Angus and Geordie, as well. Janet found some of Meg's old toys while she was helping Mrs. Finley turn out the nursery cupboards, and we thought the boys would enjoy having them."

The butler returned with refreshments, and a book in a red leather slipcase. "Here is the volume you requested, madam."

"Thank you, Braedon." She took the book and invited Hugh to sit beside her. "Lady Helena sent this to me. I set it aside to peruse and then forgot all about it until a few minutes ago."

"Then let us have a cordial while you examine it," Hugh suggested. She let him pour a dollop of Meg's headache remedy into hers, then removed the book from its slipcase.

"Oh! *The Churches of Rome: An Illustrated Guide to Their History and Architecture.* I do hope it has an illustration of San Marcello al Corso, where Alistair and I were wed. It had the most amazing frescoes."

"I should like to see it." He sipped his drink and watched her while she found the index and went down it quickly. "Page forty-three," she said in triumph. But when she turned to the illustration it was totally unfamiliar to her. "How disappointing; this isn't it."

"But the caption," Hugh pointed out, "claims that it is. The name is very unusual—Saint Marcellus in the Thicket."

"Perhaps there is another of the same designation dedicated to him."

The preacher shook his head. "I don't believe that is possible within the same diocese. Perhaps you have confused the name. There are so many saints in the Church of Rome."

Grace laughed. "Lady Helena said something similar to me in Rome—but my Italian is quite good, I assure you. And you must allow that any woman would recall the name of the church in which she was wed. But this is clearly not the church where Alistair and I were married. It was much more intimate, and the frescoes were much more beautiful. Such gorgeous colors, enhanced with gold leaf."

She turned the page. "Ah! Here it is." She looked at the caption. "Stella Maris. Star of the Sea. How odd! They must have reversed the titles on the two illustrations."

Hugh Kinsale bent closer to the page. "But look—'Stella Maris' is written in the letters above the altar. And there in the fresco above the altar is the Virgin Mary as the Star of the Sea." He pointed to the footnote. "The church was deconsecrated in 1856. It is under renovation as a museum, to house the collection of Antonio Frascati, brother of Count Lorenzo Borromini."

Grace was dumbfounded. "But . . . I don't understand. It says quite clearly on our marriage certificate that the officiating priest was Brother Antonio and the church was San Marcello Al Corso."

She saw that he was staring at her. "What is it?"

The cleric rubbed a hand along his jaw. "He was not perhaps called *Padre* Frascati?"

"No. I am certain of it." She put her hand on Hugh's sleeve and lowered her voice. "Please! You must tell me what is wrong!"

"A brother is not a priest, but a layman," Hugh blurted out. "He cannot officiate at a marriage."

Grace felt the blood drain from her cheeks. "Then I have made a mistake," she said slowly. *A terrible mistake.*

She had looked at her marriage lines a hundred times. Or rather, what she had thought of as her marriage lines. They must be as false as the "priest" who had presided over the ceremony. As false as the man she called her husband had proven to be. Everything he'd told her yesterday—no, everything he'd told her from the very beginning, was nothing but a web of lies. And like a foolish dragonfly, she'd repeatedly stumbled into it, enmeshing herself in his plans.

She fought for control as her world crumbled around her.

"My dear Grace! You have gone white as flour. Let me ring for your maid."

"No, no! It is just a passing dizzyness," she protested. "I . . . I am quite all right."

Grace cocked her head, then jumped up so quickly the room spun. Hugh was there to grasp her arm. "Steady now! Really, Grace, you must go up to your room and rest."

She shook her head. "If I am not mistaken, that is Lady Helena Ainsley arriving from the train station in Inverness."

She went to the window and looked out in dismay. There would be no quick escape to her room now. A traveling carriage was pulled up in front of the door, with a second luggage vehicle holding an extremely elegant lady's maid and more luggage than she and Alistair both had taken along on their honeymoon. The groom opened the door and Lady Helena descended in an aubergine ensemble straight from the House of Worth.

To Grace's great surprise, a second woman exited the vehicle. The newcomer's head was averted, but she was stylishly dressed in a traveling outfit of bronze wool, with a matching hat perched upon her blond hair. She hadn't the faintest idea as to whom the woman might be.

A moment later the door opened and Braedon entered.

"Lady Helena Ainsley and Mrs. Dearing," he announced into the sudden silence.

The peeress swanned into the drawing room with the medium behind her. "I ran into Mrs. Dearing at the train station, and invited her to join me in the carriage. You do not mind to have two guests descend upon you a little early?"

Grace took her hands in hers. "Of course not! We are delighted to have you both with us." And she was. Anything to prove an added distraction. "Braedon, inform Mr. McLean that our guests have arrived, and have Mrs. Finley send in refreshments."

"Of course, madam." He bowed out of the drawing room

as Grace greeted Mrs. Dearing. "I understand we are to have a séance while you are with us. I hope you will not find it too exhausting."

The medium's blue eyes searched hers. "Not at all, my dear Mrs. McLean. I admit I am most eager to conduct it as soon as possible."

"Excellent," Lady Helena proclaimed.

"I am also looking forward to the seance. Your reputation is well known to me, Mrs. Dearing," said Hugh.

"You are very kind," the medium said with a small smile. "I am afraid that our host is not convinced of my talents," she said. "I hope to win him over during my stay."

Grace's mind was in utter turmoil. *Alistair deceived me. Dear God, what am I to do?* Her good breeding came to the rescue. "It is a long journey from the train station to Rossmor. Let me take you up to your rooms so that you might refresh yourselves and rest before dinner."

Lady Helena waved her hand airily. "I am sure Mrs. Dearing would be glad of a rest. You must take her up straightaway, Grace. However, I wish to visit with Hugh a while longer."

"Of course. Mrs. Dearing?"

"I should like nothing better than a cup of tea and a nap," the unexpected guest confessed.

Grace led her up to the Gold Bedchamber, which was in the medieval wing of the house. She was still unsteady on her feet but managed her duties as hostess well enough. Mrs. Dearing took in the latticed windows, the high carved bed with its gold and crimson hangings, and the gilded mirror over the fireplace with approval.

"Charming. Quite charming. And very atmospheric! I am so glad I have come to Rossmor, Mrs. McLean."

"As are we to receive you," Grace murmured. She pulled aside a curtain to reveal a tastefully furnished dressing area. "And here is the bell cord, should you require anything.

I'll ring for one of the maids to bring water and help you out of your traveling garments."

"In a moment. But first I should like a word with you in private." The medium shut the door and all her feigned weariness was gone. She turned to Grace briskly. "Be careful to whom you give your trust," she said. "I have received a message for you from beyond the veil. You are in very great danger!"

"Danger?" Grace was taken aback. "From whom?"

"I am not certain, so I will say no more at the moment."

"Perhaps you are a bit late with your warning." Grace gave a shaky laugh. "It was yesterday that I was grazed by a poacher's bullet."

Mrs. Dearing shook her head. "There is worse to come."

Impatience burned in Grace's breast, masking the fear. "If you have something specific to tell me, I would appreciate it. However, I am not interested in vague mumbo-jumbo."

"That is a very strange thing for you to say, Mrs. McLean, when you and I share something in common. Yes," she went on, as Grace's eyes widened. "I know that you are, like myself, a 'sensitive.' Your gift is raw and untrained, but it is very strong. Like a sword, it can cut both ways. If you do not learn to harness it sufficiently, you could suffer great harm."

Grace took a deep breath, trying to ease the hammering of her heart. "I see. And this is the danger of which you speak?"

"No, my dear. You are in peril from forces around you. She says that she has been trying to warn you and that you have sensed her presence on several occasions."

"She?" Grace asked the question, although she already knew the answer. "Who is it who has told you this?"

Mrs. Dearing sighed. "A woman who went over to the other side before her time. She claims that she was once—as you are now—mistress of Rossmor. Her name is Finnula."

Chapter Twenty-five

The maid came in response to Grace's tug on the bellpull, and she left Mrs. Dearing to her ministrations. On the way back she saw the door to the estate room was ajar. McLean looked up as she entered. "My dear, you should be resting."

"We have guests," she said. "Hugh Kinsale is in the drawing room with Lady Helena—and Mrs. Dearing is upstairs recruiting her strength after the journey."

"What do you think of her?"

"I have not come to discuss Mrs. Dearing," Grace said coldly. "I have come to tell you that I am leaving you."

He stared at her. "What nonsense is this?"

"What nonsense was that in Rome?" she demanded. "A deconsecrated church, a false priest, and a certificate of a sham marriage!"

He didn't deny it. His blue eyes regarded her warily, and she sensed his mind racing, wondering the best way to handle the situation.

This was his worst nightmare come true. McLean knew he couldn't bluff his way out of it. "Perhaps it is best that everything is out in the open. I am sorry that you have found out in this way. Indeed, I had hoped you never would."

The moment the words were out he wished that he could

call them back. They were rusted nails in the coffin of his hopes.

Grace felt ill. She realized that, on some level, she had hoped he would not only deny everything, but produce evidence to convince her otherwise. The pain of his betrayal was so overwhelming she could scarcely bear up beneath its weight.

"My God, Grace! Don't look at me as if I were a monster! I did what I had to do to save your reputation. If we could have been married in Rome in time, I would have moved heaven and earth to do it. It was impossible under the circumstances. That is why I'd spoken to you of repeating our vows before Hugh. We would have been properly married and you none the wiser for it."

"Oh, I am wise now," she said bitterly.

He came around the desk. "We'll say our vows before Hugh, I swear it! Tomorrow, if you like, and make our union legal in the eyes of God and the law. But vows or no, Grace, you are my wife!"

"I thought I was," she whispered. "But you made me your *whore!*"

He went white. "No! I love you, Grace. I swear it! I would do anything if we could go back in time and begin anew . . ."

"Ah, so would I!" she cried, turning away. "Anything that would have kept me from such folly. I wish I had never met you!"

"Wait! You cannot leave without hearing what I have to say. You owe me at least that."

Fury poured through her. "Don't," she said. "I cannot bear it. I have listened to enough of your lies. I owe you nothing! Everything I thought you gave me was an illusion. You, who took me out to the island in the loch, and preached to me of loyalty! This was the ultimate betrayal. A sham marriage, a travesty of love!"

He reached out and caught her wrists in his iron grip.

She wrenched her hands away. "Don't touch me! Don't ever touch me again!"

"Grace!"

"I will stay until the séance. For Janet's sake. You will never see me again."

She ran from the room as if fleeing a plague. He stood there, haggard and worn, but made no attempt to follow her. He knew that there was nothing he could ever do or say to win her back.

Grace went back to her room in a daze. She locked the door, then went to the one leading into the sitting room and slid that bolt home, too. If she had the strength she would have begun packing the few things she intended to take with her, but she couldn't even attempt it. A strange lassitude had come over her and the room looked—*strange.*

The walls seemed to move in and out with her heartbeat. *Almost,* she thought, *as if they are breathing!*

A moment later she was stumbling toward the basin, where she was horribly ill. She retched until she brought up nothing but bitter bile. Once it was over with, she felt better. After rinsing her mouth and washing her face, she made her way to the bed and laid down upon the quilt and closed her eyes.

Her lids were so heavy she couldn't lift them. Not when she heard the voice whisper her name or felt cool fingers brush lightly over her forehead. So lightly that it might have been nothing but her imagination.

Or perhaps a bit of trailing mist.

Chapter Twenty-six

Dinner was an informal and extremely strained affair. Meg and Gordon and Lady Helena tried to carry on the conversation over the medallions of pheasant and rack of lamb, with scant help from the rest. Mrs. Dearing was preoccupied, Hugh distressed. McLean and Grace were like mannequins, moving and speaking and all of it just the pulling of strings.

She could scarcely look at him. The man she had grown to love and trust, who had betrayed her so cruelly. The man who knew every inch of her body so intimately, and so wantonly.

It was difficult to meet the others' eyes as well—as if she feared they would see "harlot" written in scarlet letters across her forehead. Hugh knew or guessed enough, that was evident. He hadn't shared his discovery with either Meg or Lady Helena. It was plain that they were both perplexed. She wondered if she should write a note to Meg before she left Rossmor, explaining her reasons, and decided it was better not to attempt it. What could she say? Nothing would make it right.

Janet was another matter. Grace had felt such a pang when the girl had kissed her good-night, knowing they would soon be parted. Heaven only knew what excuse Alistair would make up to explain her departure to his daughter. *No doubt he will come up with some plausible lie.* It broke her heart to think of it.

After the dessert course was removed, Grace rose and led the ladies from the room. Braedon hovered outside the drawing room to intercept them. "If it pleases you, madam, Mr. McLean has arranged for a fire to be lit in the solar. We are instructed to bring the tea cart there later."

Lady Helena clapped her hands. "How delightful! I love the solar, and it is so rarely used for entertaining."

Grace was a little startled but led her guests through to the older wing. The lamps had been lit in the Old Hall and they went up the stairs, past the gallery, and into the cozy room. Flames leapt high in the hearth, chasing away the evening chill. She saw that extra chairs had been brought in and set around the table where Janet liked to play at building her card houses.

Mrs. Dearing smiled. "I see your husband is wasting no time in putting my talents to the test, Mrs. McLean."

"What do you mean?"

Lady Helena laughed. "My dear Grace, it appears we are going to have a séance!"

He is as anxious to be rid of me as I am to go, Grace thought. She strolled around the room, with its ancient tapestries and old court cupboard. *Strange to think that this is the last time I shall ever be in this room.*

Lady Helena did a turn about the chamber. "How easy it is to imagine that we are back in time three hundred years."

The medium nodded but was rather distracted. "What is that lovely scent?" she asked finally. "I smell lavender and—I think—rose. But what is the other fragrance blended with it?"

At first Grace didn't smell anything but the woodsmoke on the hearth. Then it grew around her like a cloud of mist and she recognized it. It was the scent that accompanied the voice and the visions. Finnula's potpourri. She shivered.

It was Meg who answered. "It is bergamot," she said slowly. "It has been many years since I've smelt it, but it is unmistakable. I have never cared for the combination, but Finnula used it for her own perfume and sachets. She claimed to have re-created it from an old recipe handed down from Freya."

"Finnula had a talent for such things," Lady Helena remarked. "I remember that Gordon used to bring her all sorts of scented oils and exotic herbs for her potpourri and tonics, and clever glass bottles from Egypt and India. Alas, I never had the knack for mixing them. Hers were light and elegant, while mine always came out smelling like a chemist's shop—or worse. Once I mixed too much civet and we had to air the stillroom out for days."

The men arrived, fresh from a round of port. "I hear we are to have a séance tonight," said Hugh.

"Bah!" Gordon laughed. "Table-tapping and tipping! It is all done with accomplices and cymbals sewn to . . . ah, one's clothing."

"You needn't be afraid to say 'garters' in our presence," Helena chided. "We are not children. And I doubt if any of us will have accomplices here. Most especially Mrs. Dearing, who is the only one of us who is not related in some way."

Mrs. Dearing smiled. "Very graciously said, Lady Helena. Thank you."

McLean herded them over to the table. "Let us try our luck at raising the spirits," he said. "Then you may ask them if *they* have cymbals on their garters."

But Gordon had drawn Elspeth away from the others. "Something is wrong between Alistair and Grace."

"Nonsense!"

"Earlier today I dropped by to speak with Alistair. They were in the estate room, quarreling rather violently."

Elspeth looked shocked. "I didn't know you were the sort of person to listen at keyholes, Gordon!"

"You know damned well that I am not. A deaf man would have heard the raised voices. I couldn't tell what they were saying, but Grace fled the room looking distraught." He rubbed his jaw. "And one of the servants told me that he has moved out of their room."

"Servants' gossip!" Elspeth's voice rang with disdain. "Grace was almost shot by a poacher yesterday as she rode home from the vicarage. It was a very near thing. Alistair slept in another room out of consideration for her rest."

Gordon smiled and gave a gusty sigh of relief. "I hadn't heard. That explains it, then. But the valet said he'd taken all his belongings with him, and I jumped to the conclusion that they were estranged. I couldn't imagine any other reason for him to do so."

Lights of excitement danced in Elspeth's eyes. "Can't you? I can think of one very good reason. Alistair has always wanted a houseful of children, and you know that poor Finnula suffered several miscarriages. Perhaps Grace is in an interesting condition." She smiled happily. "Time will tell if I am right or not."

"Right about what?" Hugh had come up beside them.

"Elspeth thinks there may soon be the announcement that a new little McLean is coming into the world."

"Well, well, well!" Hugh glanced back at Grace. "I hadn't even considered the possibility."

Lady Helena rose from her chair and went to them. "You are slippery as eels. Everytime we try to get everyone seated, someone slips away." She tucked one arm through Gordon's and the other through Hugh's. "Now you have no choice but to come with me, or be excessively rude!"

Everyone laughed and they went to take up their places at the table.

McLean was edgy. He didn't want anything to go wrong, and tried to work it so Grace was at his right side. She eluded him, and took up her place almost opposite, with Hugh on one side and Mrs. Dearing on the other.

McLean was displeased, but took Lady Helena on his right with Gordon beside her, and Meg on his left.

"Do we turn out the lights and hold hands?" Lady Helena asked.

"That is the accepted mode," Mrs. Dearing replied.

"Then we will link hands first," McLean announced, "so there is no question of anyone holding a stuffed glove in the darkness. I will have Braedon put out the lamps before he leaves."

A expectant silence fell over the little group as they held hands. Braedon tiptoed around the room. One by one the lamps were snuffed. The only light was the red-gold glow from the hearth, but even the flames had been banked. At Mrs. Dearing's request a screen was placed in front of it.

"I do not know if my guide will come tonight," she announced. "However, even should he not make an appearance, I will still receive messages from the spirit world. Open your minds, and close your eyes . . ."

Grace closed her eyes with the others, then peeked out beneath her lashes. The chamber was very dark. She could barely discern the outlines of the people sitting around the circular table.

"Now we will remain silent," Mrs. Dearing said, "while I summon my guide. Do not break the contact except under the most dire circumstances! I have no desire to be left wandering about an astral plane, with no way of returning." After a good deal of shifting about and clearing of throats, the medium began.

"There are two spirits here," she said in a voice that seemed somehow altered. "Both women. One is the guardian spirit of this place. She cannot see us nor we, her. The spirit is benevolent. The other one is trying to communicate. I can feel her trying to enter my body. Mr. Kinsale . . . You must play the part of interlocutor . . ."

Mrs. Dearing's voice trailed off.

Grace could hear the susurrus of her blood moving in

her veins and arteries. It grew from the rustling of silk and satin to the loud beating of wings, then fell into profound silence.

"Who is there?" Hugh asked firmly. "Will you speak to us?"

There was only rustling silence and the crackle of the fire. "Who are you?" he asked again. "Speak! I command you. What is it you wish to tell us?"

The answer came low and full. "Murder . . ."

"What is your name?"

There was no answer. "I command you to speak your name," Hugh said.

Lady Helena leaned forward. "Ask it if Freya . . ."

The voice that spoke was soft, yet echoing. *"I am not Freya, although she is here among us . . . I am Finnula!"*

"Finnula! Why are you here?" McLean's voice was ragged. "What is it you want of us?"

"Justice!"

A tremor ran through the linked hands but no one let go. "Justice for what?" Lady Helena asked breathlessly.

The voice was cool and distant, but filled with arcane power. *"For my death. I did not jump from Freya's Tower . . . He lifted me over the parapet, dashed me to the rocks below . . .*

"Seek your vengeance. Name your murderer!" Hugh exclaimed.

"Vengeance . . . yes. He is here among you tonight . . ."

There was a sharp rap and the table lifted, then twisted violently sideways. A woman screamed. Chairs scraped back on the ancient floor and there was a good deal of shouting and confusion. Someone hurried to light the lamps.

When they were lit, only two people were still seated at the table: Mrs. Dearing was slumped forward, her head resting on her arms. Grace was rigid, her eyes staring, and it was from her lips that the voice of Finulla was issuing.

"I will tell you his name that you may bring him to justice. It was . . ."

The table took a big jump sideways and tipped over. McLean grabbed Grace and lifted her out of the way. He carried her to the settee and knelt beside her.

"Grace! Grace, wake up, my love!"

She came to slowly. Her head seemed filled with fog. Meg and Elspeth leaned over her anxiously, while Lady Helena issued orders to Hugh and Gordon. "Gordon, ring for Braedon and Mrs. Finley."

"What . . . what has happened?" Grace asked dazedly. "Why are we in the solar?"

"We were conducting a séance, darling. You fell into a trance state," McLean said. "I thought it was a trick, that Mrs. Dearing was pretending that she'd been taken over by a spirit from beyond."

"Then—was it trickery or was it real? Did she contact someone from beyond the veil?"

He held her hands tightly in his. "Finnula spoke to us," he said gravely. "Her voice was unmistakable. But she did not speak through Mrs. Dearing, love. She spoke through you."

Meg stood up. "Where is Mrs. Dearing? She seems to have vanished!"

It was only then, that Hugh spied the medium on the floor between the table and the wall. "She appears to have fainted!"

Lady Helena bent over the woman, saw the thick wet blood that mingled freely with Mrs. Dearing's pale hair, and straightened up with a most inelegant shriek.

"Mrs. Dearing is injured! Send for the surgeon down in the village."

"Better yet," Gordon said, "I'll fetch him myself. My new team can cover the ground twice as quickly."

But McLean had left Grace's side to kneel beside the medium. He placed his fingers over the pulse spot at her throat. "I am afraid there is no need for the surgeon. She's dead."

Chapter Twenty-seven

It was a subdued party that sat in the drawing room as the clock struck eleven. Grace was stunned, Meg in tears, and Lady Helena, for once, silenced. Hugh sat beside his wife, holding her hand.

"She must have slipped and hit her head on that marble statue during the commotion," he said for the fifth time.

"That poor woman, come all this way to suffer such a tragedy!" Elspeth said.

They heard carriage wheels on the drive, and Braedon entered solemnly to announce that the vicarage carriage was ready, and Mr. Gordon McLean's, as well.

"I don't feel that I should leave you," Meg said.

"Nonsense," Lady Helena said, regaining her assertiveness. "You need to be under your own roof with your children tonight."

Hugh led his wife out. "If you need anything, you only have to send for me and I shall come, no matter the hour."

Grace nodded. "Thank you. I shall let you know what the arrangments are tomorrow."

She escorted them to the drawing room door. "Where is Gordon?"

"Off conferring with Alistair, I believe. I'll go and see what is keeping them."

She went up the staircase toward the small bedroom

where Mrs. Dearing had been laid out. Gordon McLean came along the corridor to join her. "Excellent timing," he said. "I was just coming in search of you. Janet had a terrible nightmare. The maid left her to fetch a glass of warm milk—and when she came back, Janet was gone!"

"Rouse the servants! We'll search the house . . ."

"Calm down. Alistair has already given the orders. You had best go back to your guests."

"No, I must help find her. Poor child, she'll be frightened to death."

The words had an ominous chill after the evening's events.

"Then I'll go with you."

"Look!" Grace pointed to where a tapestry billowed in the draft. "The door to the medieval wing is open. She must have gone there. When she's upset, she goes to the solar . . ."

They raced along the corridor and into the gallery above the Great Hall. Grace couldn't shake the uncanny sensation of being followed. It didn't take long to figure out where the girl was headed. The door to Freya's Tower stood open and an icy draft swirled through the air.

"Oh, how cold it is here," Grace gasped. She felt as if she'd been plunged into a vast pool of ice. The warmth was sucked from her very bones, and she found her limbs responding awkwardly when she needed to be swift and sure.

"It is the shock that makes you feel the cold so," Gordon told her. "Stay here where it's safe and warm. I'll find Janet if she's up here, and bring her down!" He vanished into the ascending darkness.

Grace hesitated.

Grace.

"Yes?" She glanced over her shoulder, thinking Elspeth had called her. There was nothing behind her but shadows. She couldn't bear to stand waiting to know if Janet had gone up to the ramparts, and followed Gordon. She could hear his footsteps echoing above.

Grace. Go back!

She whirled around. Still nothing. *It is my imagination,* she told herself. But with every step the sensation that she was not wanted here grew stronger.

"I see her!" Gordon called out. "By the battlements. No, Janet! No!"

Grace raced up the last of the circular steps after him. At the top of the stairs the open door showed a rectangle of stars half-obscured by mist. As she approached it, the mist thickened. Coalesced into a moving, luminous fog. A woman formed of light, the details of her garments barely discernible. Only enough to show that it was not a flowing gown she wore, but a winding sheet.

The shrouded figure blocked the way, and Grace was almost paralyzed with terror. *Go back! Grace . . .*

"No!"

A high-pitched scream from beyond the door galvanized her. Gathering her courage, Grace forced her way through the luminous mass and came out onto the top of Freya's Tower.

Gordon stood near the edge of the battlements, his hands reaching out toward Janet. Grace could see the fabric of her white nightgown reflecting the starlight. But when she arrived at the spot there was no sign of Janet. A piece of white cloth fluttered in the breeze.

"Why, it's nothing but a bit of lace curtain . . . Why on earth would anyone put it here?"

"I did," Gordon said. "To lure you up here."

"But . . . why?"

"It is nothing personal, my dear. I am quite fond of you. But I find myself in dire financial straits, and there is only one way out of it. Someone must die—and I really would rather it isn't me."

Grace bit her lip. He looked the same except for his eyes.

They were the eyes of a madman. "What have you done with Janet?"

"Nothing that will harm her. She is safe enough, drugged and sleeping in one of the empty guest rooms. Don't worry, I was careful not to give her too much. She'll be fine in the morning after a good night's sleep."

Grace whirled on him. "What? Are you insane?"

Alistair stepped between them. "I am afraid that he is. Insane with jealousy! He has always coveted Rossmor. Until tonight I didn't realize that he wanted it badly enough to commit murder—again! It was you who aggravated Finnula's mental problems, whispering through the old speaking tubes your father put in. Putting drugs in her tonics. It was you who lured her up to the tower—and pushed her over. What was the rest of your plan?"

"I really underestimated the power of your reputation," Gordon replied suavely. "I expected that you would be arrested and hanged for her murder. And then little Janet and her fortune would be in my hands. I didn't mean for her to become ill, you know. I'm very fond of her."

Alistair had been moving closer as he listened. Suddenly he stepped in front of Grace. "Run! Head for the other turret!"

"It's locked from the inside," Gordon said, pulling a dueling pistol from his pocket. "This is loaded and on a hair trigger. From your own gunroom, Alistair. Don't try anything foolish. You might get hurt."

"I don't imagine either of us is intended to get down from here alive in any case."

"You were always quick-witted, nephew. Perhaps you think that you know everything?"

McLean edged slowly away from Grace. "I know that you are deeply in debt. I know that you were always upset that Rossmor and all its lovely collections and lands came to me. And that my mother's uncle left me his fortune from his inventions, as well."

"It is highly unfair that you should have both. You've had them quite long enough. I had only intended to dispose of your bride tonight, but this strange affair of your marriage—or shall I say non-marriage—gives me the perfect excuse to accelerate my plans. How distraught I shall be at your deaths. Murder and suicide," he said calmly. "The only quandary is which of you should be which?"

"And what of my daughter?" McLean said raggedly. "How do you intend to dispose of her?"

"You forget. Janet doesn't come into her majority until the age of twenty-five, according to your will—and I am named her trustee in it. That gives me sufficient time to bring myself about."

McLean regarded him stonily. "And what then? Will you dispose of her as you did her mother?"

"So you have guessed that, too." He shook his head. "I wanted no more heirs to Rossmor clouding my future. I have no children of my own, other than a natural son who emigrated to Canada—a most expensive and unsatisfactory lad! He has been a drain on my purse. On the other hand, I have always been exceedingly fond of Janet. If I succeed in putting my affairs in good order, there might be no need to ever consider an act which I would find extremely distressful."

"Noble of you!" Grace snapped.

Gordon rounded on her. "You may be as sarcastic as you like, my dear, but it will not be for long. The rain will fall soon—and so will you! Your body will be found upon the rocks at the foot of the tower. Just like Finnula. But this time there will be no doubt in anyone's mind of Alistair's guilt in either case."

She fought against the sickening sensation his words wrought in her. "You're mad. There is no way you can throw me off and place the blame upon my husband—and then dispose of him, too."

"Can't I?"

"He is younger and stronger than you," Grace said. "You cannot hope to throw him over the tower as easily."

"Alistair," Gordon pronounced airily, "will kill himself in remorse after your battered body lies bleeding upon on the rocks."

"He would never do that!"

"Perhaps not in actuality. But I assure you that people will be convinced that he did." Gordon smiled. "Especially when he is found with a bullet through his head—and his gun beside him."

Alistair laughed. "It won't happen that way. I will distract him, Grace, while you run back the way we came. I can hold him that long."

Gordon was enraged. "You fool! What is to prevent me from shooting you and her both!"

In the moonlight Alistair's face was a silver mask, his eyes gleaming diamonds. "The fact that a dueling pistol has only one shot in it!"

He launched himself at the other man. "Run, Grace!"

She was too stunned to move for a few vital seconds. A shot rang out. "No! *Alistair!*" He fell heavily against the parapet and Gordon lunged toward him. McLean managed to roll and throw the other man off, but the odds were against him, wounded as he was. His shoulder gleamed wetly in the starlight.

Instead of running for the door, she ran toward the two figures grappling against the ramparts. She looked around for the stout stick that normally propped the heavy door open. It had grown very dark as the clouds moved in, but the moon suddenly revealed itself in a wash of pale light.

The stick lay to one side. Grace grabbed it up in two hands, and entered the fray. She would never know for sure if Alistair could have saved himself. He had Gordon by the throat, but the older man had the advantage—blood drenched the side of Alistair's shirt.

Without stopping to think, Grace lifted the heavy piece

of wood and swung it two-handed, like a warrior queen wielding a battle sword. The whirling blackthorn stick hit Gordon's shoulder and the side of his face with a sickening thud just as McLean lurched to his feet. He grasped at his uncle's arm as the older man's body crumpled against the parapet.

It was all so fast she could never recall exactly what happened next. One moment there were three of them upon the ramparts of Rossmor, the next only two. Gordon McLean had tumbled backward over the edge of the tower, his jacket billowing out like the wings of a great black bird as he fell to the rocks below.

Braedon came running up onto the battlements, with Hugh and several of the menservants. They were met by a shocking sight: Grace kneeling in a pool of spreading dark liquid, beside McLean's still form.

Hugh ran to them. "What in God's name has happened here?"

"There has been an accident," she said shakily. She knelt beside Alistair's still form. She knew then that she loved him with an undying passion. He had done what he had done to save his daughter. And he had risked his life—or even rendered it up—to save her.

She could no longer doubt his love.

"But where is Gordon?" Lady Helena exclaimed.

"He has fallen from the tower," Grace answered.

"Great heavens. He'll never have survived the fall!"

"No. He has gone the route he intended for me."

Grace took charge. "Braedon, have Mrs. Finley meet us in the master chamber with bandages and hot water. Hugh, help Braedon carry Alistair to our bedchamber."

Alistair opened his eyes and looked up at her. "Don't leave me, Grace."

She cradled his head against her breast. "I never will, my darling. I swear it."

"I shall hold you to your promise," he said with a weak smile, and passed out in her arms.

Epilogue

Meg and the twins sat at one end of the drawing room at Rossmor, working a wooden puzzle with Janet. Beyond the open terrace doors, the glen was in bloom, and across the room Grace reclined on the sofa with an open book on her lap, watching Elspeth read her mail.

Grace couldn't stand it any longer: "I hope that Count Borromini is well?"

"Quite well," Elspeth said, and kept reading. But two spots of high color rose on her cheeks.

Grace and Meg exchanged glances. Count Borromini had joined them the day following the double tragedy at Rossmor, and had stayed on to comfort them. He and Elspeth had struck up a great friendship over the course of his stay. Ever since, letters had been traveling back and forth between Rossmor and London, where the count had taken a large house just outside London, much to the surprise of his relations in Rome.

Meg smiled. "I wonder how long he intends to remain in England?"

Elspeth's blush deepened. "At least to the end of June. He intends to invite us all to be his guests after Easter Week. Do you think Alistair would consent to go?"

He came in through the terrace doors. "Go where?"

"To London at month's end, as the guests of Count Borromini."

"Good Lord! Lorenzo knows how I hate leaving Rossmor at this time of year!"

Elspeth's gasp of dismay made him laugh. "I am only teasing you, my dear cousin. He has already written to me, inviting us to stay a few weeks with him. I think it would be very good for all of us. I know your aversion to London, however, so you need not accompany us if you don't wish to do so, Elspeth."

Her face went from red to white. Then McLean took pity on her. "I am teasing you again, Elspeth. Grace and I have every intention of accepting his kind offer." His smile flashed, tinged with affection and a touch of mischief. "After all, we would not want to blight your chances of becoming a countess."

Elspeth rose with great dignity and opened her mouth to make a cutting retort. Instead she hesitated and blushed again. "I . . . I do think he is inclined to favor my company," she said awkwardly, sounding like a young girl in the throes of her first love. "However, only a fool would read anything into it!"

"My dear Elspeth," McLean said, "I am no fool. The man is head over heels. If he doesn't come up to scratch, I shall horsewhip him through Trafalgar Square!"

It was even odds as to whether Elspeth would laugh or stalk off in a temper. "Leave her alone, Alistair," Grace said. "She has no need of you to champion her." Meg exchanged another look with Grace and her brother. Elspeth kept her own counsel, but they both believed that there would be an announcement, in the very near future, that she was going to become the Countess Borromini. Grace realized that she would miss her dreadfully. *What a difference a few months can make!*

Alistair came over to his wife and kissed her cheek. "Have you told Janet and Meg's monsters the news?"

"Your father and I wish very much that we could have had you and the rest of the family with us in Rome. Since you were not, we are going to renew our vows at St. Declan's at the end of the month."

"Will it be like a wedding?"

McLean smiled at Grace, then kissed his daughter. "Exactly so, my darling girl. Now that our six months of mourning is over, we will do it up in style. And you and Angus and Geordie will all be members of the wedding party."

Janet laughed and clapped her hands in excitement. "Angus and Geordie will be our ring-bearers," Grace explained as the twins listened eagerly, "and each will carry a pillow with one of the rings down the aisle for us to exchange during the vows."

"If they don't stick them in their ears, or drop them down a drain, or lose them outside the church," Alistair interjected.

Everyone laughed. Grace saw the look of excited expectancy on Janet's face. "And you shall be the flower girl," she told Janet. "Elspeth is making you a dress of white silk trimmed with silver embroidery and blue ribbons, to match your eyes. And you shall have a chaplet of matching silk flowers on your hair, and a posy in a silver holder."

Janet laughed and clapped her hands. "And will there be a party after, with dancing in the Old Hall, and all the neighbors and servants in attendance?"

"If you wish," Grace told her, smiling. "And you may stay up until midnight if you like."

Janet threw her arms around Grace. "Oh, thank you, Mama!"

It was the first time Janet had ever called her that, and Grace's eyes sparkled with happy tears. McLean came to their side and kissed them both. "With apologies to Meg, but I shall have the most beautiful ladies of all at my side."

His eyes met Grace's. "Always and ever," she said. They

had started anew from that horrible night in the tower. Now the foundation of their marriage would be based on love and truth. And loyalty.

McLean turned to answer a question from one of the twins and Janet danced away to play with the kitten again.

The sunshine grew brighter on the far side of the room, where Grace had ordered Finnula's portrait to be put back in its original place. She glanced up at it as the light grew to an almost blinding brilliance that seemed to sparkle as if it were filled with tiny, glowing stars.

No one else seemed to notice anything. Grace looked at Finnula's portrait and realized that the menacing shadows were gone. The young woman in the painting no longer looked fearful, but content. At peace.

Grace . . .

She heard her name called clearly, but this time there was no fear in her. Rising, she went toward the portrait, stepping into the circle of golden light.

It is time for me to leave. Take care of Janet. She is your daughter now . . .

"I shall. Good-bye, Finnula," Grace whispered. "Godspeed—and safe journey home."

The light flared to incredible brilliance and winked out, and nothing but sunshine—and the warmth in Grace's heart—remained.

McLean came over to her. "Talking to yourself, love?"

"No. I was saying good-bye to Finnula. She is gone now. She is at peace."

He smiled and pulled her into his arms, ignoring the interested stares of his young nephews, and kissed her soundly. "So am I, my dearest love. So am I."

TEMPT ME TWICE

BARBARA DAWSON SMITH

New York Times Bestselling Author of
ROMANCING THE ROGUE

A rogue shrouded in mystery, Lord Gabriel Kenyon returns from abroad to find himself guardian of Kate Talisford, the girl he had betrayed four years earlier. Now sworn to protect her, he fights his attraction to the spirited young woman. Although Kate wants nothing to do with the scoundrel who had once scorned her, Gabriel is the only man who can help her recover a priceless artifact stolen from her late father. On a quest to outwit a murderous villain, she soon discovers her true adventure lies with Gabriel himself, a seducer whose tempting embrace offers an irresistible challenge—to uncover his secrets and claim his heart forever...

"Barbara Dawson Smith is wonderful!"
— *Affaire de Coeur*

"Barbara Dawson Smith makes magic."
— *Romantic Times*